Courtney Crumrin

By Ted Naifeh

The Twilight Kingdom

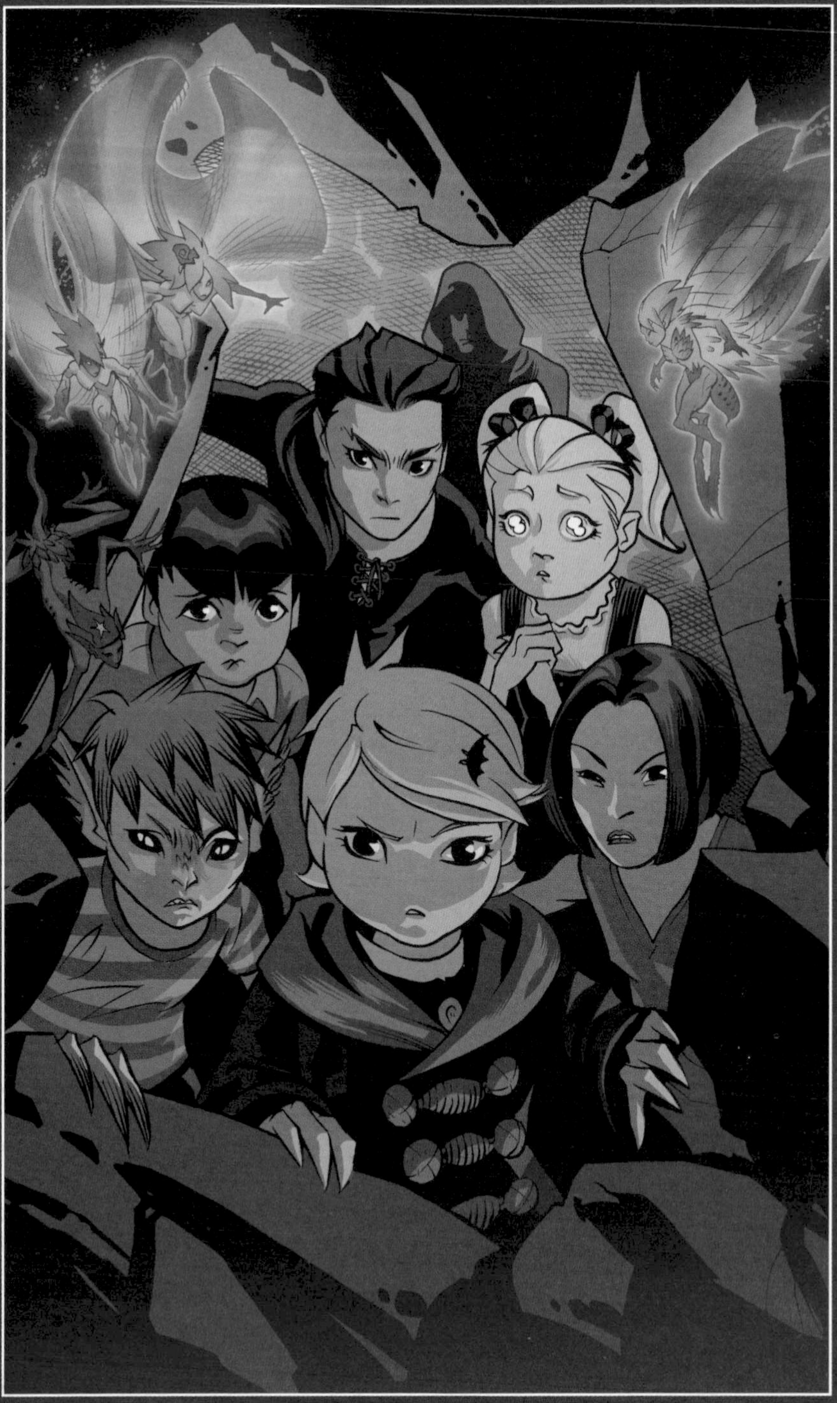

Courtney

By Ted Naifeh

Crumrin

The Twilight Kingdom

Written & Illustrated by

→ ❖ TED NAIFEH ❖ ←

Colored by

WARREN WUCINICH

Original Series edited by

JOE NOZEMACK, JAMES LUCAS JONES, AND JILL BEATON

Collection edited by

ROBIN HERRERA

Design by

KEITH WOOD AND ANGIE KNOWLES

Oni Press, Inc.
founder & chief financial officer, JOE NOZEMACK
publisher, JAMES LUCAS JONES
v.p. of creative & business development, CHARLIE CHU
director of operations, BRAD ROOKS
director of publicity, MELISSA MESZAROS
director of sales, MARGOT WOOD
marketing manager, RACHEL REED
director of design & production, TROY LOOK
senior graphic designer, HILARY THOMPSON
junior graphic designer, KATE Z. STONE
junior graphic designer, SONJA SYNAK
digital prepress lead, ANGIE KNOWLES
executive editor, ARI YARWOOD
senior editor, ROBIN HERRERA
associate editor, DESIREE WILSON
administrative assistant, ALISSA SALLAH
logistics associate, JUNG LEE

Originally published as issues 1-4 of the Oni Press comic series
Courtney Crumrin and the Twilight Kingdom.

Courtney Crumrin: The Twilight Kingdom. June 2018. Published by Oni Press, Inc. 1319
SE Martin Luther King, Jr. Blvd., Suite 240, Portland, OR 97214. Courtney Crumrin is ™
& © 2018 Ted Naifeh. All rights reserved. Oni Press logo and icon ™ & © 2018 Oni Press,
Inc. Oni Press logo and icon artwork created by Keith A. Wood. The events, institutions, and
characters presented in this book are fictional. Any resemblance to actual persons, living or
dead, is purely coincidental. No portion of this publication may be reproduced, by any means,
without the express written permission of the copyright holders.

1319 SE Martin Luther King Jr. Blvd.
Suite 240
Portland, OR 97214

onipress.com · tednaifeh.com
facebook.com/onipress · twitter.com/onipress
onipress.tumblr.com · instagram.com/onipress

First Edition: June 2018

ISBN 978-1-62010-518-4
eISBN 978-1-62010-029-5

1 3 5 7 9 10 8 6 4 2

Library of Congress Control Number: 2012956143

Printed in China.

For Julie and for Corinne

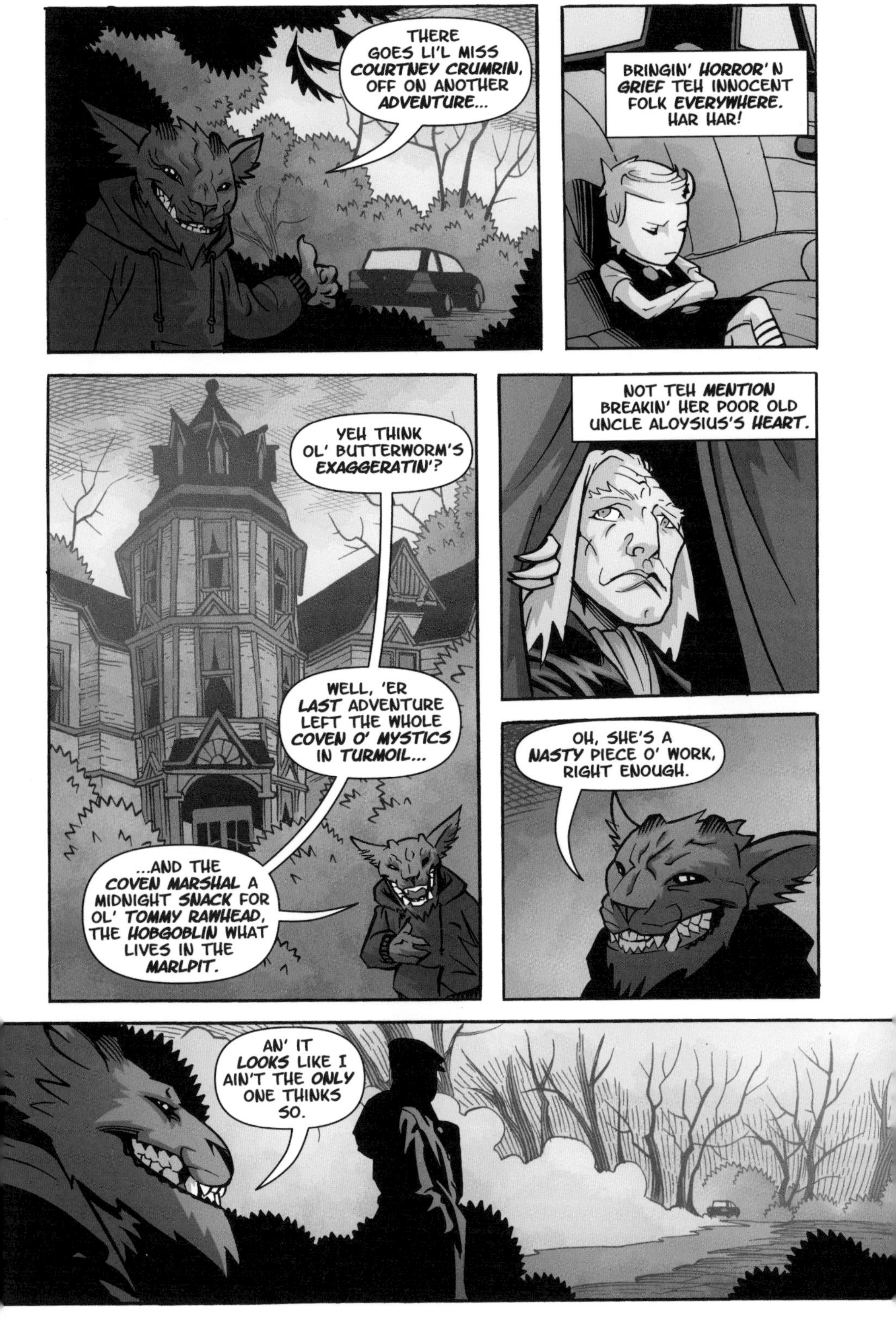

THERE GOES LI'L MISS COURTNEY CRUMRIN, OFF ON ANOTHER ADVENTURE...
BRINGIN' HORROR'N GRIEF TEH INNOCENT FOLK EVERYWHERE. HAR HAR!
YEH THINK OL' BUTTERWORM'S EXAGGERATIN'?
WELL, 'ER LAST ADVENTURE LEFT THE WHOLE COVEN O' MYSTICS IN TURMOIL...
...AND THE COVEN MARSHAL A MIDNIGHT SNACK FOR OL' TOMMY RAWHEAD, THE HOBGOBLIN WHAT LIVES IN THE MARLPIT.
NOT TEH MENTION BREAKIN' HER POOR OLD UNCLE ALOYSIUS'S HEART.
OH, SHE'S A NASTY PIECE O' WORK, RIGHT ENOUGH.
AN' IT LOOKS LIKE I AIN'T THE ONLY ONE THINKS SO.

Chapter One

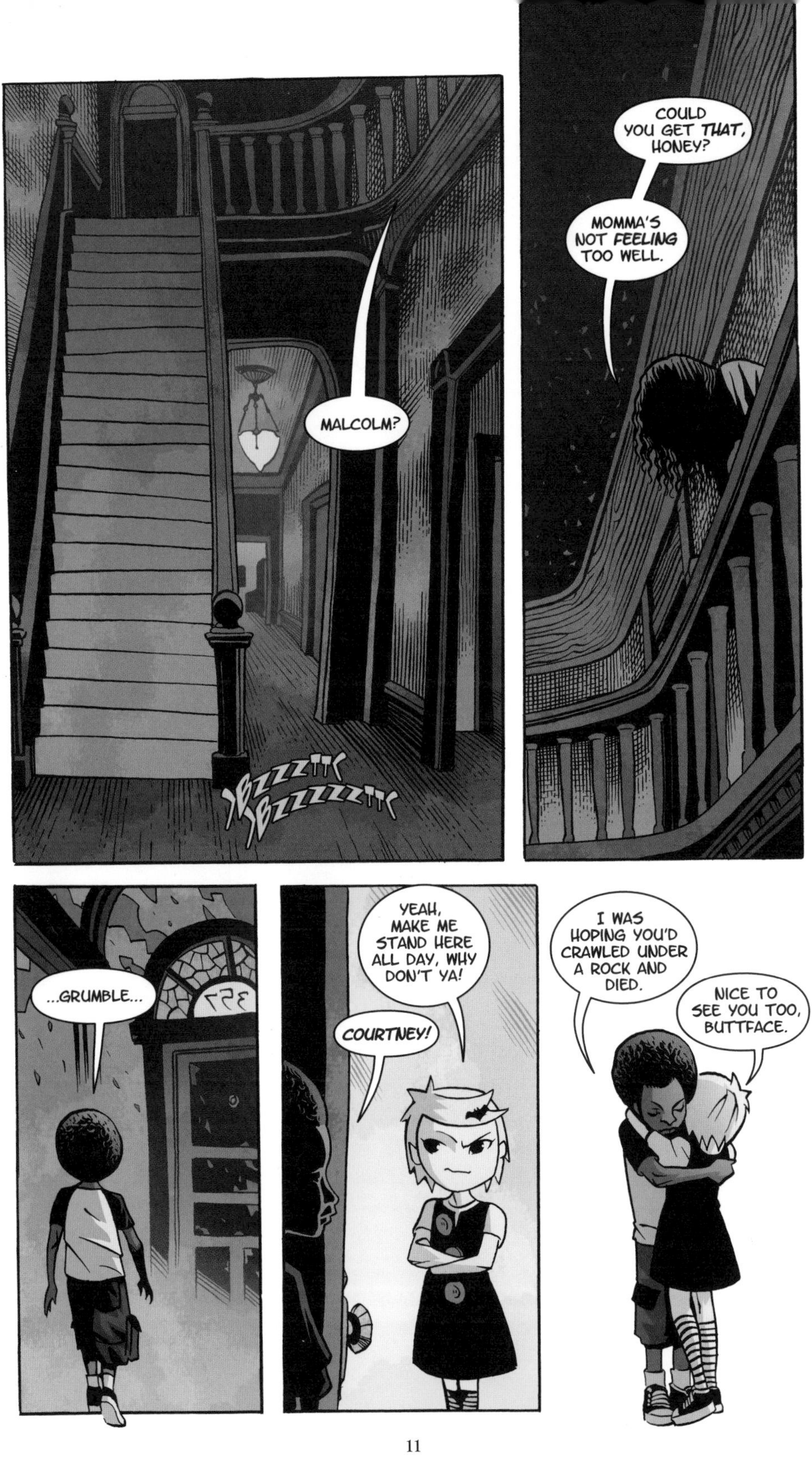
MALCOLM?
BZZZZTT
BZZZZZZTT
COULD YOU GET THAT, HONEY?
MOMMA'S NOT FEELING TOO WELL.
...GRUMBLE...
357
YEAH, MAKE ME STAND HERE ALL DAY, WHY DON'T YA!
COURTNEY!
I WAS HOPING YOU'D CRAWLED UNDER A ROCK AND DIED.
NICE TO SEE YOU TOO, BUTTFACE.

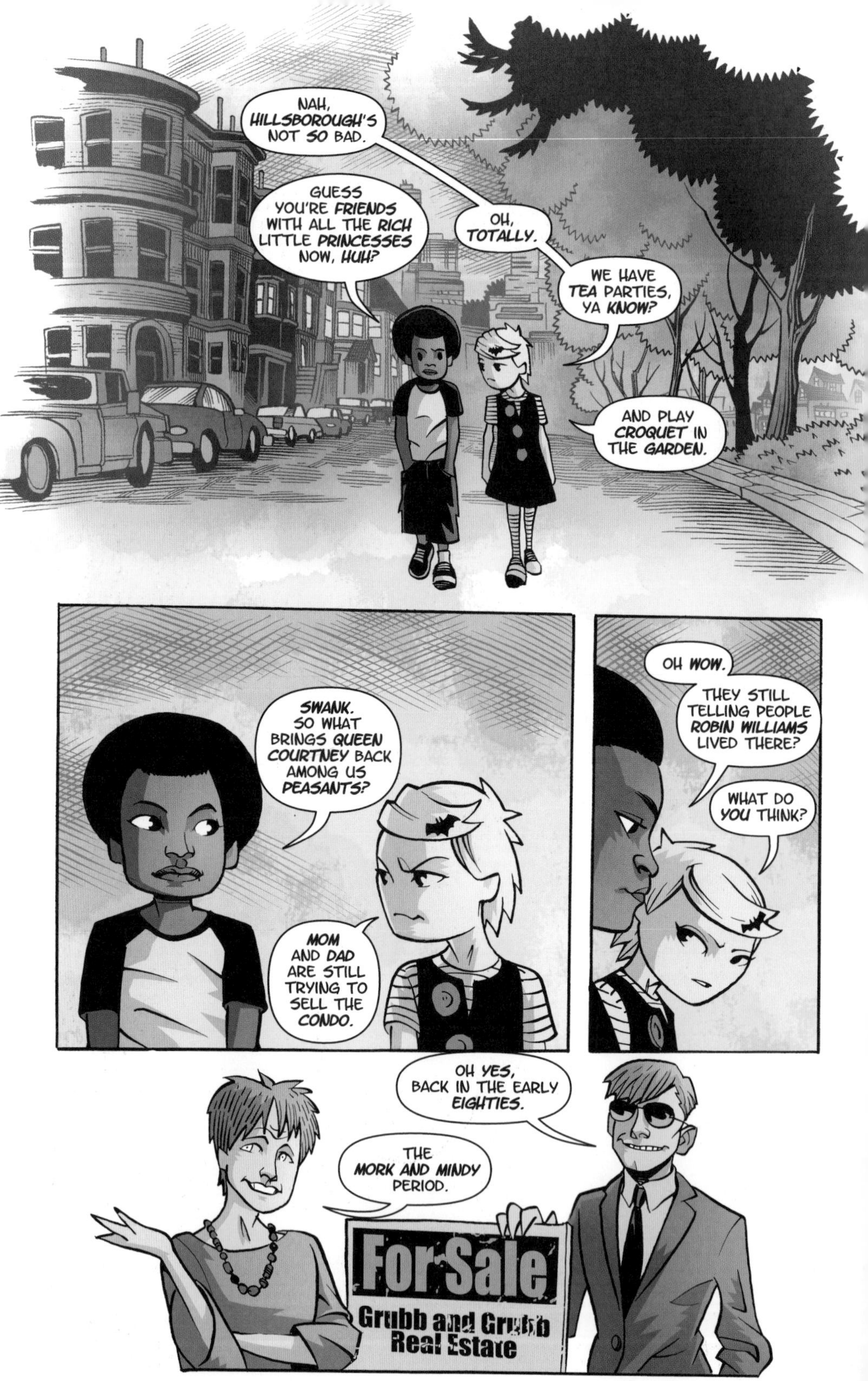
NAH, HILLSBOROUGH'S NOT SO BAD.
GUESS YOU'RE FRIENDS WITH ALL THE RICH LITTLE PRINCESSES NOW, HUH?
OH, TOTALLY.
WE HAVE TEA PARTIES, YA KNOW?
AND PLAY CROQUET IN THE GARDEN.
SWANK. SO WHAT BRINGS QUEEN COURTNEY BACK AMONG US PEASANTS?
MOM AND DAD ARE STILL TRYING TO SELL THE CONDO.
OH WOW.
THEY STILL TELLING PEOPLE ROBIN WILLIAMS LIVED THERE?
WHAT DO YOU THINK?
OH YES, BACK IN THE EARLY EIGHTIES.
THE MORK AND MINDY PERIOD.
For Sale
Grubb and Grubb
Real Estate

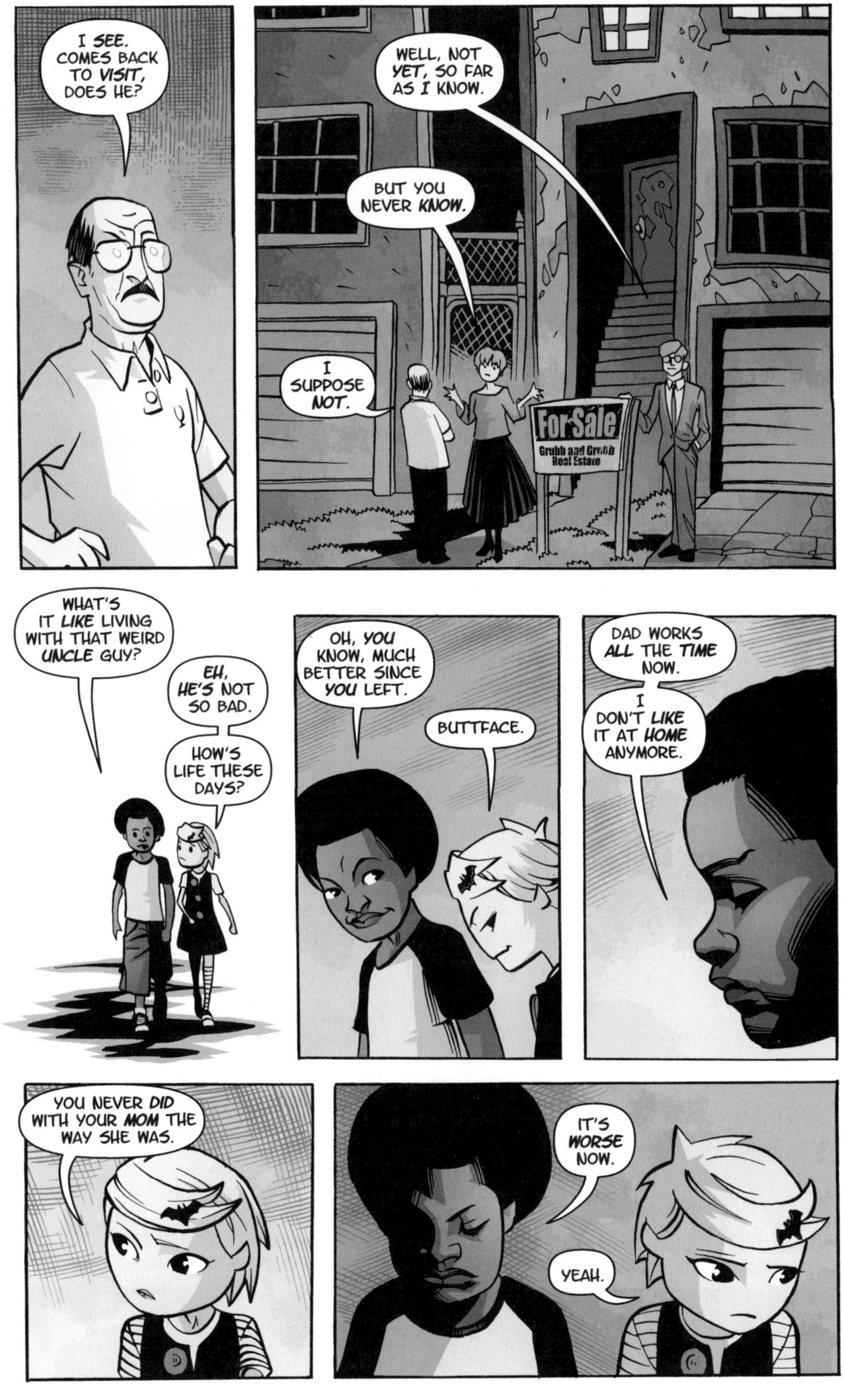
I SEE. COMES BACK TO VISIT, DOES HE?
WELL, NOT YET, SO FAR AS I KNOW.
BUT YOU NEVER KNOW.
I SUPPOSE NOT.
For Sale
Grubb and Grubb Real Estate
WHAT'S IT LIKE LIVING WITH THAT WEIRD UNCLE GUY?
EH, HE'S NOT SO BAD.
HOW'S LIFE THESE DAYS?
OH, YOU KNOW, MUCH BETTER SINCE YOU LEFT.
BUTTFACE.
DAD WORKS ALL THE TIME NOW.
I DON'T LIKE IT AT HOME ANYMORE.
YOU NEVER DID WITH YOUR MOM THE WAY SHE WAS.
IT'S WORSE NOW.
YEAH.

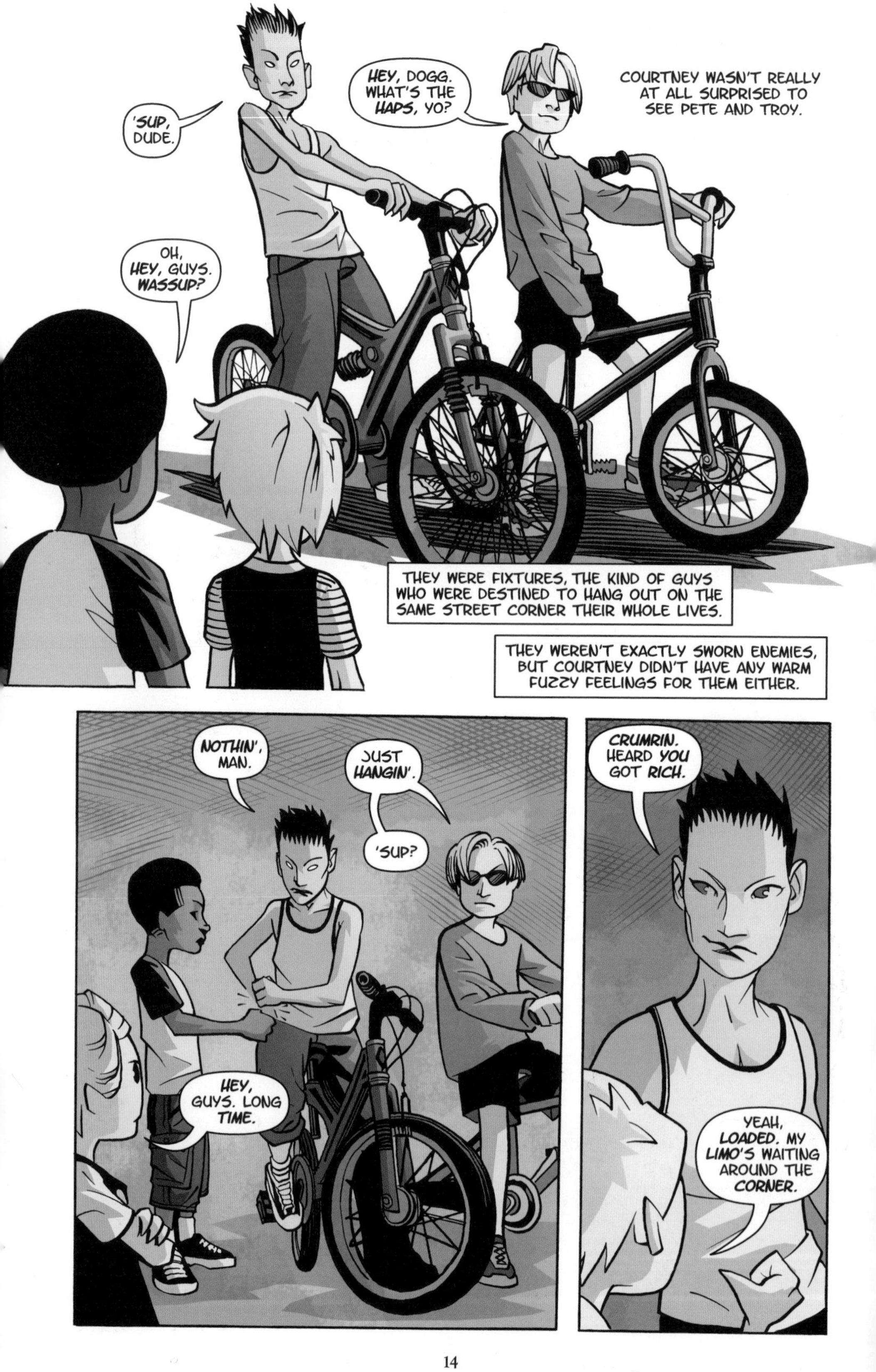
'SUP, DUDE.
HEY, DOGG. WHAT'S THE HAPS, YO?
COURTNEY WASN'T REALLY AT ALL SURPRISED TO SEE PETE AND TROY.
OH, HEY, GUYS. WASSUP?
THEY WERE FIXTURES, THE KIND OF GUYS WHO WERE DESTINED TO HANG OUT ON THE SAME STREET CORNER THEIR WHOLE LIVES.
THEY WEREN'T EXACTLY SWORN ENEMIES, BUT COURTNEY DIDN'T HAVE ANY WARM FUZZY FEELINGS FOR THEM EITHER.
NOTHIN', MAN.
JUST HANGIN'.
'SUP?
HEY, GUYS. LONG TIME.
CRUMRIN. HEARD YOU GOT RICH.
YEAH, LOADED. MY LIMO'S WAITING AROUND THE CORNER.

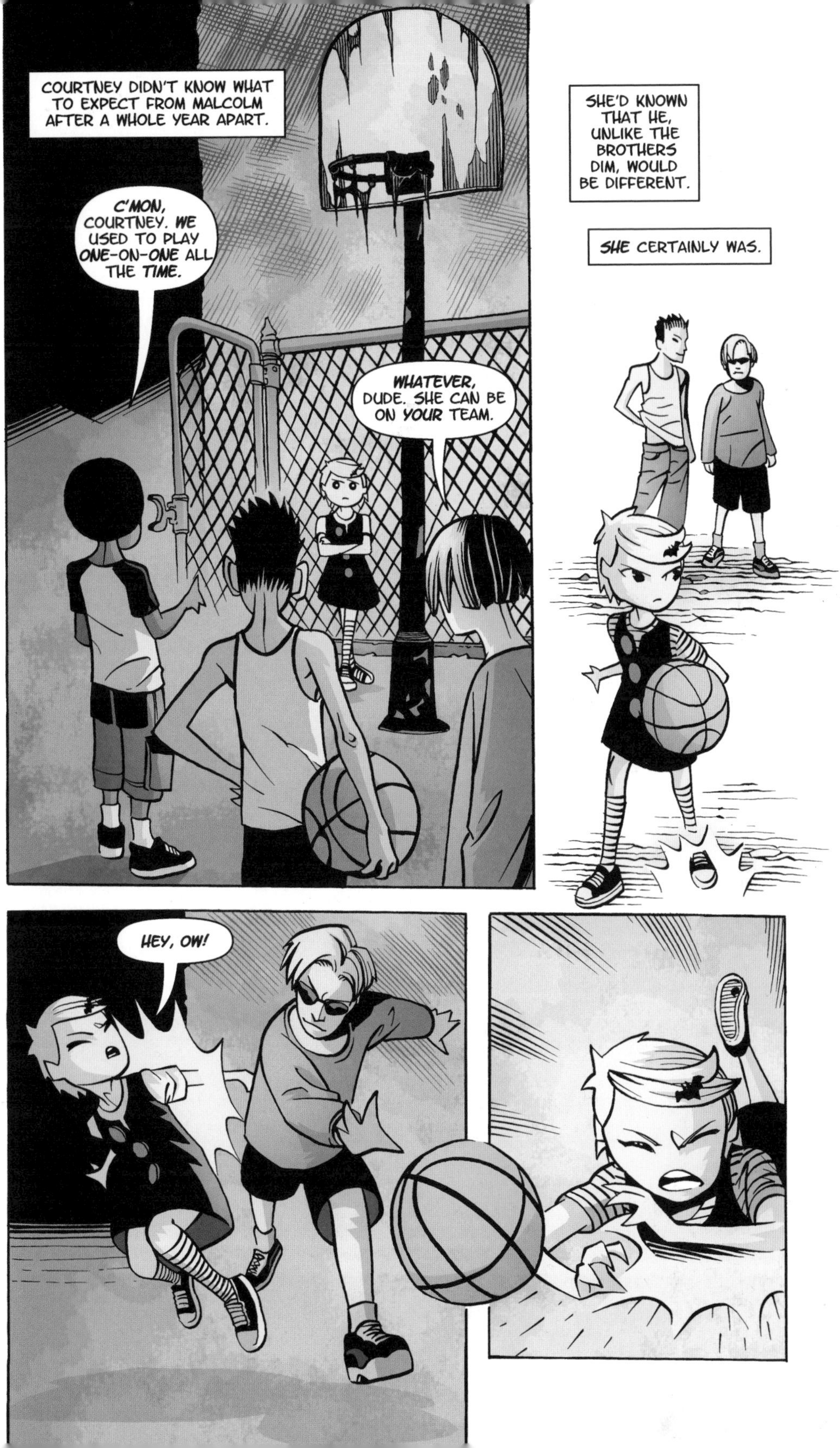
COURTNEY DIDN'T KNOW WHAT TO EXPECT FROM MALCOLM AFTER A WHOLE YEAR APART.
C'MON, COURTNEY. WE USED TO PLAY ONE-ON-ONE ALL THE TIME.
WHATEVER, DUDE. SHE CAN BE ON YOUR TEAM.
SHE'D KNOWN THAT HE, UNLIKE THE BROTHERS DIM, WOULD BE DIFFERENT.
SHE CERTAINLY WAS.
HEY, OW!

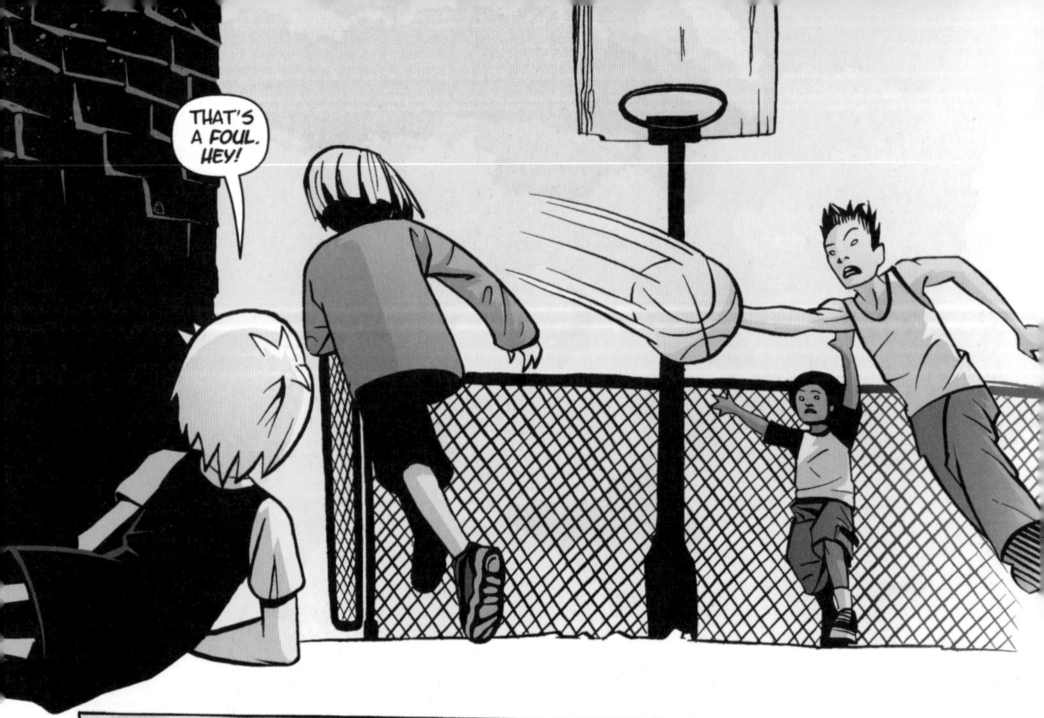
THAT'S A FOUL. HEY!

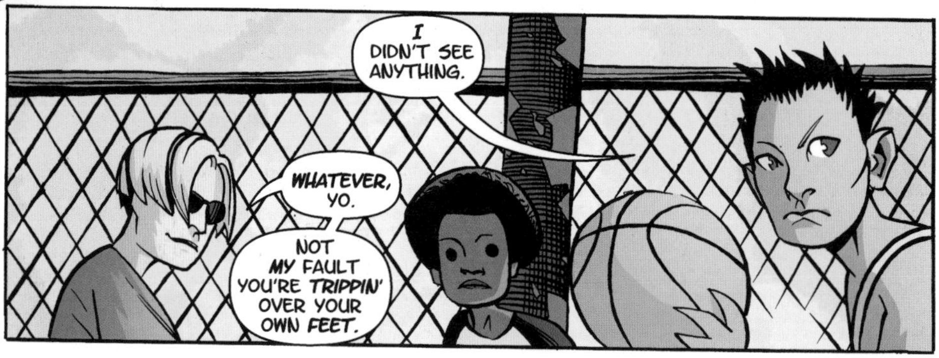
I DIDN'T SEE ANYTHING.
WHATEVER, YO.
NOT MY FAULT YOU'RE TRIPPIN' OVER YOUR OWN FEET.

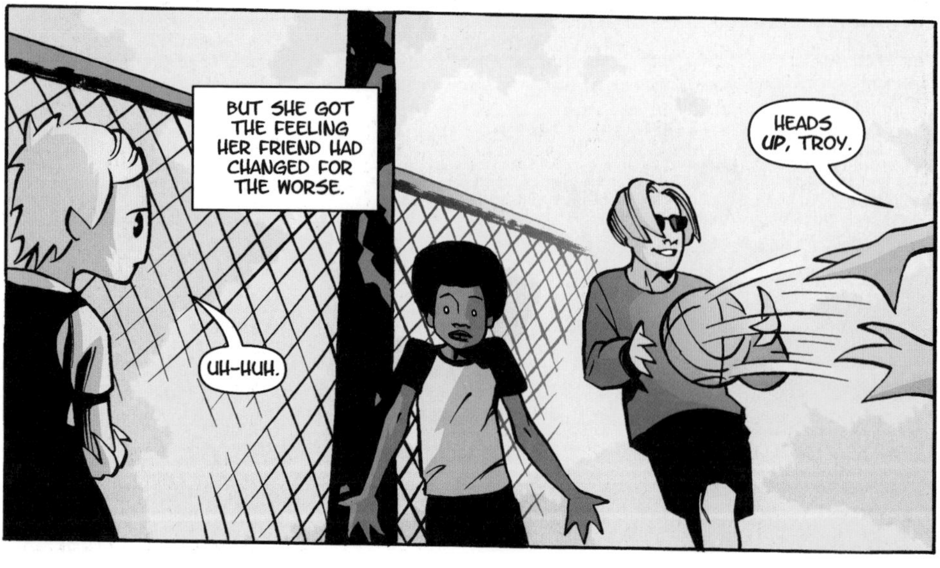
BUT SHE GOT THE FEELING HER FRIEND HAD CHANGED FOR THE WORSE.
HEADS UP, TROY.
UH-HUH.

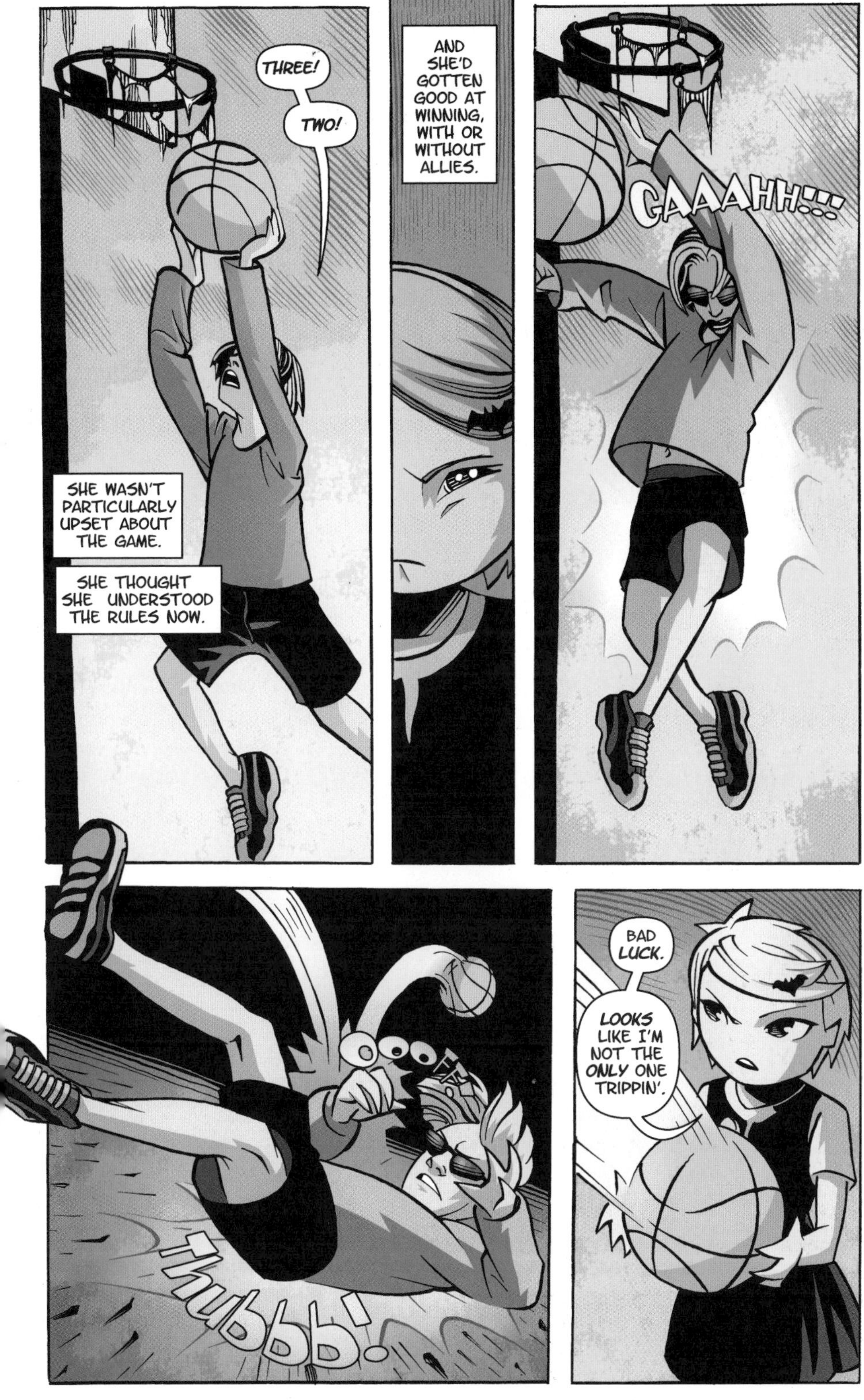
THREE!
TWO!
SHE WASN'T PARTICULARLY UPSET ABOUT THE GAME.
SHE THOUGHT SHE UNDERSTOOD THE RULES NOW.
AND SHE'D GOTTEN GOOD AT WINNING, WITH OR WITHOUT ALLIES.
GAAAHH!!!
THUBBB!
BAD LUCK.
LOOKS LIKE I'M NOT THE ONLY ONE TRIPPIN'.

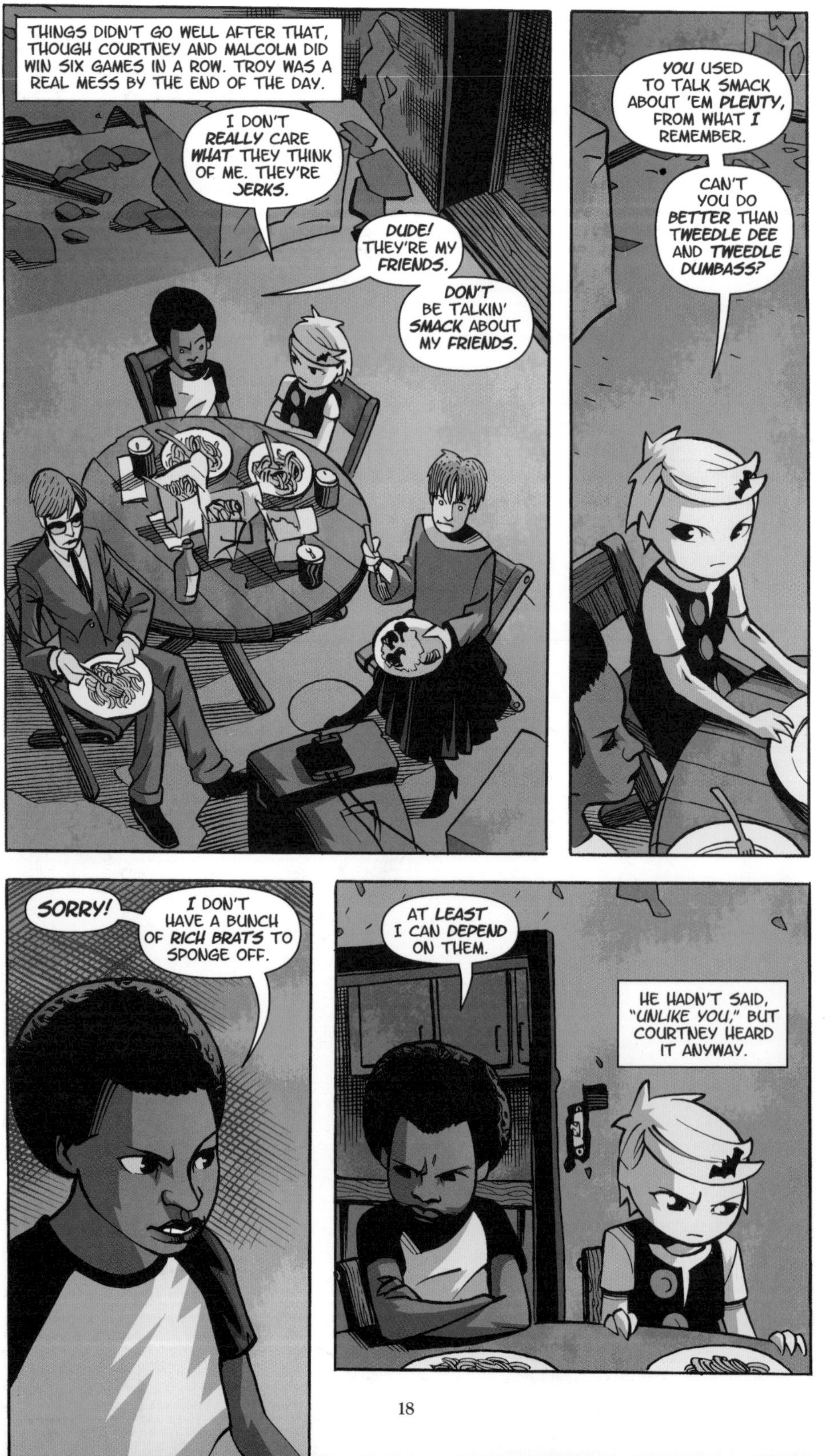
THINGS DIDN'T GO WELL AFTER THAT, THOUGH COURTNEY AND MALCOLM DID WIN SIX GAMES IN A ROW. TROY WAS A REAL MESS BY THE END OF THE DAY.
I DON'T REALLY CARE WHAT THEY THINK OF ME. THEY'RE JERKS.
DUDE! THEY'RE MY FRIENDS.
DON'T BE TALKIN' SMACK ABOUT MY FRIENDS.
YOU USED TO TALK SMACK ABOUT 'EM PLENTY, FROM WHAT I REMEMBER.
CAN'T YOU DO BETTER THAN TWEEDLE DEE AND TWEEDLE DUMBASS?
SORRY!
I DON'T HAVE A BUNCH OF RICH BRATS TO SPONGE OFF.
AT LEAST I CAN DEPEND ON THEM.
HE HADN'T SAID, "UNLIKE YOU," BUT COURTNEY HEARD IT ANYWAY.

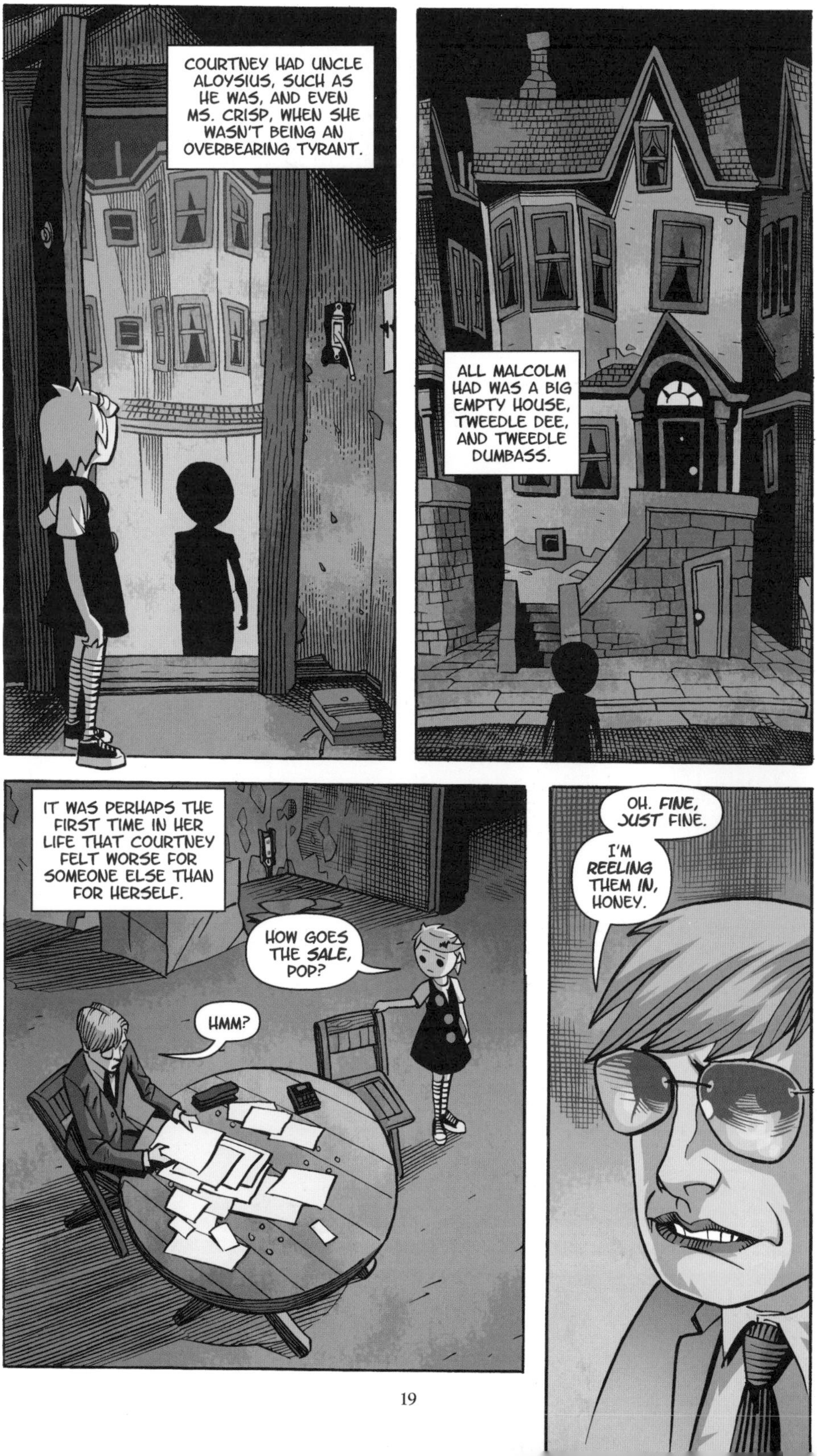
COURTNEY HAD UNCLE ALOYSIUS, SUCH AS HE WAS, AND EVEN MS. CRISP, WHEN SHE WASN'T BEING AN OVERBEARING TYRANT.
ALL MALCOLM HAD WAS A BIG EMPTY HOUSE, TWEEDLE DEE, AND TWEEDLE DUMBASS.
IT WAS PERHAPS THE FIRST TIME IN HER LIFE THAT COURTNEY FELT WORSE FOR SOMEONE ELSE THAN FOR HERSELF.
HOW GOES THE SALE, POP?
HMM?
OH. FINE, JUST FINE.
I'M REELING THEM IN, HONEY.

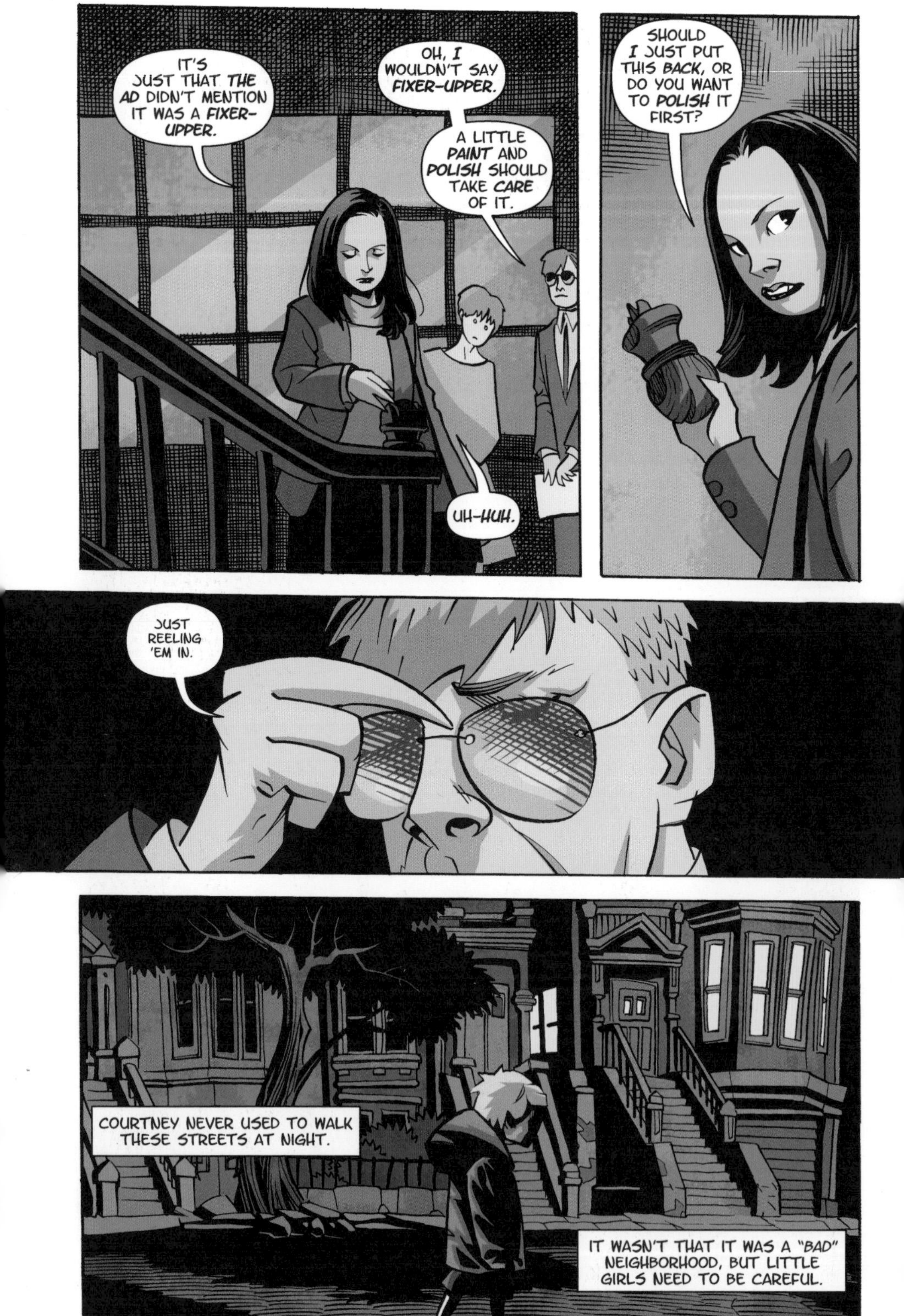
IT'S JUST THAT THE AD DIDN'T MENTION IT WAS A FIXER-UPPER.
OH, I WOULDN'T SAY FIXER-UPPER.
A LITTLE PAINT AND POLISH SHOULD TAKE CARE OF IT.
UH-HUH.
SHOULD I JUST PUT THIS BACK, OR DO YOU WANT TO POLISH IT FIRST?
JUST REELING 'EM IN.
COURTNEY NEVER USED TO WALK THESE STREETS AT NIGHT.
IT WASN'T THAT IT WAS A "BAD" NEIGHBORHOOD, BUT LITTLE GIRLS NEED TO BE CAREFUL.

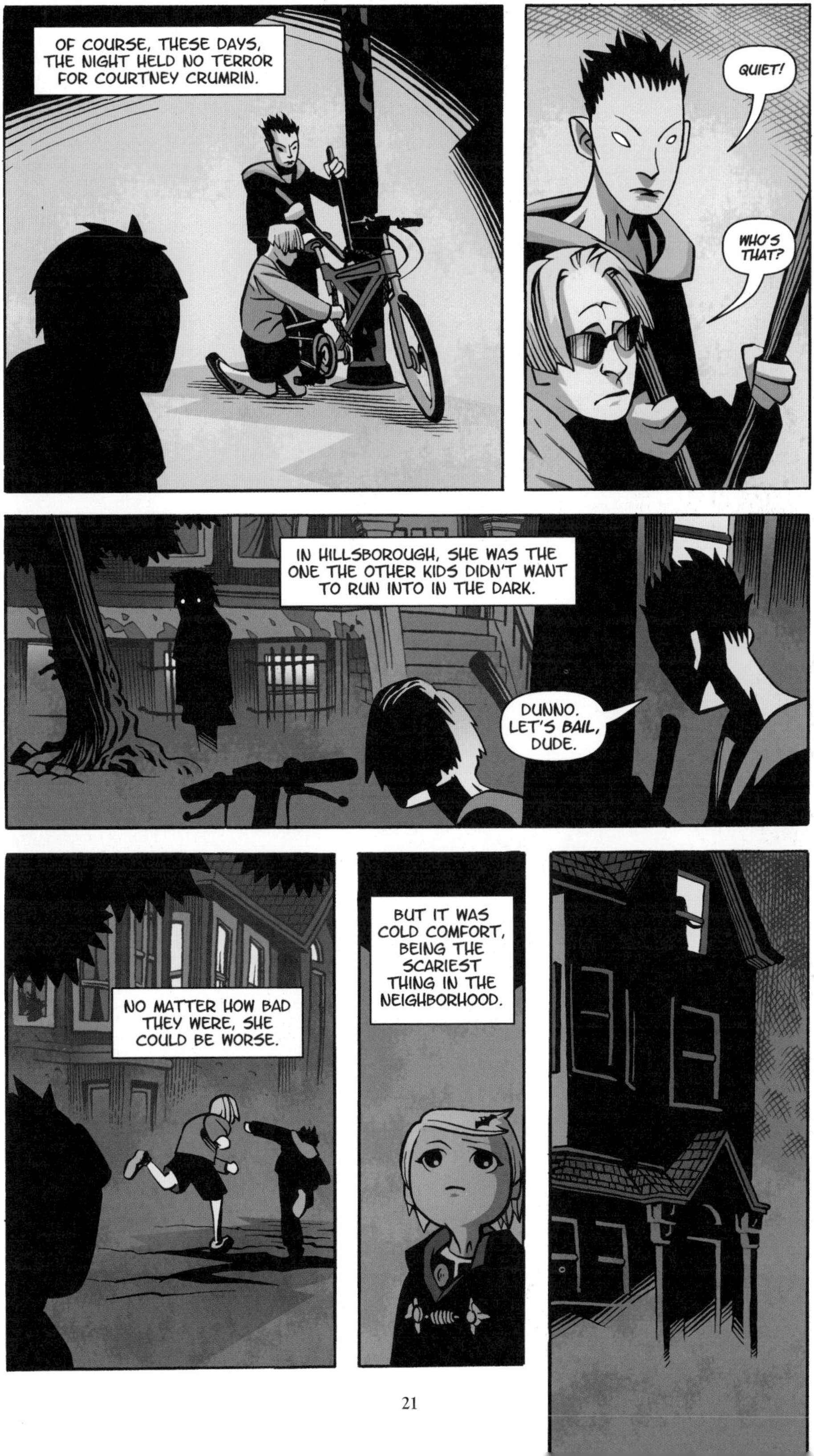
OF COURSE, THESE DAYS, THE NIGHT HELD NO TERROR FOR COURTNEY CRUMRIN.
QUIET!
WHO'S THAT?
IN HILLSBOROUGH, SHE WAS THE ONE THE OTHER KIDS DIDN'T WANT TO RUN INTO IN THE DARK.
DUNNO. LET'S BAIL, DUDE.
NO MATTER HOW BAD THEY WERE, SHE COULD BE WORSE.
BUT IT WAS COLD COMFORT, BEING THE SCARIEST THING IN THE NEIGHBORHOOD.

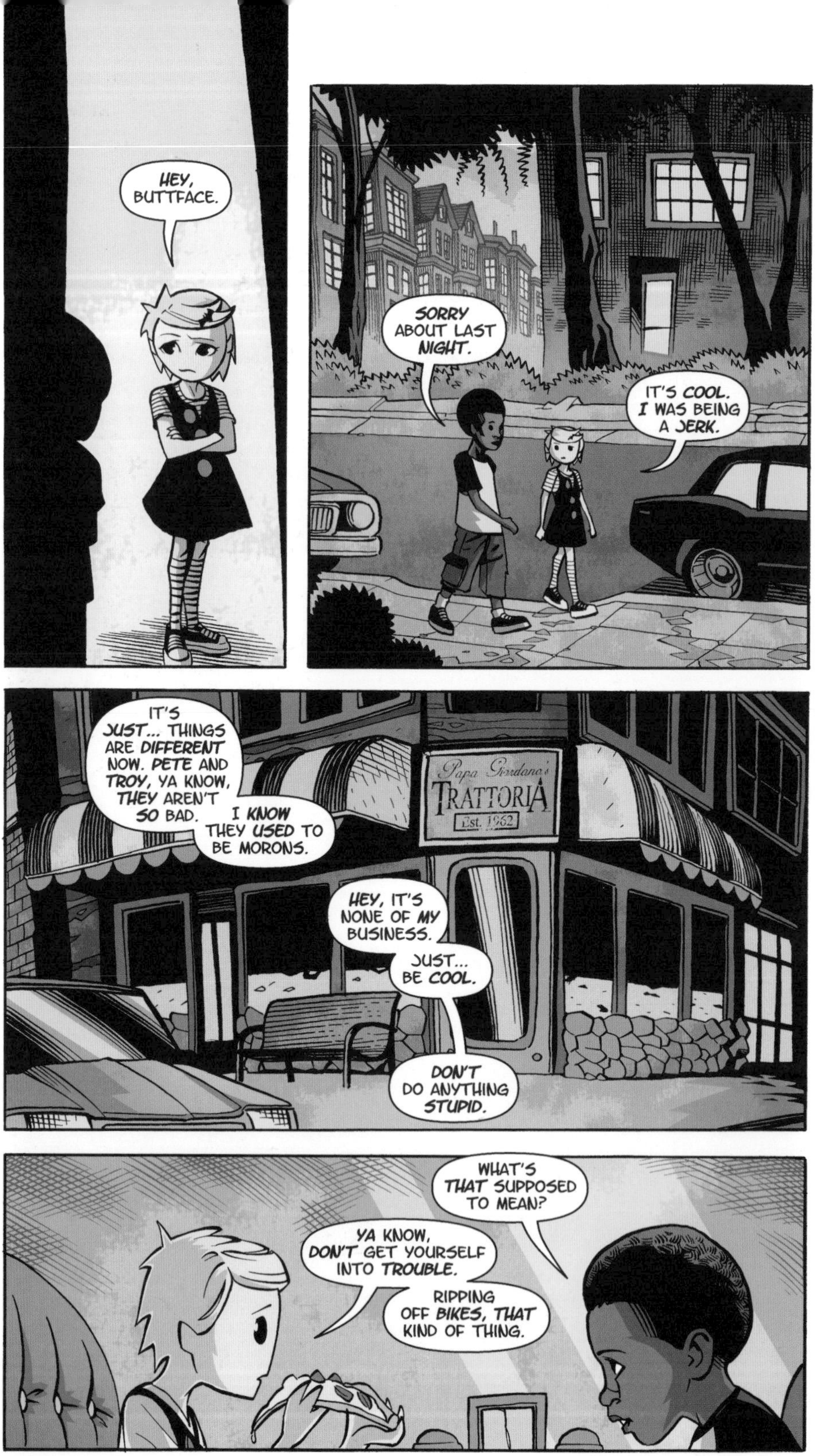
HEY, BUTTFACE.
SORRY ABOUT LAST NIGHT.
IT'S COOL. I WAS BEING A JERK.
IT'S JUST... THINGS ARE DIFFERENT NOW. PETE AND TROY, YA KNOW, THEY AREN'T SO BAD.
I KNOW THEY USED TO BE MORONS.
Papa Giordano's TRATTORIA Est. 1962
HEY, IT'S NONE OF MY BUSINESS.
JUST... BE COOL.
DON'T DO ANYTHING STUPID.
WHAT'S THAT SUPPOSED TO MEAN?
YA KNOW, DON'T GET YOURSELF INTO TROUBLE.
RIPPING OFF BIKES, THAT KIND OF THING.

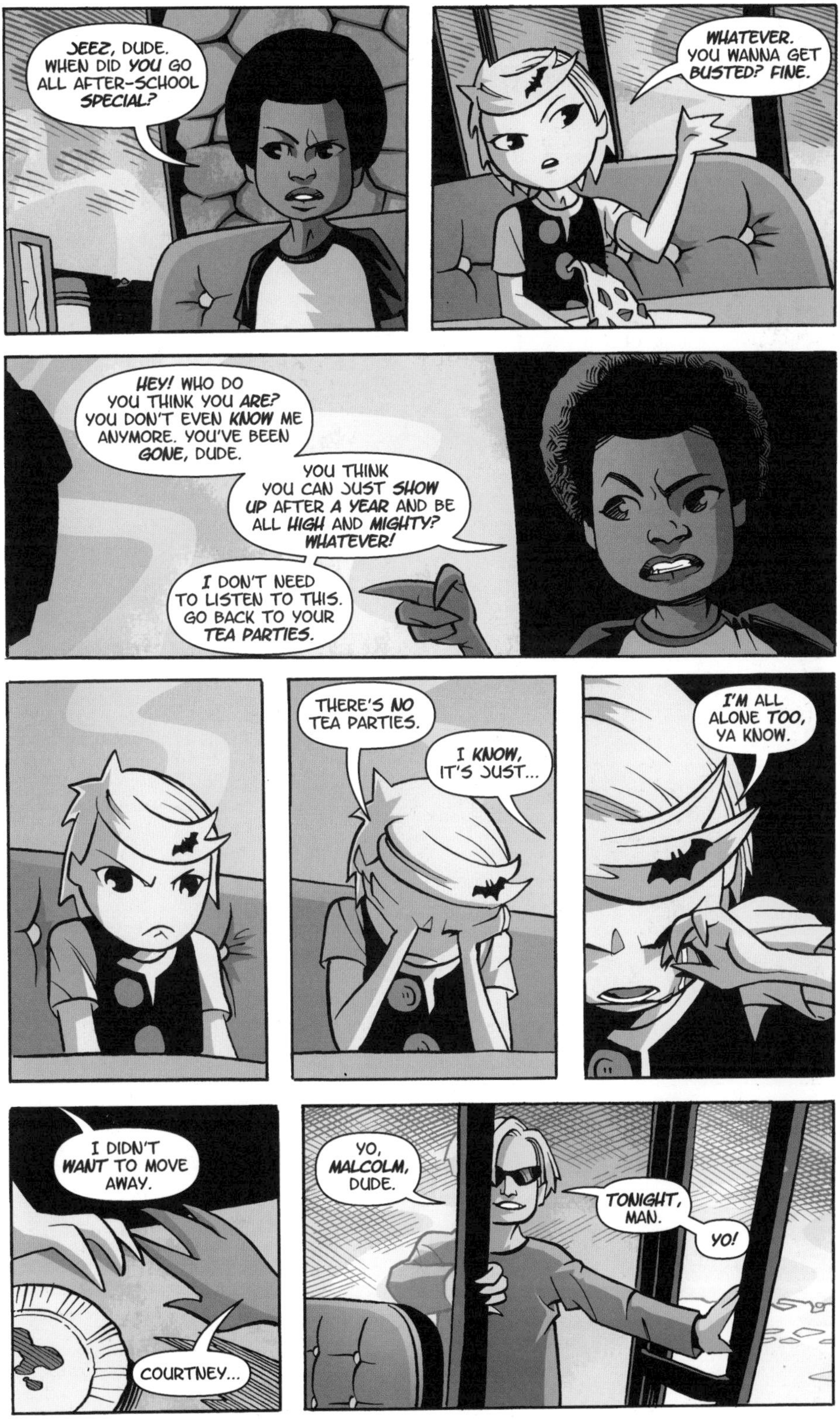
JEEZ, DUDE. WHEN DID YOU GO ALL AFTER-SCHOOL SPECIAL?
WHATEVER. YOU WANNA GET BUSTED? FINE.
HEY! WHO DO YOU THINK YOU ARE? YOU DON'T EVEN KNOW ME ANYMORE. YOU'VE BEEN GONE, DUDE.
YOU THINK YOU CAN JUST SHOW UP AFTER A YEAR AND BE ALL HIGH AND MIGHTY? WHATEVER!
I DON'T NEED TO LISTEN TO THIS. GO BACK TO YOUR TEA PARTIES.
THERE'S NO TEA PARTIES.
I KNOW, IT'S JUST...
I'M ALL ALONE TOO, YA KNOW.
I DIDN'T WANT TO MOVE AWAY.
COURTNEY...
YO, MALCOLM, DUDE.
TONIGHT, MAN.
YO!

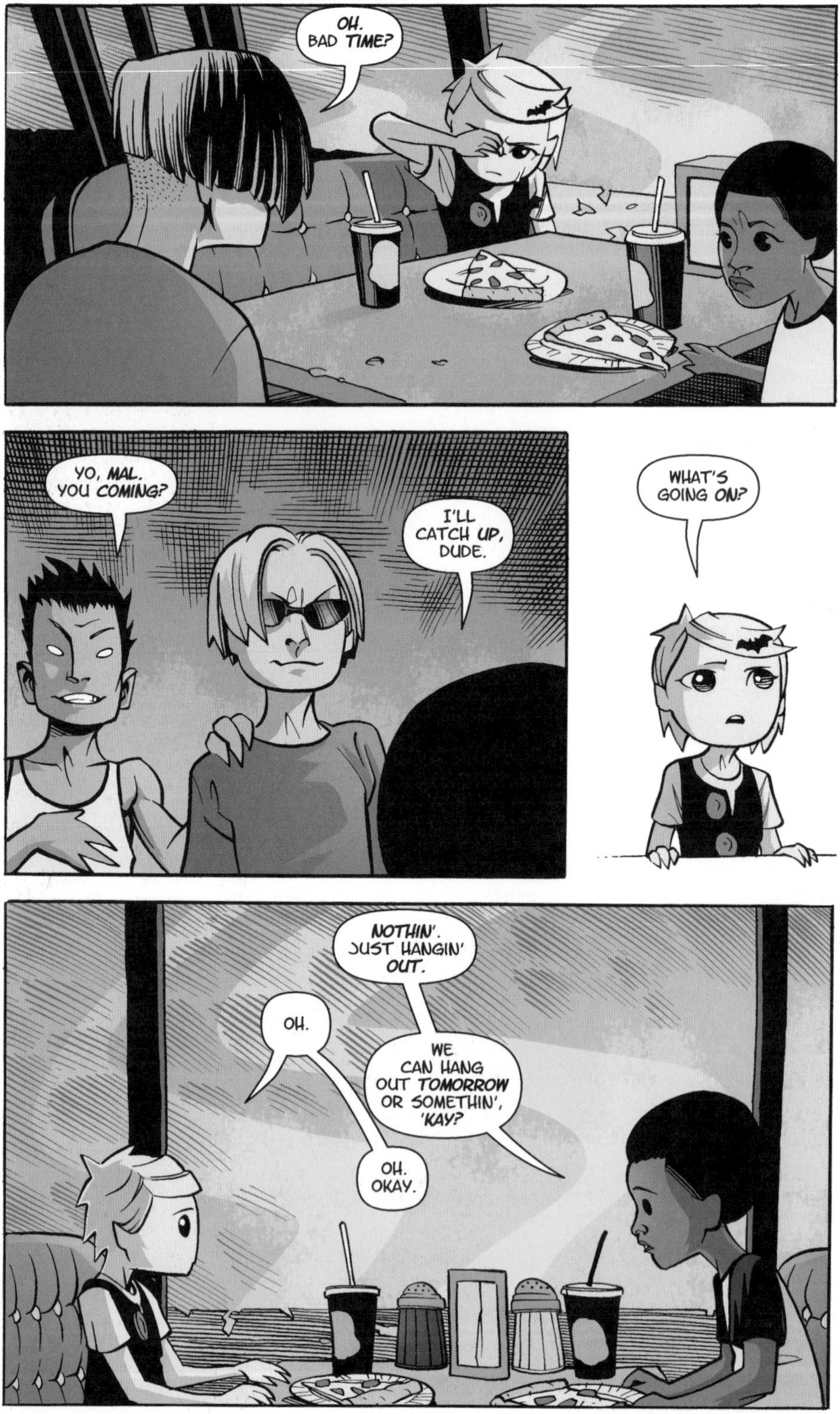
OH.
BAD TIME?
YO, MAL.
YOU COMING?
I'LL
CATCH UP,
DUDE.
WHAT'S
GOING ON?
NOTHIN'.
JUST HANGIN'
OUT.
WE
CAN HANG
OUT TOMORROW
OR SOMETHIN',
'KAY?
OH.
OH.
OKAY.

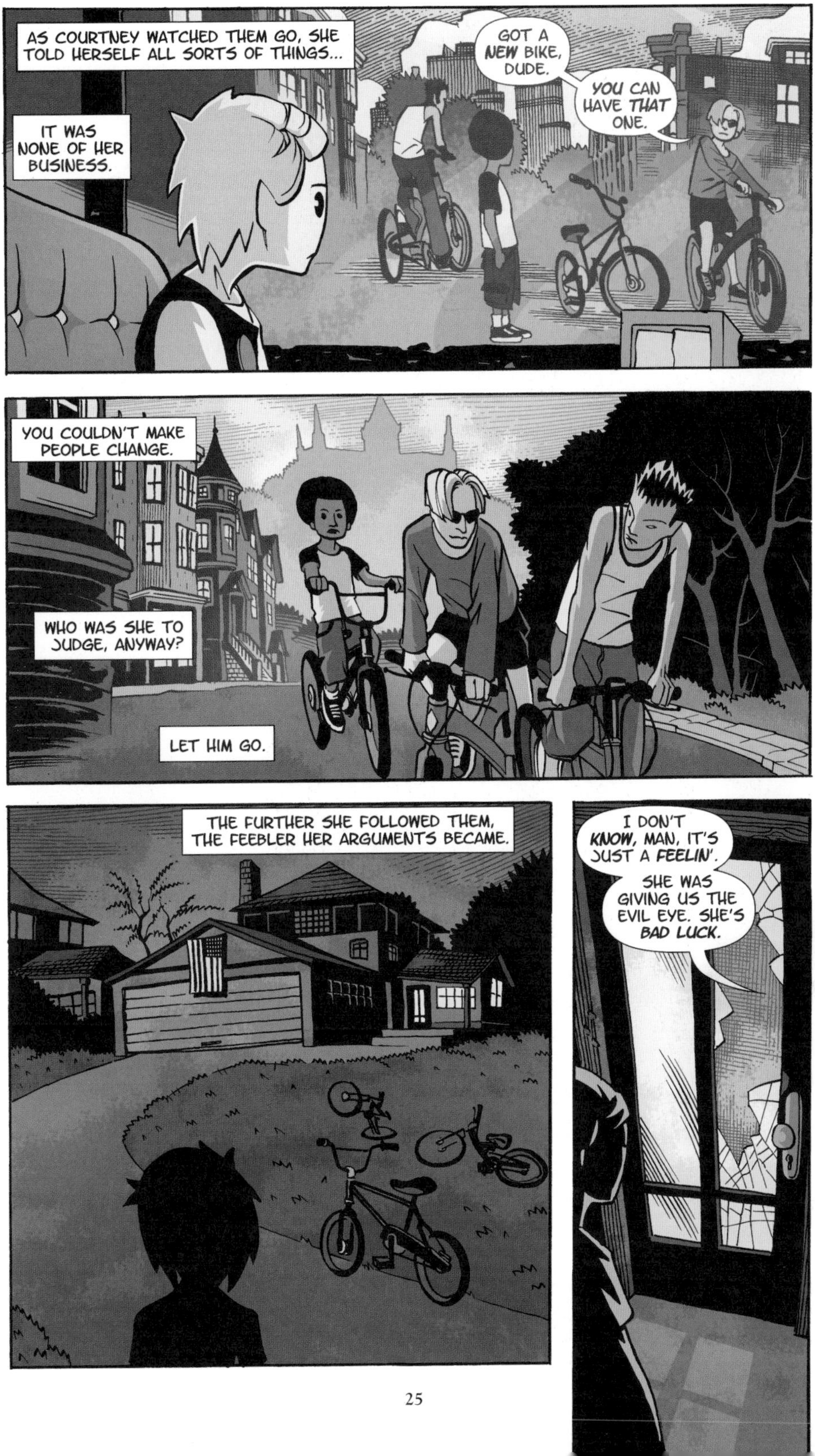
AS COURTNEY WATCHED THEM GO, SHE TOLD HERSELF ALL SORTS OF THINGS...
IT WAS NONE OF HER BUSINESS.
GOT A NEW BIKE, DUDE.
YOU CAN HAVE THAT ONE.
YOU COULDN'T MAKE PEOPLE CHANGE.
WHO WAS SHE TO JUDGE, ANYWAY?
LET HIM GO.
THE FURTHER SHE FOLLOWED THEM, THE FEEBLER HER ARGUMENTS BECAME.
I DON'T KNOW, MAN, IT'S JUST A FEELIN'.
SHE WAS GIVING US THE EVIL EYE. SHE'S BAD LUCK.

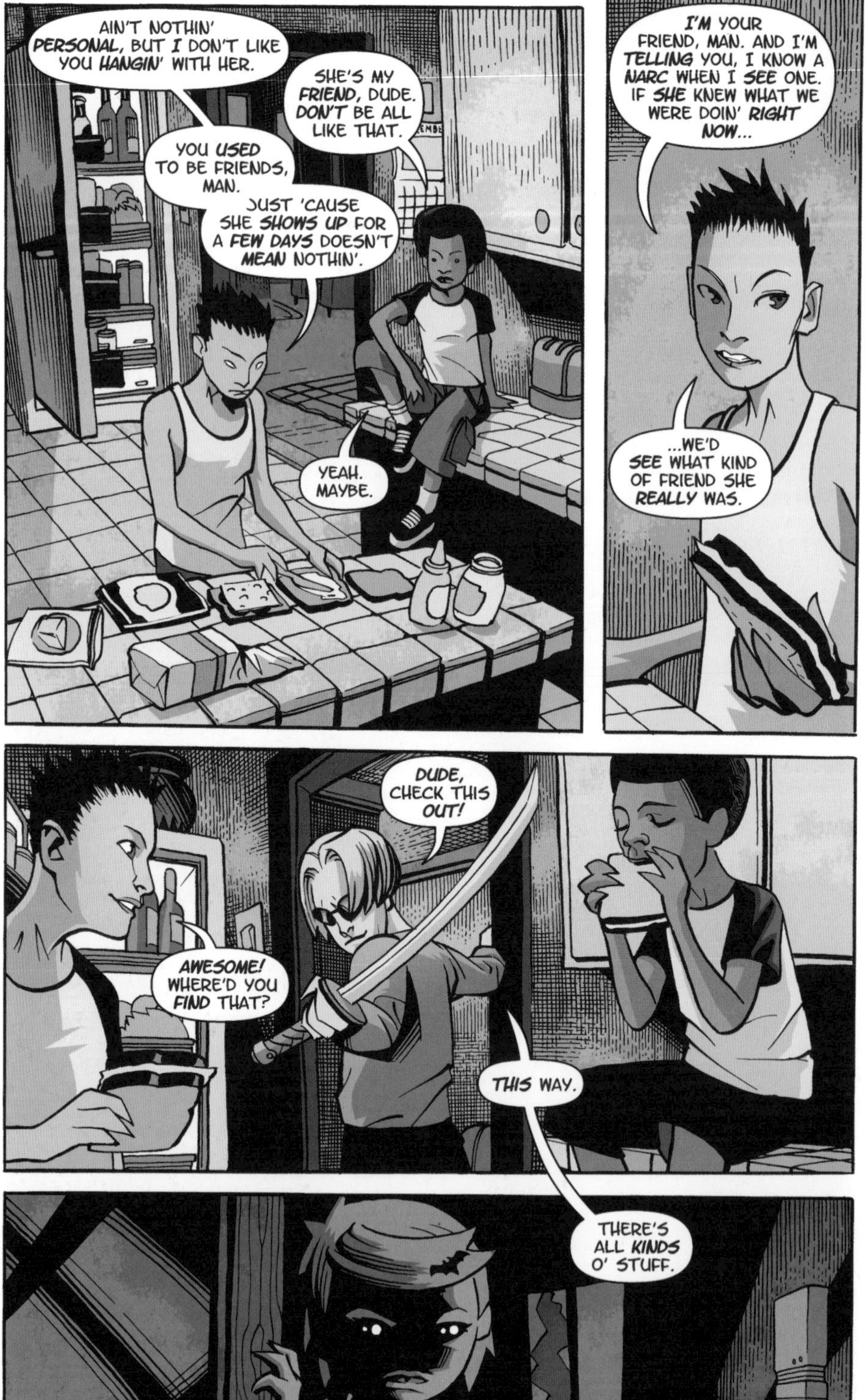
AIN'T NOTHIN' PERSONAL, BUT I DON'T LIKE YOU HANGIN' WITH HER.
SHE'S MY FRIEND, DUDE. DON'T BE ALL LIKE THAT.
YOU USED TO BE FRIENDS, MAN.
JUST 'CAUSE SHE SHOWS UP FOR A FEW DAYS DOESN'T MEAN NOTHIN'.
YEAH. MAYBE.
I'M YOUR FRIEND, MAN. AND I'M TELLING YOU, I KNOW A NARC WHEN I SEE ONE. IF SHE KNEW WHAT WE WERE DOIN' RIGHT NOW...
...WE'D SEE WHAT KIND OF FRIEND SHE REALLY WAS.
DUDE, CHECK THIS OUT!
AWESOME! WHERE'D YOU FIND THAT?
THIS WAY.
THERE'S ALL KINDS O' STUFF.

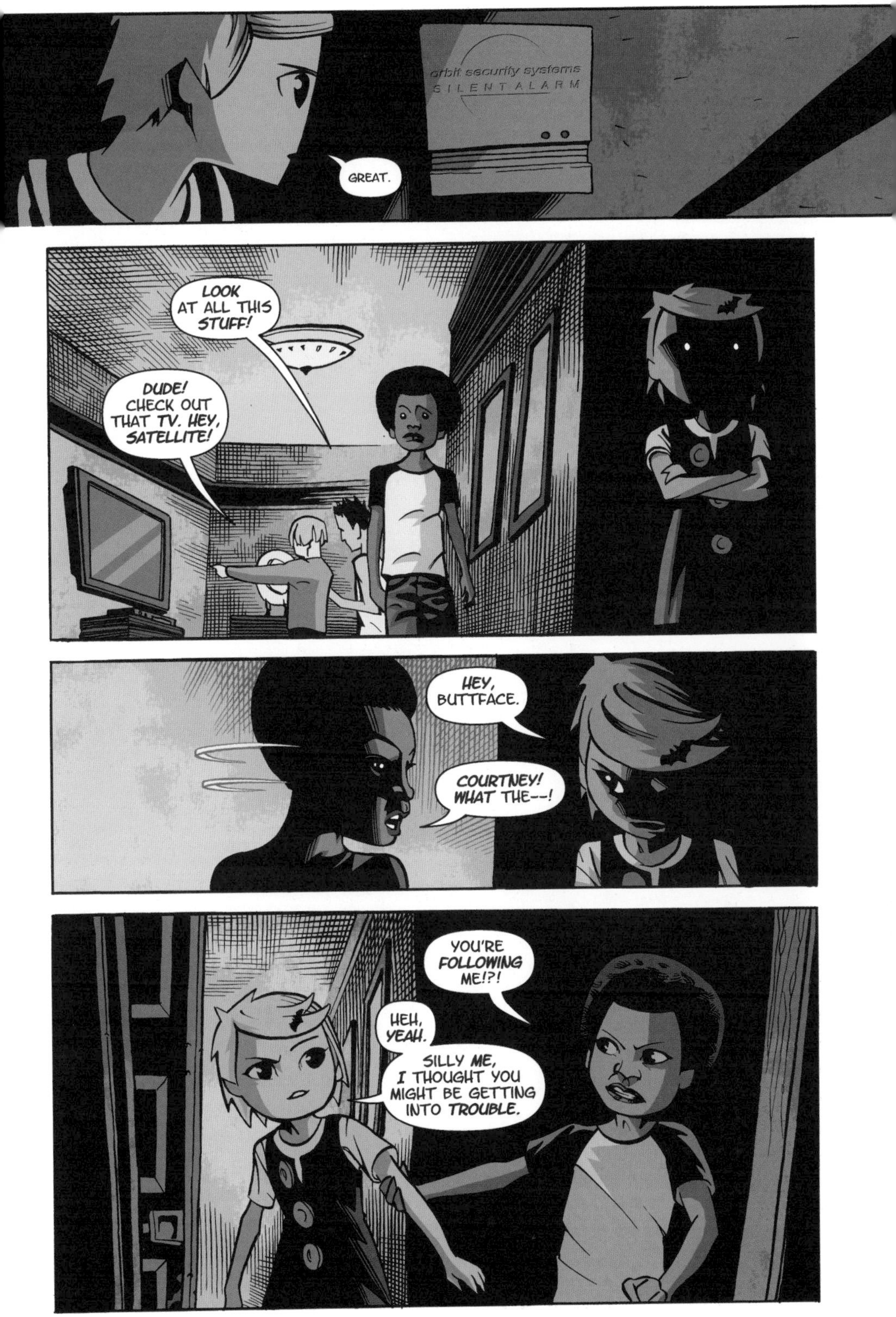
orbit security systems
SILENT ALARM
GREAT.
LOOK AT ALL THIS STUFF!
DUDE! CHECK OUT THAT TV. HEY, SATELLITE!
HEY, BUTTFACE.
COURTNEY! WHAT THE--!
YOU'RE FOLLOWING ME!?!
HEH, YEAH.
SILLY ME, I THOUGHT YOU MIGHT BE GETTING INTO TROUBLE.

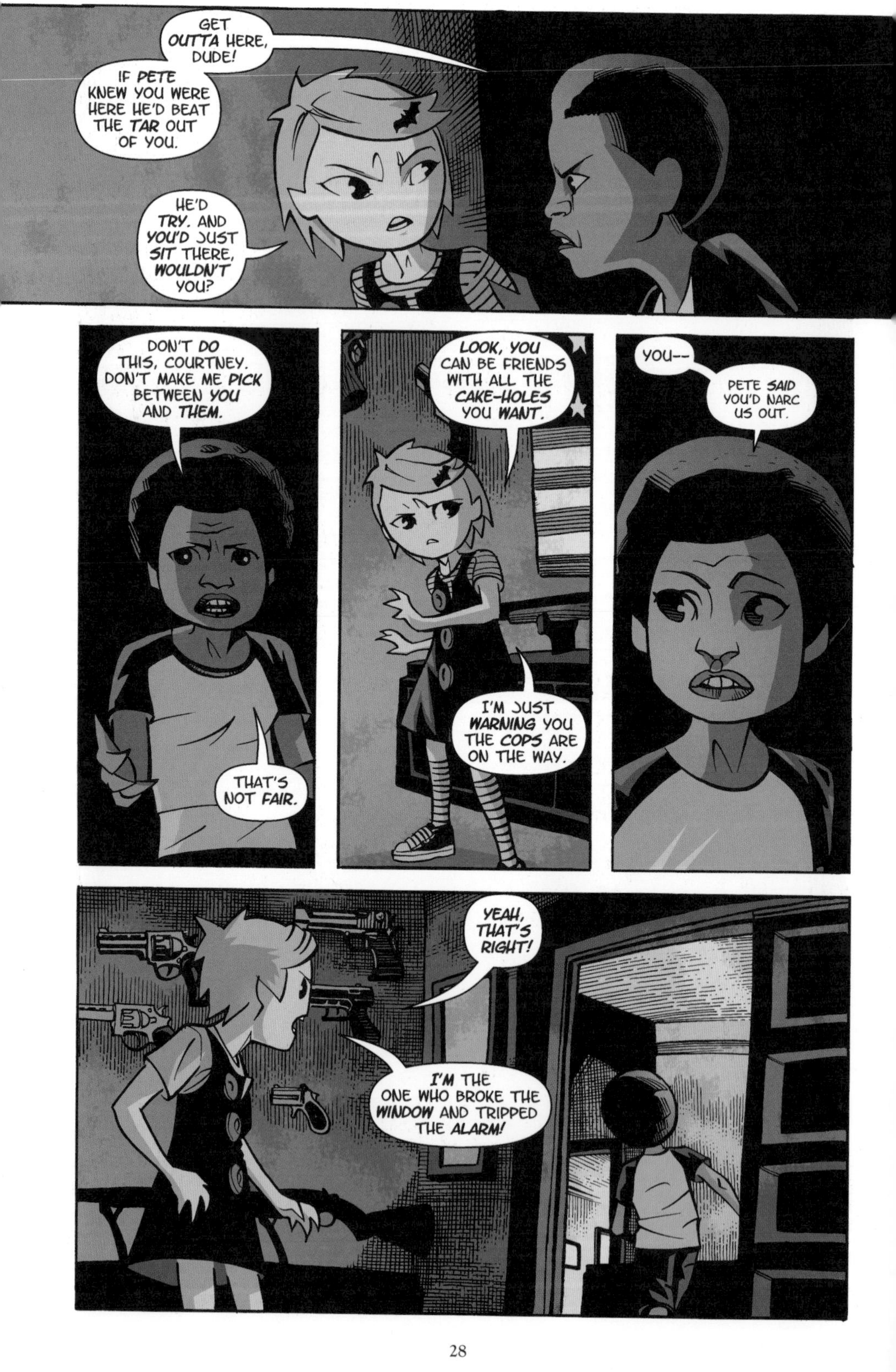
GET OUTTA HERE, DUDE!
IF PETE KNEW YOU WERE HERE HE'D BEAT THE TAR OUT OF YOU.
HE'D TRY. AND YOU'D JUST SIT THERE, WOULDN'T YOU?
DON'T DO THIS, COURTNEY. DON'T MAKE ME PICK BETWEEN YOU AND THEM.
THAT'S NOT FAIR.
LOOK, YOU CAN BE FRIENDS WITH ALL THE CAKE-HOLES YOU WANT.
I'M JUST WARNING YOU THE COPS ARE ON THE WAY.
YOU--
PETE SAID YOU'D NARC US OUT.
YEAH, THAT'S RIGHT!
I'M THE ONE WHO BROKE THE WINDOW AND TRIPPED THE ALARM!

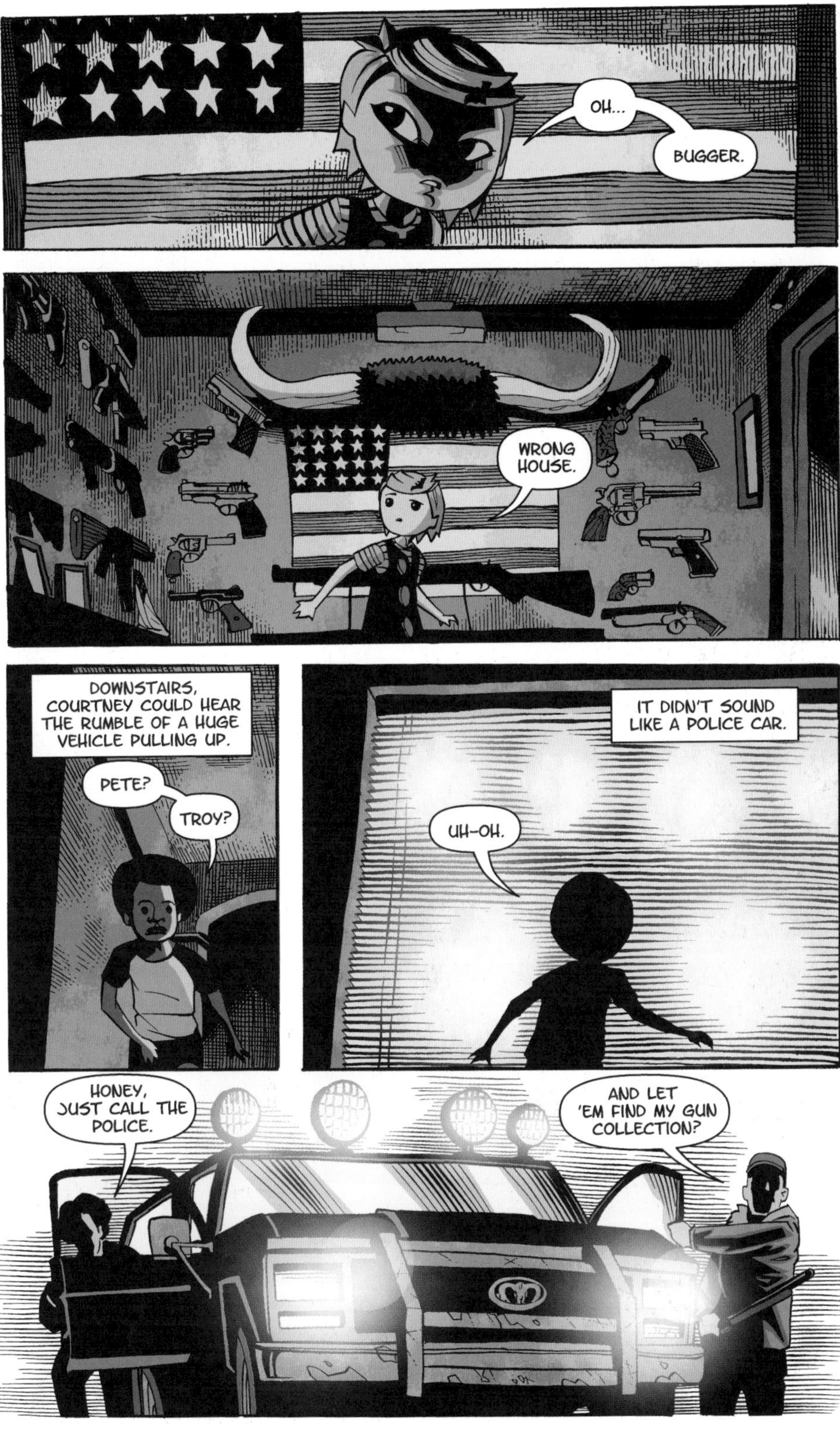
OH...
BUGGER.
WRONG HOUSE.
DOWNSTAIRS, COURTNEY COULD HEAR THE RUMBLE OF A HUGE VEHICLE PULLING UP.
PETE?
TROY?
IT DIDN'T SOUND LIKE A POLICE CAR.
UH-OH.
HONEY, JUST CALL THE POLICE.
AND LET 'EM FIND MY GUN COLLECTION?

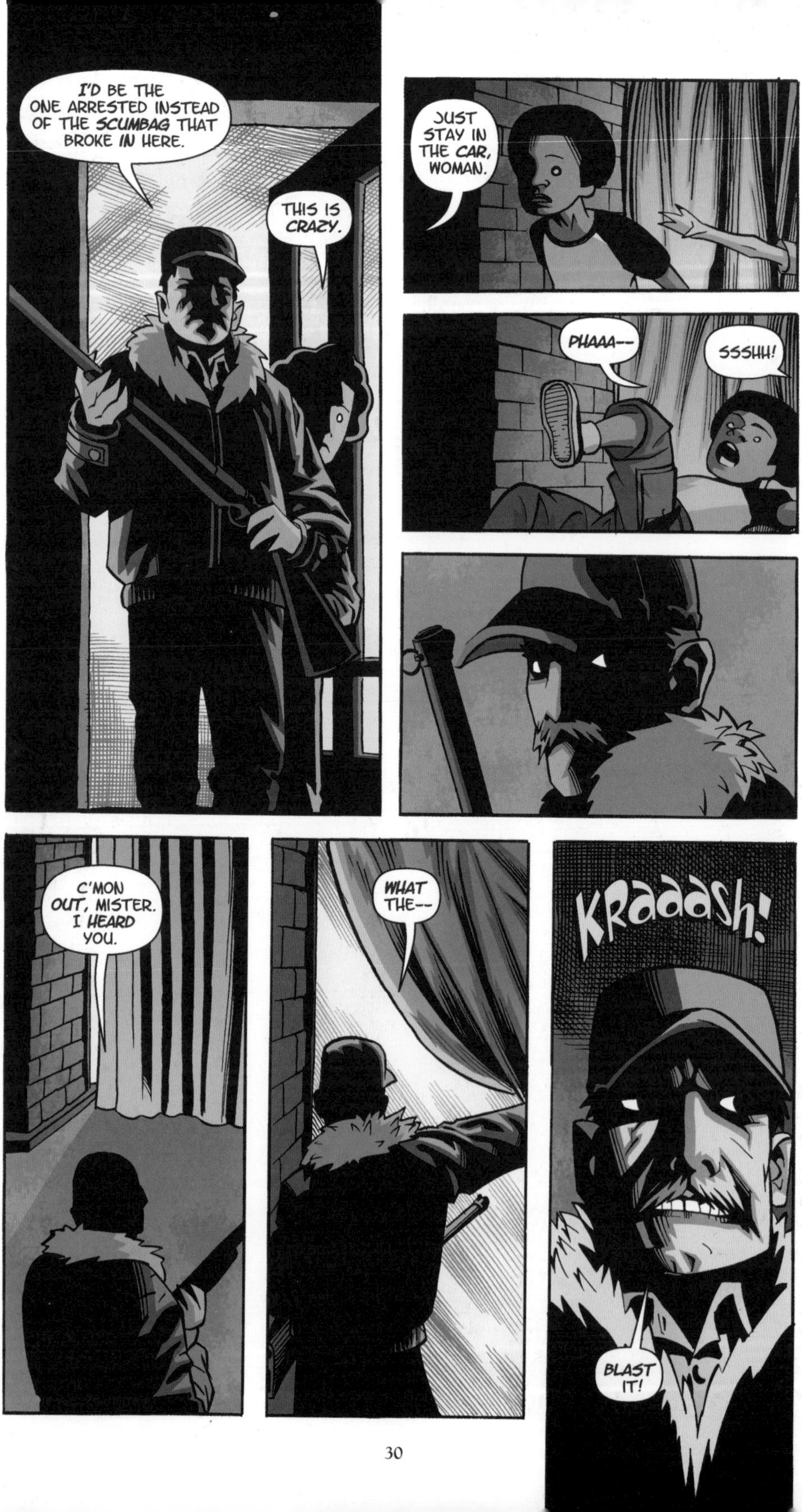
I'D BE THE ONE ARRESTED INSTEAD OF THE SCUMBAG THAT BROKE IN HERE.
THIS IS CRAZY.
JUST STAY IN THE CAR, WOMAN.
PHAAA--
SSSHH!
C'MON OUT, MISTER. I HEARD YOU.
WHAT THE--
KRAAASH!
BLAST IT!

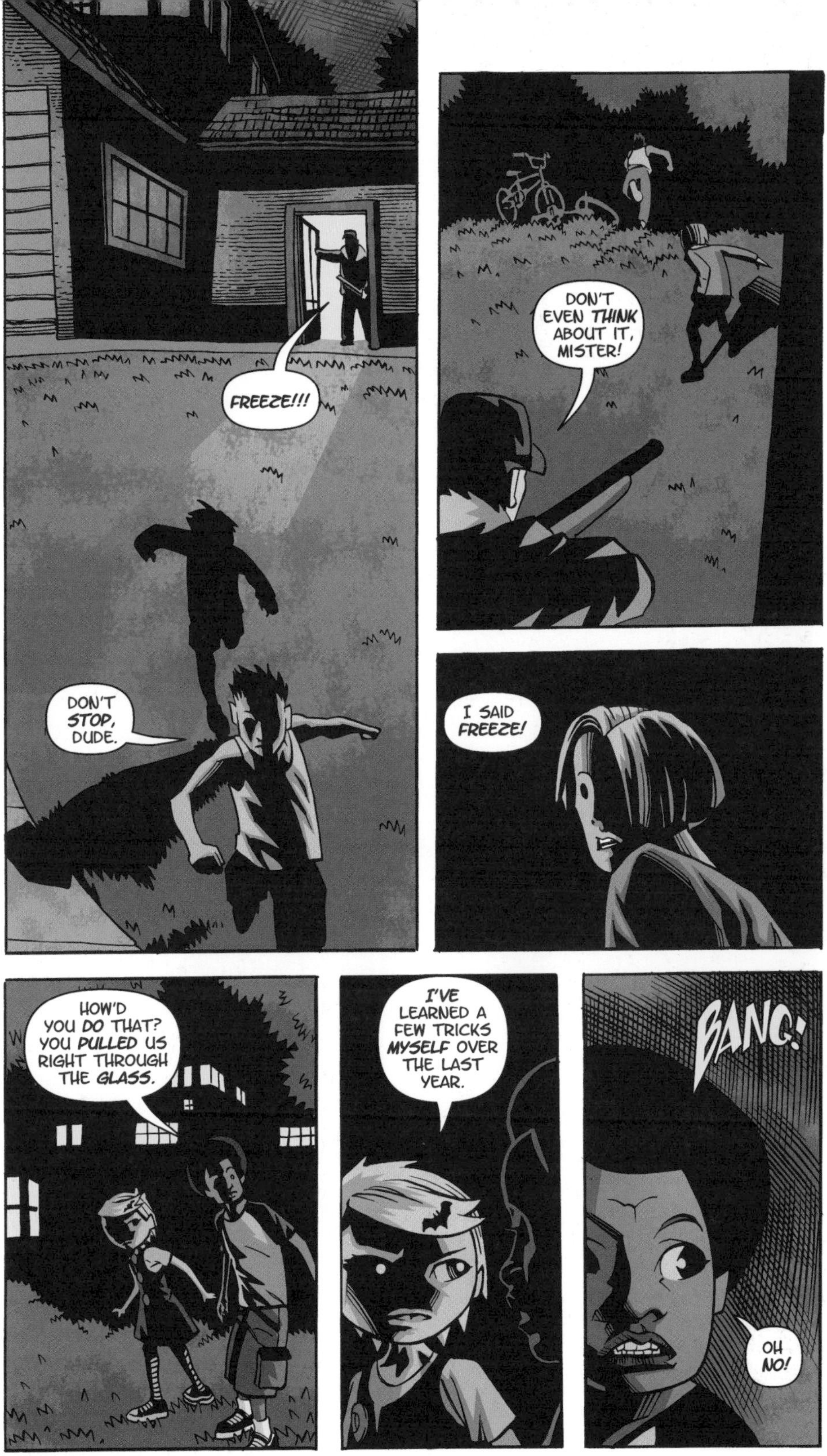
FREEZE!!!
DON'T STOP, DUDE.
DON'T EVEN THINK ABOUT IT, MISTER!
I SAID FREEZE!
HOW'D YOU DO THAT? YOU PULLED US RIGHT THROUGH THE GLASS.
I'VE LEARNED A FEW TRICKS MYSELF OVER THE LAST YEAR.
BANG!
OH NO!

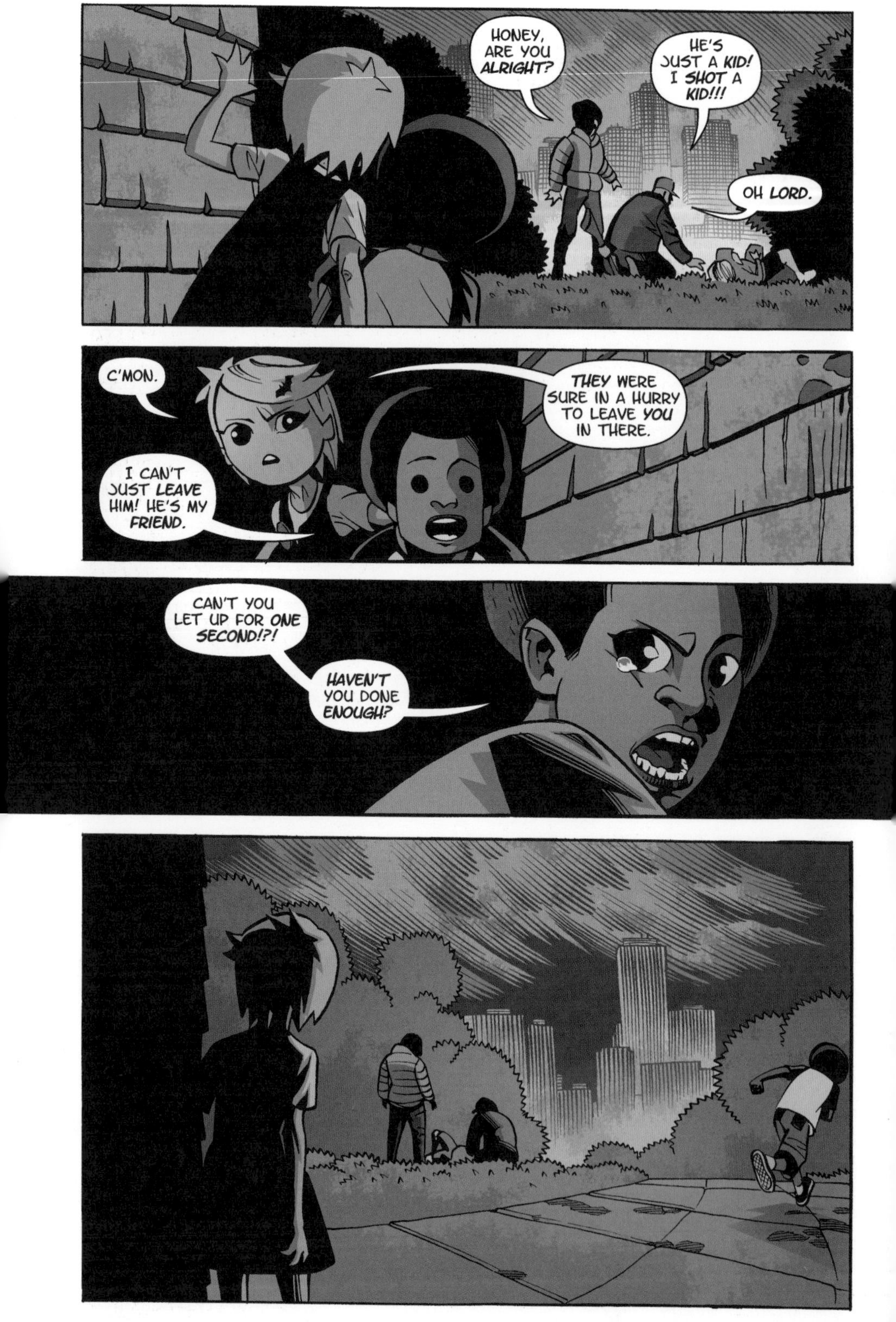
HONEY, ARE YOU ALRIGHT?
HE'S JUST A KID! I SHOT A KID!!!
OH LORD.
C'MON.
THEY WERE SURE IN A HURRY TO LEAVE YOU IN THERE.
I CAN'T JUST LEAVE HIM! HE'S MY FRIEND.
CAN'T YOU LET UP FOR ONE SECOND!?!
HAVEN'T YOU DONE ENOUGH?

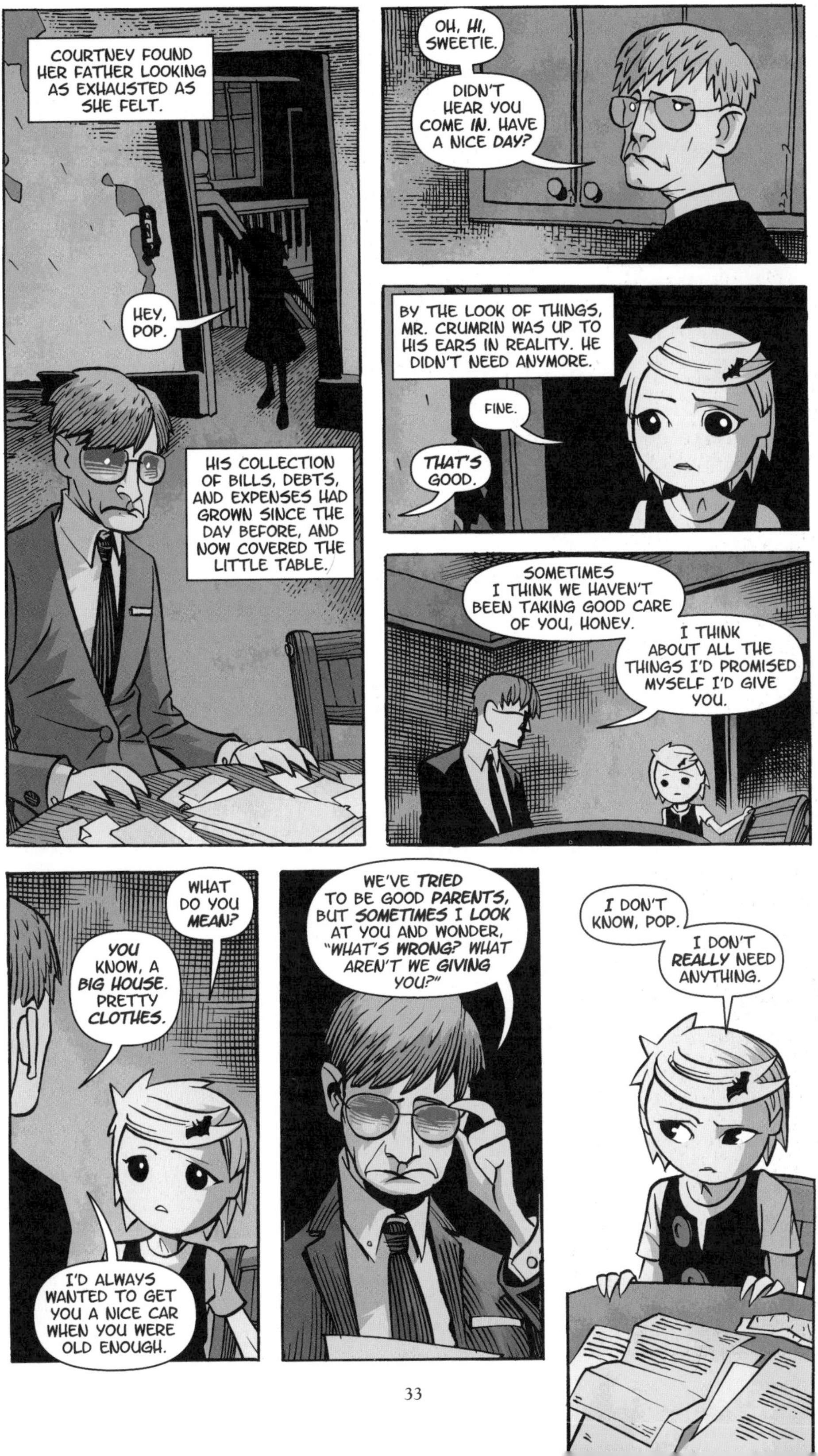
COURTNEY FOUND HER FATHER LOOKING AS EXHAUSTED AS SHE FELT.
HEY, POP.
HIS COLLECTION OF BILLS, DEBTS, AND EXPENSES HAD GROWN SINCE THE DAY BEFORE, AND NOW COVERED THE LITTLE TABLE.
OH, HI, SWEETIE.
DIDN'T HEAR YOU COME IN. HAVE A NICE DAY?
BY THE LOOK OF THINGS, MR. CRUMRIN WAS UP TO HIS EARS IN REALITY. HE DIDN'T NEED ANYMORE.
FINE.
THAT'S GOOD.
SOMETIMES I THINK WE HAVEN'T BEEN TAKING GOOD CARE OF YOU, HONEY.
I THINK ABOUT ALL THE THINGS I'D PROMISED MYSELF I'D GIVE YOU.
WHAT DO YOU MEAN?
YOU KNOW, A BIG HOUSE. PRETTY CLOTHES.
I'D ALWAYS WANTED TO GET YOU A NICE CAR WHEN YOU WERE OLD ENOUGH.
WE'VE TRIED TO BE GOOD PARENTS, BUT SOMETIMES I LOOK AT YOU AND WONDER, "WHAT'S WRONG? WHAT AREN'T WE GIVING YOU?"
I DON'T KNOW, POP.
I DON'T REALLY NEED ANYTHING.

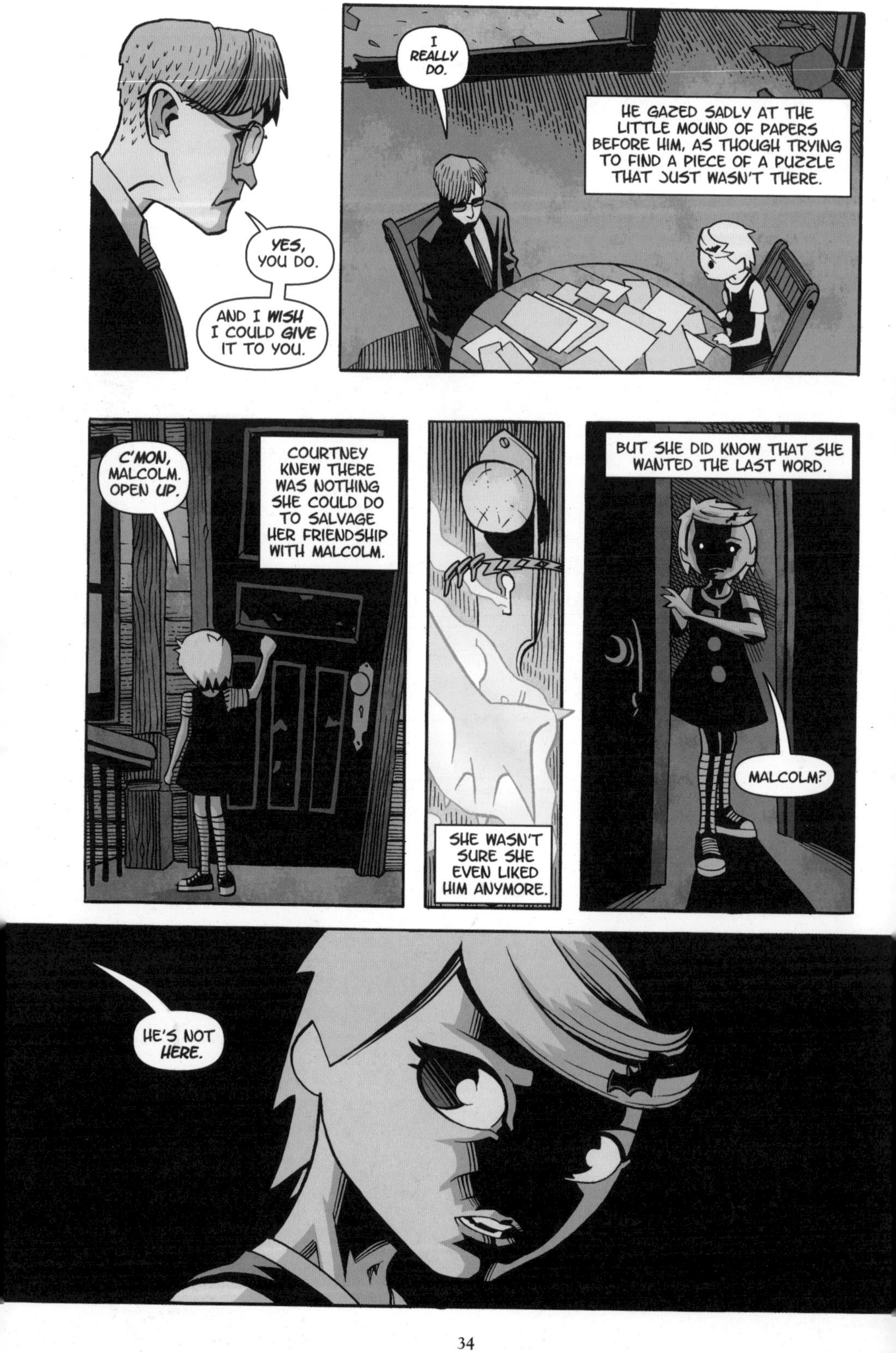
YES, YOU DO.
AND I WISH I COULD GIVE IT TO YOU.
I REALLY DO.
HE GAZED SADLY AT THE LITTLE MOUND OF PAPERS BEFORE HIM, AS THOUGH TRYING TO FIND A PIECE OF A PUZZLE THAT JUST WASN'T THERE.
C'MON, MALCOLM. OPEN UP.
COURTNEY KNEW THERE WAS NOTHING SHE COULD DO TO SALVAGE HER FRIENDSHIP WITH MALCOLM.
SHE WASN'T SURE SHE EVEN LIKED HIM ANYMORE.
BUT SHE DID KNOW THAT SHE WANTED THE LAST WORD.
MALCOLM?
HE'S NOT HERE.

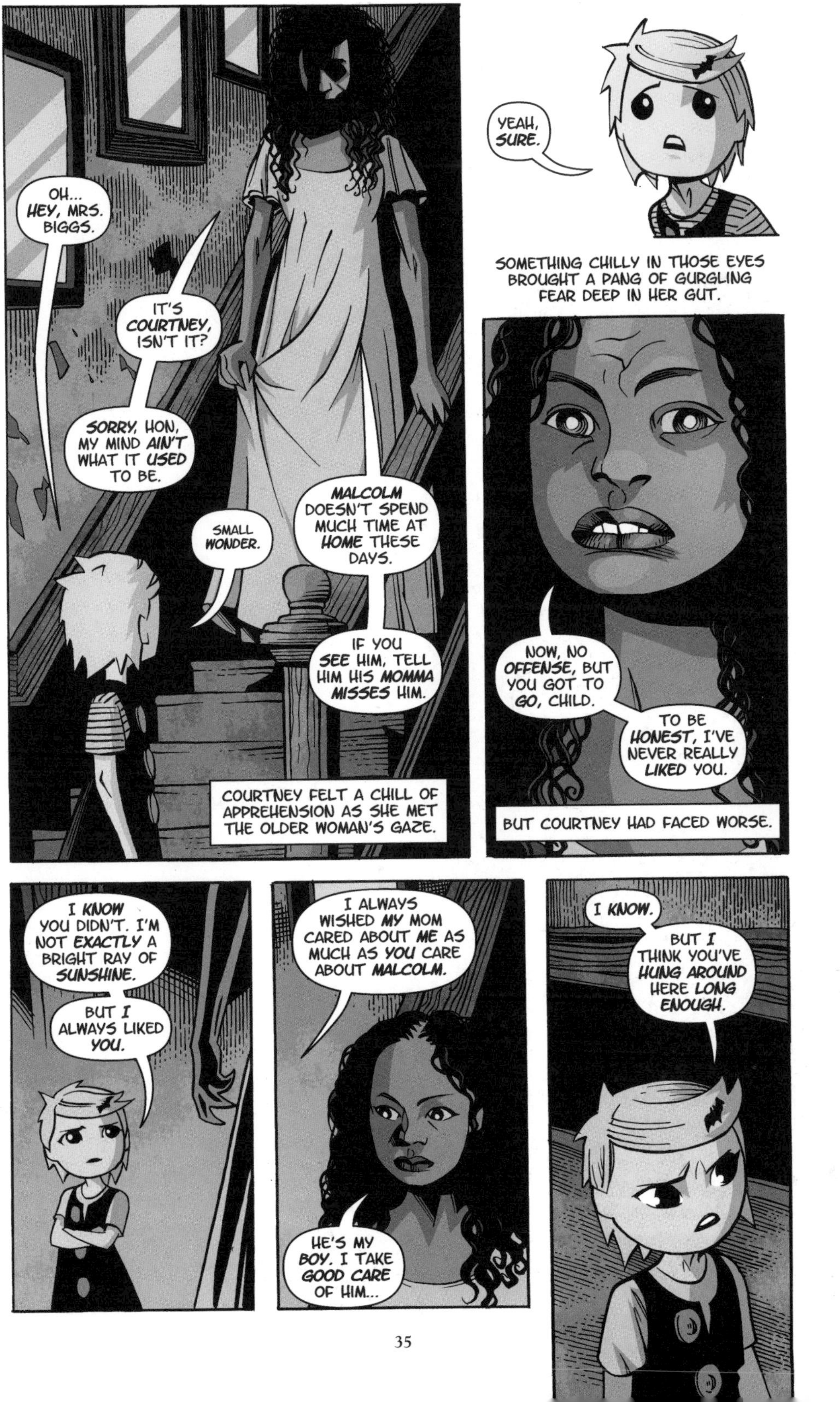
OH... HEY, MRS. BIGGS.
IT'S COURTNEY, ISN'T IT?
SORRY, HON, MY MIND AIN'T WHAT IT USED TO BE.
SMALL WONDER.
MALCOLM DOESN'T SPEND MUCH TIME AT HOME THESE DAYS.
IF YOU SEE HIM, TELL HIM HIS MOMMA MISSES HIM.
COURTNEY FELT A CHILL OF APPREHENSION AS SHE MET THE OLDER WOMAN'S GAZE.
YEAH, SURE.
SOMETHING CHILLY IN THOSE EYES BROUGHT A PANG OF GURGLING FEAR DEEP IN HER GUT.
NOW, NO OFFENSE, BUT YOU GOT TO GO, CHILD.
TO BE HONEST, I'VE NEVER REALLY LIKED YOU.
BUT COURTNEY HAD FACED WORSE.
I KNOW YOU DIDN'T. I'M NOT EXACTLY A BRIGHT RAY OF SUNSHINE.
BUT I ALWAYS LIKED YOU.
I ALWAYS WISHED MY MOM CARED ABOUT ME AS MUCH AS YOU CARE ABOUT MALCOLM.
HE'S MY BOY. I TAKE GOOD CARE OF HIM...
I KNOW.
BUT I THINK YOU'VE HUNG AROUND HERE LONG ENOUGH.

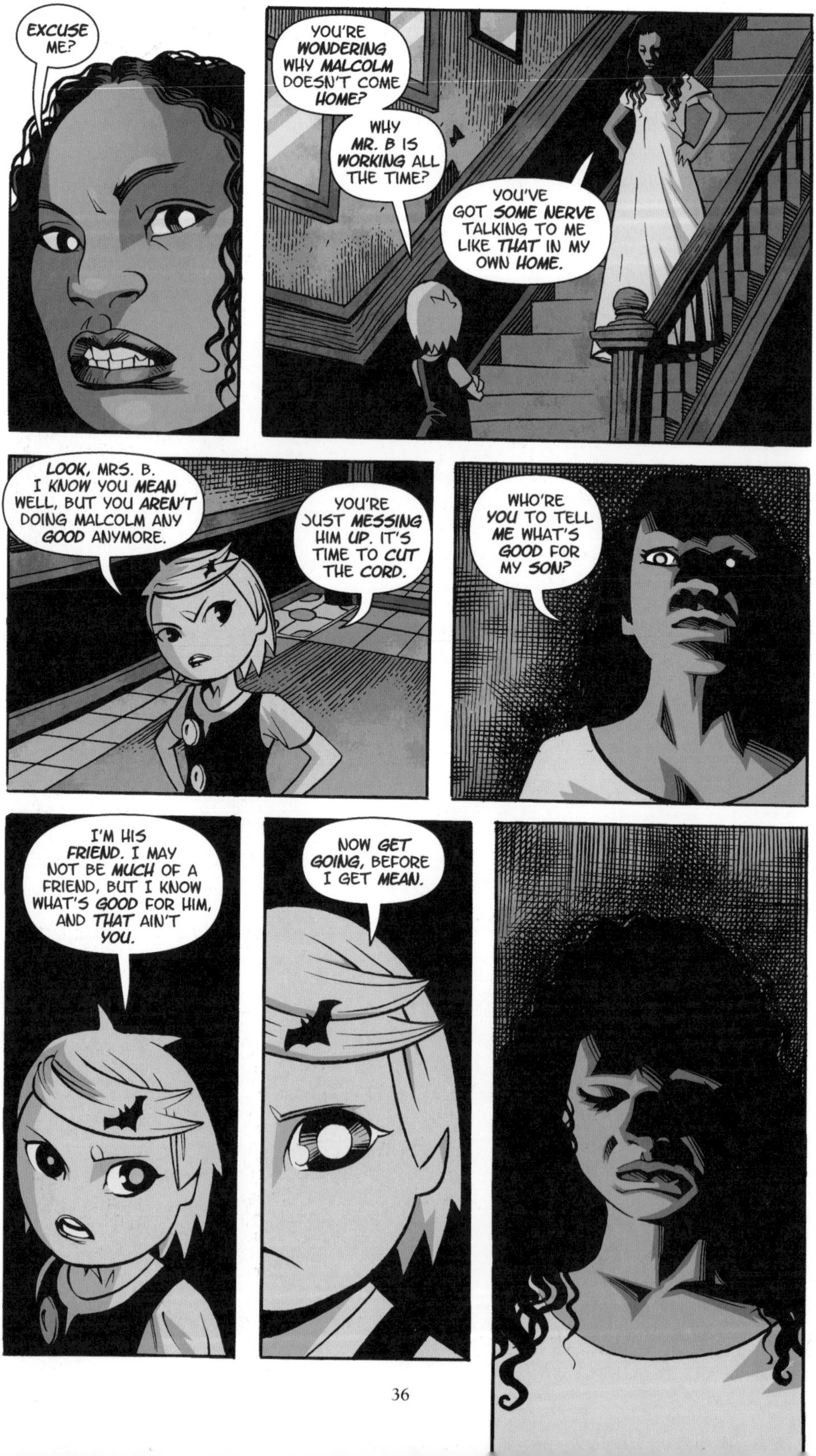
EXCUSE ME?
YOU'RE WONDERING WHY MALCOLM DOESN'T COME HOME?
WHY MR. B IS WORKING ALL THE TIME?
YOU'VE GOT SOME NERVE TALKING TO ME LIKE THAT IN MY OWN HOME.
LOOK, MRS. B. I KNOW YOU MEAN WELL, BUT YOU AREN'T DOING MALCOLM ANY GOOD ANYMORE.
YOU'RE JUST MESSING HIM UP. IT'S TIME TO CUT THE CORD.
WHO'RE YOU TO TELL ME WHAT'S GOOD FOR MY SON?
I'M HIS FRIEND. I MAY NOT BE MUCH OF A FRIEND, BUT I KNOW WHAT'S GOOD FOR HIM, AND THAT AIN'T YOU.
NOW GET GOING, BEFORE I GET MEAN.

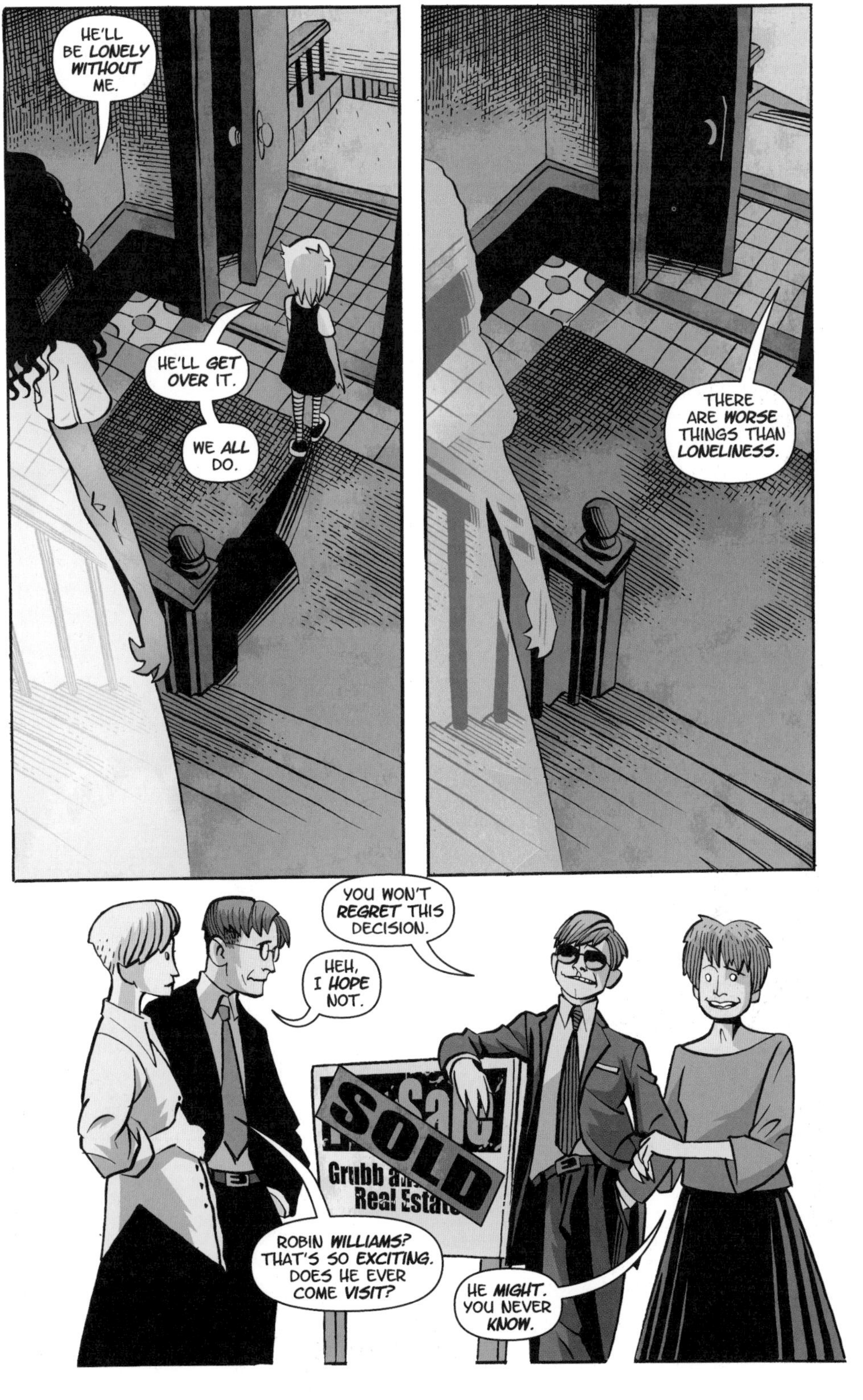
HE'LL BE LONELY WITHOUT ME.
HE'LL GET OVER IT.
WE ALL DO.
THERE ARE WORSE THINGS THAN LONELINESS.
YOU WON'T REGRET THIS DECISION.
HEH, I HOPE NOT.
SOLD
ROBIN WILLIAMS? THAT'S SO EXCITING. DOES HE EVER COME VISIT?
HE MIGHT. YOU NEVER KNOW.

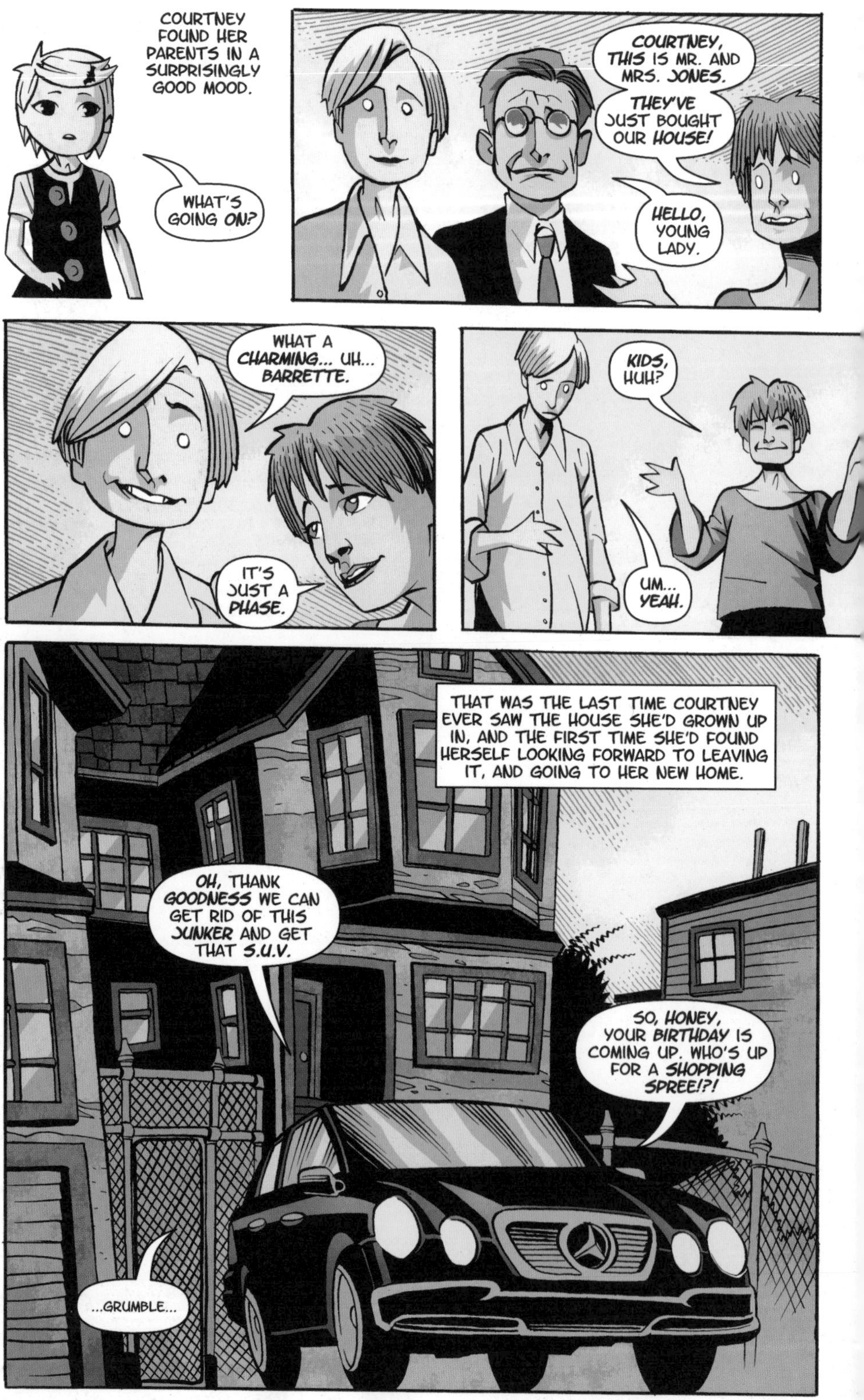
COURTNEY FOUND HER PARENTS IN A SURPRISINGLY GOOD MOOD.
WHAT'S GOING ON?
COURTNEY, THIS IS MR. AND MRS. JONES.
THEY'VE JUST BOUGHT OUR HOUSE!
HELLO, YOUNG LADY.
WHAT A CHARMING... UH... BARRETTE.
IT'S JUST A PHASE.
KIDS, HUH?
UM... YEAH.
THAT WAS THE LAST TIME COURTNEY EVER SAW THE HOUSE SHE'D GROWN UP IN, AND THE FIRST TIME SHE'D FOUND HERSELF LOOKING FORWARD TO LEAVING IT, AND GOING TO HER NEW HOME.
OH, THANK GOODNESS WE CAN GET RID OF THIS JUNKER AND GET THAT S.U.V.
SO, HONEY, YOUR BIRTHDAY IS COMING UP. WHO'S UP FOR A SHOPPING SPREE!?!
...GRUMBLE...

Chapter Two

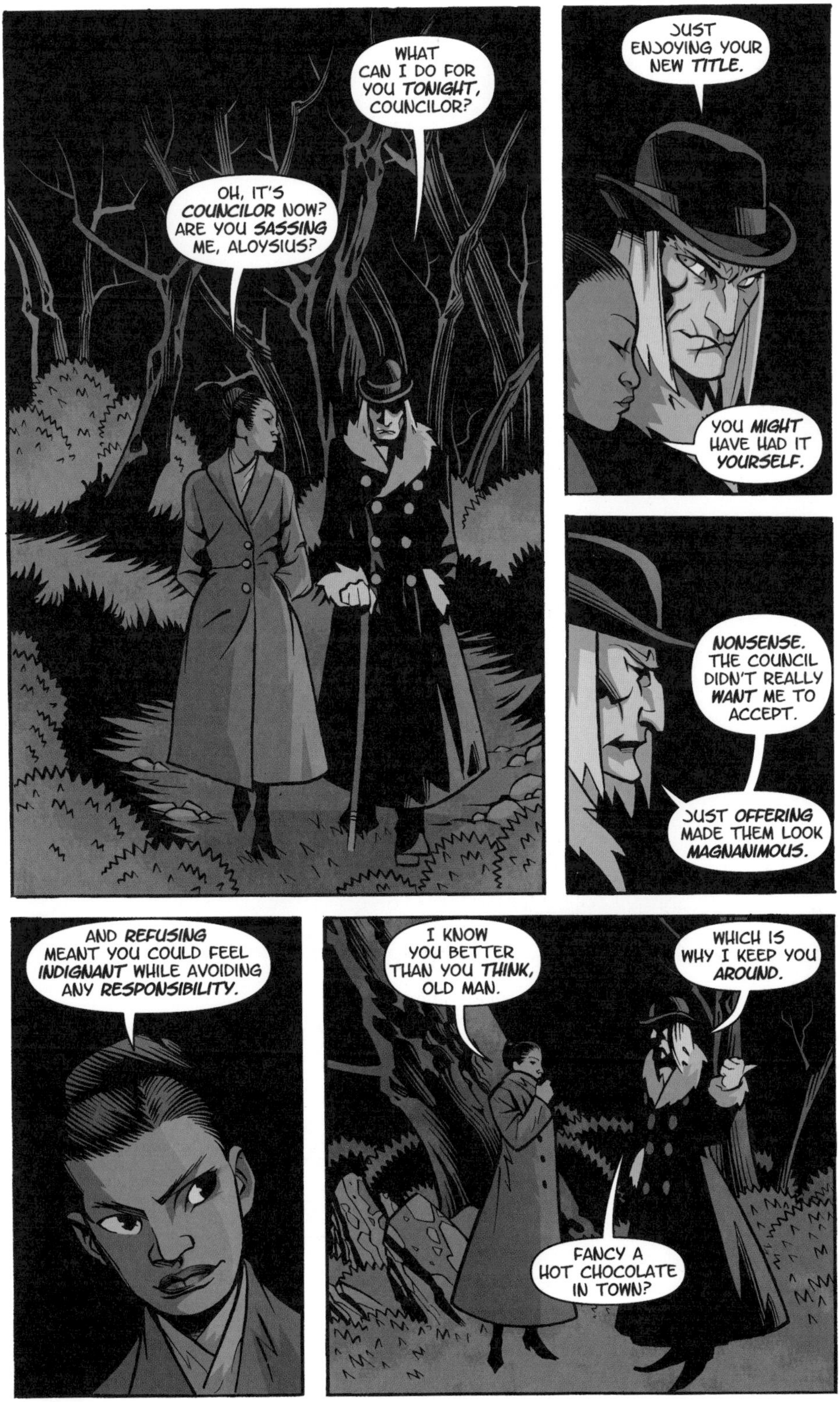
WHAT CAN I DO FOR YOU TONIGHT, COUNCILOR?
OH, IT'S COUNCILOR NOW? ARE YOU SASSING ME, ALOYSIUS?
JUST ENJOYING YOUR NEW TITLE.
YOU MIGHT HAVE HAD IT YOURSELF.
NONSENSE. THE COUNCIL DIDN'T REALLY WANT ME TO ACCEPT.
JUST OFFERING MADE THEM LOOK MAGNANIMOUS.
AND REFUSING MEANT YOU COULD FEEL INDIGNANT WHILE AVOIDING ANY RESPONSIBILITY.
I KNOW YOU BETTER THAN YOU THINK, OLD MAN.
WHICH IS WHY I KEEP YOU AROUND.
FANCY A HOT CHOCOLATE IN TOWN?

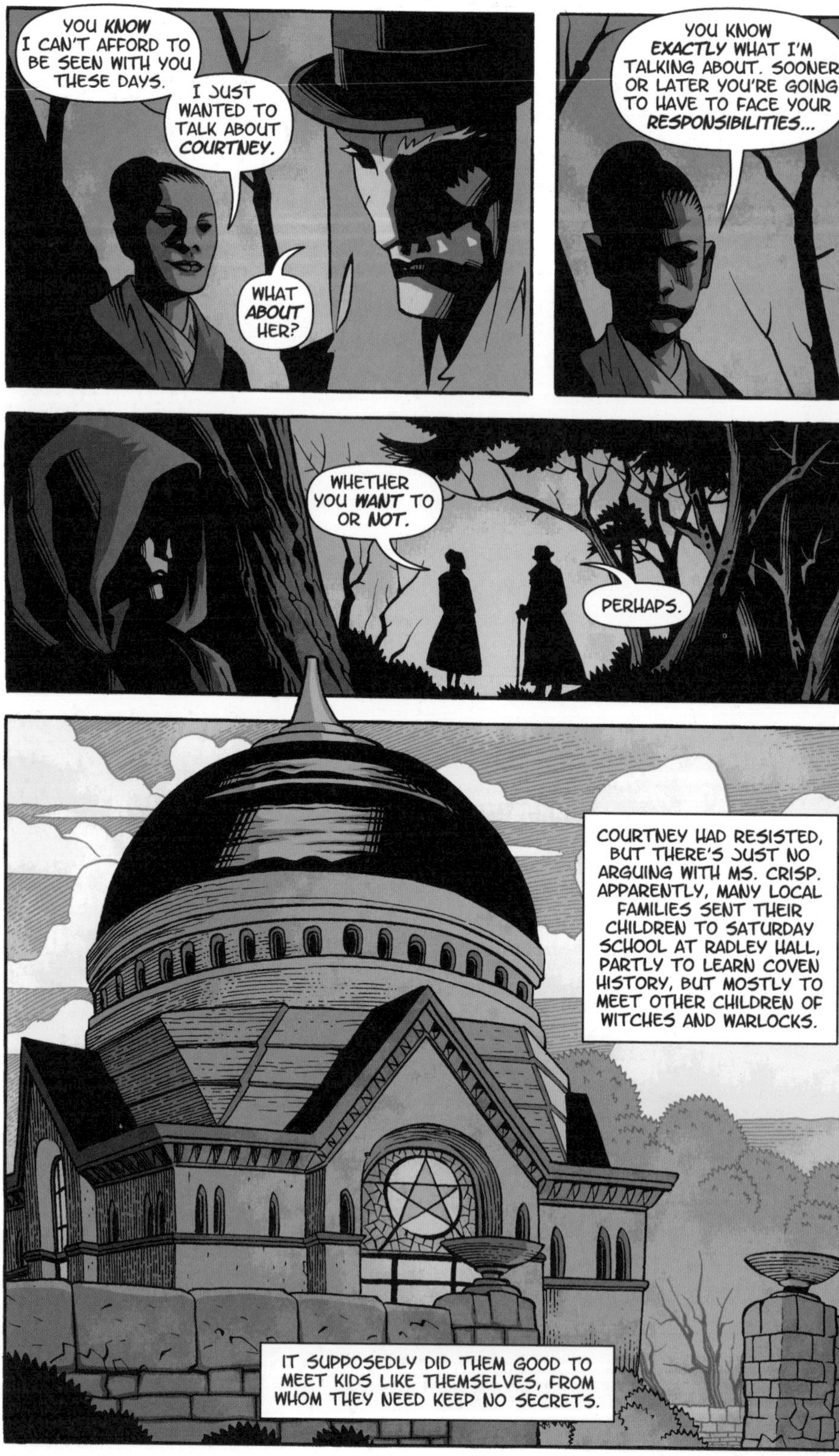
YOU KNOW I CAN'T AFFORD TO BE SEEN WITH YOU THESE DAYS.
I JUST WANTED TO TALK ABOUT COURTNEY.
WHAT ABOUT HER?
YOU KNOW EXACTLY WHAT I'M TALKING ABOUT. SOONER OR LATER YOU'RE GOING TO HAVE TO FACE YOUR RESPONSIBILITIES...
WHETHER YOU WANT TO OR NOT.
PERHAPS.
COURTNEY HAD RESISTED, BUT THERE'S JUST NO ARGUING WITH MS. CRISP. APPARENTLY, MANY LOCAL FAMILIES SENT THEIR CHILDREN TO SATURDAY SCHOOL AT RADLEY HALL, PARTLY TO LEARN COVEN HISTORY, BUT MOSTLY TO MEET OTHER CHILDREN OF WITCHES AND WARLOCKS.
IT SUPPOSEDLY DID THEM GOOD TO MEET KIDS LIKE THEMSELVES, FROM WHOM THEY NEED KEEP NO SECRETS.

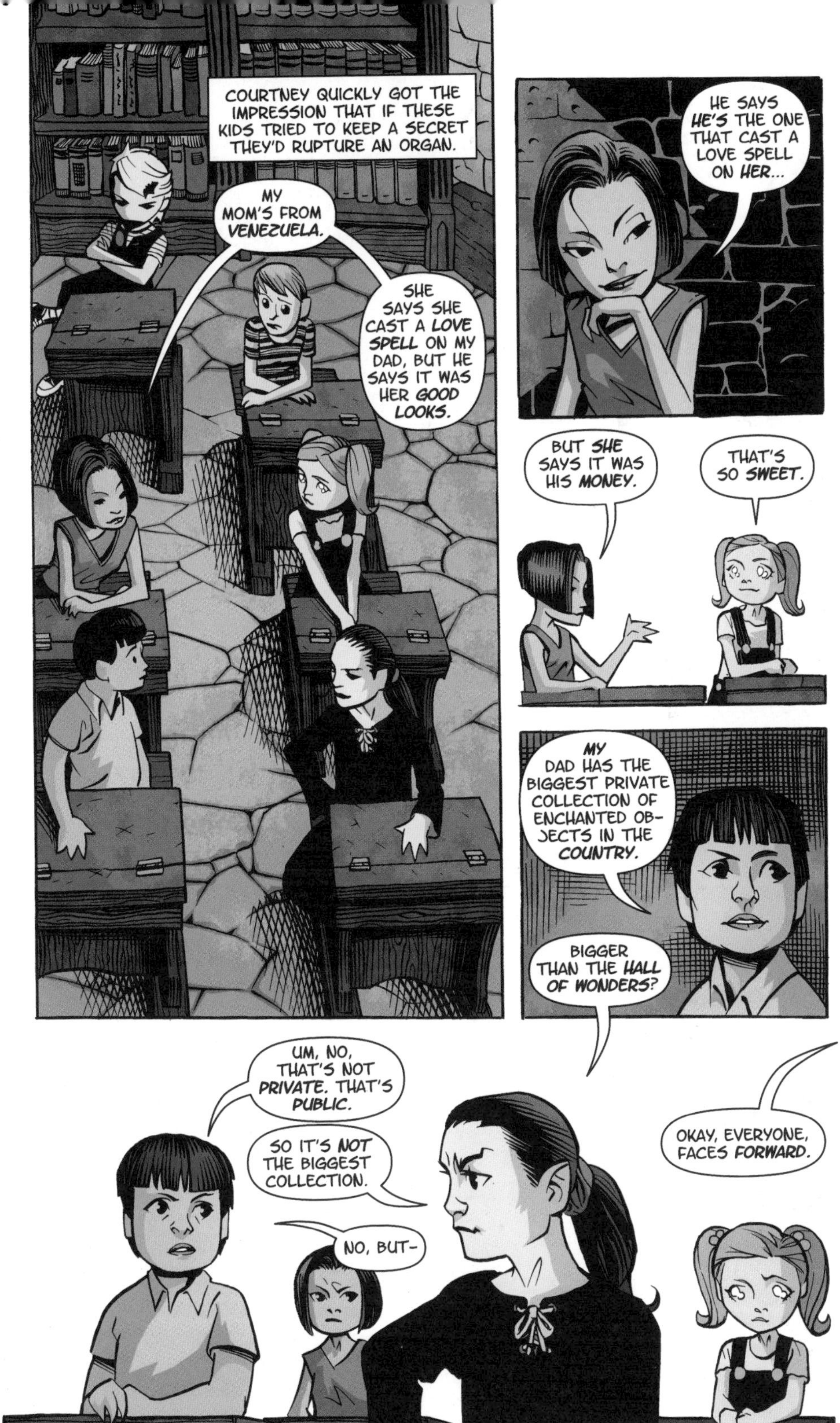
COURTNEY QUICKLY GOT THE IMPRESSION THAT IF THESE KIDS TRIED TO KEEP A SECRET THEY'D RUPTURE AN ORGAN.
MY MOM'S FROM VENEZUELA.
SHE SAYS SHE CAST A LOVE SPELL ON MY DAD, BUT HE SAYS IT WAS HER GOOD LOOKS.
HE SAYS HE'S THE ONE THAT CAST A LOVE SPELL ON HER...
BUT SHE SAYS IT WAS HIS MONEY.
THAT'S SO SWEET.
MY DAD HAS THE BIGGEST PRIVATE COLLECTION OF ENCHANTED OB-JECTS IN THE COUNTRY.
BIGGER THAN THE HALL OF WONDERS?
UM, NO, THAT'S NOT PRIVATE. THAT'S PUBLIC.
SO IT'S NOT THE BIGGEST COLLECTION.
NO, BUT-
OKAY, EVERYONE, FACES FORWARD.

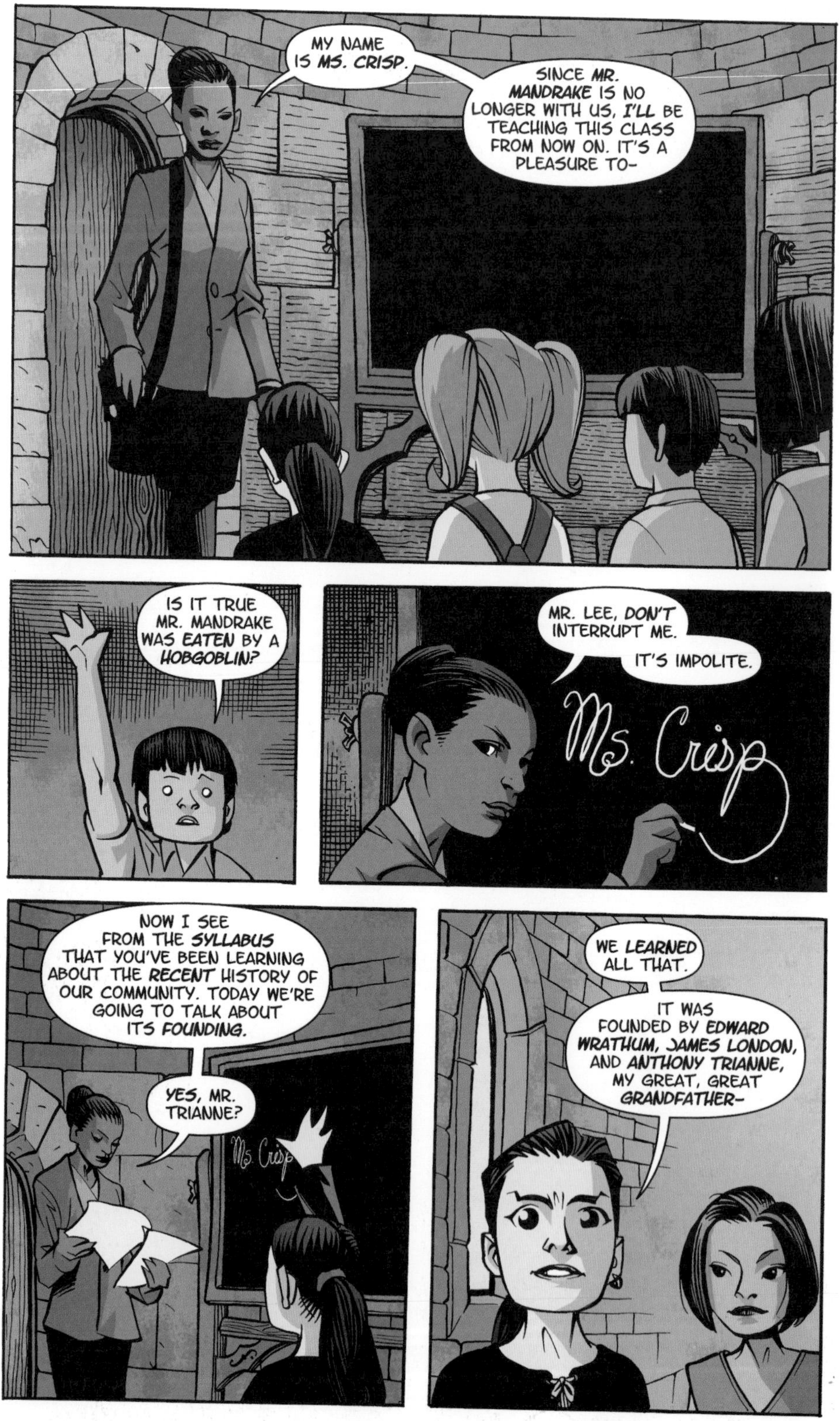
MY NAME IS MS. CRISP.
SINCE MR. MANDRAKE IS NO LONGER WITH US, I'LL BE TEACHING THIS CLASS FROM NOW ON. IT'S A PLEASURE TO-
IS IT TRUE MR. MANDRAKE WAS EATEN BY A HOBGOBLIN?
MR. LEE, DON'T INTERRUPT ME.
IT'S IMPOLITE.
Ms. Crisp
NOW I SEE FROM THE SYLLABUS THAT YOU'VE BEEN LEARNING ABOUT THE RECENT HISTORY OF OUR COMMUNITY. TODAY WE'RE GOING TO TALK ABOUT ITS FOUNDING.
YES, MR. TRIANNE?
Ms. Crisp
WE LEARNED ALL THAT.
IT WAS FOUNDED BY EDWARD WRATHUM, JAMES LONDON, AND ANTHONY TRIANNE, MY GREAT, GREAT GRANDFATHER-

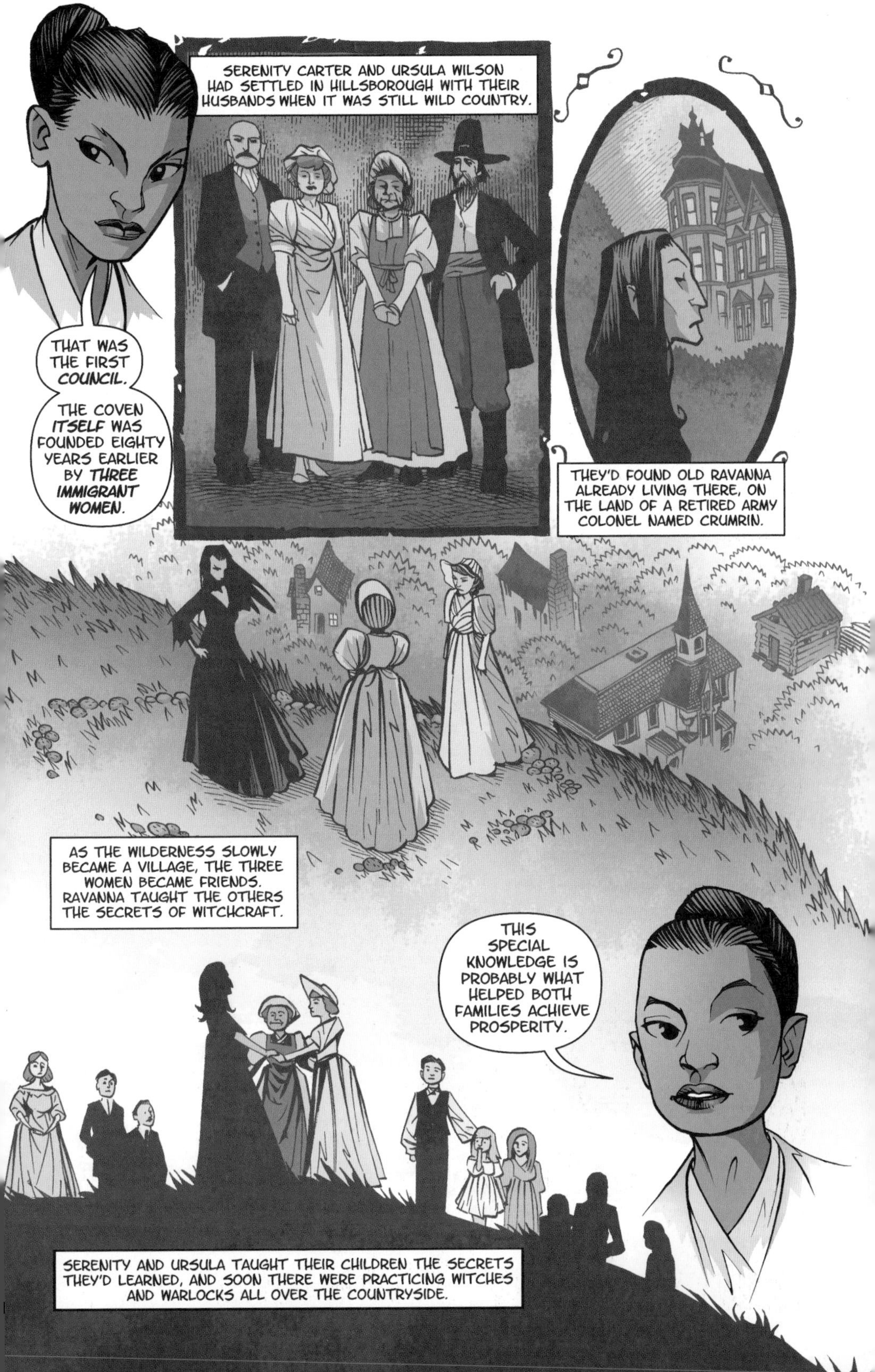

SERENITY CARTER AND URSULA WILSON HAD SETTLED IN HILLSBOROUGH WITH THEIR HUSBANDS WHEN IT WAS STILL WILD COUNTRY.
THAT WAS THE FIRST COUNCIL.
THE COVEN ITSELF WAS FOUNDED EIGHTY YEARS EARLIER BY THREE IMMIGRANT WOMEN.
THEY'D FOUND OLD RAVANNA ALREADY LIVING THERE, ON THE LAND OF A RETIRED ARMY COLONEL NAMED CRUMRIN.
AS THE WILDERNESS SLOWLY BECAME A VILLAGE, THE THREE WOMEN BECAME FRIENDS. RAVANNA TAUGHT THE OTHERS THE SECRETS OF WITCHCRAFT.
THIS SPECIAL KNOWLEDGE IS PROBABLY WHAT HELPED BOTH FAMILIES ACHIEVE PROSPERITY.
SERENITY AND URSULA TAUGHT THEIR CHILDREN THE SECRETS THEY'D LEARNED, AND SOON THERE WERE PRACTICING WITCHES AND WARLOCKS ALL OVER THE COUNTRYSIDE.

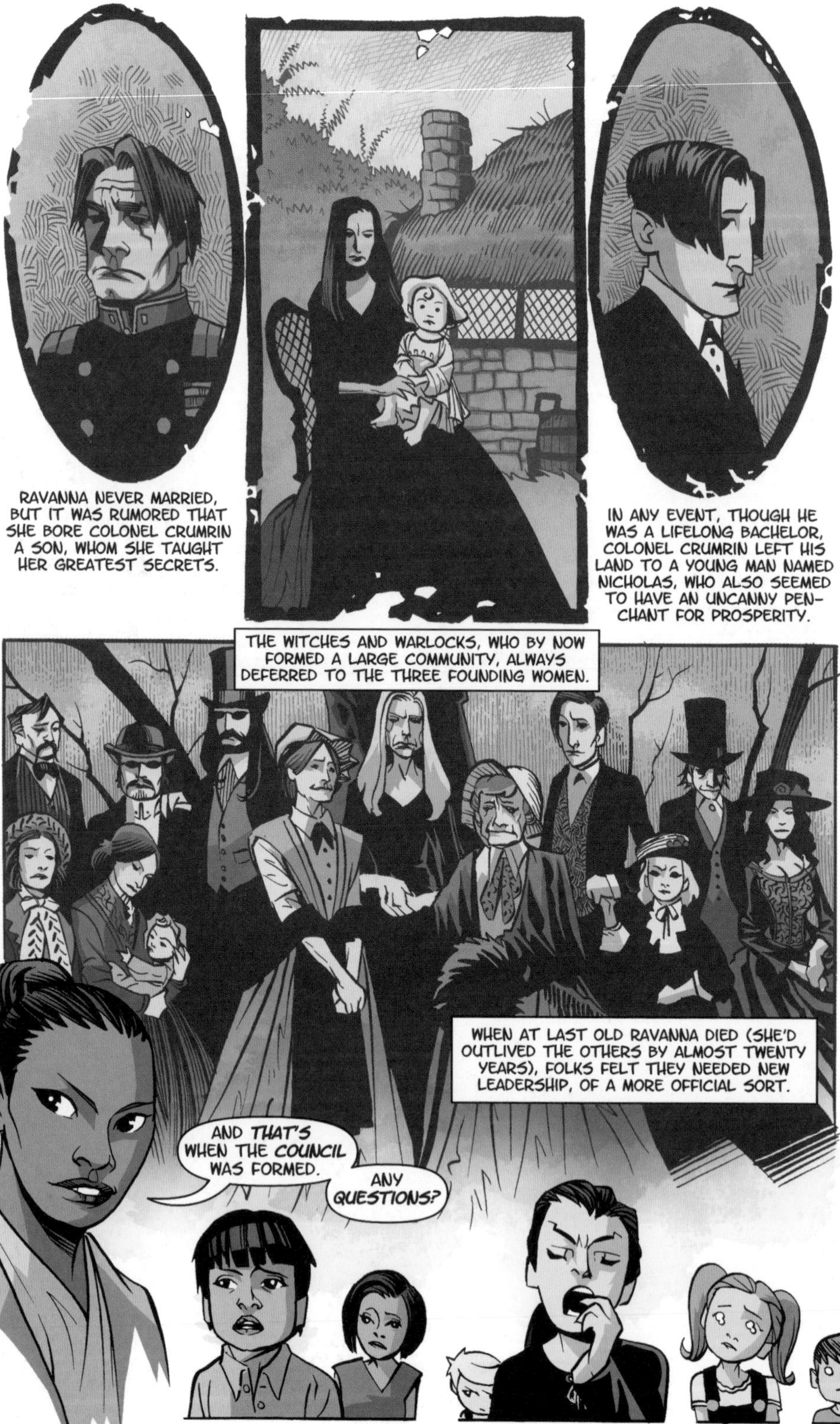
RAVANNA NEVER MARRIED, BUT IT WAS RUMORED THAT SHE BORE COLONEL CRUMRIN A SON, WHOM SHE TAUGHT HER GREATEST SECRETS.
IN ANY EVENT, THOUGH HE WAS A LIFELONG BACHELOR, COLONEL CRUMRIN LEFT HIS LAND TO A YOUNG MAN NAMED NICHOLAS, WHO ALSO SEEMED TO HAVE AN UNCANNY PEN-CHANT FOR PROSPERITY.
THE WITCHES AND WARLOCKS, WHO BY NOW FORMED A LARGE COMMUNITY, ALWAYS DEFERRED TO THE THREE FOUNDING WOMEN.
WHEN AT LAST OLD RAVANNA DIED (SHE'D OUTLIVED THE OTHERS BY ALMOST TWENTY YEARS), FOLKS FELT THEY NEEDED NEW LEADERSHIP, OF A MORE OFFICIAL SORT.
AND *THAT'S* WHEN THE *COUNCIL* WAS FORMED.
ANY *QUESTIONS?*

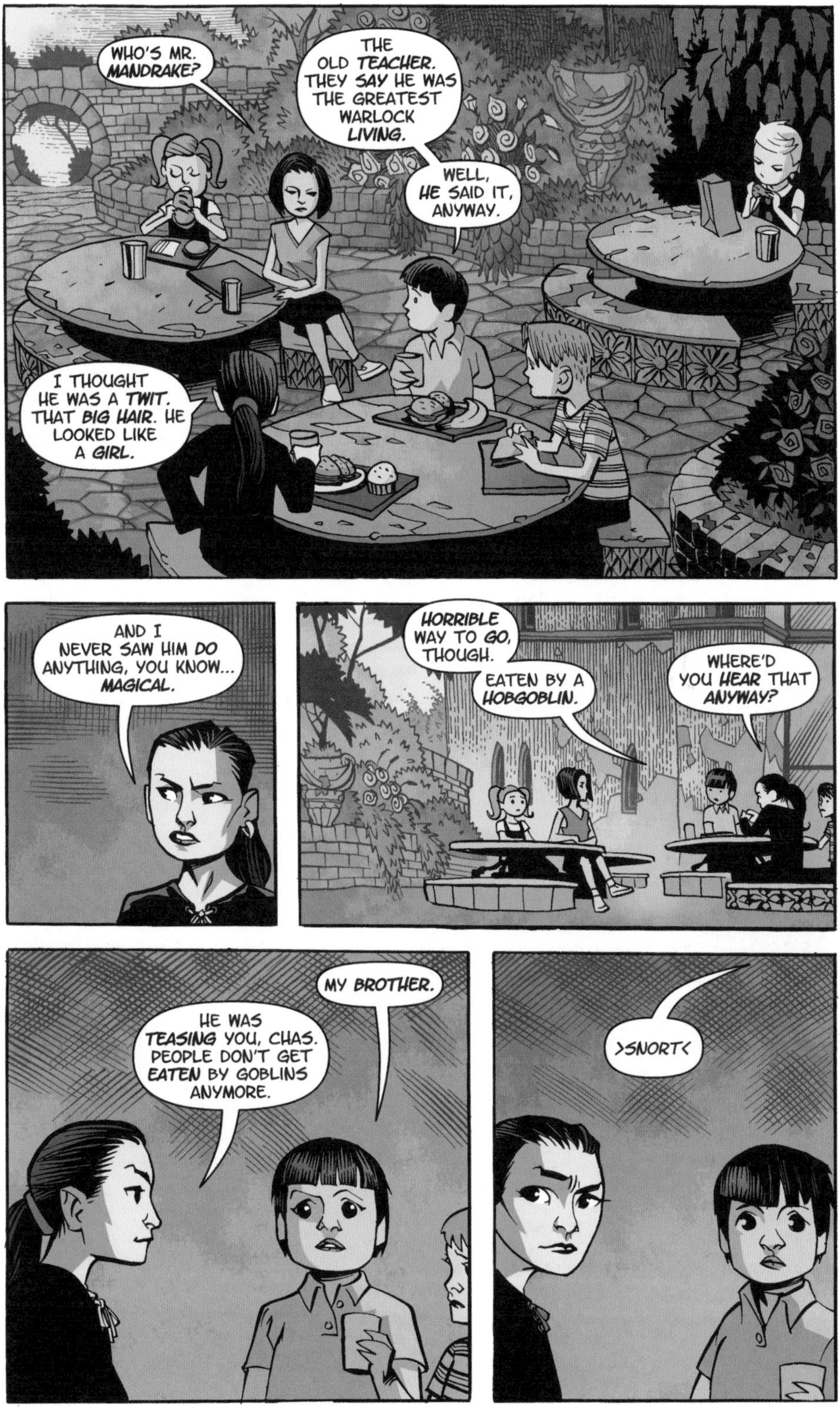

WHO'S MR. MANDRAKE?
THE OLD TEACHER. THEY SAY HE WAS THE GREATEST WARLOCK LIVING.
WELL, HE SAID IT, ANYWAY.
I THOUGHT HE WAS A TWIT. THAT BIG HAIR. HE LOOKED LIKE A GIRL.
AND I NEVER SAW HIM DO ANYTHING, YOU KNOW... MAGICAL.
HORRIBLE WAY TO GO, THOUGH.
EATEN BY A HOBGOBLIN.
WHERE'D YOU HEAR THAT ANYWAY?
MY BROTHER.
HE WAS TEASING YOU, CHAS. PEOPLE DON'T GET EATEN BY GOBLINS ANYMORE.
>SNORT<

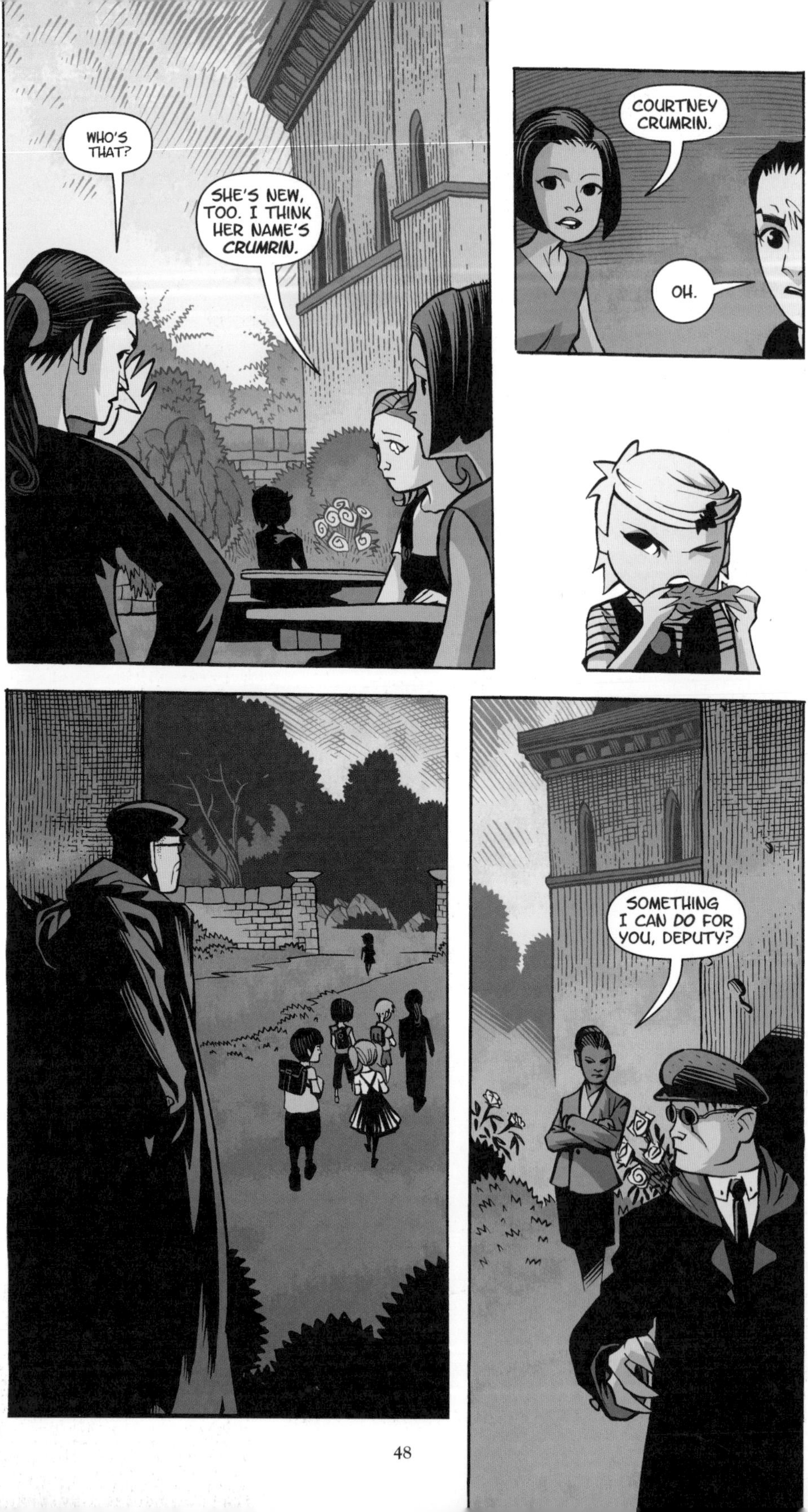
WHO'S THAT?
SHE'S NEW, TOO. I THINK HER NAME'S CRUMRIN.
COURTNEY CRUMRIN.
OH.
SOMETHING I CAN DO FOR YOU, DEPUTY?

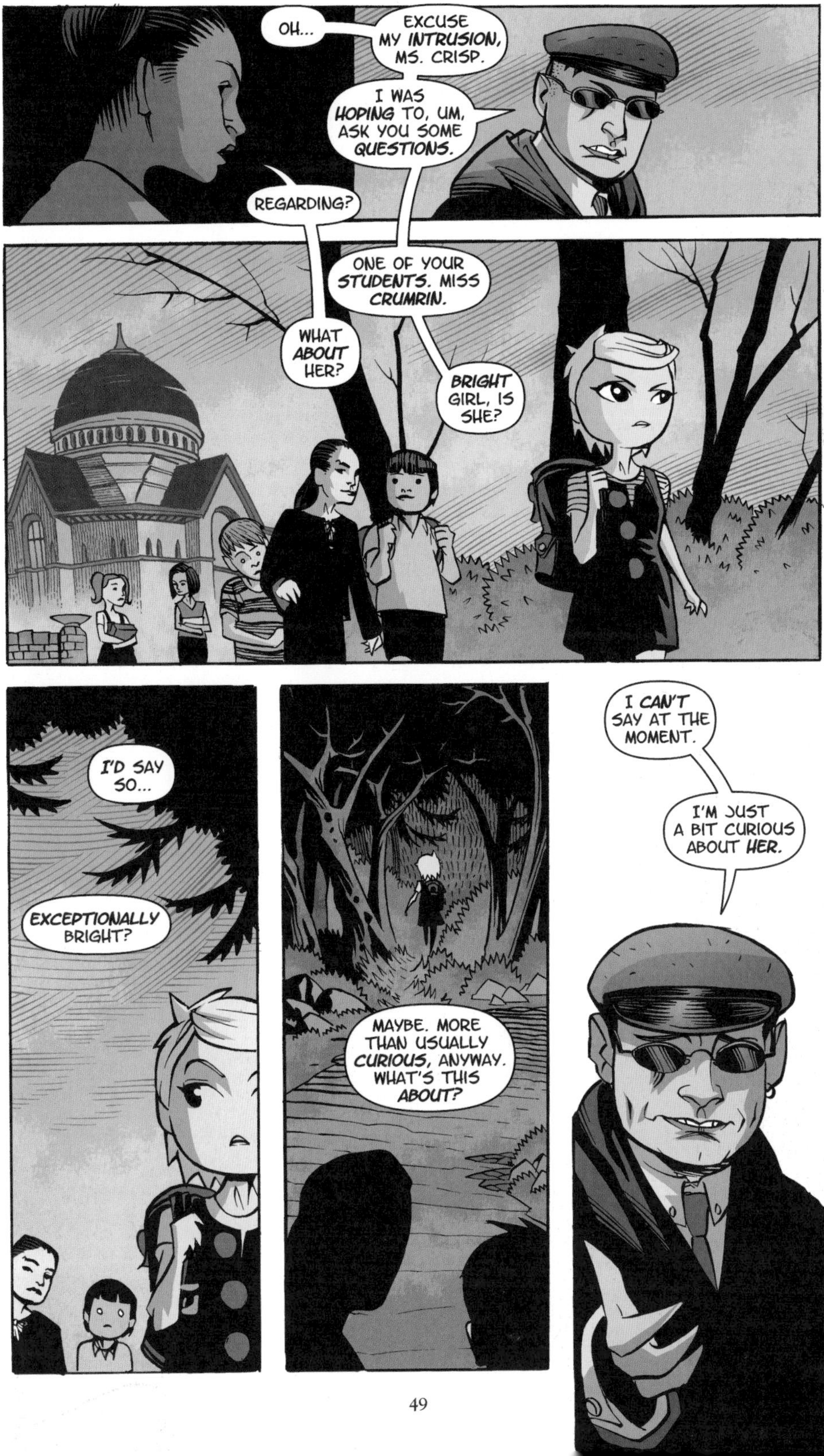
OH...
EXCUSE MY INTRUSION, MS. CRISP.
I WAS HOPING TO, UM, ASK YOU SOME QUESTIONS.
REGARDING?
ONE OF YOUR STUDENTS. MISS CRUMRIN.
WHAT ABOUT HER?
BRIGHT GIRL, IS SHE?
I'D SAY SO...
EXCEPTIONALLY BRIGHT?
MAYBE. MORE THAN USUALLY CURIOUS, ANYWAY. WHAT'S THIS ABOUT?
I CAN'T SAY AT THE MOMENT.
I'M JUST A BIT CURIOUS ABOUT HER.

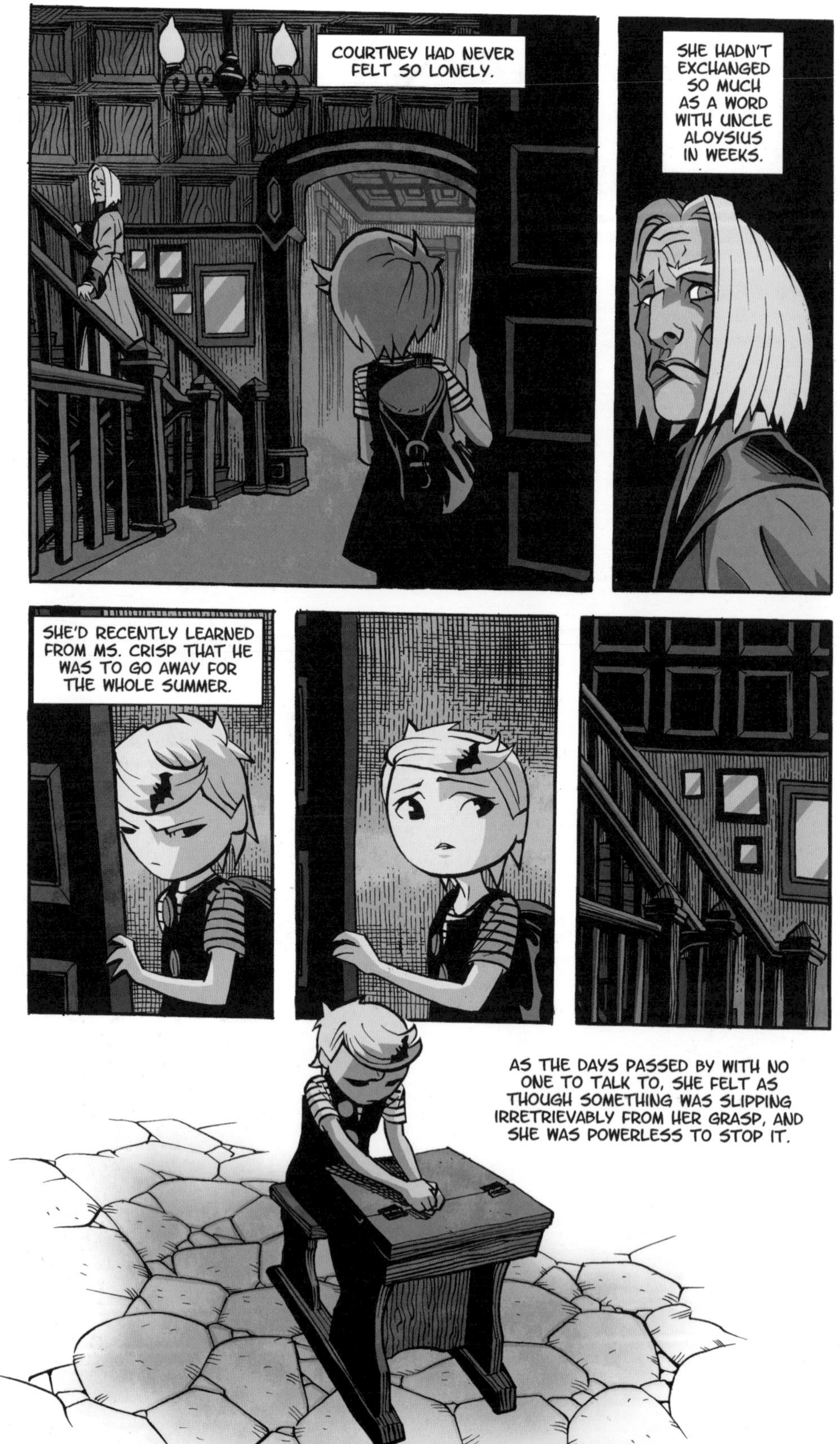
COURTNEY HAD NEVER FELT SO LONELY.
SHE HADN'T EXCHANGED SO MUCH AS A WORD WITH UNCLE ALOYSIUS IN WEEKS.
SHE'D RECENTLY LEARNED FROM MS. CRISP THAT HE WAS TO GO AWAY FOR THE WHOLE SUMMER.
AS THE DAYS PASSED BY WITH NO ONE TO TALK TO, SHE FELT AS THOUGH SOMETHING WAS SLIPPING IRRETRIEVABLY FROM HER GRASP, AND SHE WAS POWERLESS TO STOP IT.

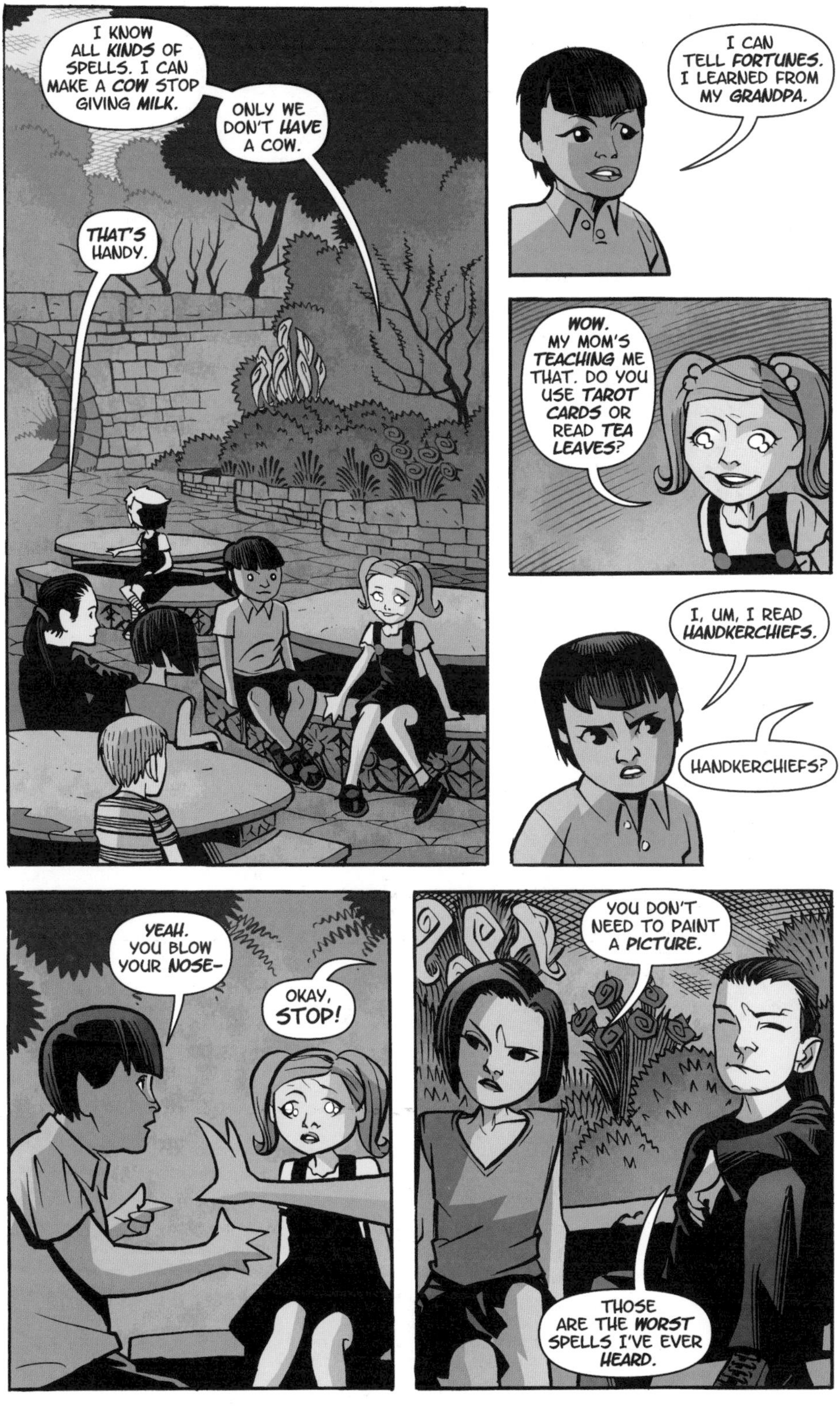

I KNOW ALL KINDS OF SPELLS. I CAN MAKE A COW STOP GIVING MILK.
ONLY WE DON'T HAVE A COW.
THAT'S HANDY.
I CAN TELL FORTUNES. I LEARNED FROM MY GRANDPA.
WOW. MY MOM'S TEACHING ME THAT. DO YOU USE TAROT CARDS OR READ TEA LEAVES?
I, UM, I READ HANDKERCHIEFS.
HANDKERCHIEFS?
YEAH. YOU BLOW YOUR NOSE-
OKAY, STOP!
YOU DON'T NEED TO PAINT A PICTURE.
THOSE ARE THE WORST SPELLS I'VE EVER HEARD.

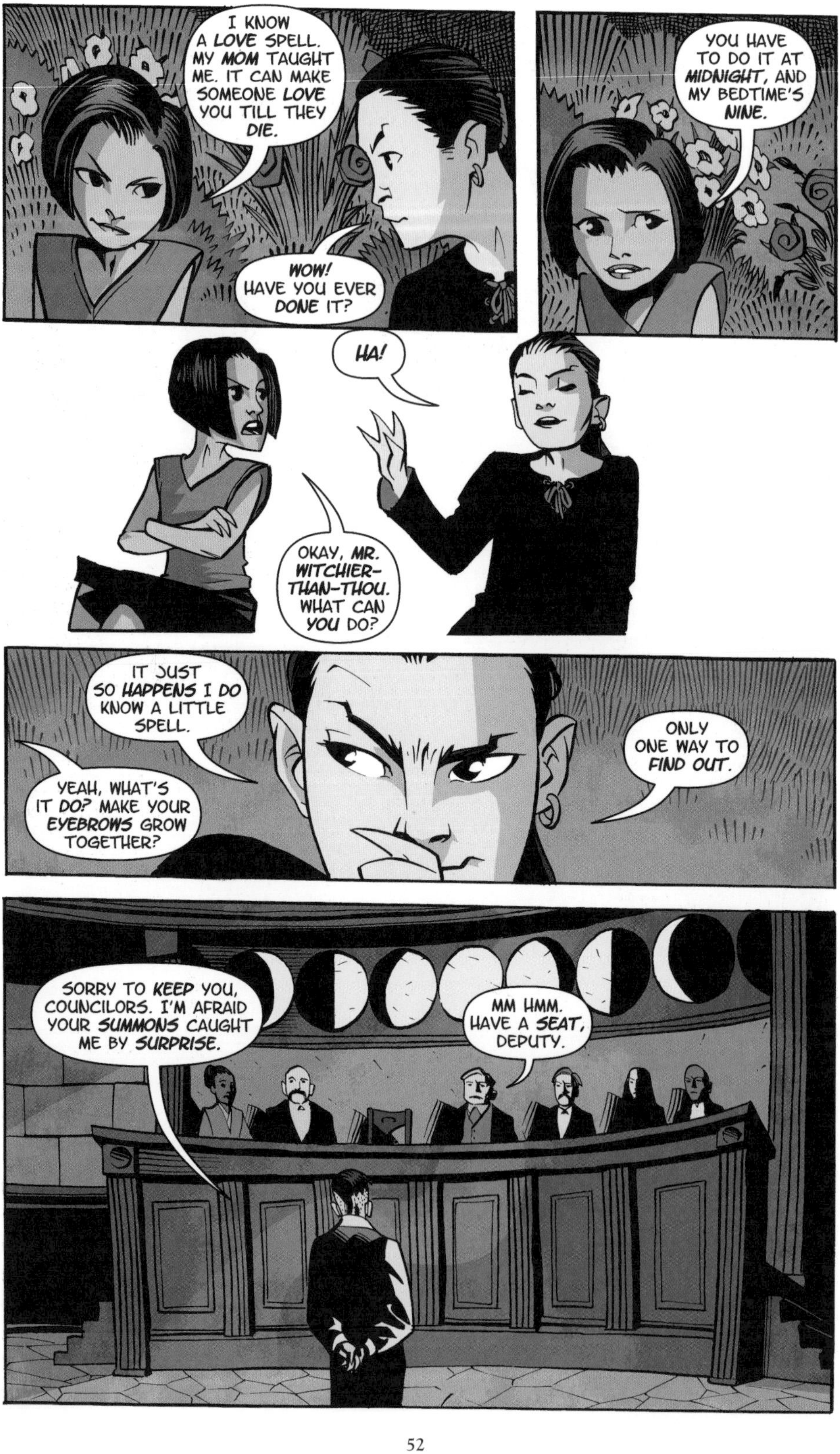

I KNOW A LOVE SPELL. MY MOM TAUGHT ME. IT CAN MAKE SOMEONE LOVE YOU TILL THEY DIE.
WOW! HAVE YOU EVER DONE IT?
YOU HAVE TO DO IT AT MIDNIGHT, AND MY BEDTIME'S NINE.
HA!
OKAY, MR. WITCHIER-THAN-THOU. WHAT CAN YOU DO?
IT JUST SO HAPPENS I DO KNOW A LITTLE SPELL.
YEAH, WHAT'S IT DO? MAKE YOUR EYEBROWS GROW TOGETHER?
ONLY ONE WAY TO FIND OUT.
SORRY TO KEEP YOU, COUNCILORS. I'M AFRAID YOUR SUMMONS CAUGHT ME BY SURPRISE.
MM HMM. HAVE A SEAT, DEPUTY.

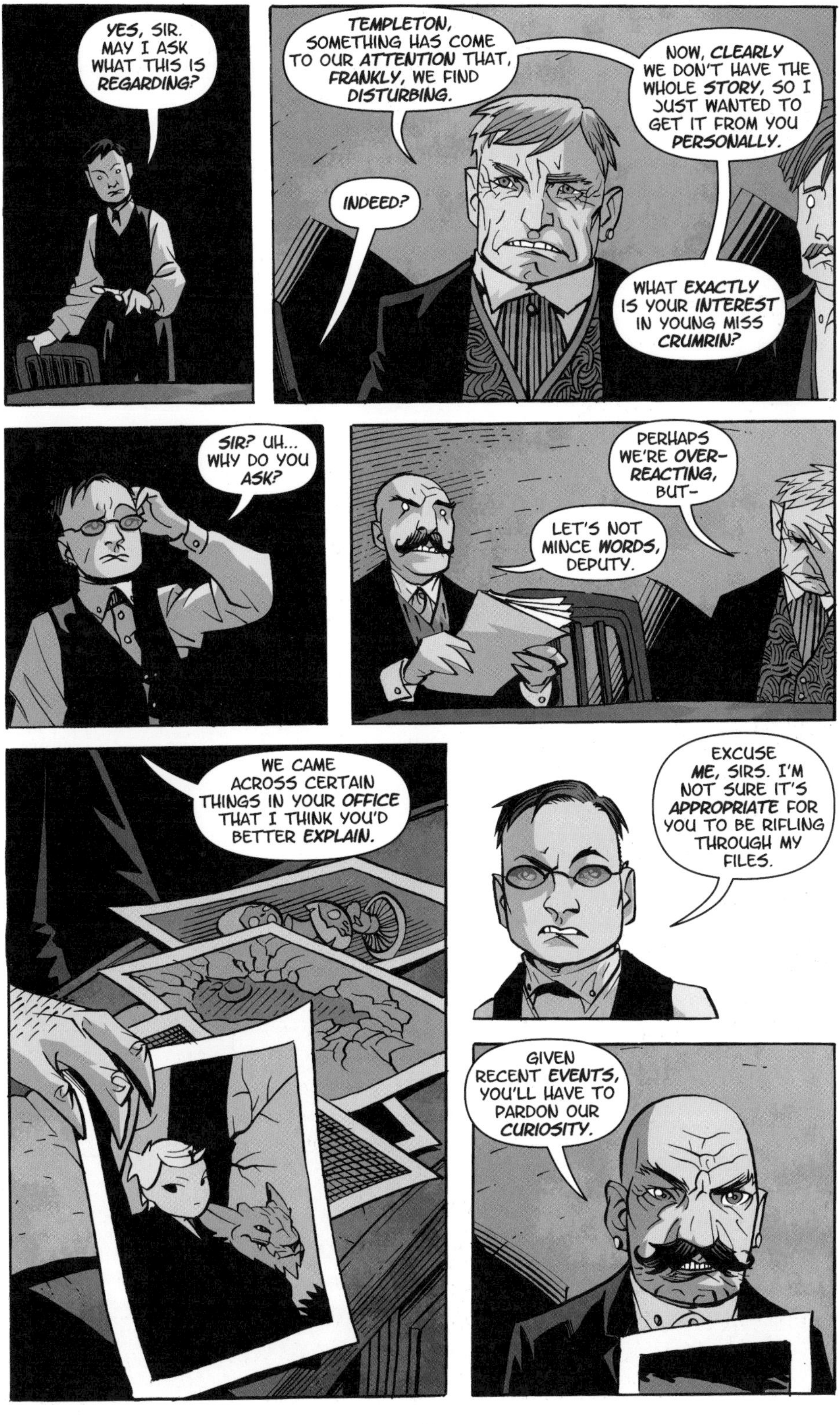
YES, SIR. MAY I ASK WHAT THIS IS REGARDING?
TEMPLETON, SOMETHING HAS COME TO OUR ATTENTION THAT, FRANKLY, WE FIND DISTURBING.
INDEED?
NOW, CLEARLY WE DON'T HAVE THE WHOLE STORY, SO I JUST WANTED TO GET IT FROM YOU PERSONALLY.
WHAT EXACTLY IS YOUR INTEREST IN YOUNG MISS CRUMRIN?
SIR? UH... WHY DO YOU ASK?
PERHAPS WE'RE OVER-REACTING, BUT-
LET'S NOT MINCE WORDS, DEPUTY.
WE CAME ACROSS CERTAIN THINGS IN YOUR OFFICE THAT I THINK YOU'D BETTER EXPLAIN.
EXCUSE ME, SIRS. I'M NOT SURE IT'S APPROPRIATE FOR YOU TO BE RIFLING THROUGH MY FILES.
GIVEN RECENT EVENTS, YOU'LL HAVE TO PARDON OUR CURIOSITY.

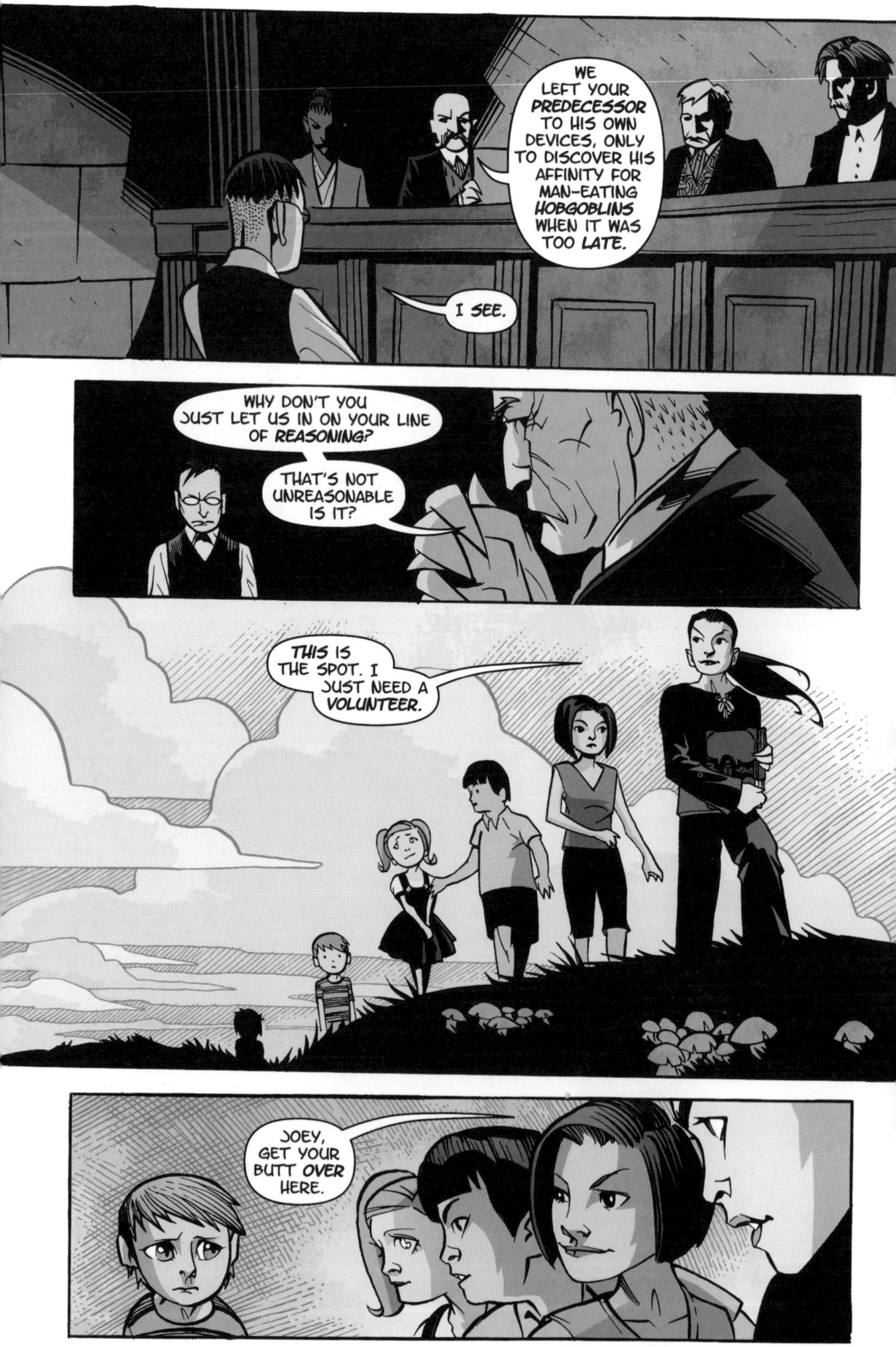
WE LEFT YOUR PREDECESSOR TO HIS OWN DEVICES, ONLY TO DISCOVER HIS AFFINITY FOR MAN-EATING HOBGOBLINS WHEN IT WAS TOO LATE.
I SEE.
WHY DON'T YOU JUST LET US IN ON YOUR LINE OF REASONING?
THAT'S NOT UNREASONABLE IS IT?
THIS IS THE SPOT. I JUST NEED A VOLUNTEER.
JOEY, GET YOUR BUTT OVER HERE.

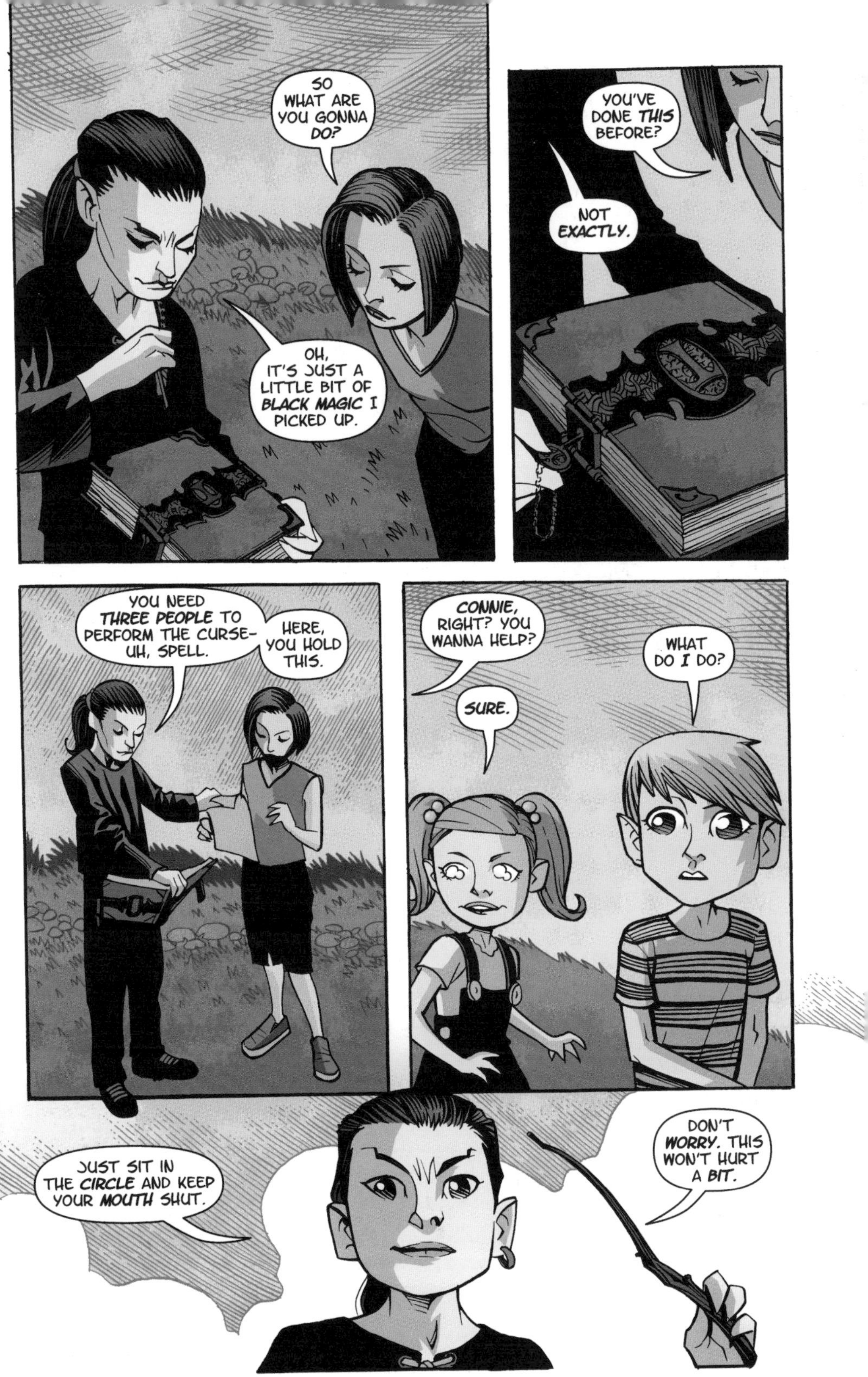
SO WHAT ARE YOU GONNA DO?
OH, IT'S JUST A LITTLE BIT OF BLACK MAGIC I PICKED UP.
YOU'VE DONE THIS BEFORE?
NOT EXACTLY.
YOU NEED THREE PEOPLE TO PERFORM THE CURSE- UH, SPELL.
HERE, YOU HOLD THIS.
CONNIE, RIGHT? YOU WANNA HELP?
SURE.
WHAT DO I DO?
JUST SIT IN THE CIRCLE AND KEEP YOUR MOUTH SHUT.
DON'T WORRY. THIS WON'T HURT A BIT.

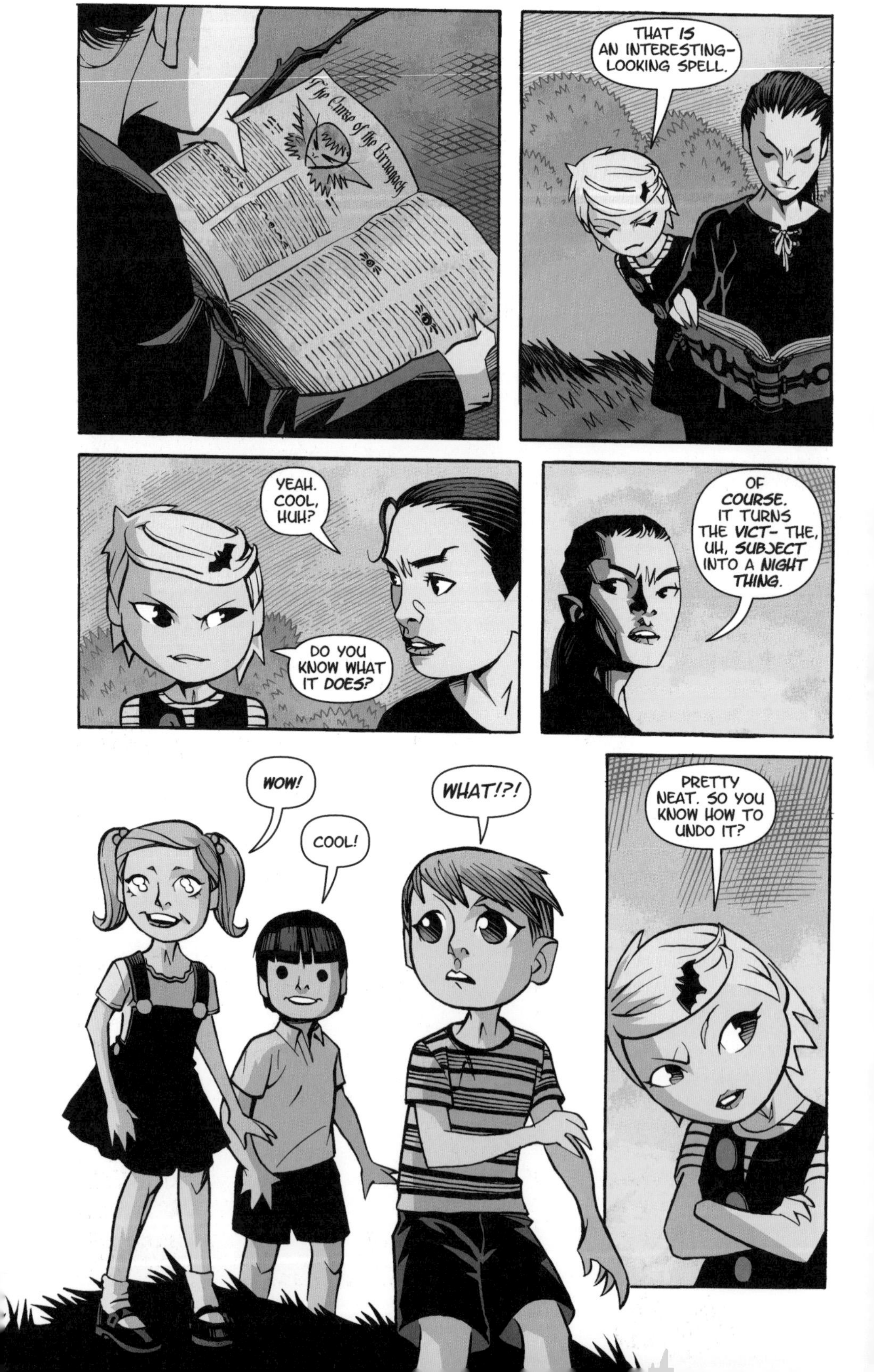
The Curse of the Grungoch
THAT IS AN INTERESTING-LOOKING SPELL.
YEAH. COOL, HUH?
DO YOU KNOW WHAT IT DOES?
OF COURSE. IT TURNS THE VICT- THE, UH, SUBJECT INTO A NIGHT THING.
WOW!
COOL!
WHAT!?!
PRETTY NEAT. SO YOU KNOW HOW TO UNDO IT?

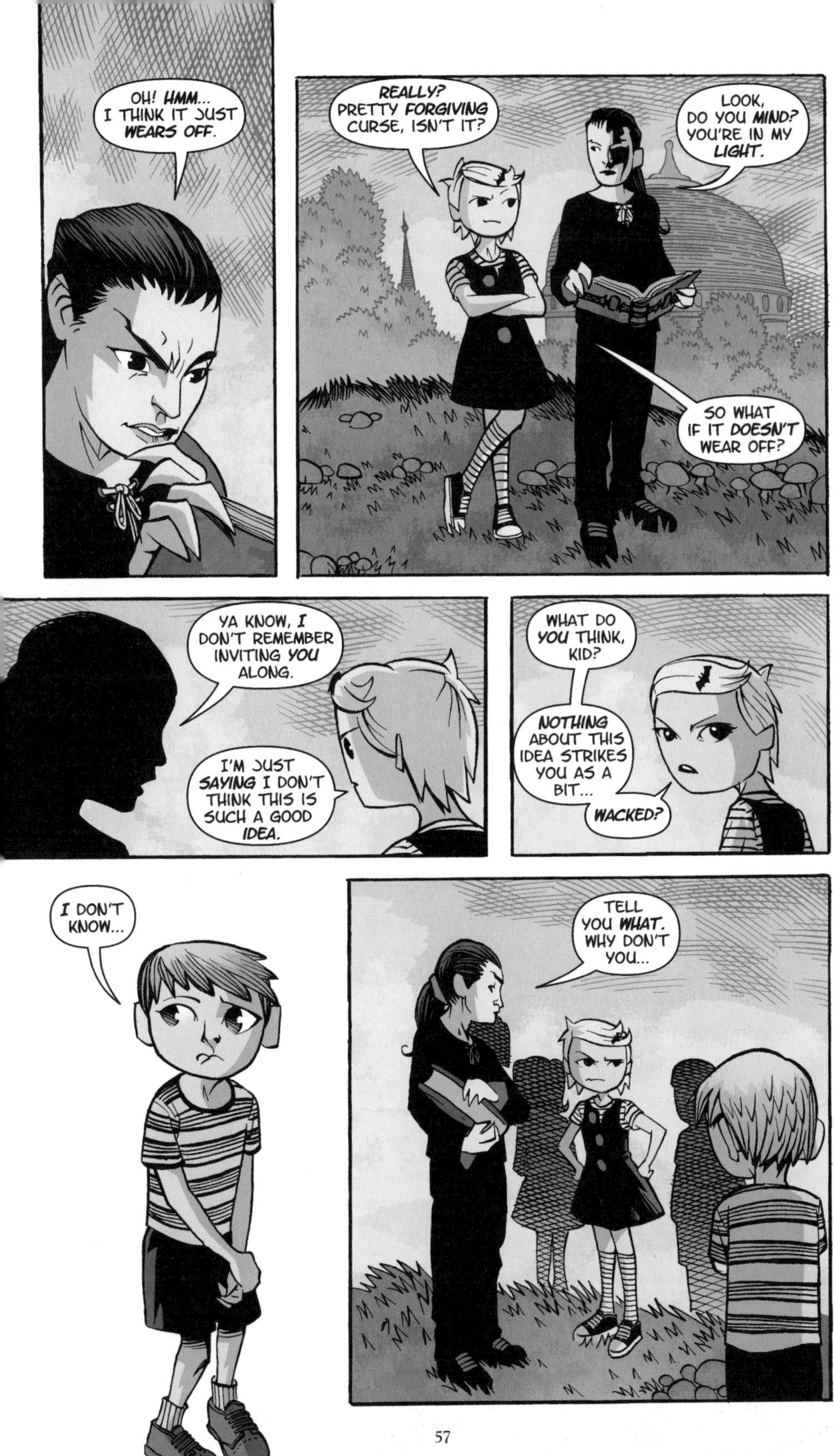
OH! HMM... I THINK IT JUST WEARS OFF.
REALLY? PRETTY FORGIVING CURSE, ISN'T IT?
LOOK, DO YOU MIND? YOU'RE IN MY LIGHT.
SO WHAT IF IT DOESN'T WEAR OFF?
YA KNOW, I DON'T REMEMBER INVITING YOU ALONG.
I'M JUST SAYING I DON'T THINK THIS IS SUCH A GOOD IDEA.
WHAT DO YOU THINK, KID?
NOTHING ABOUT THIS IDEA STRIKES YOU AS A BIT...
WACKED?
I DON'T KNOW...
TELL YOU WHAT. WHY DON'T YOU...

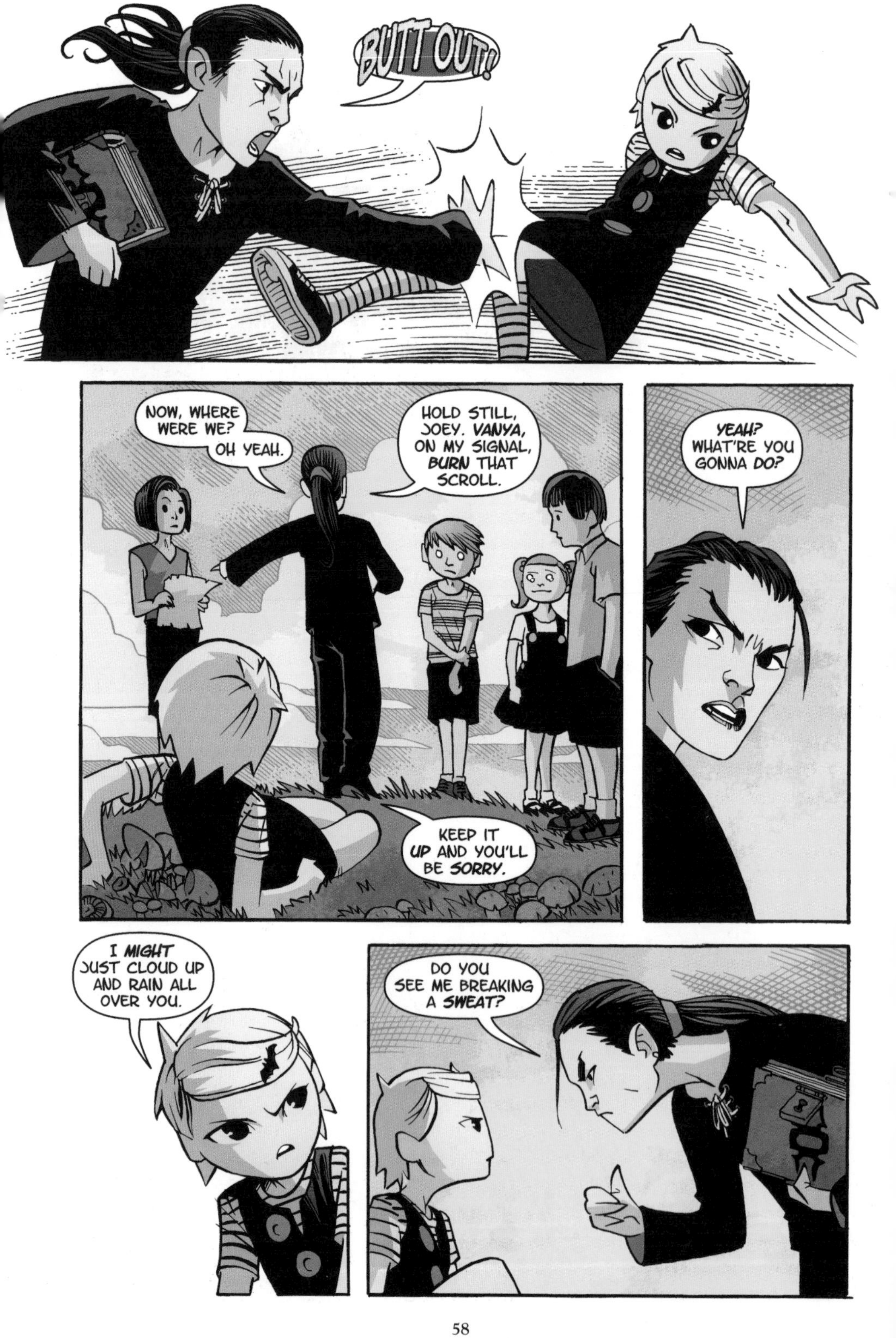
BUTT OUT!
NOW, WHERE WERE WE?
OH YEAH.
HOLD STILL, JOEY. VANYA, ON MY SIGNAL, BURN THAT SCROLL.
KEEP IT UP AND YOU'LL BE SORRY.
YEAH? WHAT'RE YOU GONNA DO?
I MIGHT JUST CLOUD UP AND RAIN ALL OVER YOU.
DO YOU SEE ME BREAKING A SWEAT?

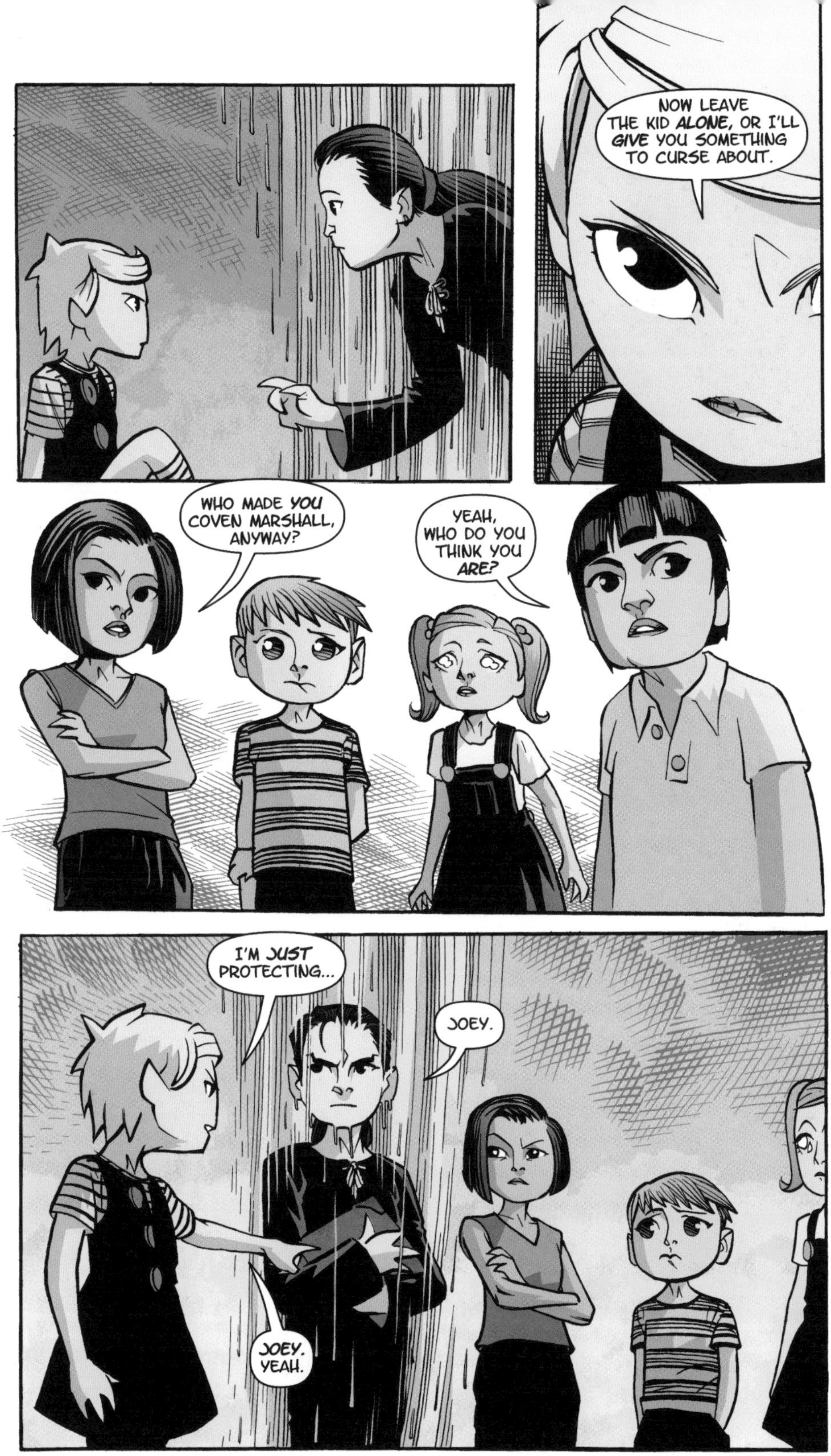
NOW LEAVE THE KID ALONE, OR I'LL GIVE YOU SOMETHING TO CURSE ABOUT.
WHO MADE YOU COVEN MARSHALL, ANYWAY?
YEAH, WHO DO YOU THINK YOU ARE?
I'M JUST PROTECTING...
JOEY.
JOEY. YEAH.

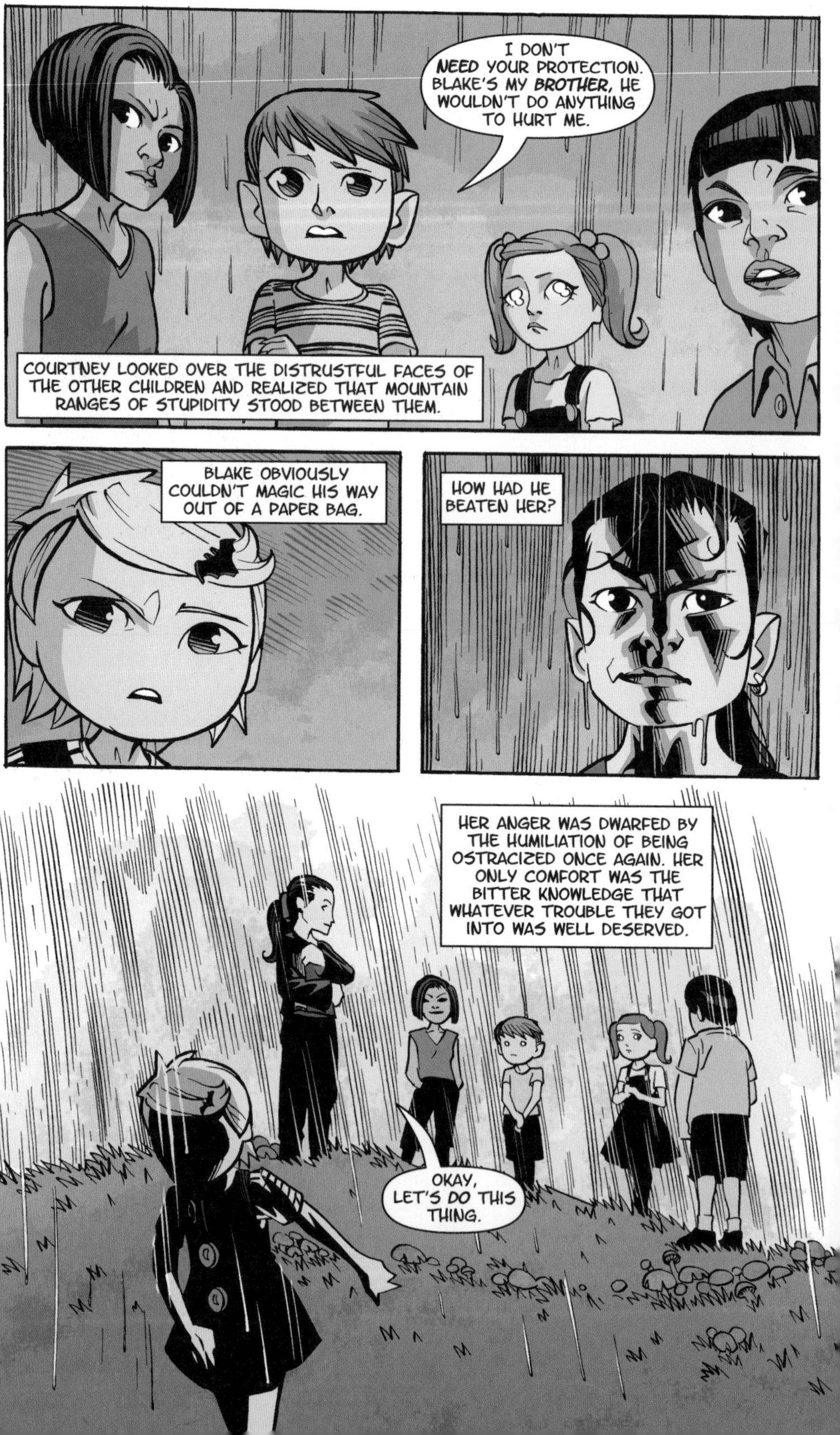
I DON'T *NEED* YOUR PROTECTION. BLAKE'S MY *BROTHER*, HE WOULDN'T DO ANYTHING TO HURT ME.
COURTNEY LOOKED OVER THE DISTRUSTFUL FACES OF THE OTHER CHILDREN AND REALIZED THAT MOUNTAIN RANGES OF STUPIDITY STOOD BETWEEN THEM.
BLAKE OBVIOUSLY COULDN'T MAGIC HIS WAY OUT OF A PAPER BAG.
HOW HAD HE BEATEN HER?
HER ANGER WAS DWARFED BY THE HUMILIATION OF BEING OSTRACIZED ONCE AGAIN. HER ONLY COMFORT WAS THE BITTER KNOWLEDGE THAT WHATEVER TROUBLE THEY GOT INTO WAS WELL DESERVED.
OKAY, LET'S *DO* THIS THING.

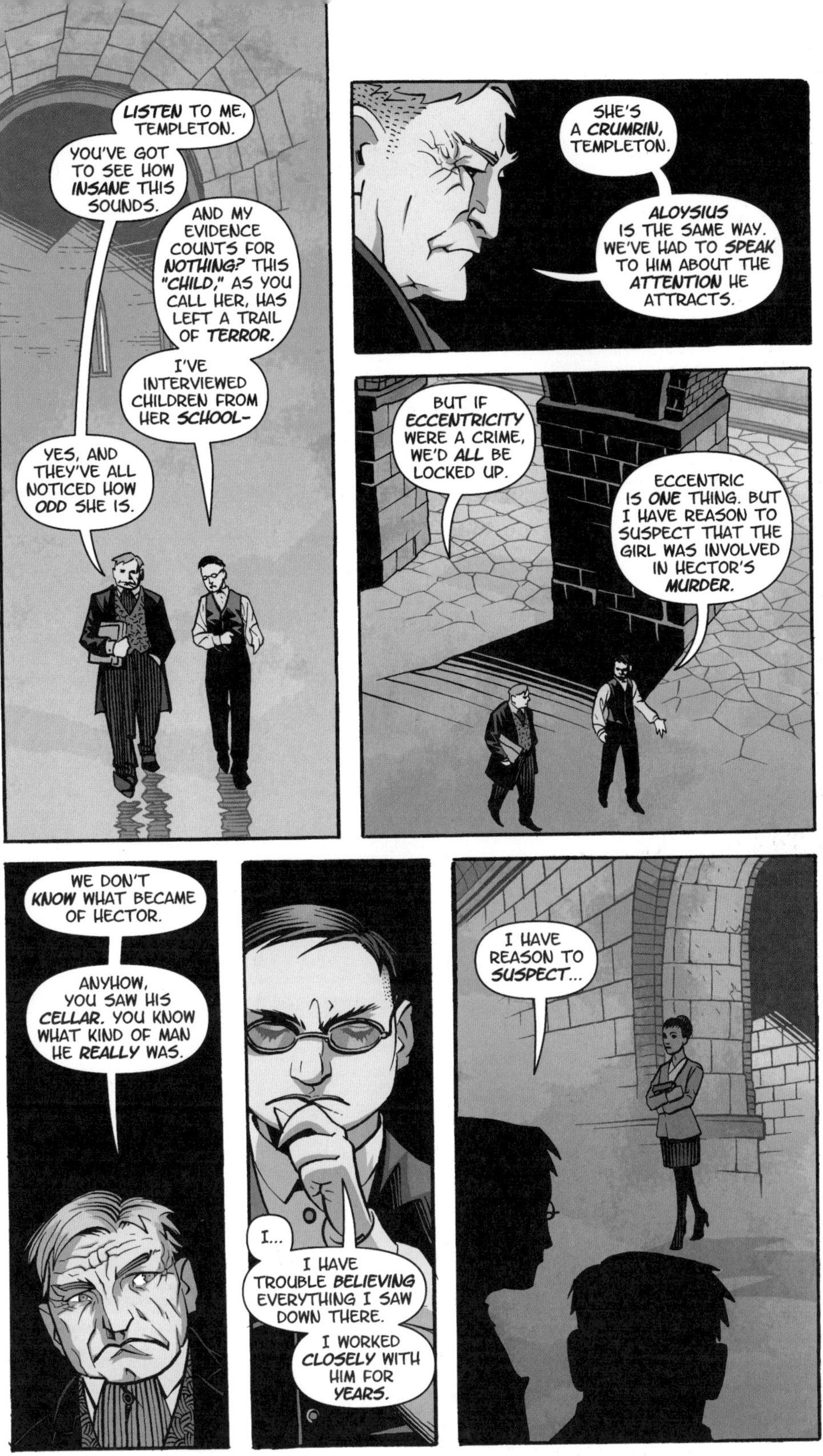
LISTEN TO ME, TEMPLETON.
YOU'VE GOT TO SEE HOW INSANE THIS SOUNDS.
AND MY EVIDENCE COUNTS FOR NOTHING? THIS "CHILD," AS YOU CALL HER, HAS LEFT A TRAIL OF TERROR.
I'VE INTERVIEWED CHILDREN FROM HER SCHOOL-
YES, AND THEY'VE ALL NOTICED HOW ODD SHE IS.
SHE'S A CRUMRIN, TEMPLETON.
ALOYSIUS IS THE SAME WAY. WE'VE HAD TO SPEAK TO HIM ABOUT THE ATTENTION HE ATTRACTS.
BUT IF ECCENTRICITY WERE A CRIME, WE'D ALL BE LOCKED UP.
ECCENTRIC IS ONE THING. BUT I HAVE REASON TO SUSPECT THAT THE GIRL WAS INVOLVED IN HECTOR'S MURDER.
WE DON'T KNOW WHAT BECAME OF HECTOR.
ANYHOW, YOU SAW HIS CELLAR. YOU KNOW WHAT KIND OF MAN HE REALLY WAS.
I...
I HAVE TROUBLE BELIEVING EVERYTHING I SAW DOWN THERE.
I WORKED CLOSELY WITH HIM FOR YEARS.
I HAVE REASON TO SUSPECT...

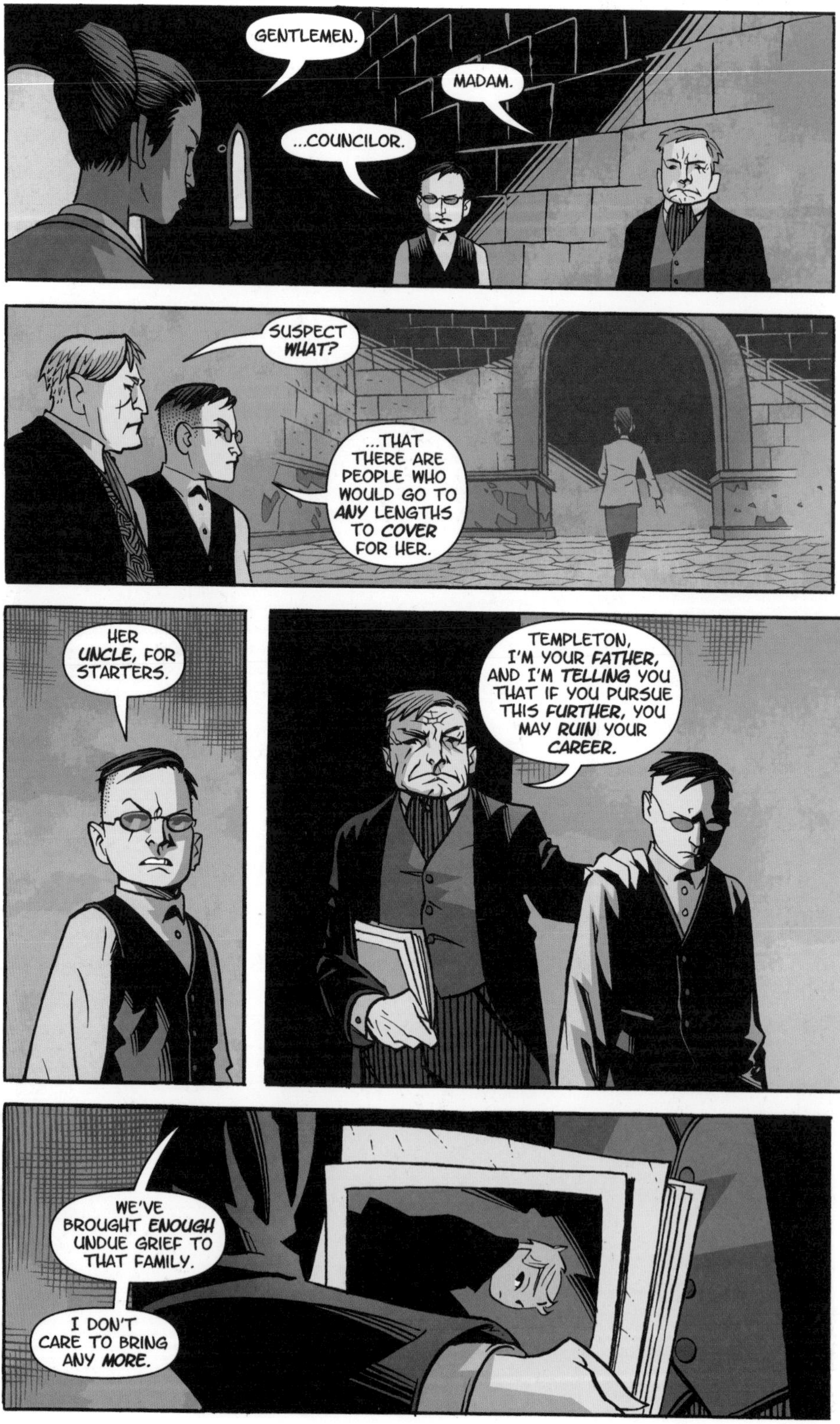
GENTLEMEN.
MADAM.
...COUNCILOR.
SUSPECT WHAT?
...THAT THERE ARE PEOPLE WHO WOULD GO TO ANY LENGTHS TO COVER FOR HER.
HER UNCLE, FOR STARTERS.
TEMPLETON, I'M YOUR FATHER, AND I'M TELLING YOU THAT IF YOU PURSUE THIS FURTHER, YOU MAY RUIN YOUR CAREER.
WE'VE BROUGHT ENOUGH UNDUE GRIEF TO THAT FAMILY.
I DON'T CARE TO BRING ANY MORE.

COURTNEY DIDN'T UNDERSTAND WHY THIS LATEST REJECTION WAS SO UPSETTING.

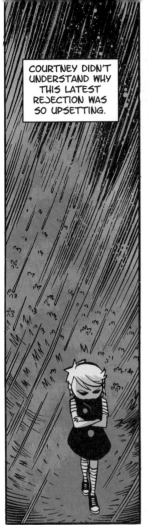

THESE COVEN CHILDREN WERE EVERY BIT AS HEARTLESS AND FOOLISH AS ALL THE OTHER KIDS OF HILLSBOROUGH.

BUT THEIR RECKLESS CURIOSITY ABOUT WITCHCRAFT SEEMED ALL TOO FAMILIAR.

SEEING THE WICKED GLEAM IN BLAKE'S EYE...

...WAS LIKE LOOKING INTO A MIRROR.

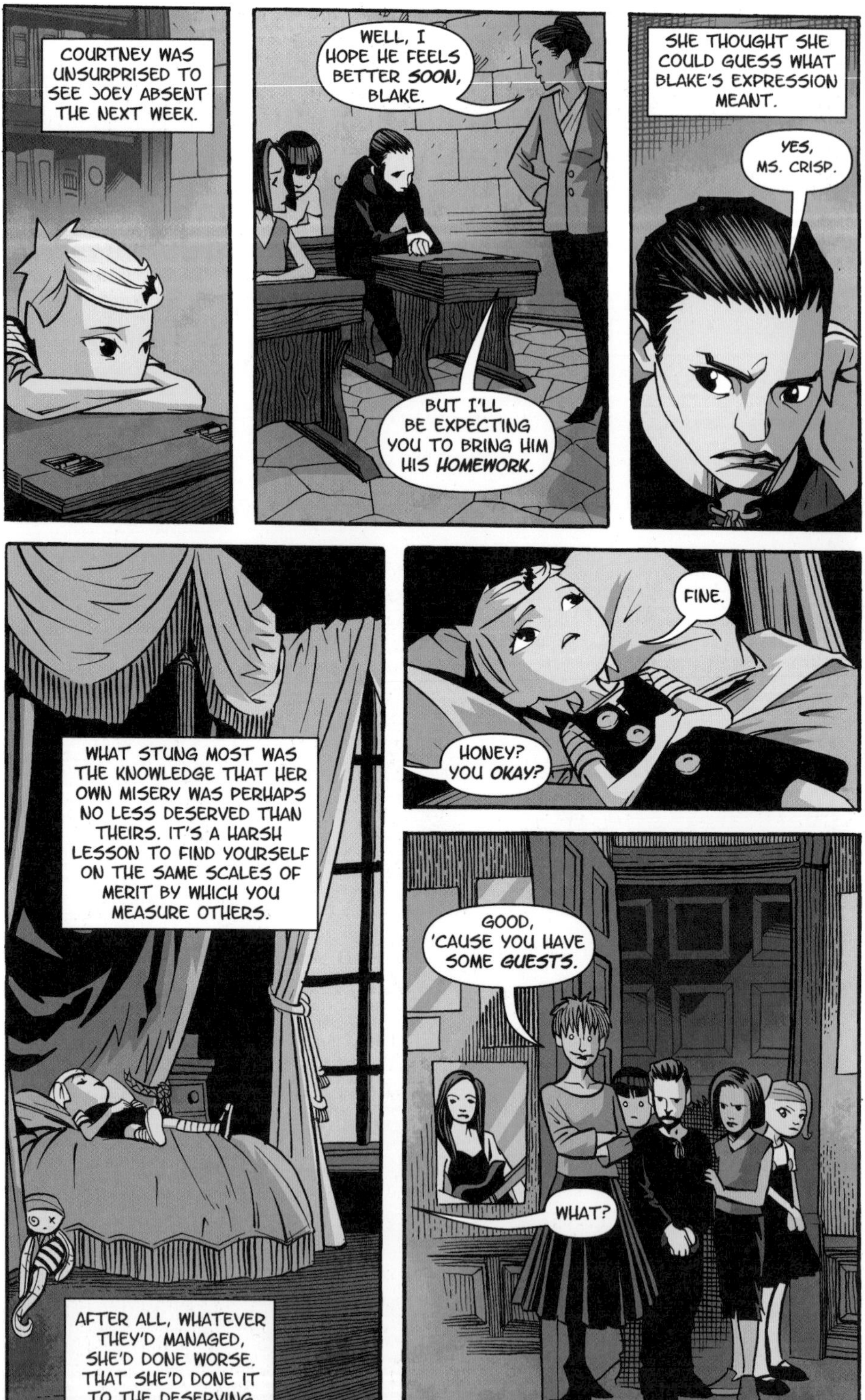
COURTNEY WAS UNSURPRISED TO SEE JOEY ABSENT THE NEXT WEEK.
WELL, I HOPE HE FEELS BETTER SOON, BLAKE.
BUT I'LL BE EXPECTING YOU TO BRING HIM HIS HOMEWORK.
SHE THOUGHT SHE COULD GUESS WHAT BLAKE'S EXPRESSION MEANT.
YES, MS. CRISP.
WHAT STUNG MOST WAS THE KNOWLEDGE THAT HER OWN MISERY WAS PERHAPS NO LESS DESERVED THAN THEIRS. IT'S A HARSH LESSON TO FIND YOURSELF ON THE SAME SCALES OF MERIT BY WHICH YOU MEASURE OTHERS.
AFTER ALL, WHATEVER THEY'D MANAGED, SHE'D DONE WORSE. THAT SHE'D DONE IT TO THE DESERVING WAS SMALL COMFORT.
HONEY? YOU OKAY?
FINE.
GOOD, 'CAUSE YOU HAVE SOME GUESTS.
WHAT?

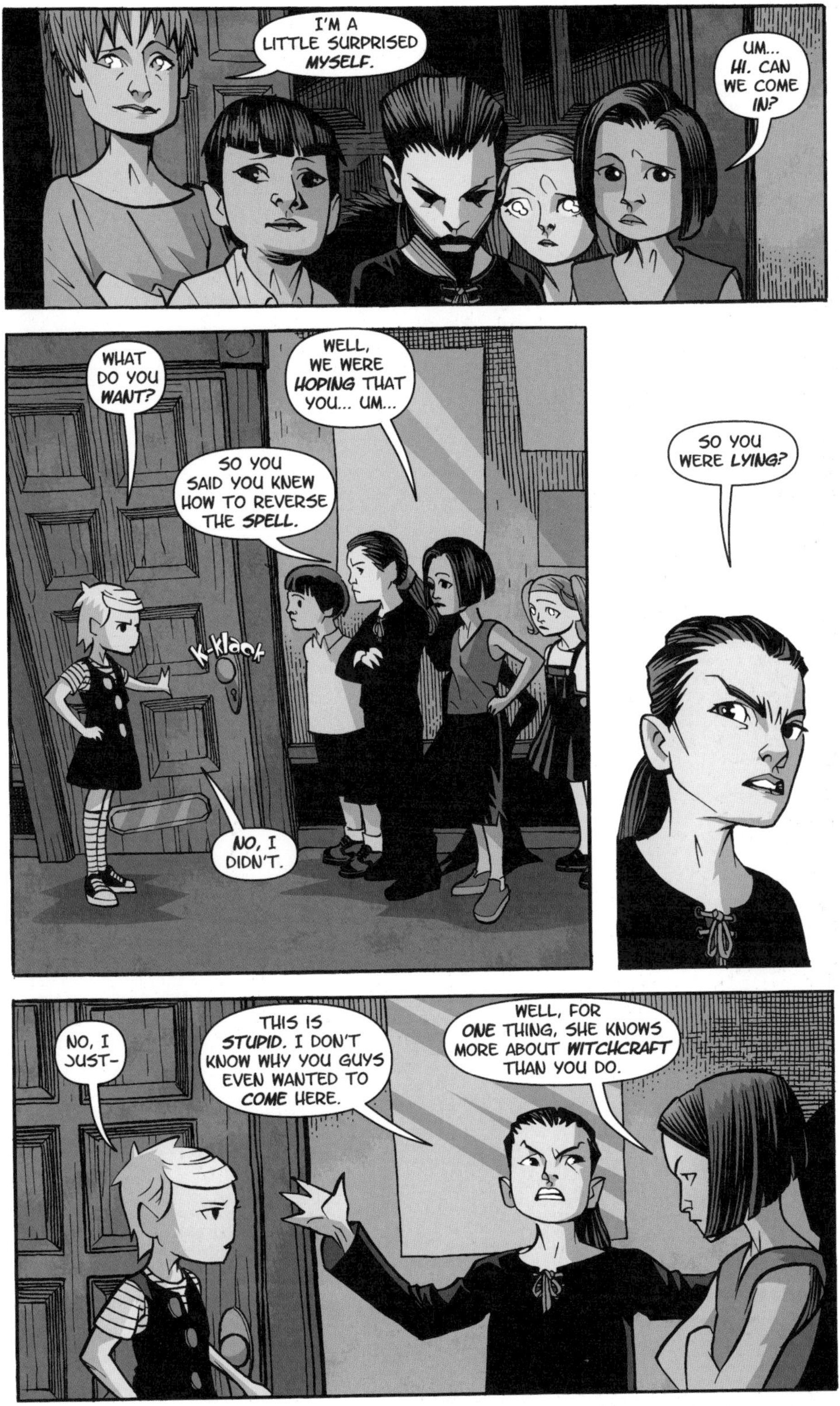
I'M A LITTLE SURPRISED MYSELF.
UM... HI. CAN WE COME IN?
WHAT DO YOU WANT?
WELL, WE WERE HOPING THAT YOU... UM...
SO YOU SAID YOU KNEW HOW TO REVERSE THE SPELL.
K-KLACK
NO, I DIDN'T.
SO YOU WERE LYING?
NO, I JUST-
THIS IS STUPID. I DON'T KNOW WHY YOU GUYS EVEN WANTED TO COME HERE.
WELL, FOR ONE THING, SHE KNOWS MORE ABOUT WITCHCRAFT THAN YOU DO.

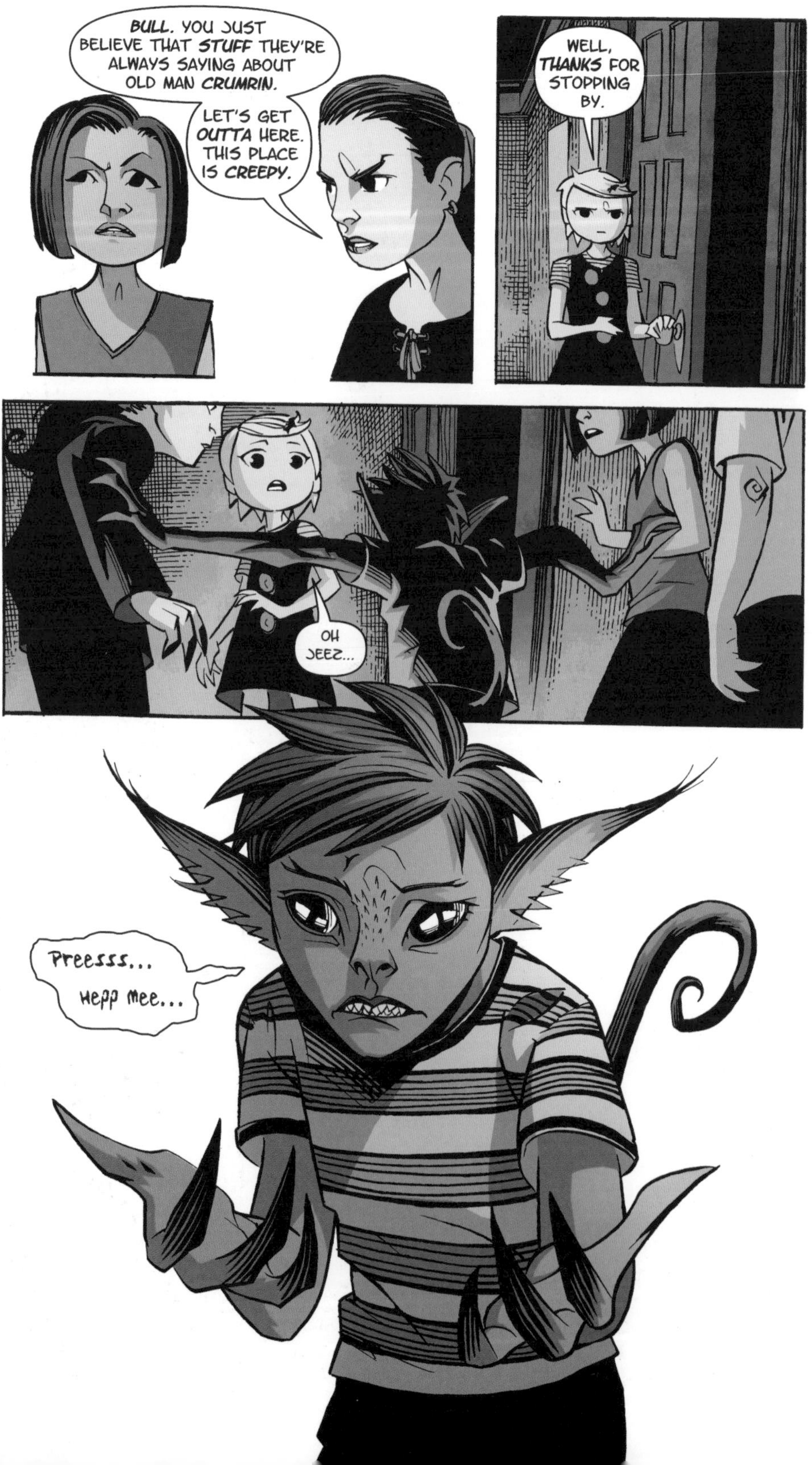
BULL. YOU JUST BELIEVE THAT STUFF THEY'RE ALWAYS SAYING ABOUT OLD MAN CRUMRIN.
LET'S GET OUTTA HERE. THIS PLACE IS CREEPY.
WELL, THANKS FOR STOPPING BY.
OH JEEZ...
Preesss... Hepp mee...

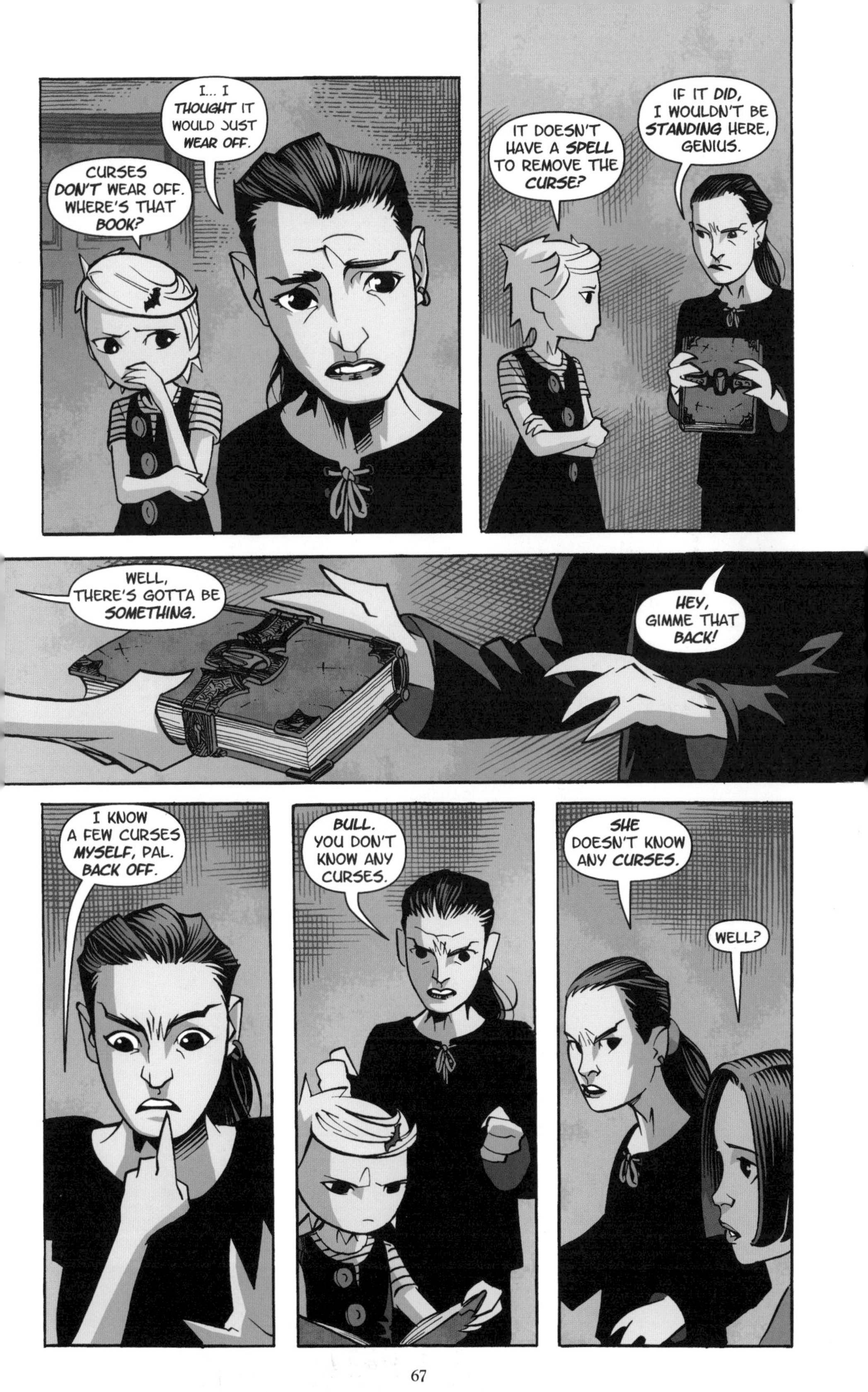
I... I THOUGHT IT WOULD JUST WEAR OFF.
CURSES DON'T WEAR OFF. WHERE'S THAT BOOK?
IT DOESN'T HAVE A SPELL TO REMOVE THE CURSE?
IF IT DID, I WOULDN'T BE STANDING HERE, GENIUS.
WELL, THERE'S GOTTA BE SOMETHING.
HEY, GIMME THAT BACK!
I KNOW A FEW CURSES MYSELF, PAL. BACK OFF.
BULL. YOU DON'T KNOW ANY CURSES.
SHE DOESN'T KNOW ANY CURSES.
WELL?

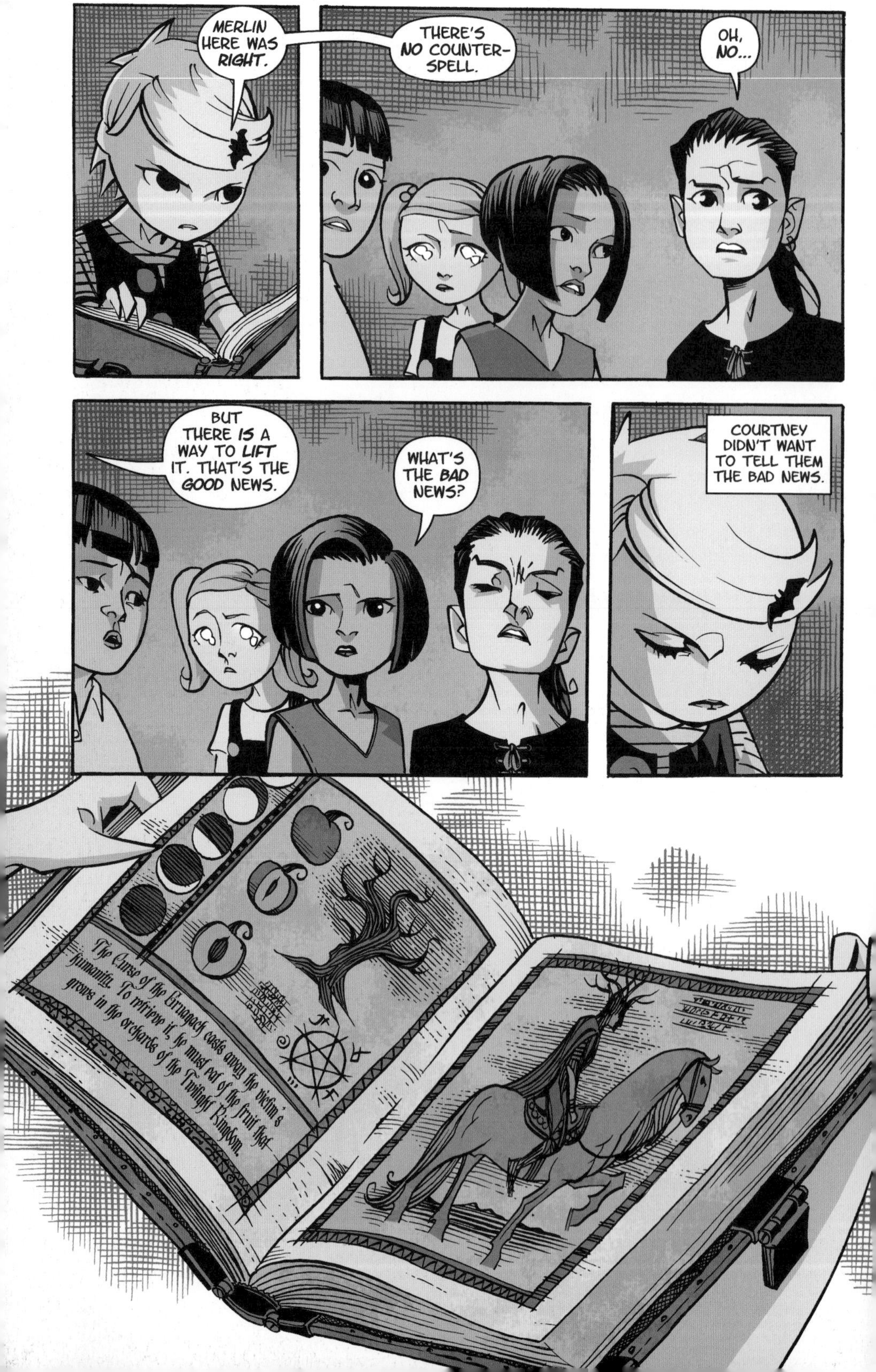
MERLIN HERE WAS RIGHT.
THERE'S NO COUNTER-SPELL.
OH, NO...
BUT THERE IS A WAY TO LIFT IT. THAT'S THE GOOD NEWS.
WHAT'S THE BAD NEWS?
COURTNEY DIDN'T WANT TO TELL THEM THE BAD NEWS.
The Curse of the Erunagach casts away the victim's humanity. To retrieve it, he must eat of the fruit that grows in the orchards of the Twilight Kingdom.

Chapter Three

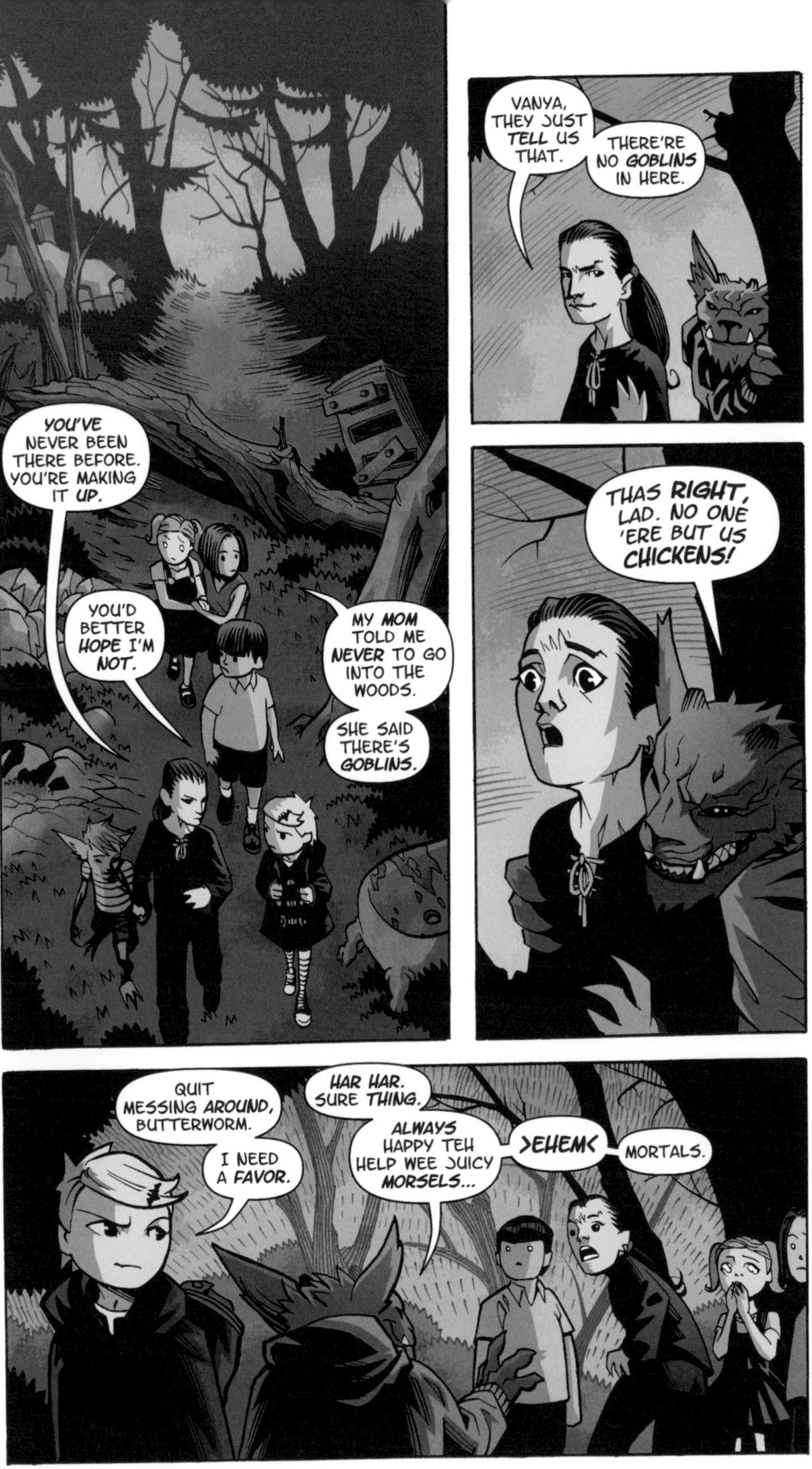
YOU'VE NEVER BEEN THERE BEFORE. YOU'RE MAKING IT UP.
YOU'D BETTER HOPE I'M NOT.
MY MOM TOLD ME NEVER TO GO INTO THE WOODS.
SHE SAID THERE'S GOBLINS.
VANYA, THEY JUST TELL US THAT.
THERE'RE NO GOBLINS IN HERE.
THAS RIGHT, LAD. NO ONE 'ERE BUT US CHICKENS!
QUIT MESSING AROUND, BUTTERWORM.
I NEED A FAVOR.
HAR HAR. SURE THING.
ALWAYS HAPPY TEH HELP WEE JUICY MORSELS...
>EHEM<
MORTALS.

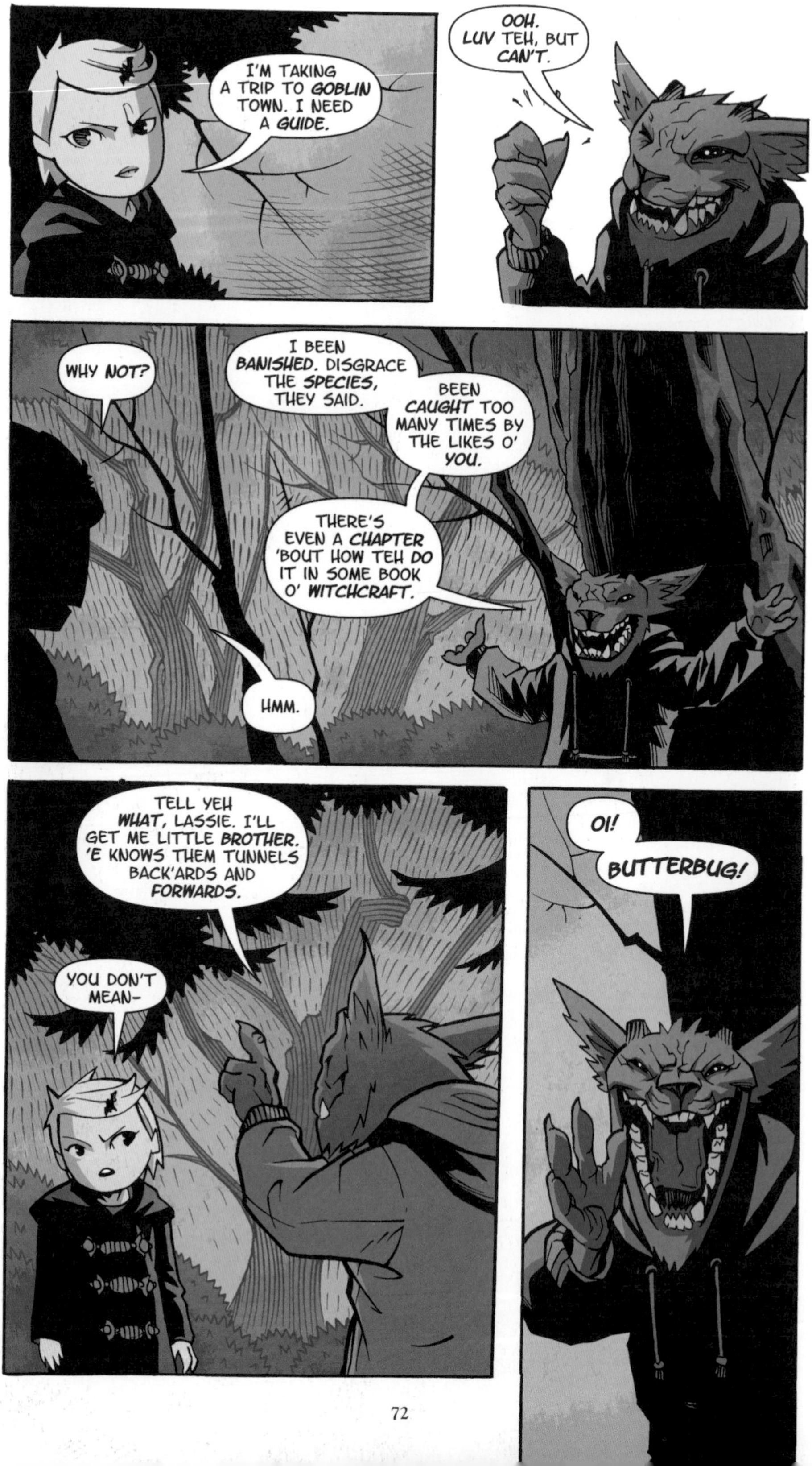
I'M TAKING A TRIP TO GOBLIN TOWN. I NEED A GUIDE.
OOH. LUV TEH, BUT CAN'T.
WHY NOT?
I BEEN BANISHED. DISGRACE THE SPECIES, THEY SAID.
BEEN CAUGHT TOO MANY TIMES BY THE LIKES O' YOU.
THERE'S EVEN A CHAPTER 'BOUT HOW TEH DO IT IN SOME BOOK O' WITCHCRAFT.
HMM.
TELL YEH WHAT, LASSIE. I'LL GET ME LITTLE BROTHER. 'E KNOWS THEM TUNNELS BACK'ARDS AND FORWARDS.
YOU DON'T MEAN–
OI!
BUTTERBUG!

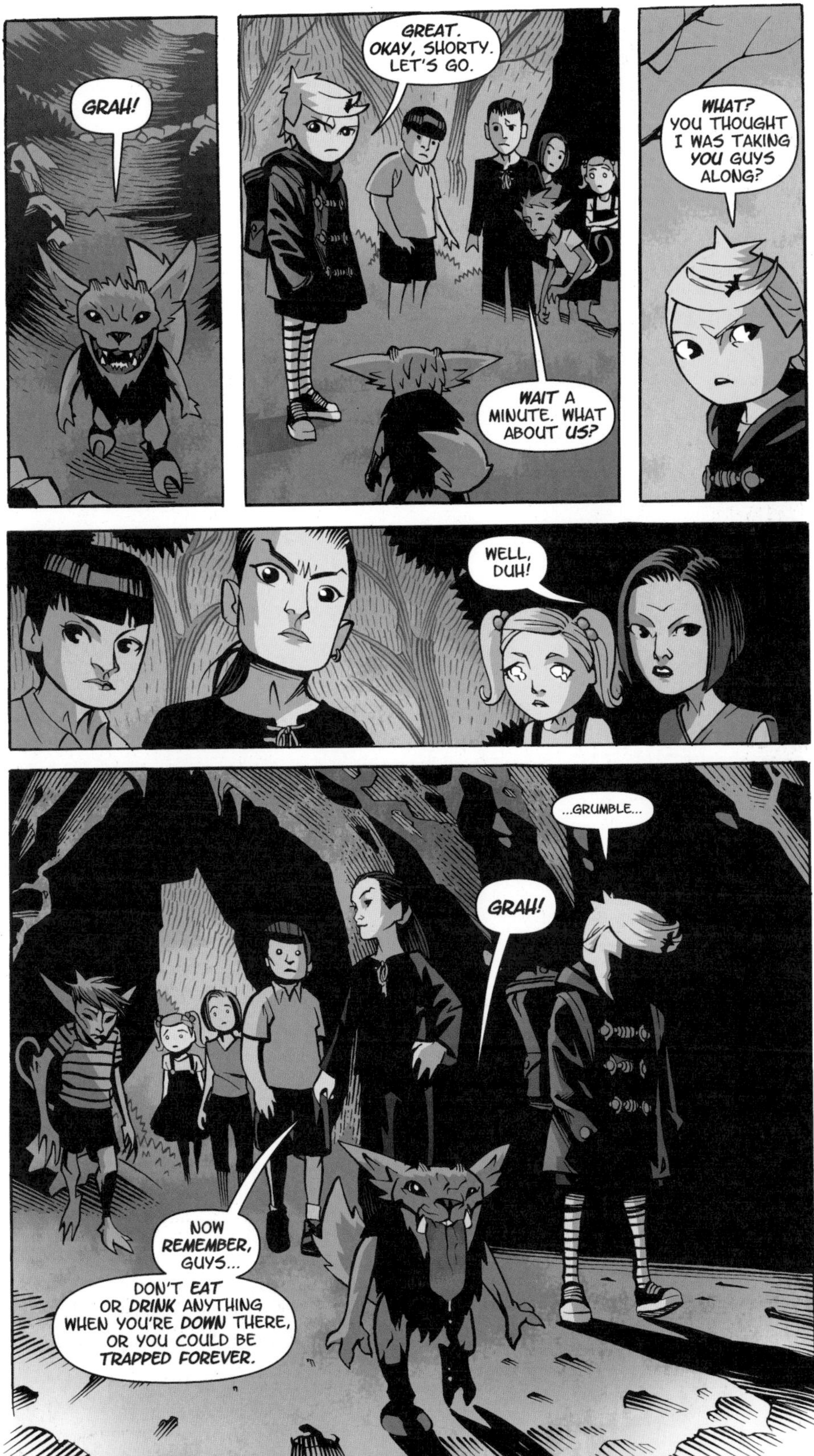
GRAH!
GREAT. OKAY, SHORTY. LET'S GO.
WAIT A MINUTE. WHAT ABOUT US?
WHAT? YOU THOUGHT I WAS TAKING YOU GUYS ALONG?
WELL, DUH!
...GRUMBLE...
GRAH!
NOW REMEMBER, GUYS...
DON'T EAT OR DRINK ANYTHING WHEN YOU'RE DOWN THERE, OR YOU COULD BE TRAPPED FOREVER.

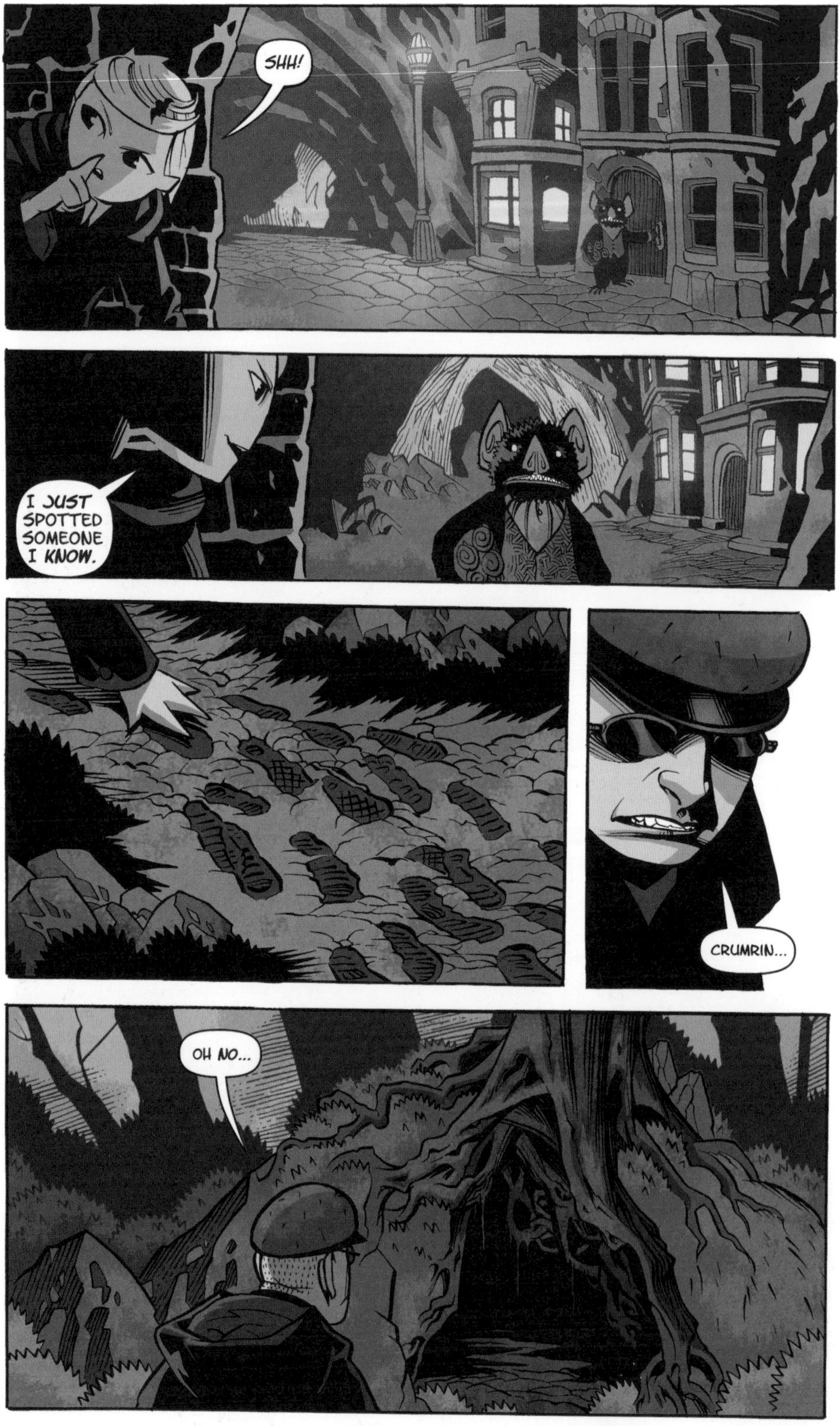
SHH!
I JUST SPOTTED SOMEONE I KNOW.
CRUMRIN...
OH NO...

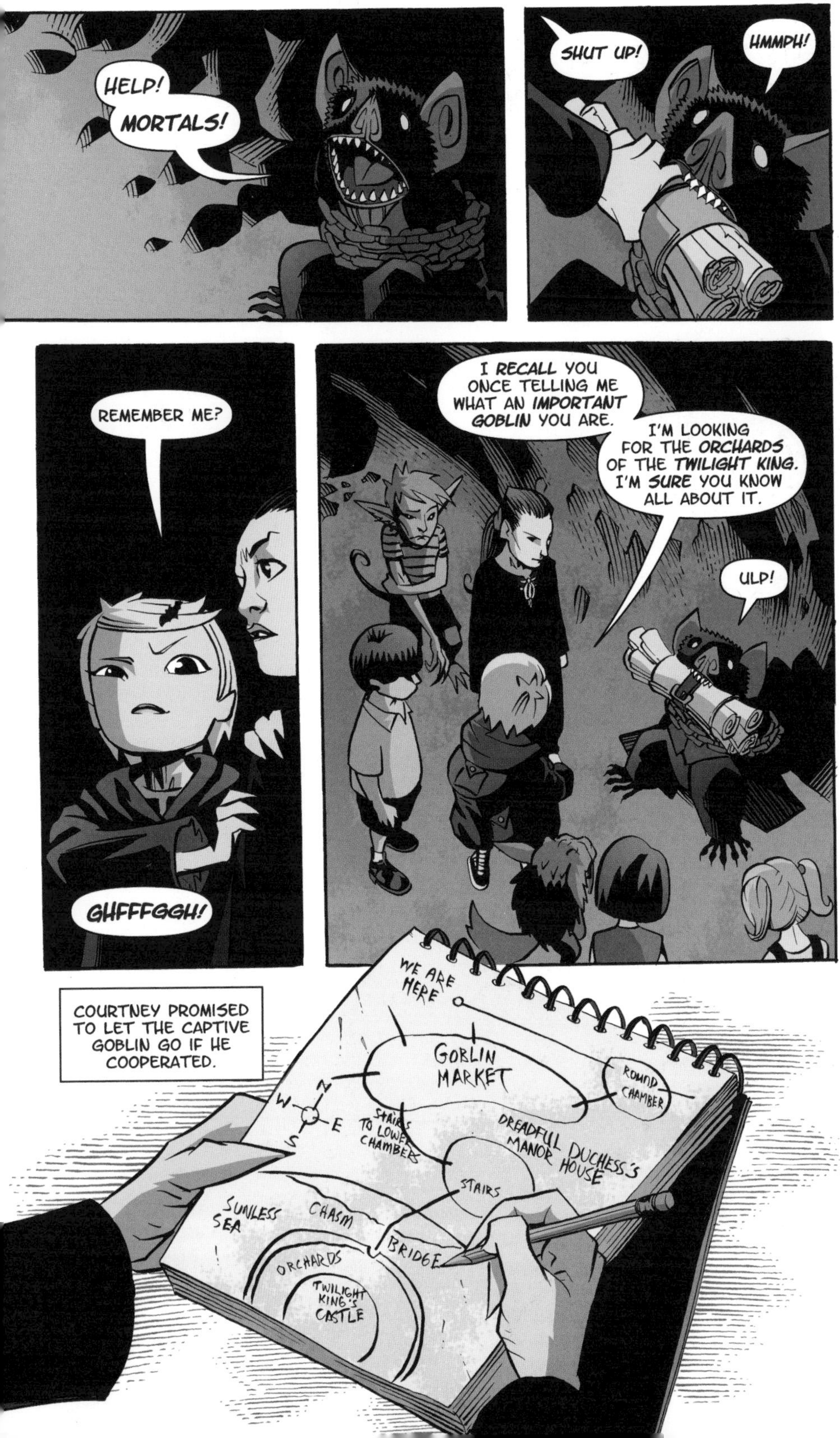
HELP!
MORTALS!
SHUT UP!
HMMPH!
REMEMBER ME?
GHFFFGGH!
I RECALL YOU ONCE TELLING ME WHAT AN IMPORTANT GOBLIN YOU ARE.
I'M LOOKING FOR THE ORCHARDS OF THE TWILIGHT KING. I'M SURE YOU KNOW ALL ABOUT IT.
ULP!
COURTNEY PROMISED TO LET THE CAPTIVE GOBLIN GO IF HE COOPERATED.
WE ARE HERE
GOBLIN MARKET
ROUND CHAMBER
N
W
E
S
STAIRS TO LOWER CHAMBERS
DREADFUL DUCHESS'S MANOR HOUSE
STAIRS
SUNLESS SEA
CHASM
BRIDGE
ORCHARDS
TWILIGHT KING'S CASTLE

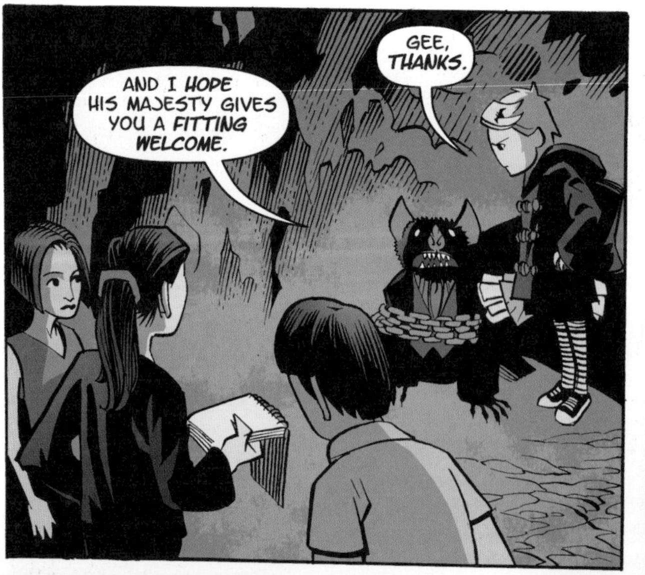
AND I HOPE HIS MAJESTY GIVES YOU A FITTING WELCOME.
GEE, THANKS.

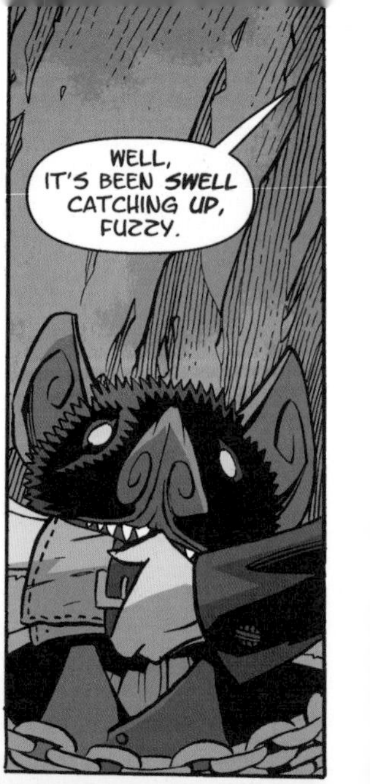
WELL, IT'S BEEN SWELL CATCHING UP, FUZZY.

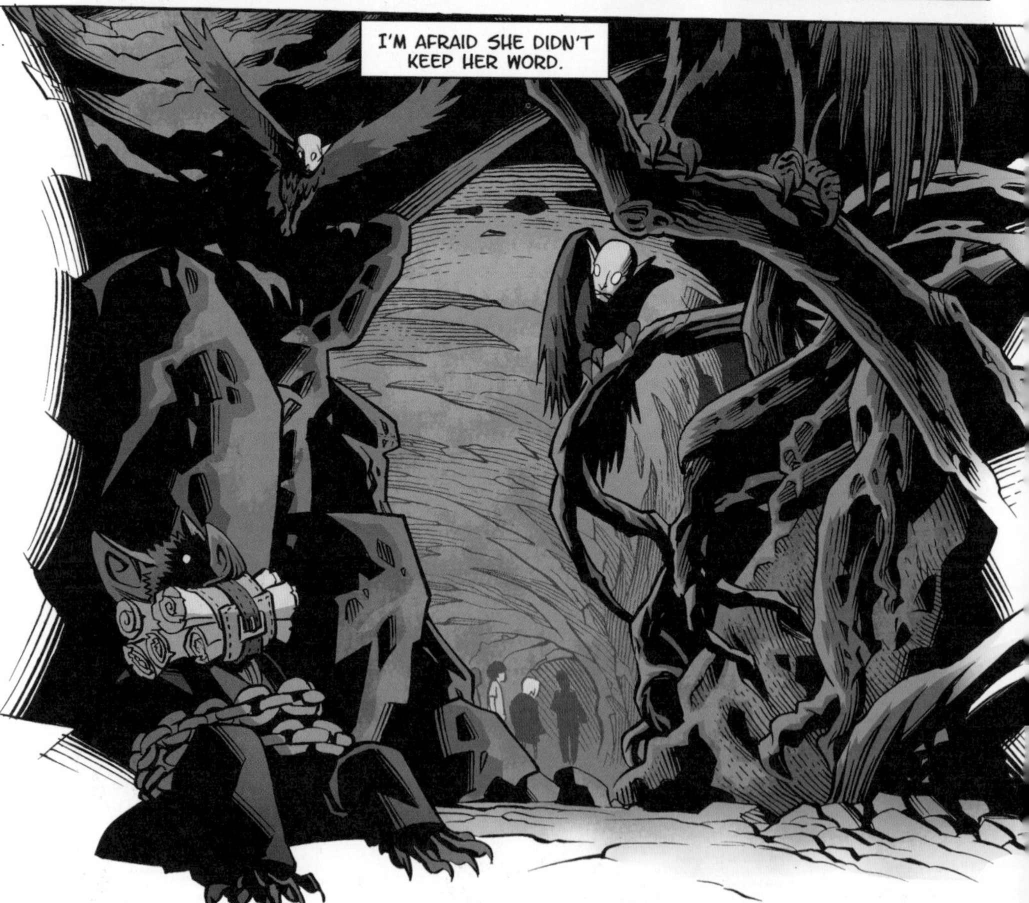
I'M AFRAID SHE DIDN'T KEEP HER WORD.

NIGHT THINGS, AFTER ALL, AREN'T CAPABLE OF ACTUALLY LYING, SO IT SOMETIMES CATCHES THEM OFF GUARD.

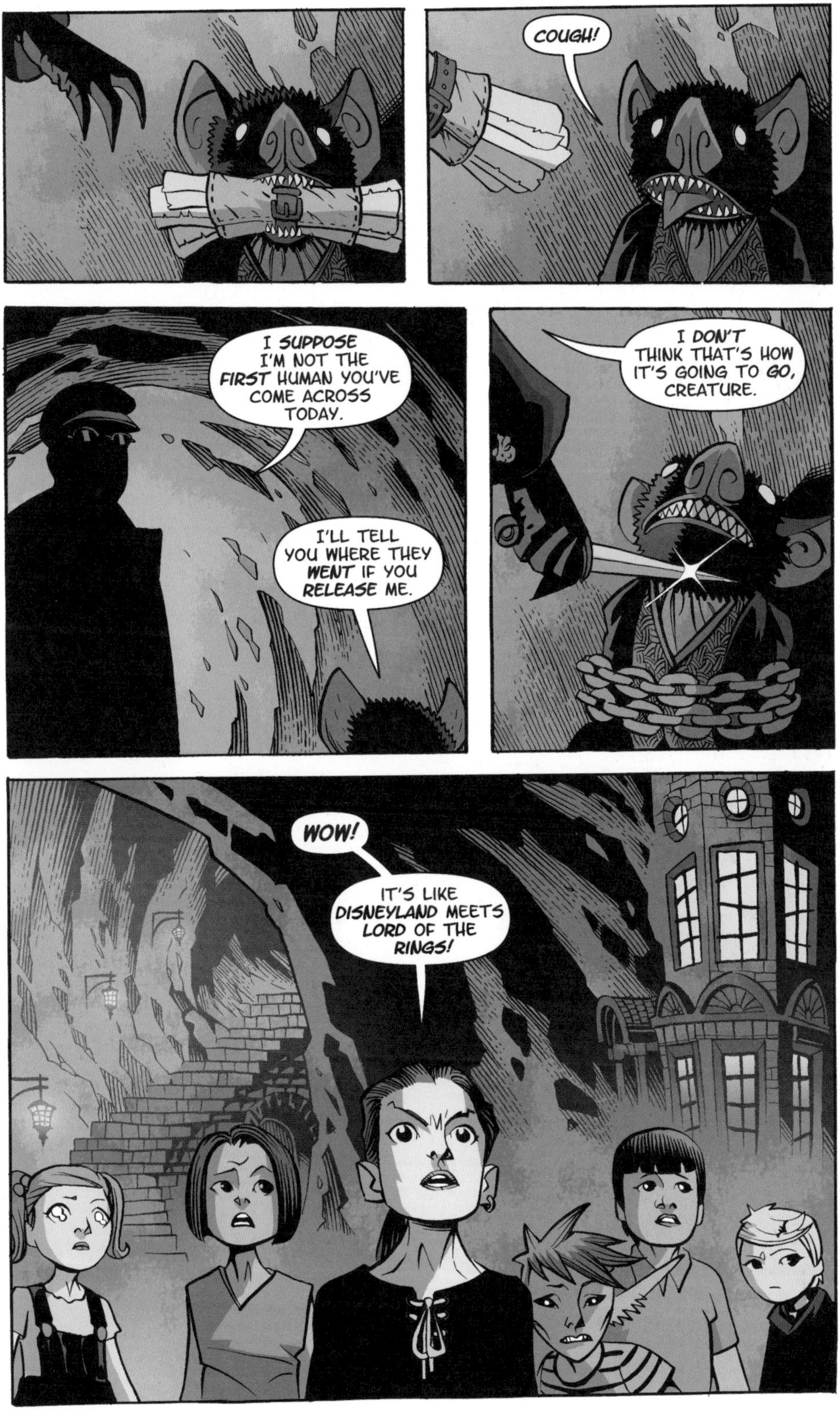
COUGH!
I SUPPOSE I'M NOT THE FIRST HUMAN YOU'VE COME ACROSS TODAY.
I'LL TELL YOU WHERE THEY WENT IF YOU RELEASE ME.
I DON'T THINK THAT'S HOW IT'S GOING TO GO, CREATURE.
WOW!
IT'S LIKE DISNEYLAND MEETS LORD OF THE RINGS!

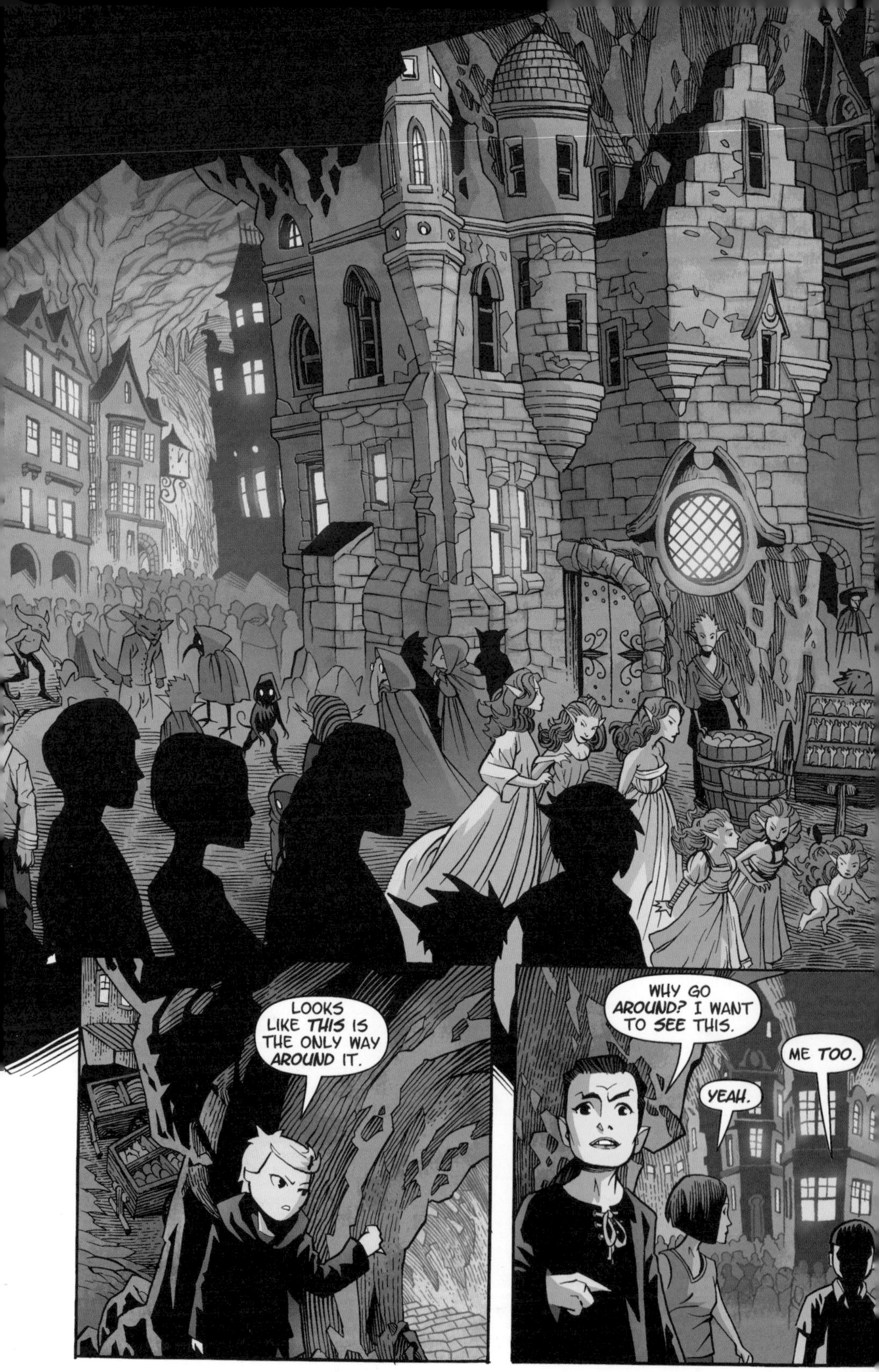
LOOKS LIKE THIS IS THE ONLY WAY AROUND IT.
WHY GO AROUND? I WANT TO SEE THIS.
YEAH.
ME TOO.

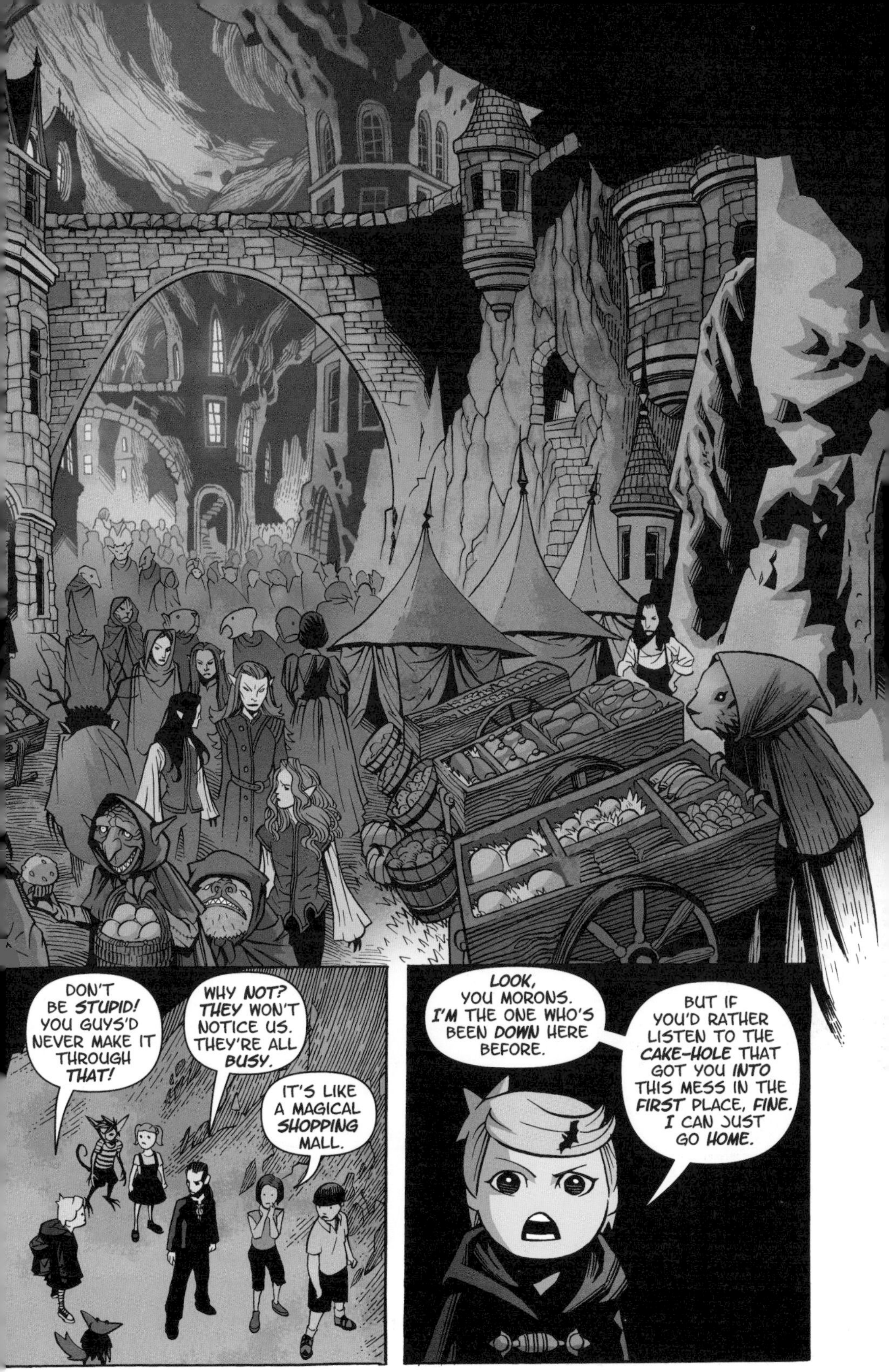
DON'T BE STUPID! YOU GUYS'D NEVER MAKE IT THROUGH THAT!
WHY NOT? THEY WON'T NOTICE US. THEY'RE ALL BUSY.
IT'S LIKE A MAGICAL SHOPPING MALL.
LOOK, YOU MORONS. I'M THE ONE WHO'S BEEN DOWN HERE BEFORE.
BUT IF YOU'D RATHER LISTEN TO THE CAKE-HOLE THAT GOT YOU INTO THIS MESS IN THE FIRST PLACE, FINE. I CAN JUST GO HOME.

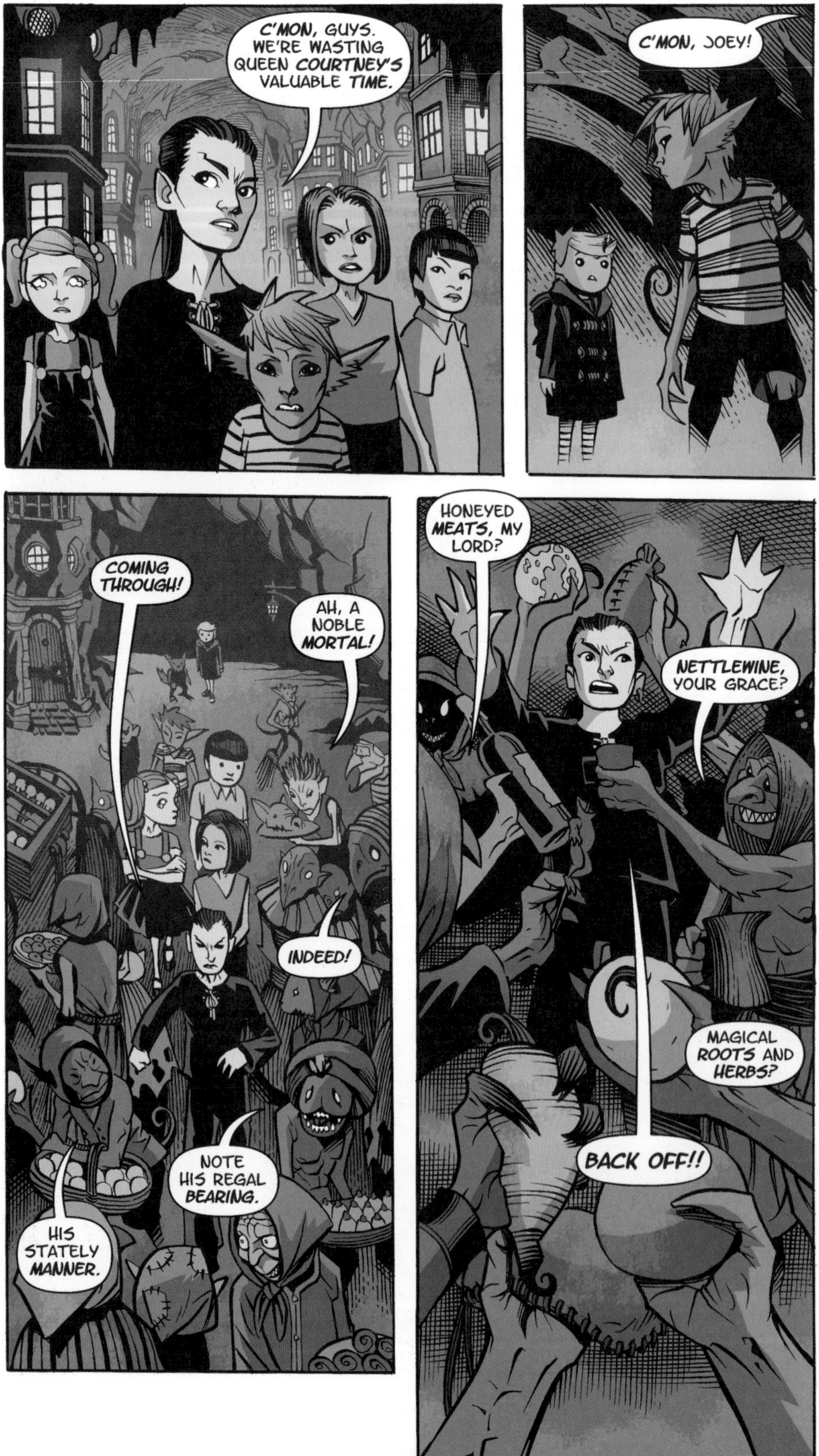
C'MON, GUYS. WE'RE WASTING QUEEN COURTNEY'S VALUABLE TIME.
C'MON, JOEY!
COMING THROUGH!
AH, A NOBLE MORTAL!
INDEED!
NOTE HIS REGAL BEARING.
HIS STATELY MANNER.
HONEYED MEATS, MY LORD?
NETTLEWINE, YOUR GRACE?
MAGICAL ROOTS AND HERBS?
BACK OFF!!

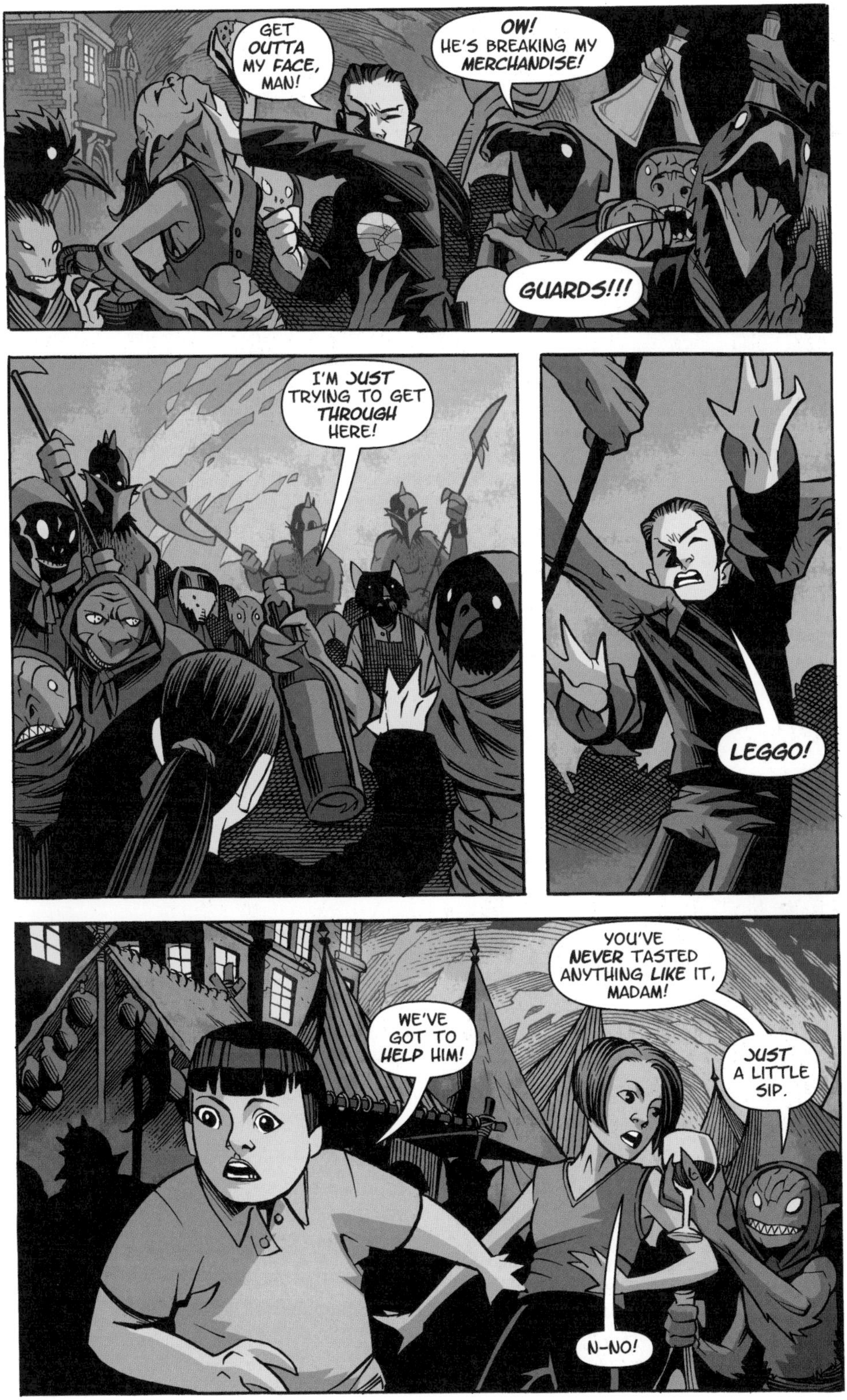
GET OUTTA MY FACE, MAN!
OW! HE'S BREAKING MY MERCHANDISE!
GUARDS!!!
I'M JUST TRYING TO GET THROUGH HERE!
LEGGO!
YOU'VE NEVER TASTED ANYTHING LIKE IT, MADAM!
WE'VE GOT TO HELP HIM!
JUST A LITTLE SIP.
N-NO!

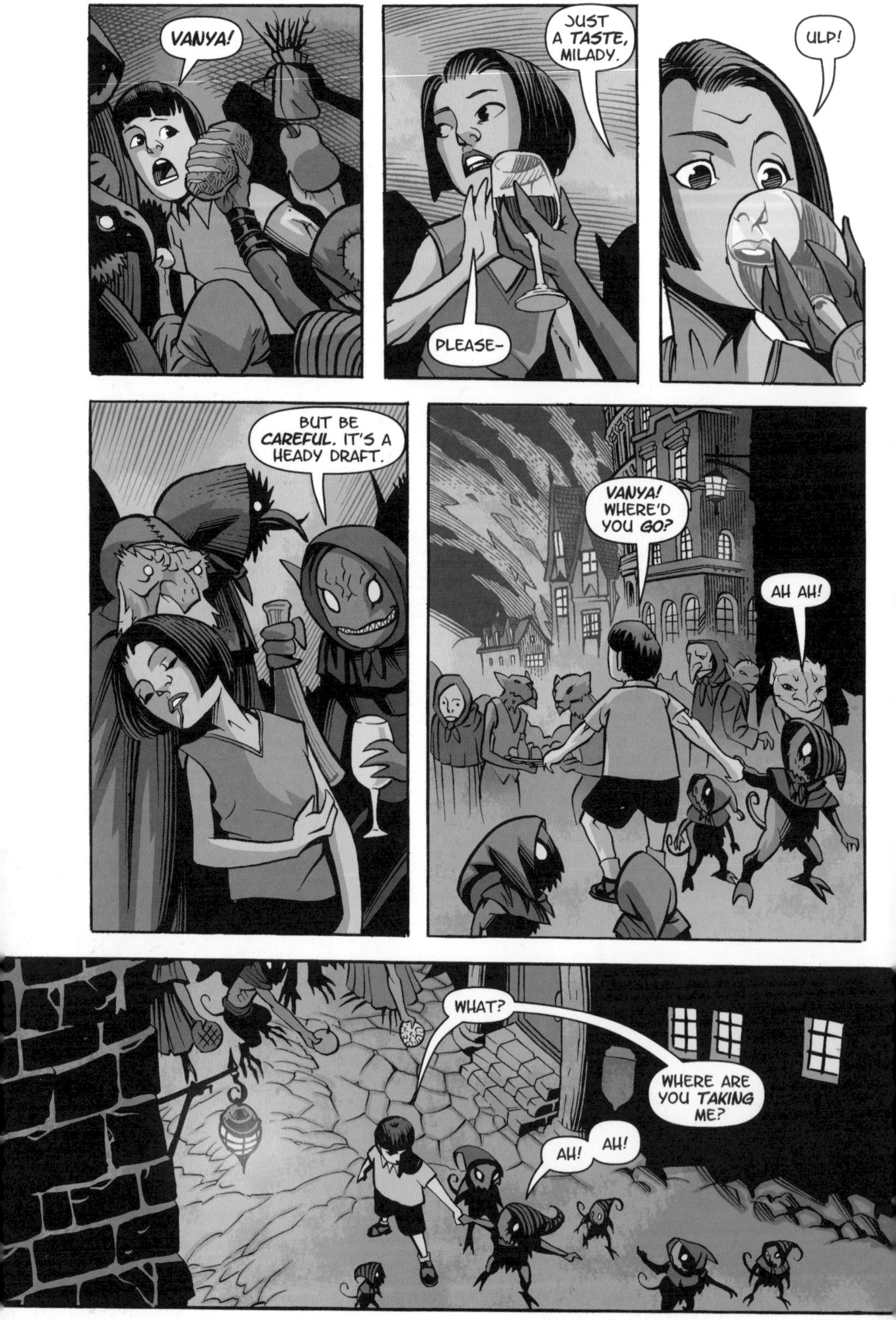
VANYA!
JUST A TASTE, MILADY.
PLEASE-
ULP!
BUT BE CAREFUL. IT'S A HEADY DRAFT.
VANYA! WHERE'D YOU GO?
AH AH!
WHAT?
WHERE ARE YOU TAKING ME?
AH!
AH!

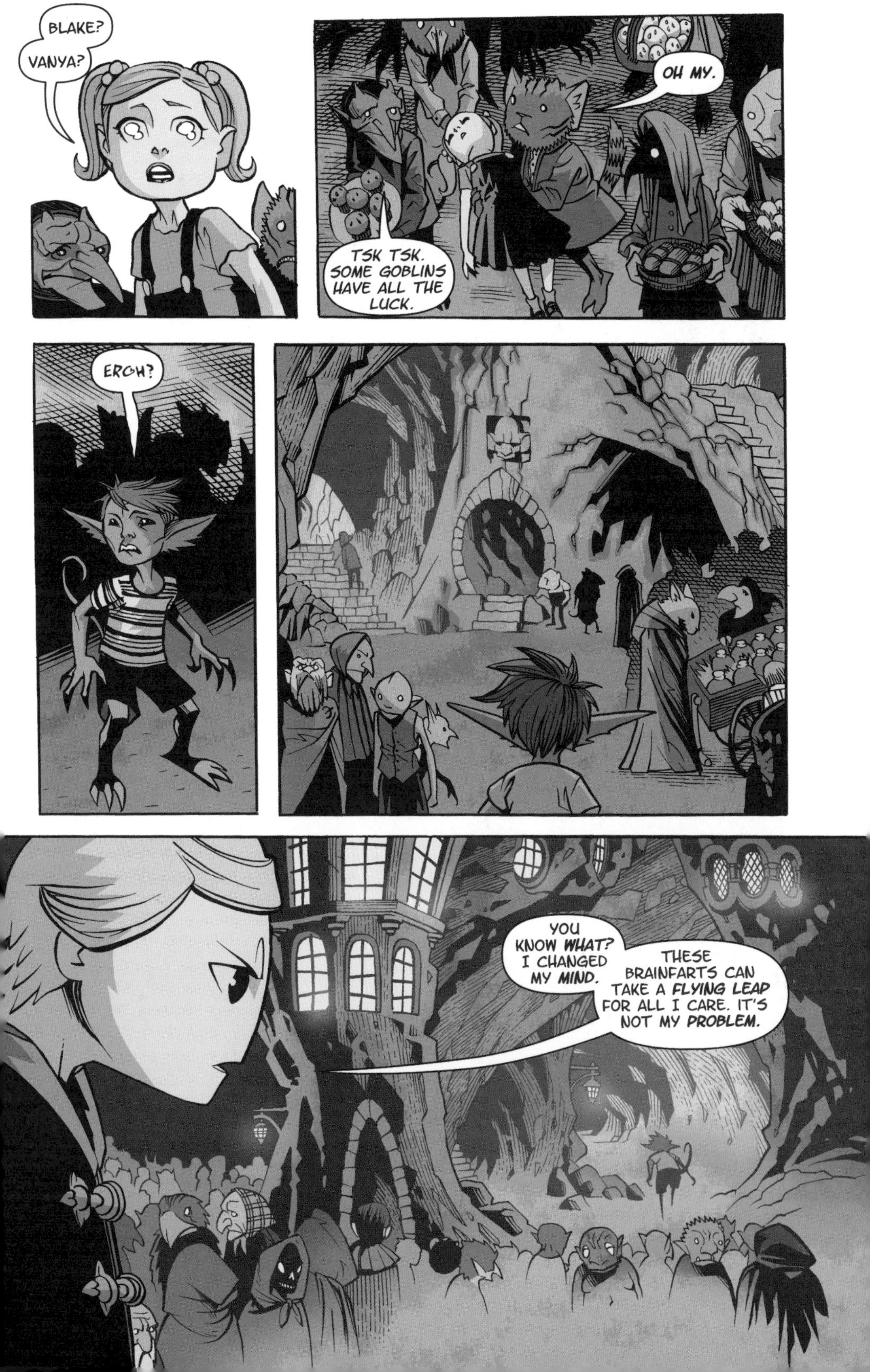
BLAKE?
VANYA?
OH MY.
TSK TSK. SOME GOBLINS HAVE ALL THE LUCK.
ERGH?
YOU KNOW WHAT? I CHANGED MY MIND.
THESE BRAINFARTS CAN TAKE A FLYING LEAP FOR ALL I CARE. IT'S NOT MY PROBLEM.

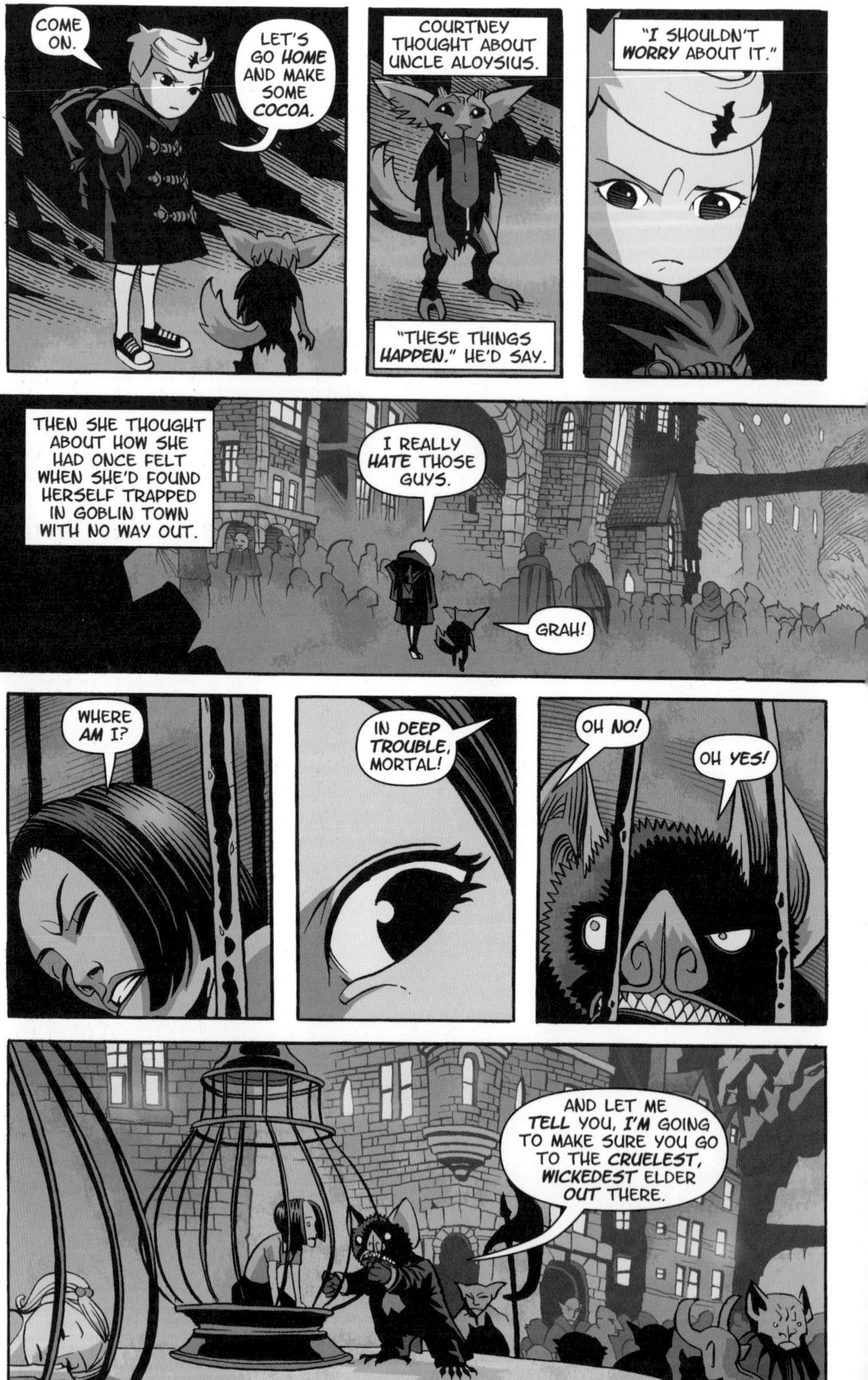
COME ON.
LET'S GO **HOME** AND MAKE SOME **COCOA.**
COURTNEY THOUGHT ABOUT UNCLE ALOYSIUS.
"THESE THINGS **HAPPEN.**" HE'D SAY.
"I SHOULDN'T **WORRY** ABOUT IT."
THEN SHE THOUGHT ABOUT HOW SHE HAD ONCE FELT WHEN SHE'D FOUND HERSELF TRAPPED IN GOBLIN TOWN WITH NO WAY OUT.
I REALLY **HATE** THOSE GUYS.
GRAH!
WHERE **AM** I?
IN **DEEP TROUBLE,** MORTAL!
OH **NO!**
OH **YES!**
AND LET ME **TELL** YOU, **I'M** GOING TO MAKE SURE YOU GO TO THE **CRUELEST, WICKEDEST** ELDER **OUT** THERE.

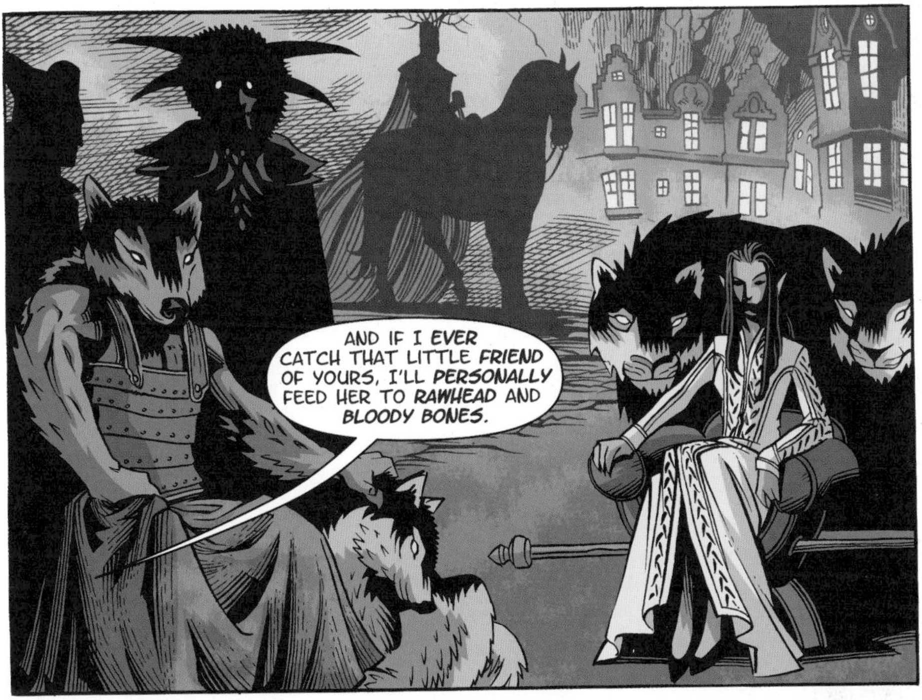
AND IF I EVER CATCH THAT LITTLE FRIEND OF YOURS, I'LL PERSONALLY FEED HER TO RAWHEAD AND BLOODY BONES.

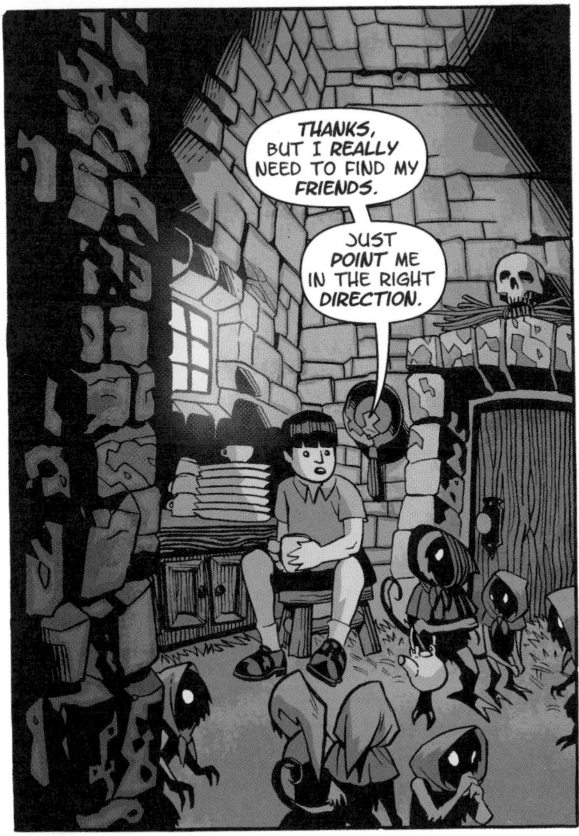
THANKS, BUT I REALLY NEED TO FIND MY FRIENDS.
JUST POINT ME IN THE RIGHT DIRECTION.

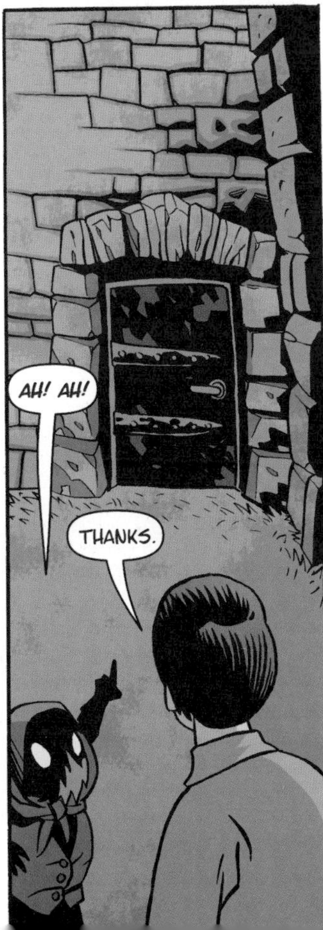
AH! AH!
THANKS.

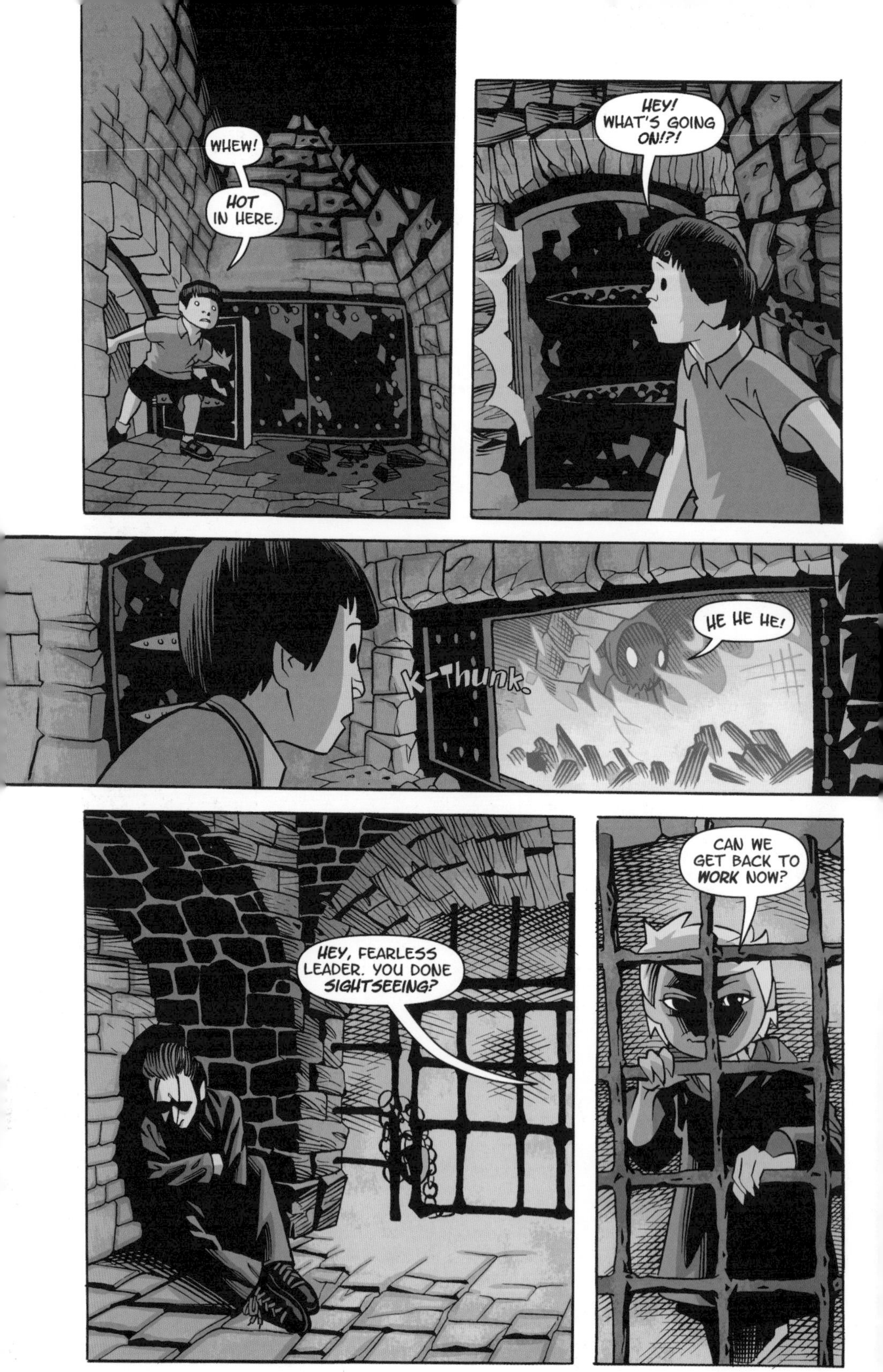
WHEW!
HOT IN HERE.
HEY! WHAT'S GOING ON!?!
HE HE HE!
K-THUNK.
HEY, FEARLESS LEADER. YOU DONE SIGHTSEEING?
CAN WE GET BACK TO WORK NOW?

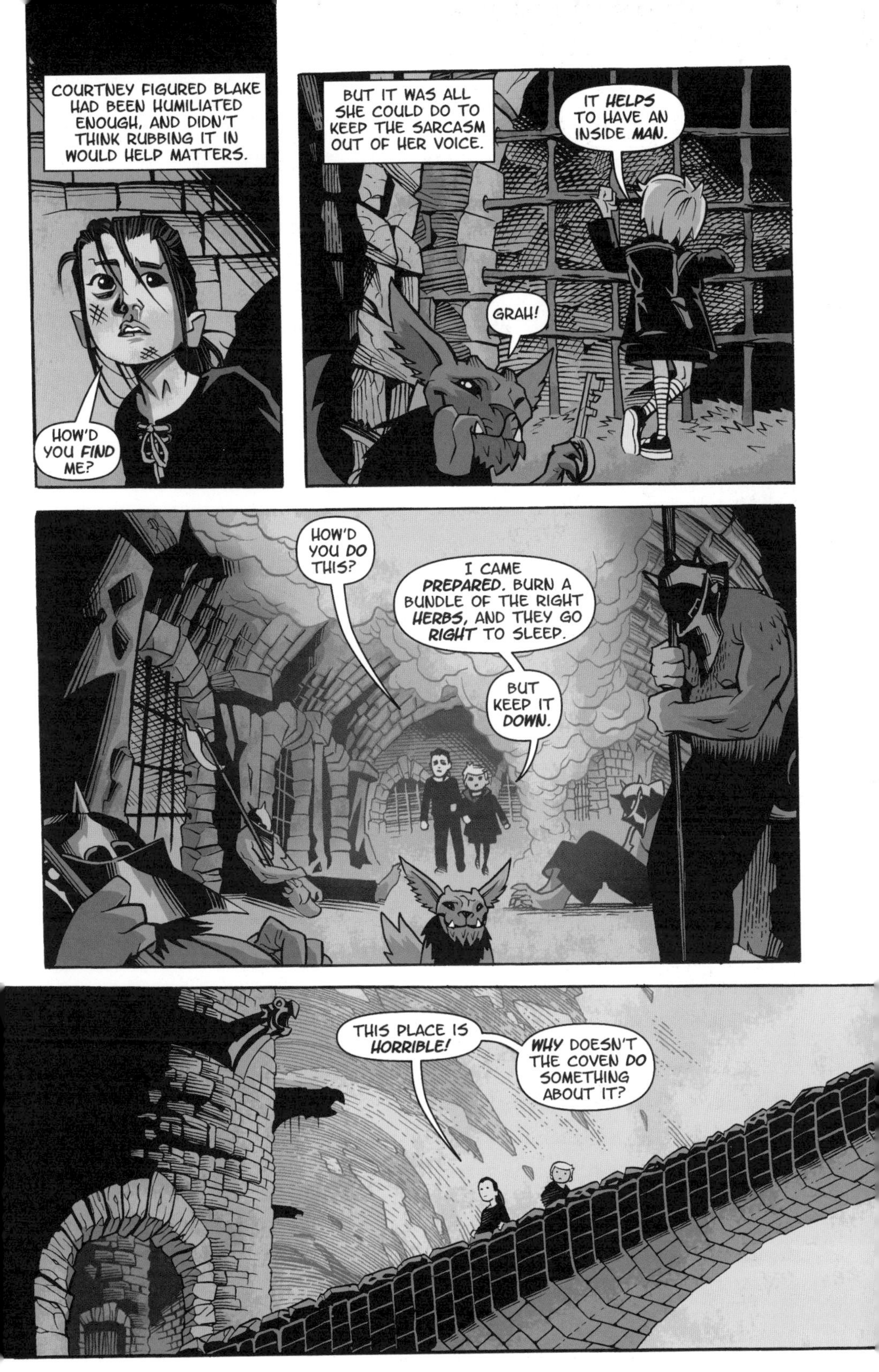
COURTNEY FIGURED BLAKE HAD BEEN HUMILIATED ENOUGH, AND DIDN'T THINK RUBBING IT IN WOULD HELP MATTERS.
HOW'D YOU FIND ME?
BUT IT WAS ALL SHE COULD DO TO KEEP THE SARCASM OUT OF HER VOICE.
IT HELPS TO HAVE AN INSIDE MAN.
GRAH!
HOW'D YOU DO THIS?
I CAME PREPARED. BURN A BUNDLE OF THE RIGHT HERBS, AND THEY GO RIGHT TO SLEEP.
BUT KEEP IT DOWN.
THIS PLACE IS HORRIBLE!
WHY DOESN'T THE COVEN DO SOMETHING ABOUT IT?

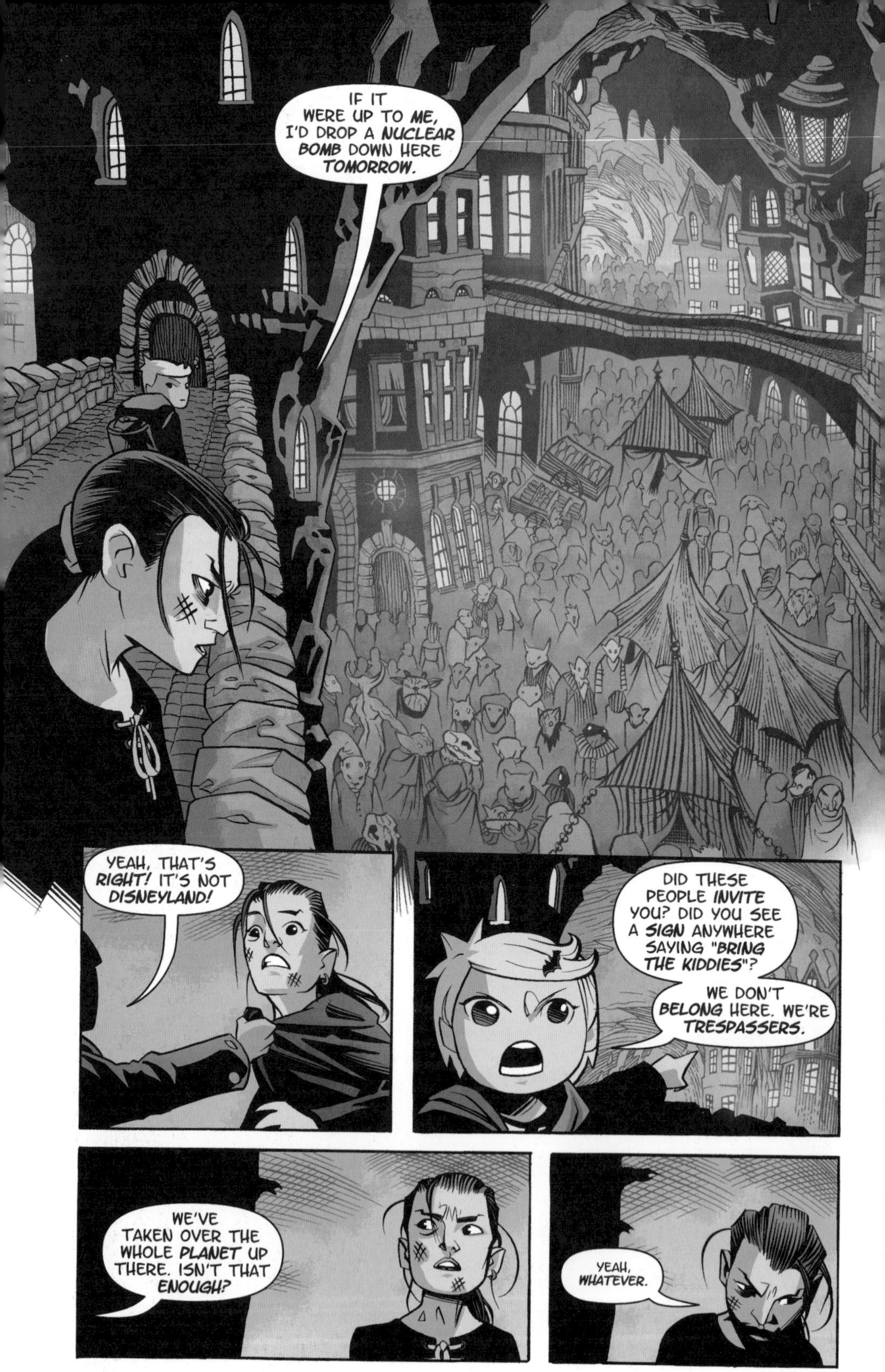
IF IT WERE UP TO ME, I'D DROP A NUCLEAR BOMB DOWN HERE TOMORROW.
YEAH, THAT'S RIGHT! IT'S NOT DISNEYLAND!
DID THESE PEOPLE INVITE YOU? DID YOU SEE A SIGN ANYWHERE SAYING "BRING THE KIDDIES"?
WE DON'T BELONG HERE. WE'RE TRESPASSERS.
WE'VE TAKEN OVER THE WHOLE PLANET UP THERE. ISN'T THAT ENOUGH?
YEAH, WHATEVER.

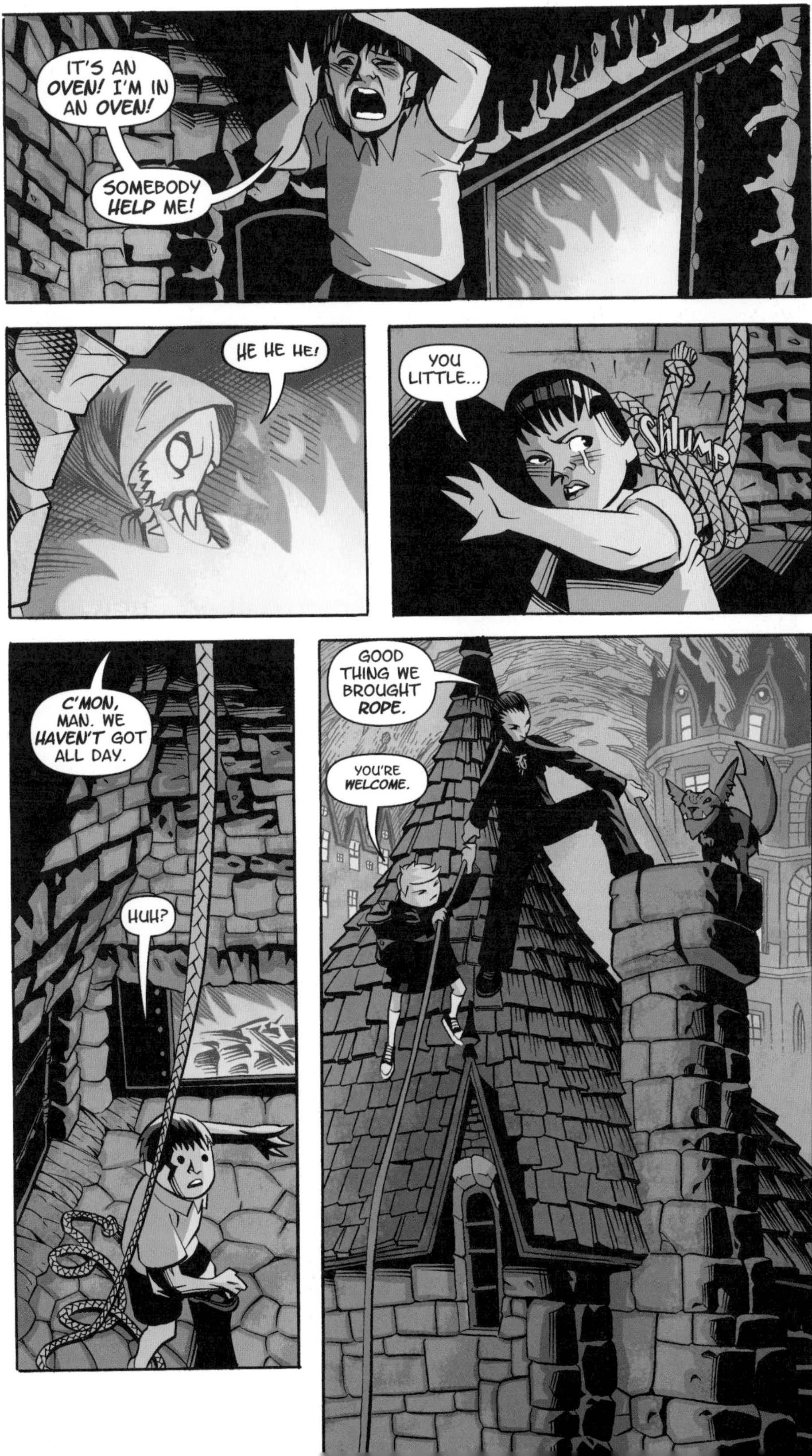
IT'S AN OVEN! I'M IN AN OVEN!
SOMEBODY HELP ME!
HE HE HE!
YOU LITTLE...
SHLUMP
C'MON, MAN. WE HAVEN'T GOT ALL DAY.
HUH?
GOOD THING WE BROUGHT ROPE.
YOU'RE WELCOME.

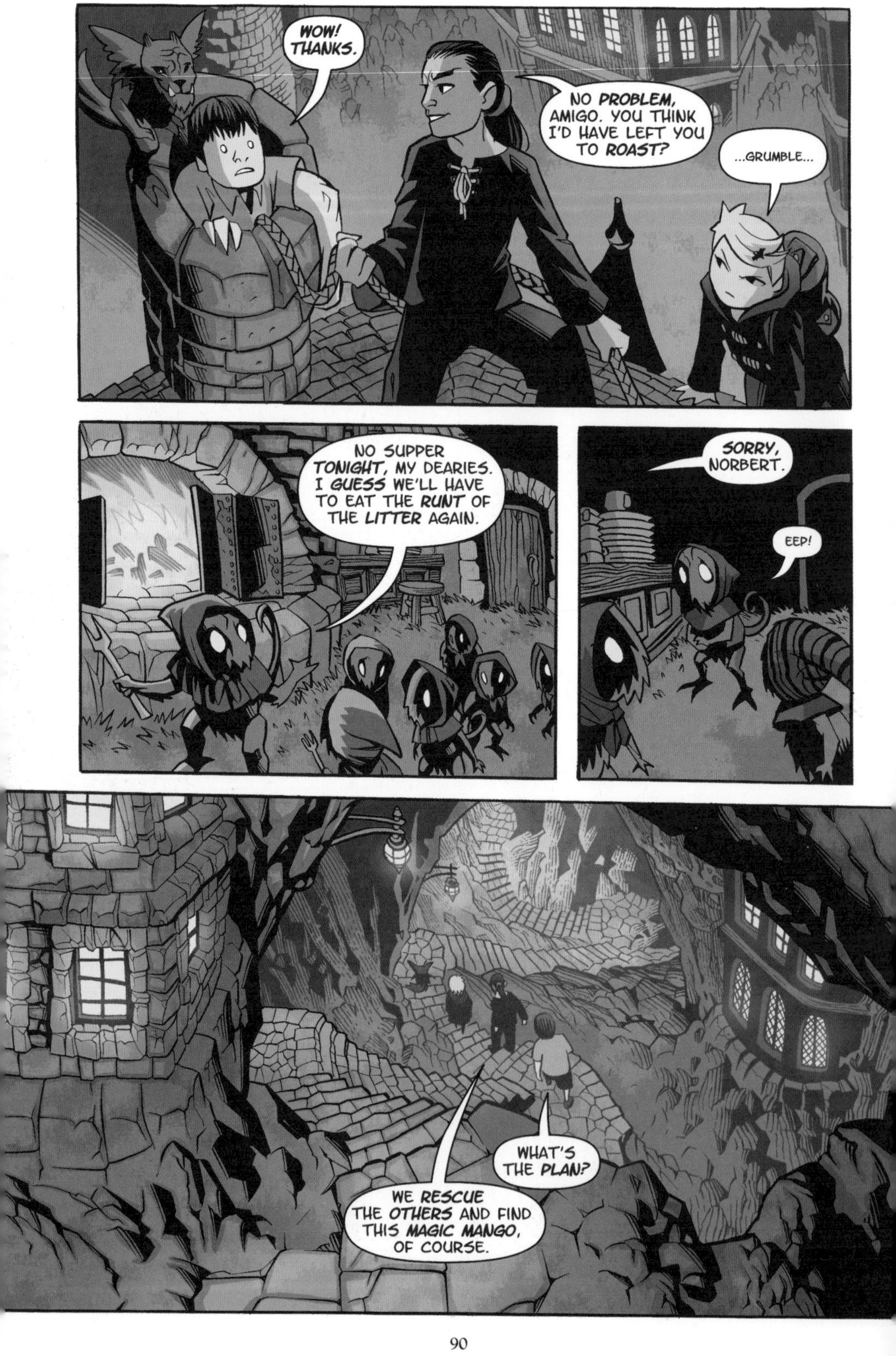
WOW! THANKS.
NO PROBLEM, AMIGO. YOU THINK I'D HAVE LEFT YOU TO ROAST?
...GRUMBLE...
NO SUPPER TONIGHT, MY DEARIES. I GUESS WE'LL HAVE TO EAT THE RUNT OF THE LITTER AGAIN.
SORRY, NORBERT.
EEP!
WHAT'S THE PLAN?
WE RESCUE THE OTHERS AND FIND THIS MAGIC MANGO, OF COURSE.

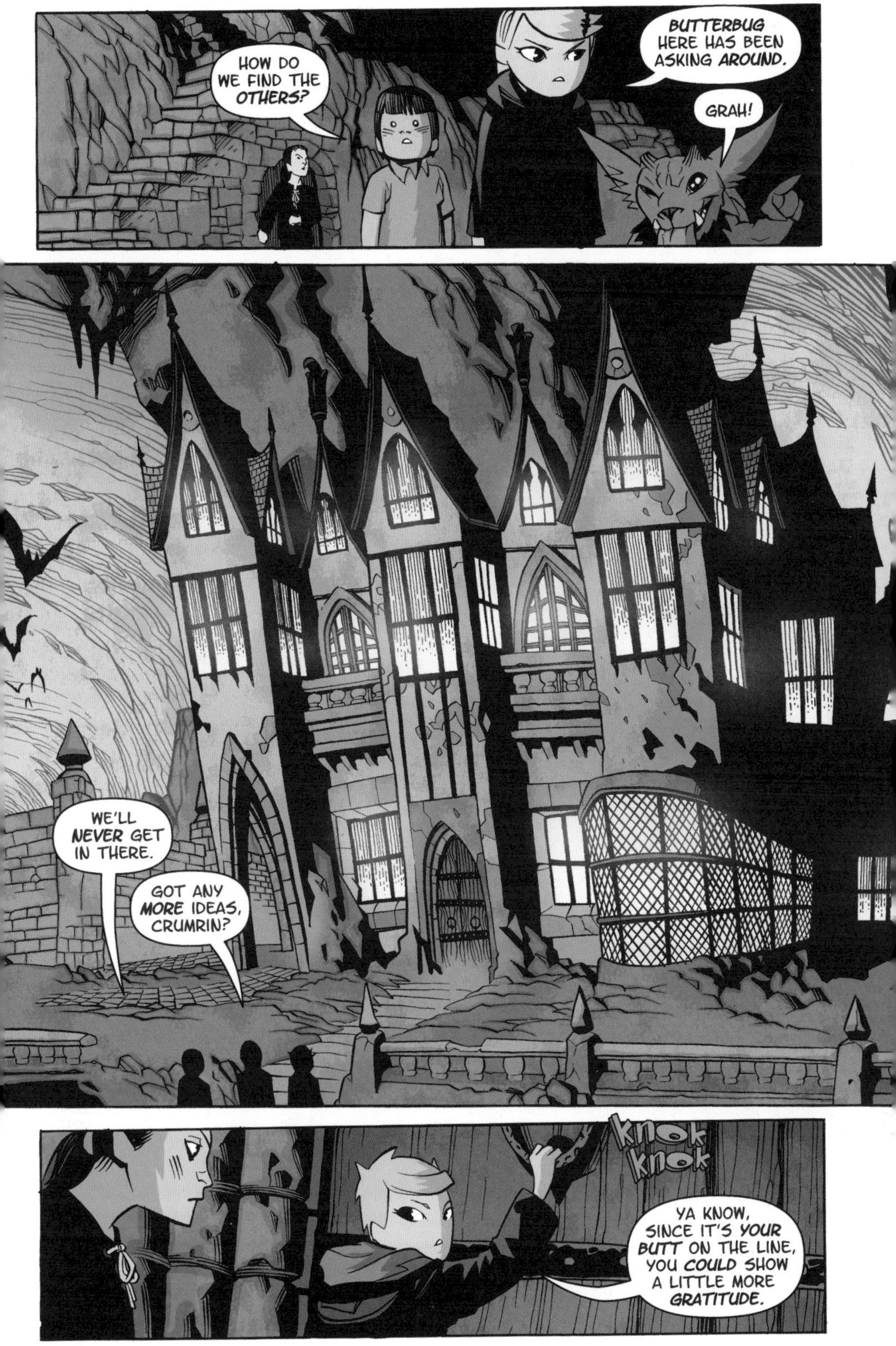
HOW DO WE FIND THE OTHERS?
BUTTERBUG HERE HAS BEEN ASKING AROUND.
GRAH!
WE'LL NEVER GET IN THERE.
GOT ANY MORE IDEAS, CRUMRIN?
knok knok
YA KNOW, SINCE IT'S YOUR BUTT ON THE LINE, YOU COULD SHOW A LITTLE MORE GRATITUDE.

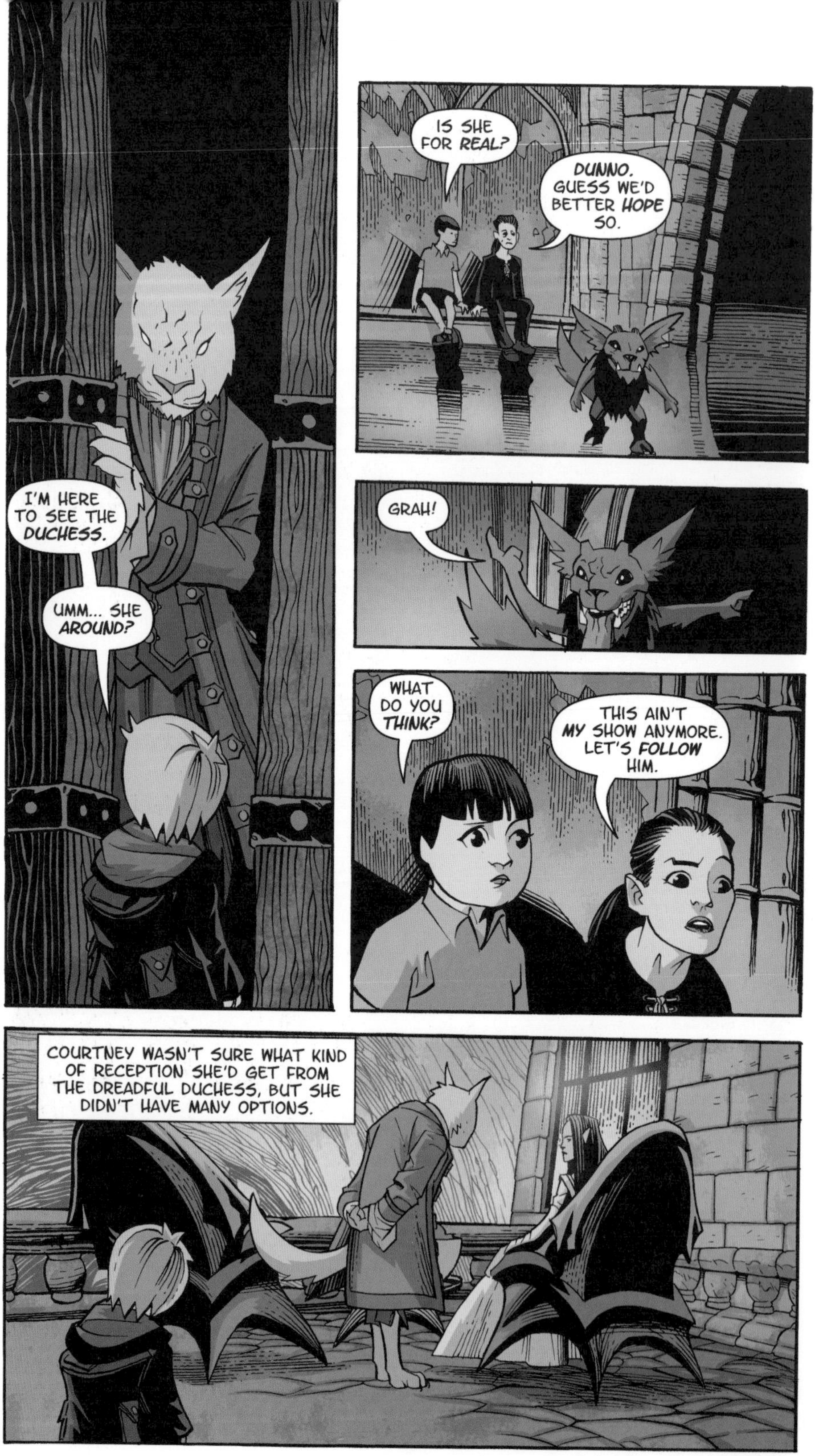
I'M HERE TO SEE THE DUCHESS.
UMM... SHE AROUND?
IS SHE FOR REAL?
DUNNO. GUESS WE'D BETTER HOPE SO.
GRAH!
WHAT DO YOU THINK?
THIS AIN'T MY SHOW ANYMORE. LET'S FOLLOW HIM.
COURTNEY WASN'T SURE WHAT KIND OF RECEPTION SHE'D GET FROM THE DREADFUL DUCHESS, BUT SHE DIDN'T HAVE MANY OPTIONS.

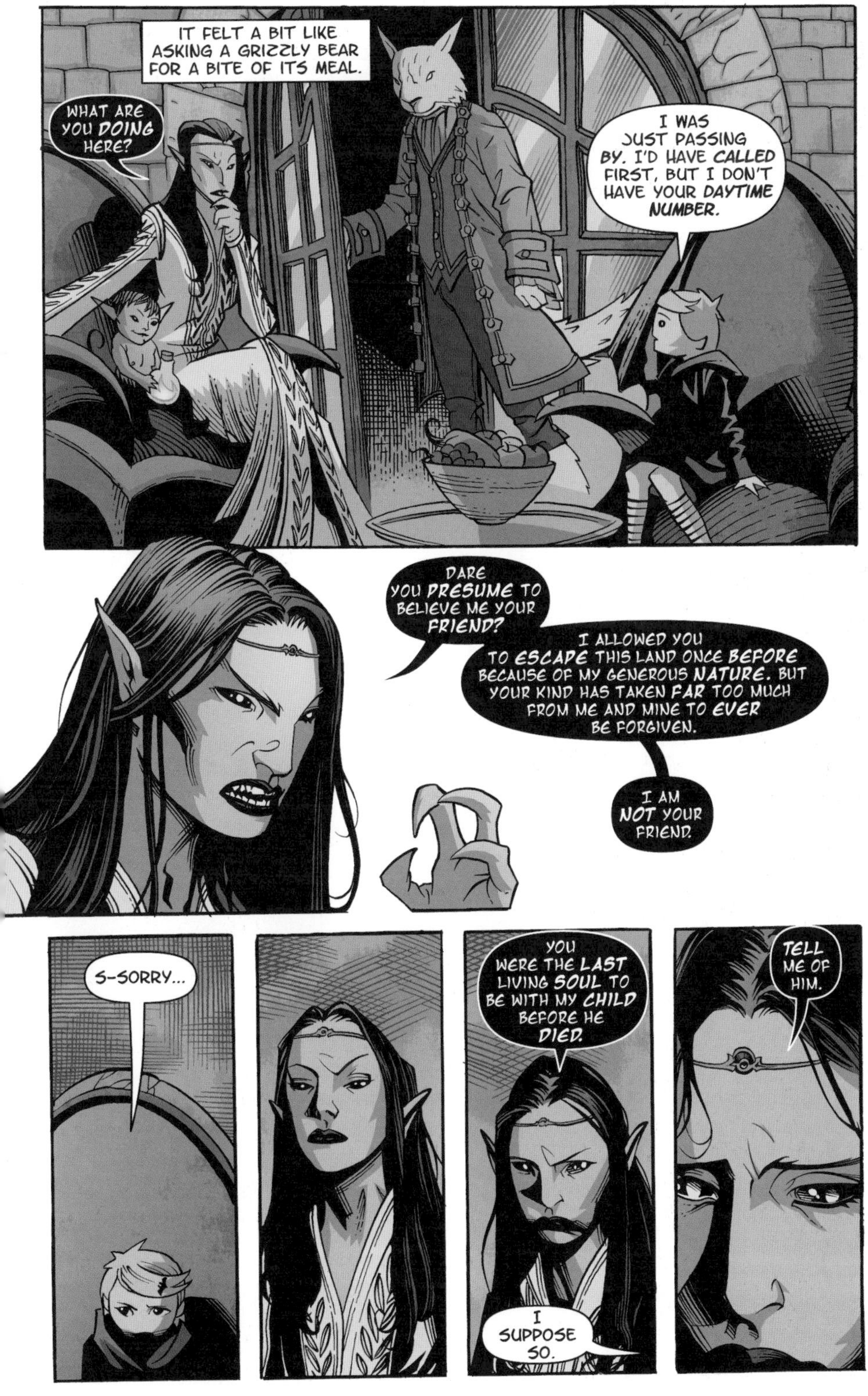
IT FELT A BIT LIKE ASKING A GRIZZLY BEAR FOR A BITE OF ITS MEAL.
WHAT ARE YOU DOING HERE?
I WAS JUST PASSING BY. I'D HAVE CALLED FIRST, BUT I DON'T HAVE YOUR DAYTIME NUMBER.
DARE YOU PRESUME TO BELIEVE ME YOUR FRIEND?
I ALLOWED YOU TO ESCAPE THIS LAND ONCE BEFORE BECAUSE OF MY GENEROUS NATURE. BUT YOUR KIND HAS TAKEN FAR TOO MUCH FROM ME AND MINE TO EVER BE FORGIVEN.
I AM NOT YOUR FRIEND.
S-SORRY...
YOU WERE THE LAST LIVING SOUL TO BE WITH MY CHILD BEFORE HE DIED.
I SUPPOSE SO.
TELL ME OF HIM.

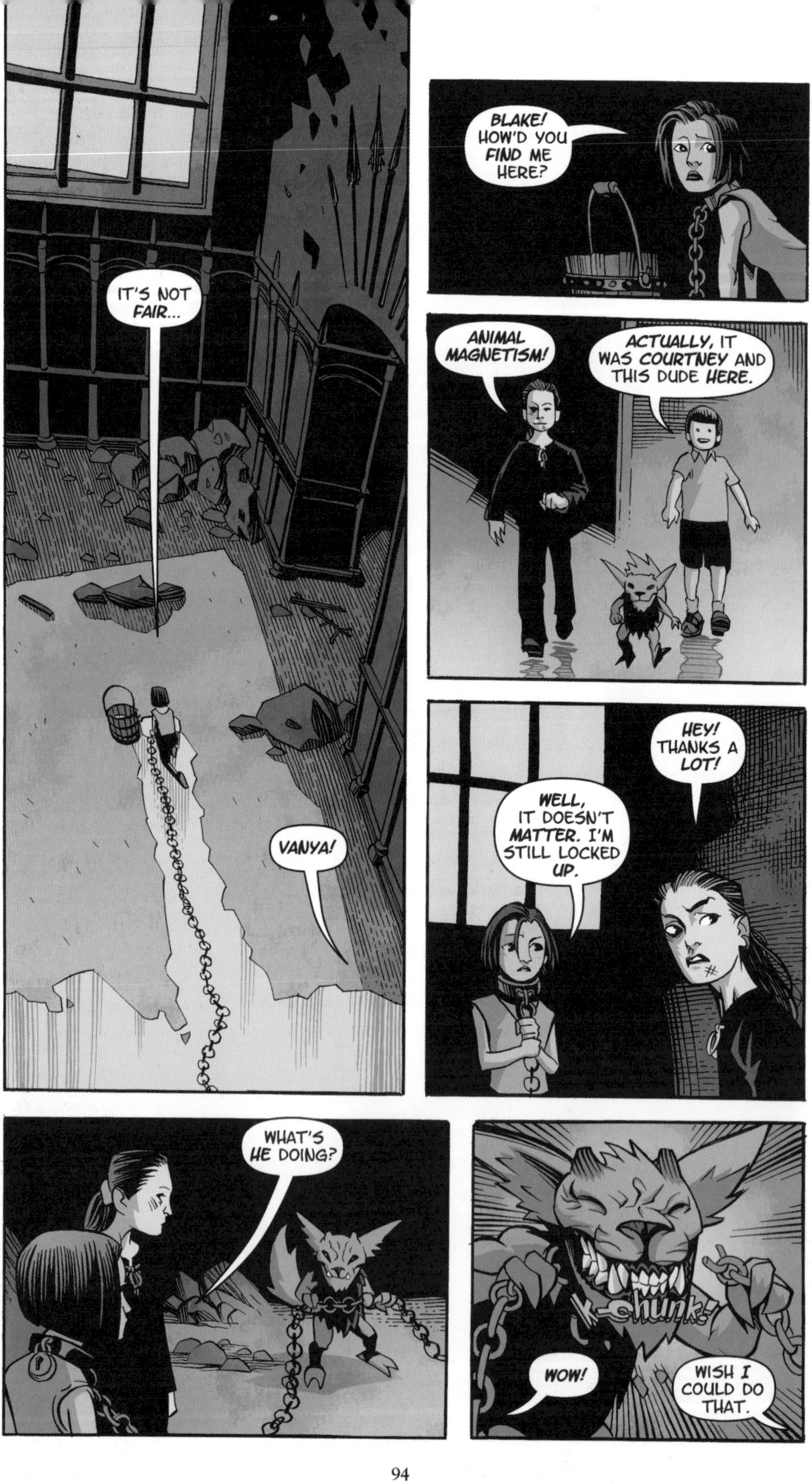
IT'S NOT FAIR...
VANYA!
BLAKE! HOW'D YOU FIND ME HERE?
ANIMAL MAGNETISM!
ACTUALLY, IT WAS COURTNEY AND THIS DUDE HERE.
HEY! THANKS A LOT!
WELL, IT DOESN'T MATTER. I'M STILL LOCKED UP.
WHAT'S HE DOING?
K-CHUNK!
WOW!
WISH I COULD DO THAT.

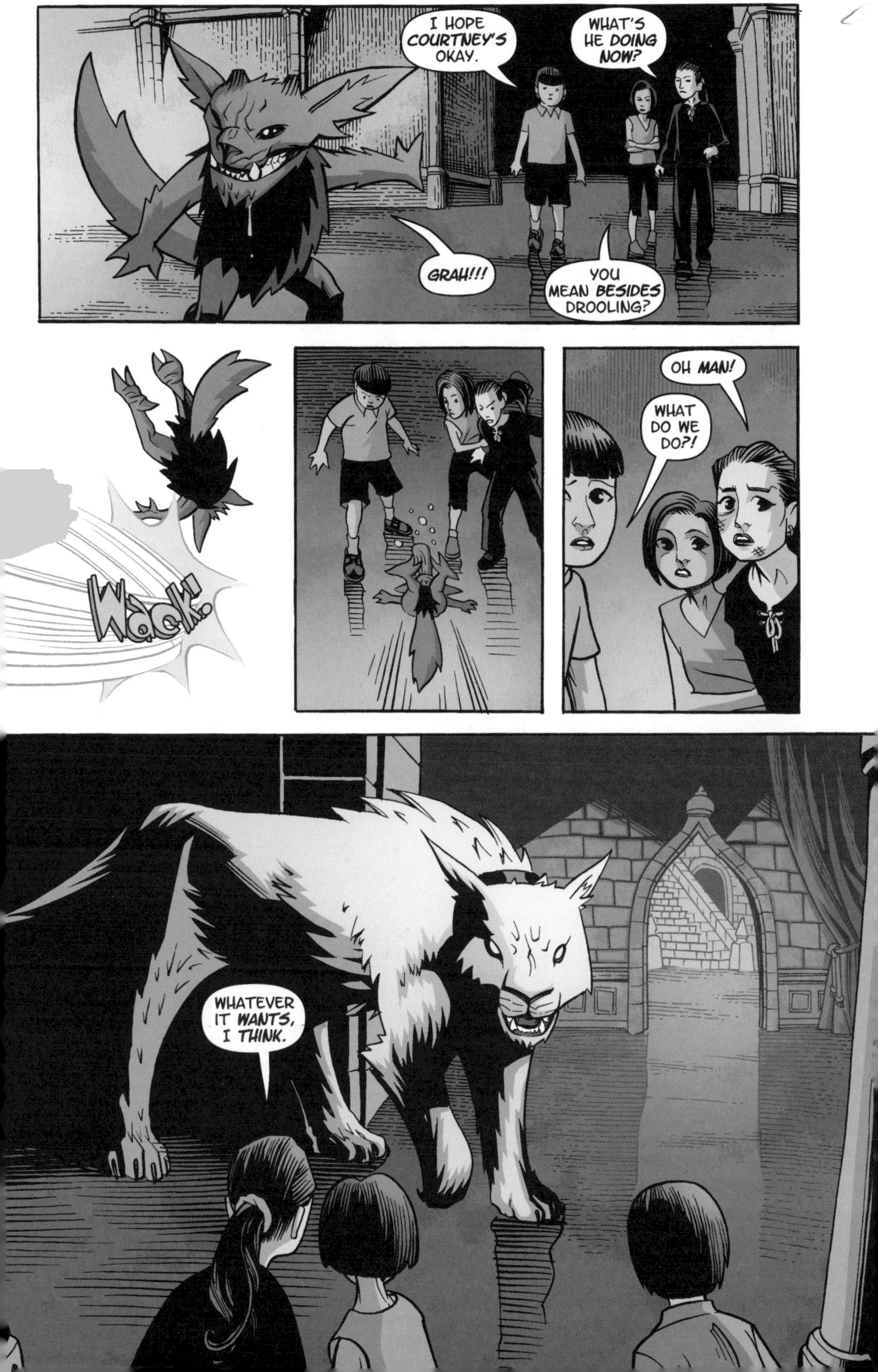
I HOPE COURTNEY'S OKAY.
WHAT'S HE DOING NOW?
GRAH!!!
YOU MEAN BESIDES DROOLING?
WACK!
OH MAN!
WHAT DO WE DO?!
WHATEVER IT WANTS, I THINK.

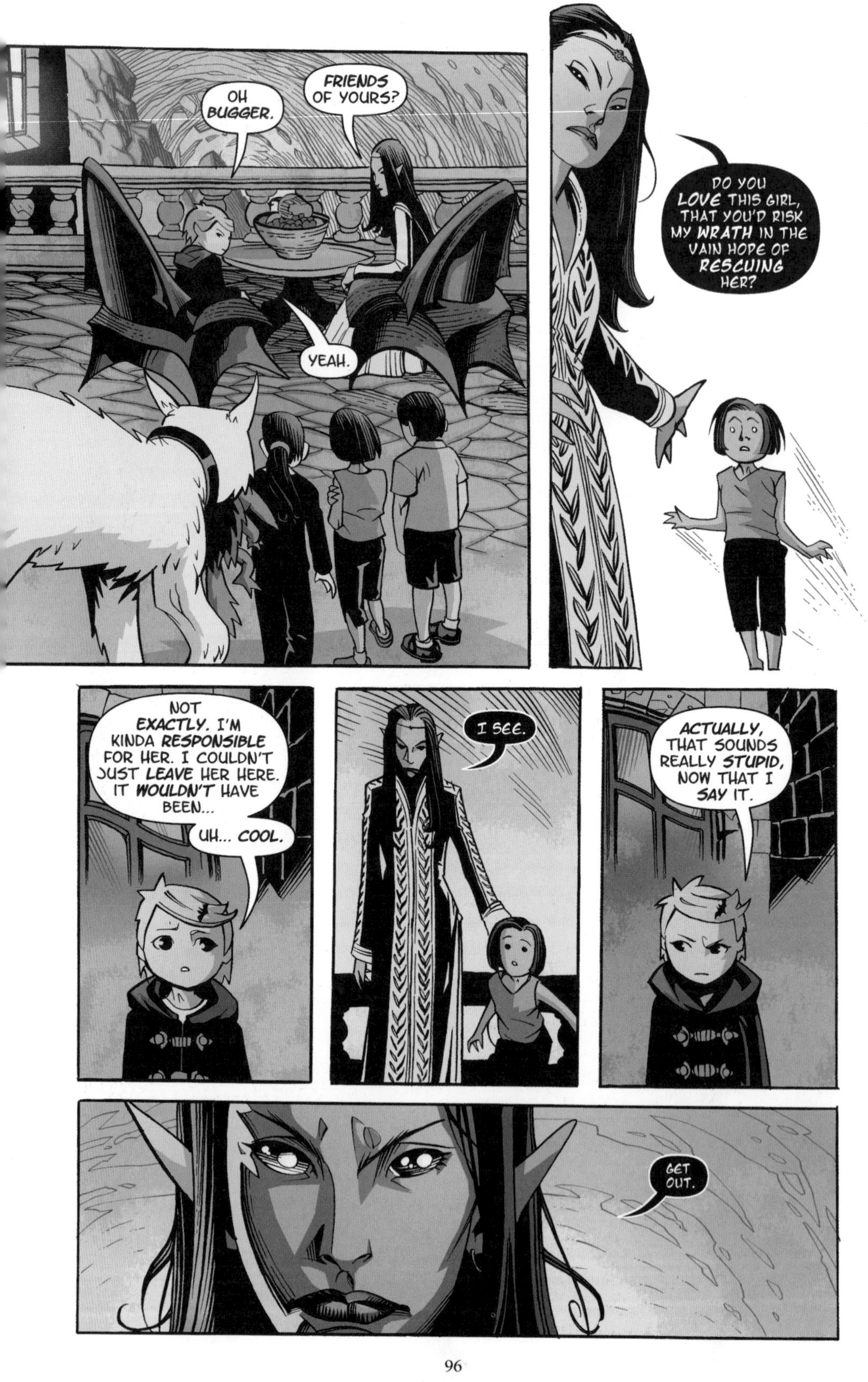
OH BUGGER.
FRIENDS OF YOURS?
YEAH.
DO YOU LOVE THIS GIRL, THAT YOU'D RISK MY WRATH IN THE VAIN HOPE OF RESCUING HER?
NOT EXACTLY. I'M KINDA RESPONSIBLE FOR HER. I COULDN'T JUST LEAVE HER HERE. IT WOULDN'T HAVE BEEN...
UH... COOL.
I SEE.
ACTUALLY, THAT SOUNDS REALLY STUPID, NOW THAT I SAY IT.
GET OUT.

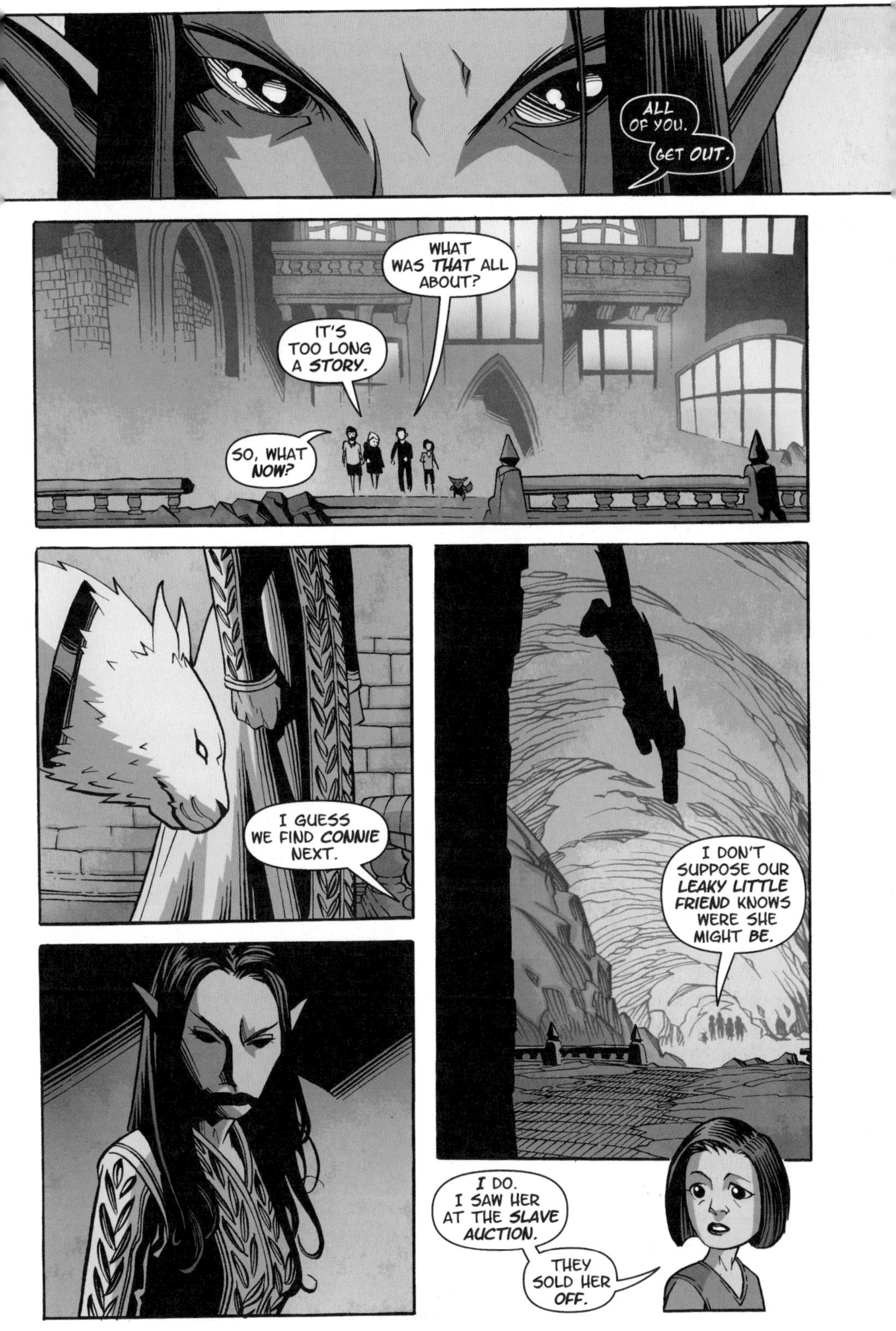
ALL OF YOU.
GET OUT.
WHAT WAS THAT ALL ABOUT?
IT'S TOO LONG A STORY.
SO, WHAT NOW?
I GUESS WE FIND CONNIE NEXT.
I DON'T SUPPOSE OUR LEAKY LITTLE FRIEND KNOWS WERE SHE MIGHT BE.
I DO. I SAW HER AT THE SLAVE AUCTION.
THEY SOLD HER OFF.

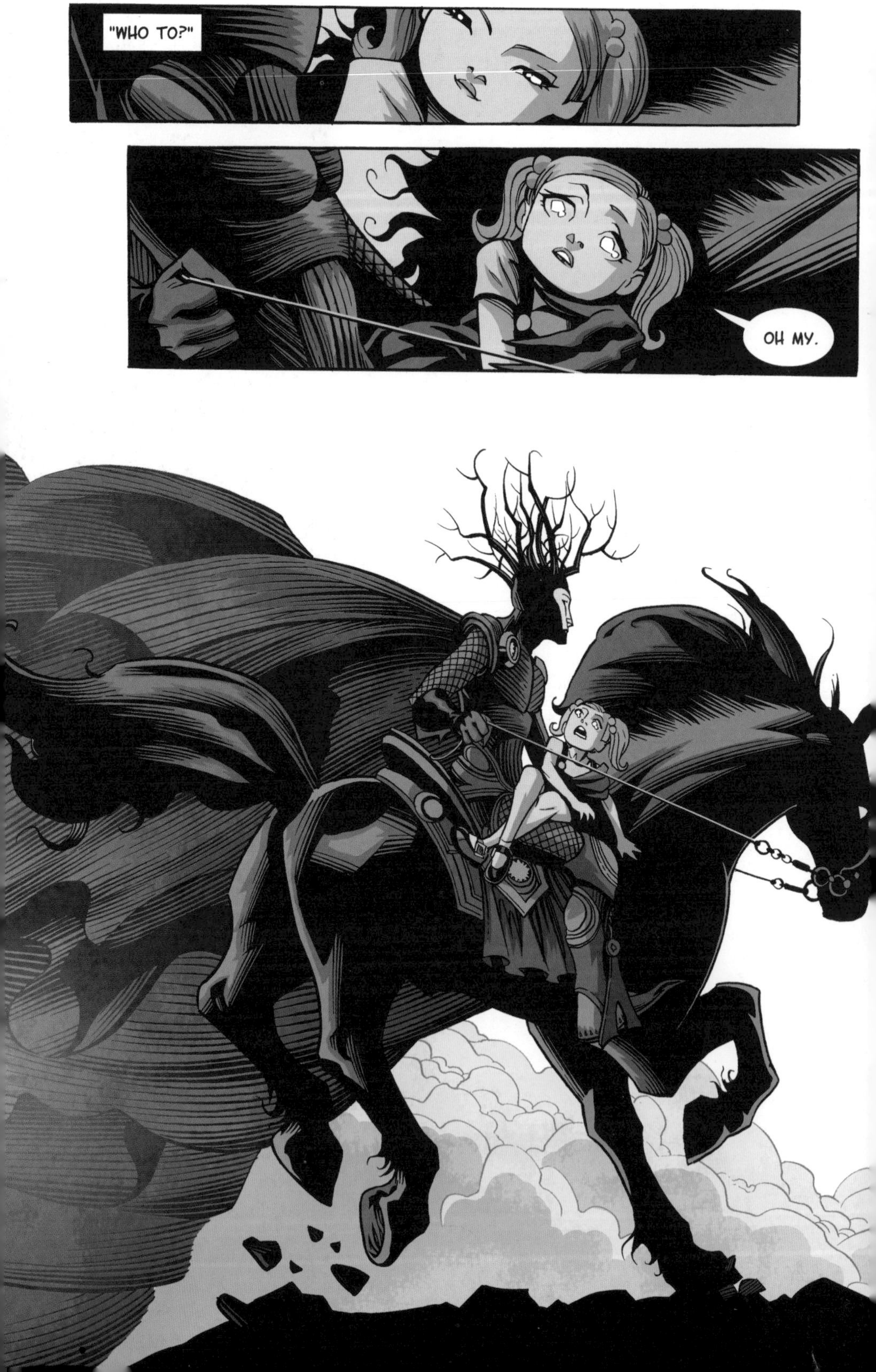
"WHO TO?"
OH MY.

Chapter Four

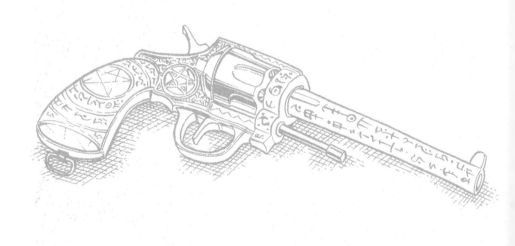

HMMMM...

Miss Crumrin & "friend"
Radley Hall 12-20

Martin...hes' Basement

OH, *EXCUSE* ME, SIR. I WAS LOOKING FOR *TEMPLETON*.

MMM-HMM.

I'VE BEEN LOOKING OVER THESE *DOCUMENTS*.

YOU KNOW, AS LUDICROUS AS IT *SOUNDS*, THIS EVIDENCE...

SIR?

BUT A *YOUNG GIRL*, DOING SUCH *TERRIBLE THINGS* ON HER OWN...

IT'S *RIDICULOUS*. UNLESS...

KEEPING AN *EYE* ON *TEMPLETON*, ARE YOU, COUNCILOR?

GIVEN HIS ATTITUDE ABOUT MY *STUDENT*, IT'D BE UNWISE *NOT* TO.

DO YOU KNOW WHERE HE MIGHT BE?

NO, AS A MATTER OF *FACT*, I DON'T...

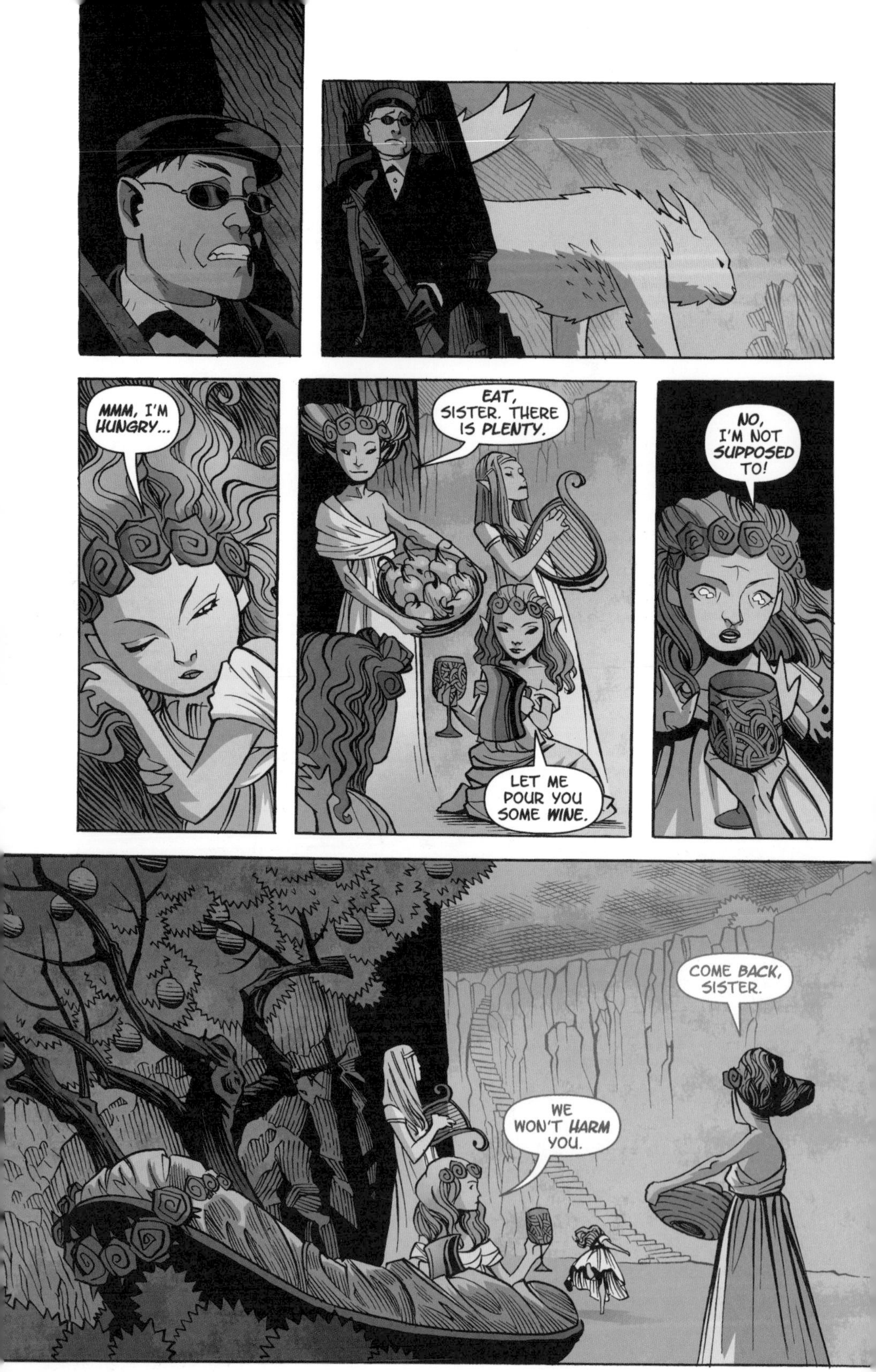
MMM, I'M HUNGRY...
EAT, SISTER. THERE IS PLENTY.
LET ME POUR YOU SOME WINE.
NO, I'M NOT SUPPOSED TO!
COME BACK, SISTER.
WE WON'T HARM YOU.

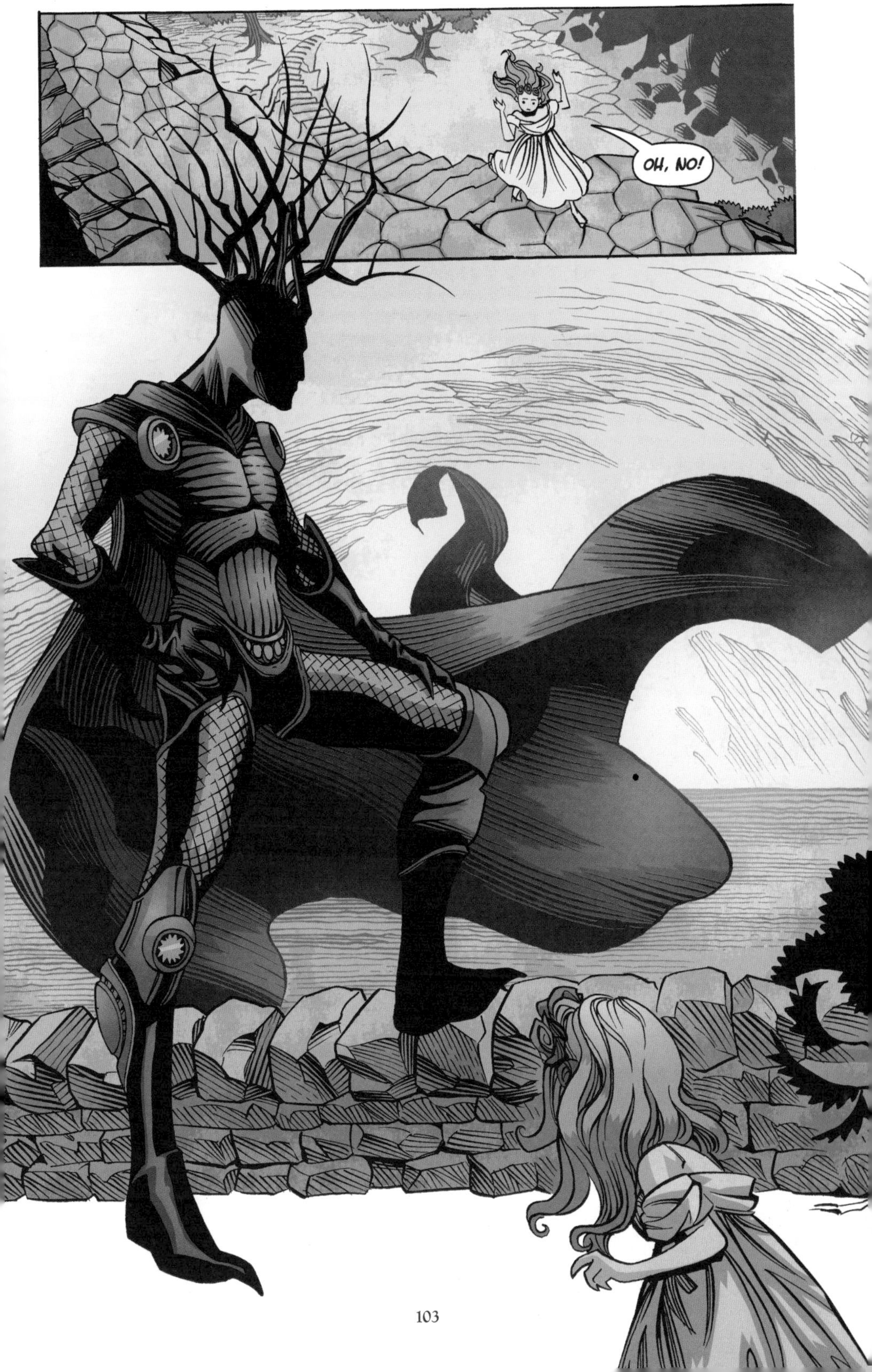
OH, NO!

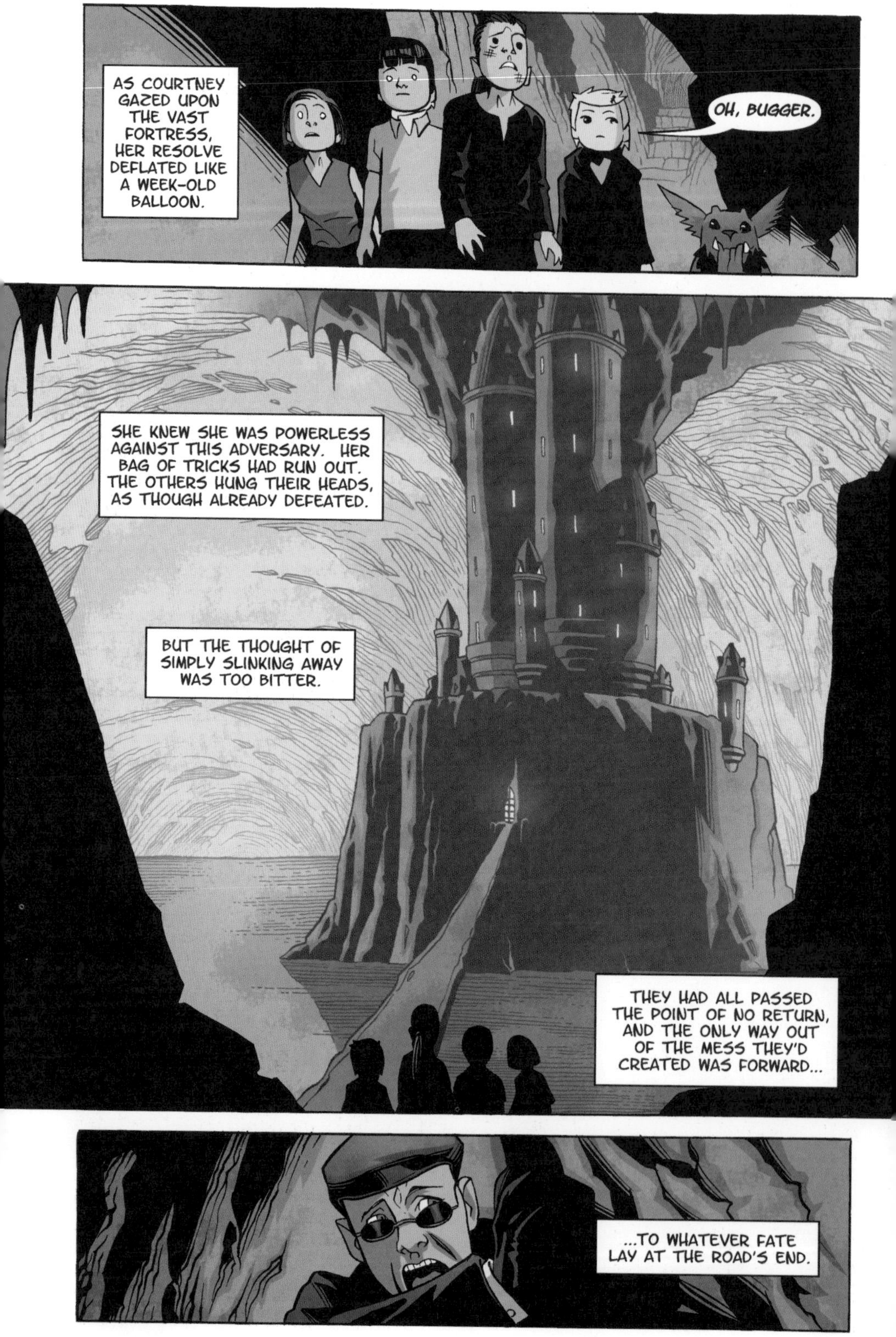
AS COURTNEY GAZED UPON THE VAST FORTRESS, HER RESOLVE DEFLATED LIKE A WEEK-OLD BALLOON.
OH, BUGGER.
SHE KNEW SHE WAS POWERLESS AGAINST THIS ADVERSARY. HER BAG OF TRICKS HAD RUN OUT. THE OTHERS HUNG THEIR HEADS, AS THOUGH ALREADY DEFEATED.
BUT THE THOUGHT OF SIMPLY SLINKING AWAY WAS TOO BITTER.
THEY HAD ALL PASSED THE POINT OF NO RETURN, AND THE ONLY WAY OUT OF THE MESS THEY'D CREATED WAS FORWARD...
...TO WHATEVER FATE LAY AT THE ROAD'S END.

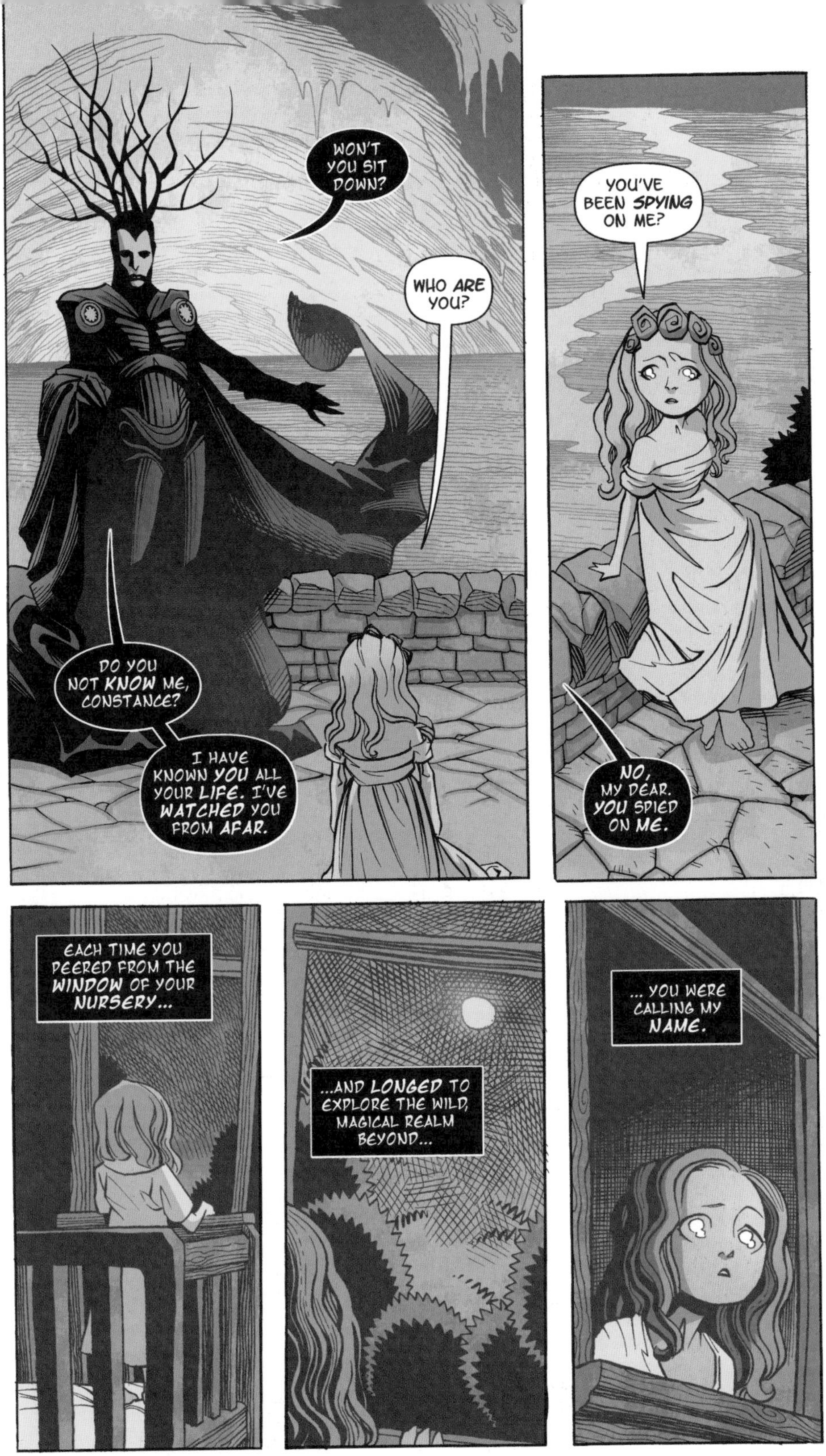
WON'T YOU SIT DOWN?
WHO ARE YOU?
DO YOU NOT KNOW ME, CONSTANCE?
I HAVE KNOWN YOU ALL YOUR LIFE. I'VE WATCHED YOU FROM AFAR.
YOU'VE BEEN SPYING ON ME?
NO, MY DEAR. YOU SPIED ON ME.
EACH TIME YOU PEERED FROM THE WINDOW OF YOUR NURSERY...
...AND LONGED TO EXPLORE THE WILD, MAGICAL REALM BEYOND...
... YOU WERE CALLING MY NAME.

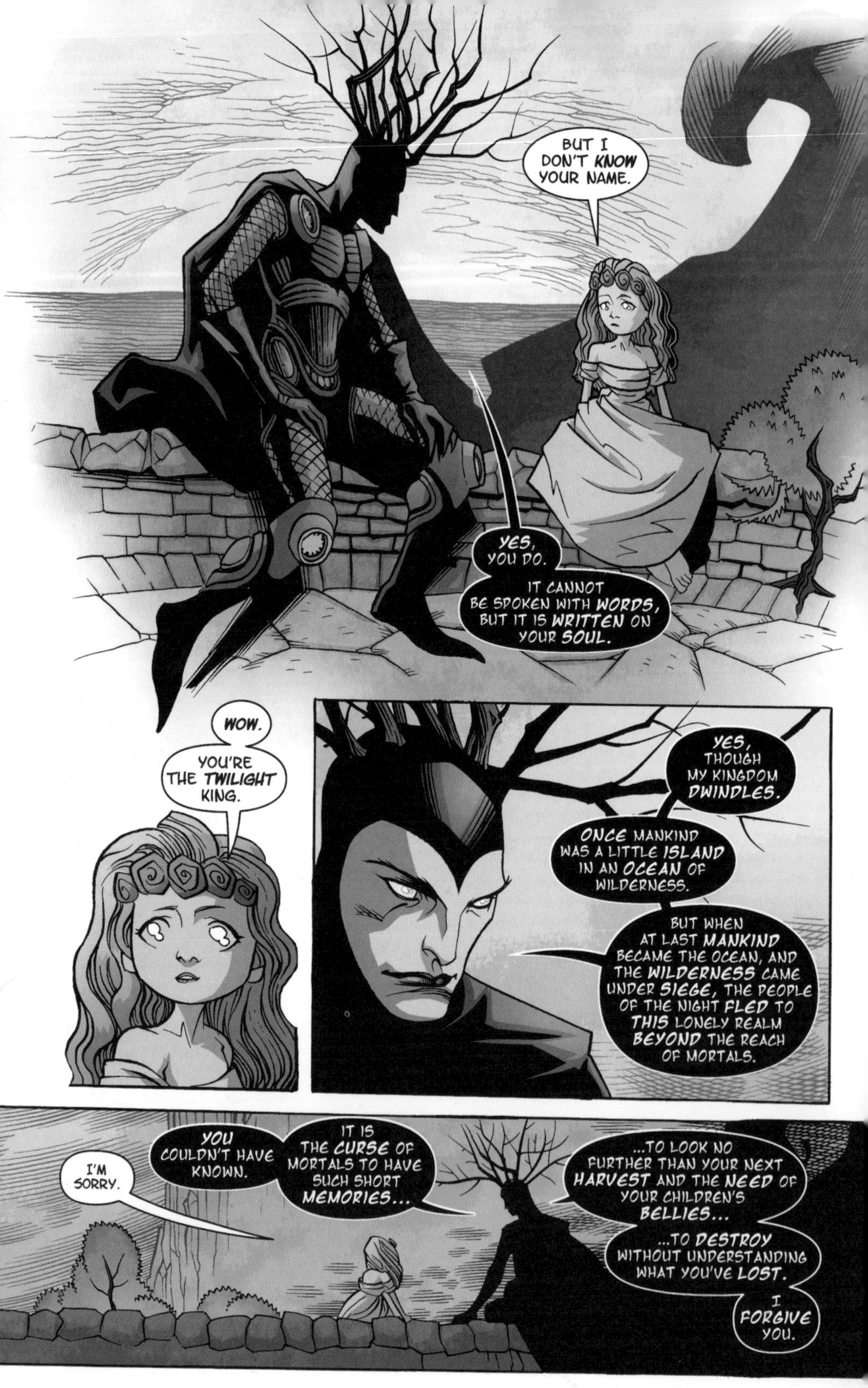
BUT I DON'T KNOW YOUR NAME.
YES, YOU DO.
IT CANNOT BE SPOKEN WITH WORDS, BUT IT IS WRITTEN ON YOUR SOUL.
WOW.
YOU'RE THE TWILIGHT KING.
YES, THOUGH MY KINGDOM DWINDLES.
ONCE MANKIND WAS A LITTLE ISLAND IN AN OCEAN OF WILDERNESS.
BUT WHEN AT LAST MANKIND BECAME THE OCEAN, AND THE WILDERNESS CAME UNDER SIEGE, THE PEOPLE OF THE NIGHT FLED TO THIS LONELY REALM BEYOND THE REACH OF MORTALS.
I'M SORRY.
YOU COULDN'T HAVE KNOWN.
IT IS THE CURSE OF MORTALS TO HAVE SUCH SHORT MEMORIES...
...TO LOOK NO FURTHER THAN YOUR NEXT HARVEST AND THE NEED OF YOUR CHILDREN'S BELLIES...
...TO DESTROY WITHOUT UNDERSTANDING WHAT YOU'VE LOST.
I FORGIVE YOU.

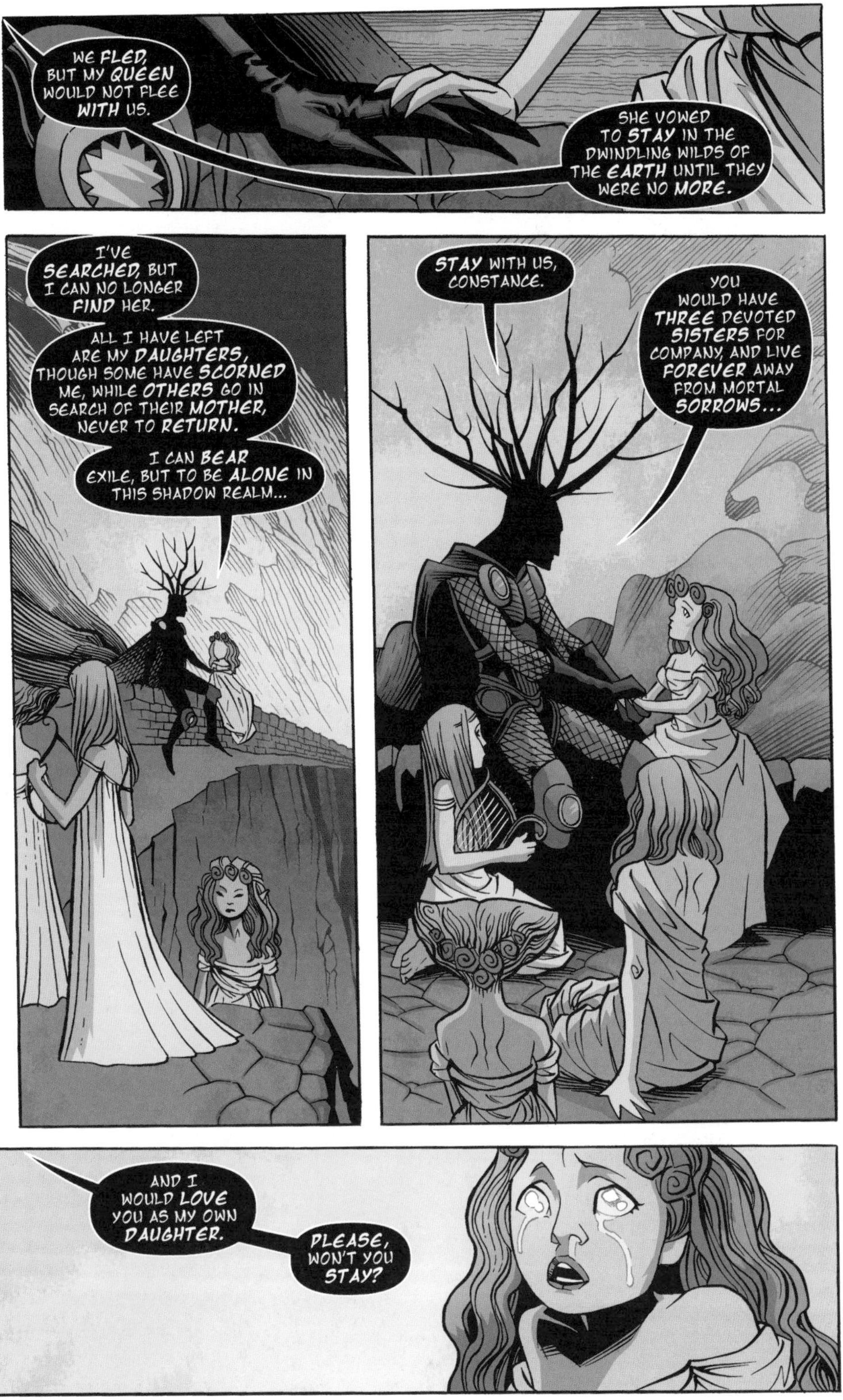
WE FLED, BUT MY QUEEN WOULD NOT FLEE WITH US.
SHE VOWED TO STAY IN THE DWINDLING WILDS OF THE EARTH UNTIL THEY WERE NO MORE.
I'VE SEARCHED, BUT I CAN NO LONGER FIND HER.
ALL I HAVE LEFT ARE MY DAUGHTERS, THOUGH SOME HAVE SCORNED ME, WHILE OTHERS GO IN SEARCH OF THEIR MOTHER, NEVER TO RETURN.
I CAN BEAR EXILE, BUT TO BE ALONE IN THIS SHADOW REALM...
STAY WITH US, CONSTANCE.
YOU WOULD HAVE THREE DEVOTED SISTERS FOR COMPANY, AND LIVE FOREVER AWAY FROM MORTAL SORROWS...
AND I WOULD LOVE YOU AS MY OWN DAUGHTER.
PLEASE, WON'T YOU STAY?

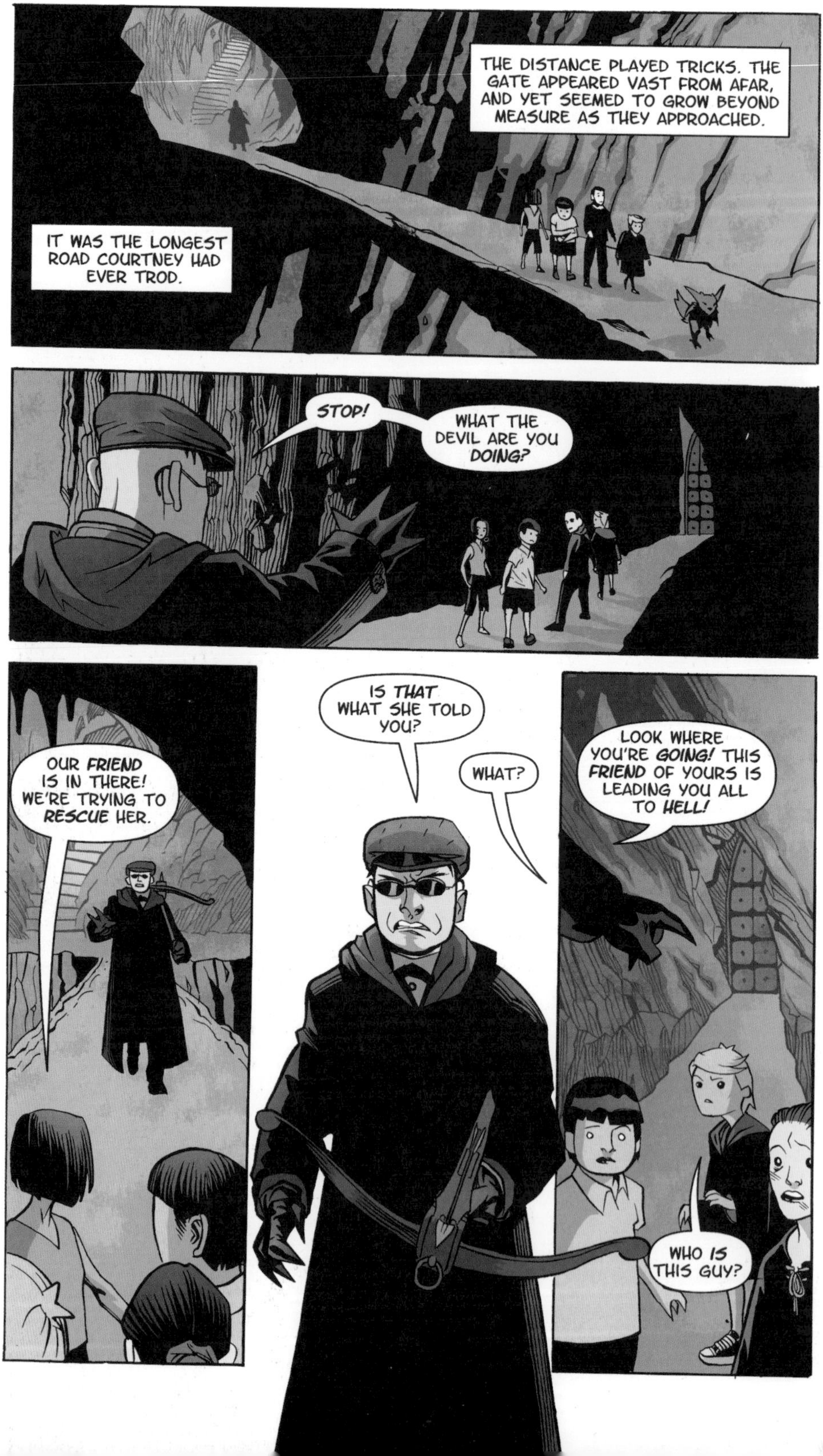
THE DISTANCE PLAYED TRICKS. THE GATE APPEARED VAST FROM AFAR, AND YET SEEMED TO GROW BEYOND MEASURE AS THEY APPROACHED.
IT WAS THE LONGEST ROAD COURTNEY HAD EVER TROD.
STOP!
WHAT THE DEVIL ARE YOU DOING?
OUR FRIEND IS IN THERE! WE'RE TRYING TO RESCUE HER.
IS THAT WHAT SHE TOLD YOU?
WHAT?
LOOK WHERE YOU'RE GOING! THIS FRIEND OF YOURS IS LEADING YOU ALL TO HELL!
WHO IS THIS GUY?

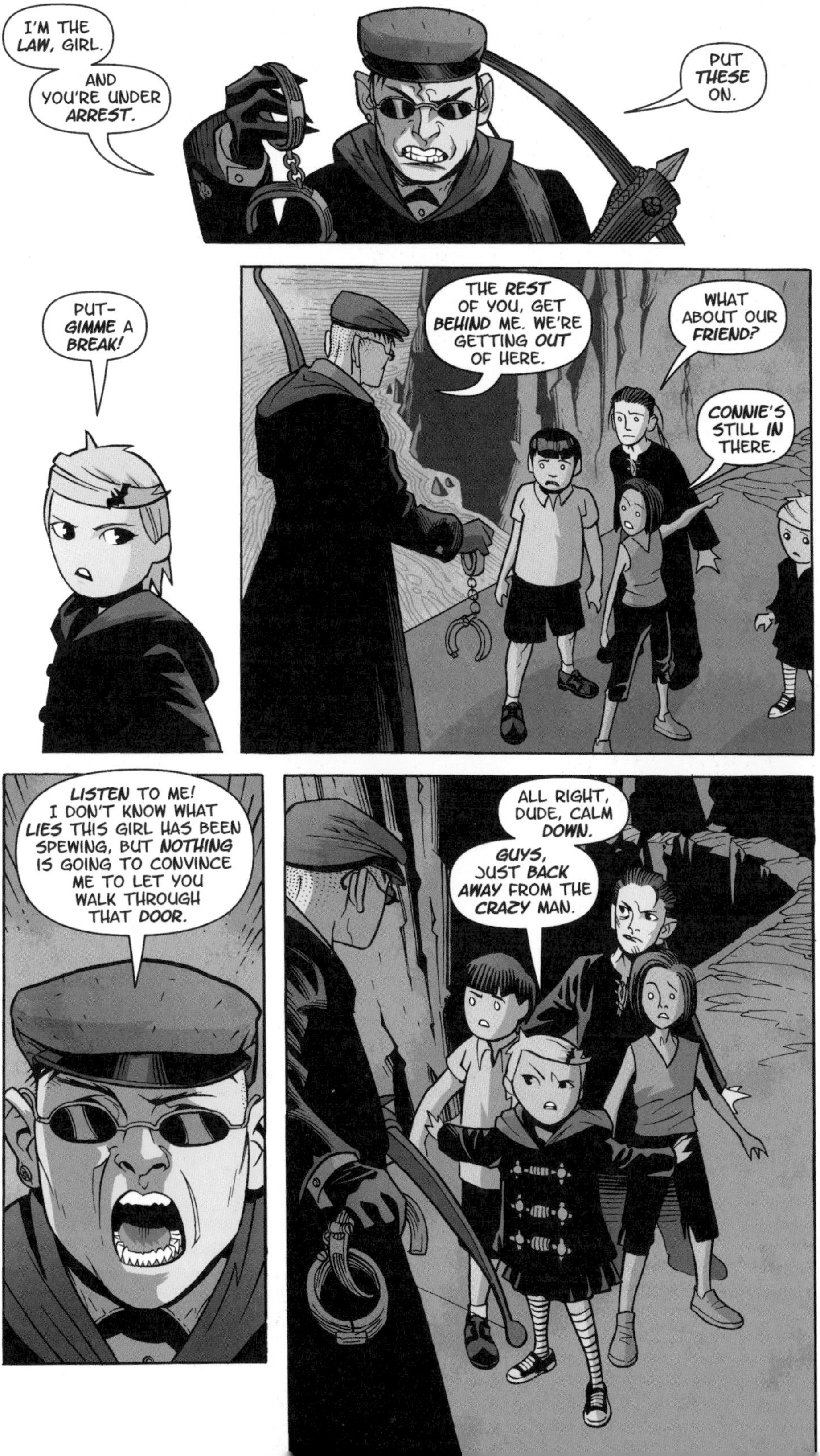
I'M THE LAW, GIRL.
AND YOU'RE UNDER ARREST.
PUT THESE ON.
PUT- GIMME A BREAK!
THE REST OF YOU, GET BEHIND ME. WE'RE GETTING OUT OF HERE.
WHAT ABOUT OUR FRIEND?
CONNIE'S STILL IN THERE.
LISTEN TO ME! I DON'T KNOW WHAT LIES THIS GIRL HAS BEEN SPEWING, BUT NOTHING IS GOING TO CONVINCE ME TO LET YOU WALK THROUGH THAT DOOR.
ALL RIGHT, DUDE, CALM DOWN.
GUYS, JUST BACK AWAY FROM THE CRAZY MAN.

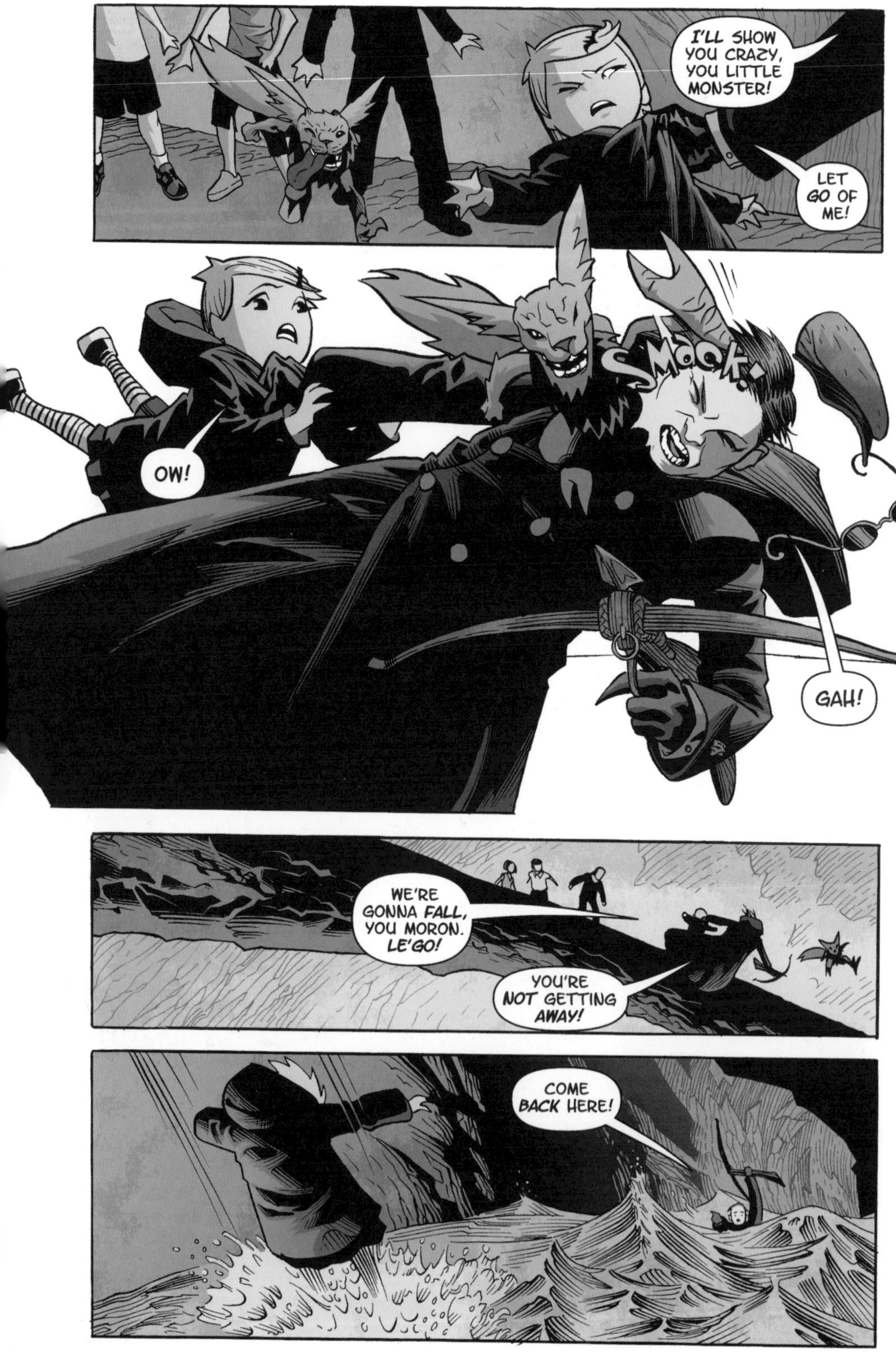
I'LL SHOW YOU CRAZY, YOU LITTLE MONSTER!
LET GO OF ME!
OW!
SMACK!
GAH!
WE'RE GONNA FALL, YOU MORON. LE'GO!
YOU'RE NOT GETTING AWAY!
COME BACK HERE!

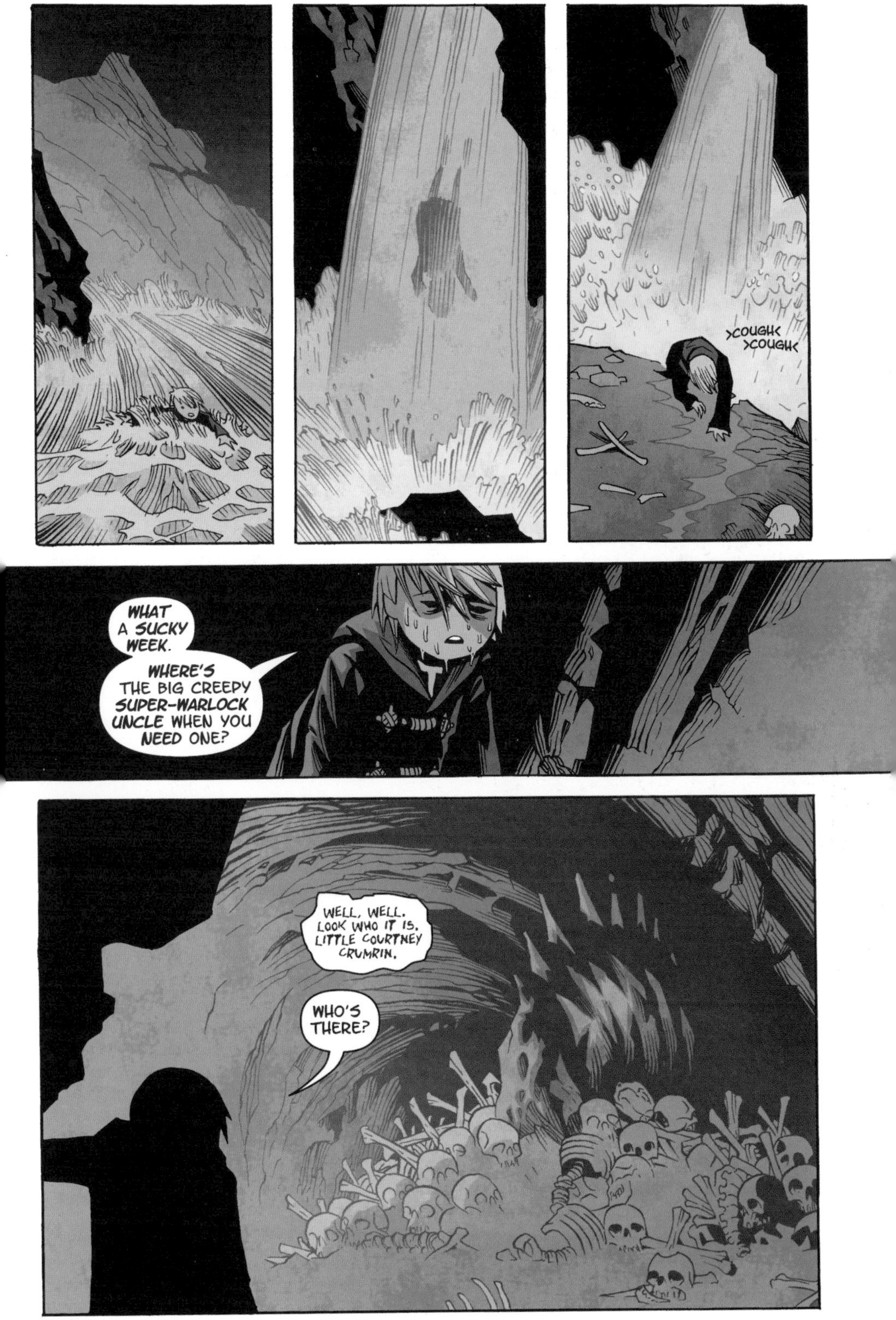
>COUGH< >COUGH<
WHAT A SUCKY WEEK.
WHERE'S THE BIG CREEPY SUPER-WARLOCK UNCLE WHEN YOU NEED ONE?
WELL, WELL. LOOK WHO IT IS. LITTLE COURTNEY CRUMRIN.
WHO'S THERE?

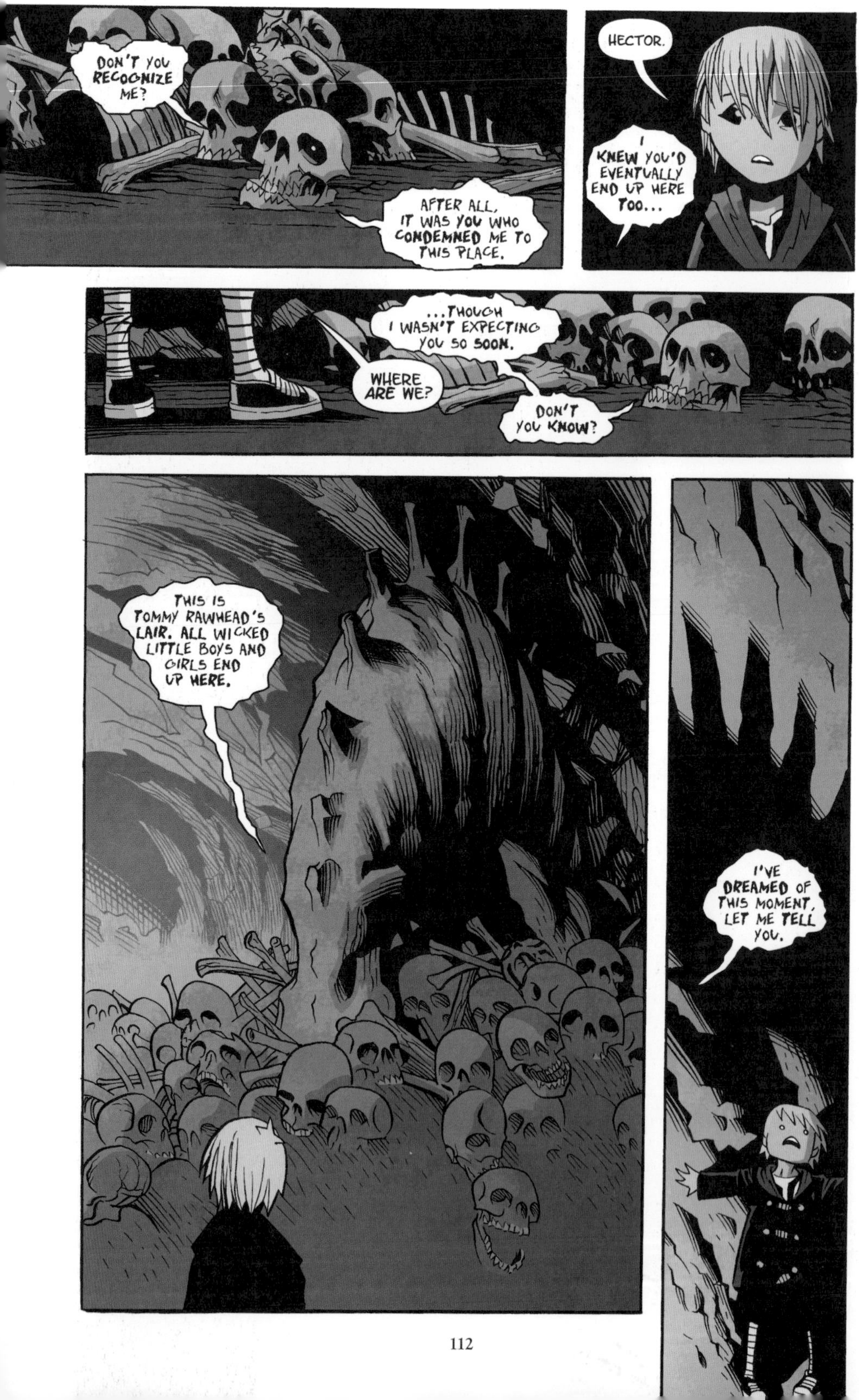
DON'T YOU RECOGNIZE ME?
AFTER ALL, IT WAS YOU WHO CONDEMNED ME TO THIS PLACE.
HECTOR.
I KNEW YOU'D EVENTUALLY END UP HERE TOO...
...THOUGH I WASN'T EXPECTING YOU SO SOON.
WHERE ARE WE?
DON'T YOU KNOW?
THIS IS TOMMY RAWHEAD'S LAIR. ALL WICKED LITTLE BOYS AND GIRLS END UP HERE.
I'VE DREAMED OF THIS MOMENT, LET ME TELL YOU.

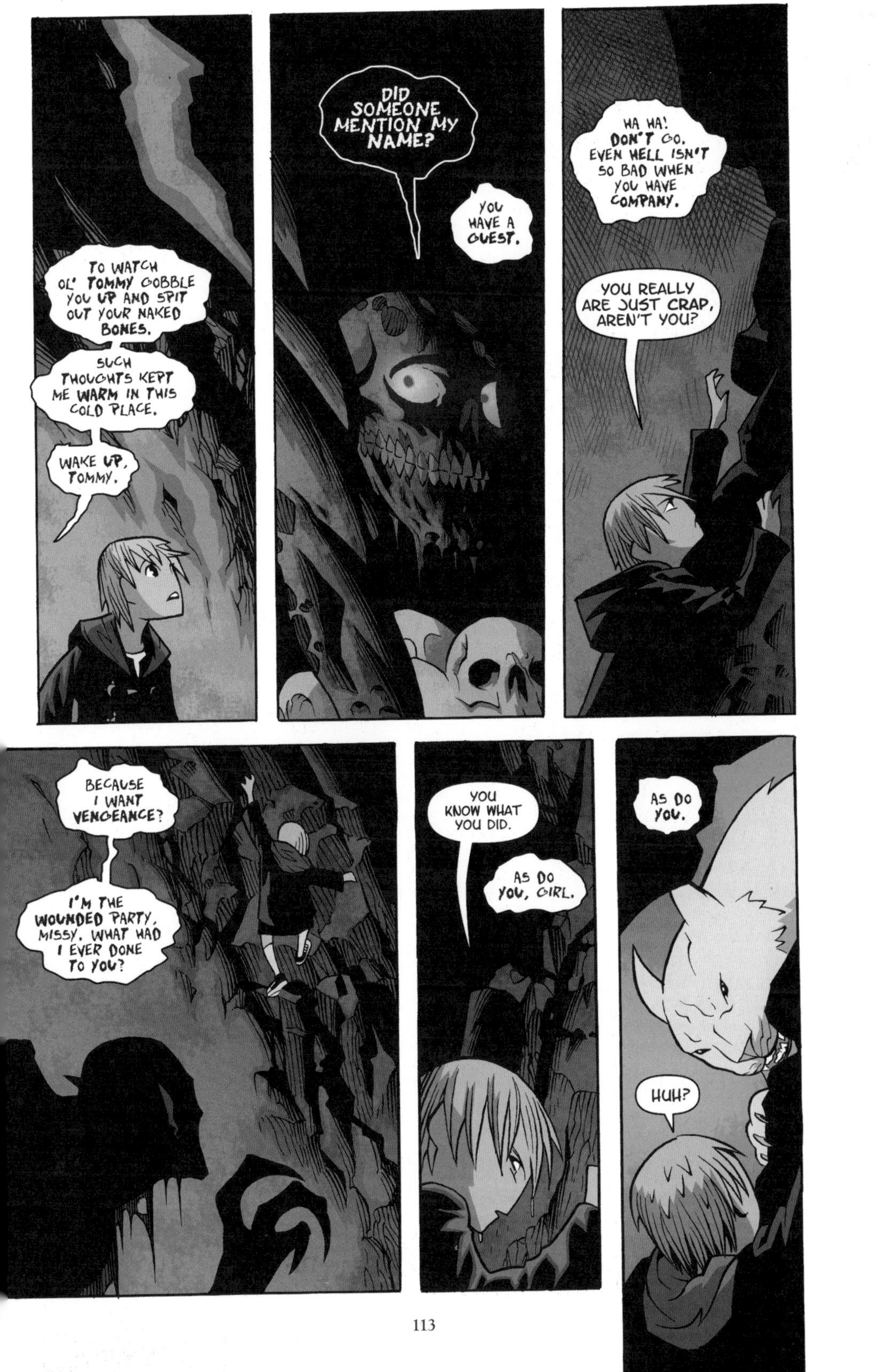
TO WATCH OL' TOMMY GOBBLE YOU UP AND SPIT OUT YOUR NAKED BONES.
SUCH THOUGHTS KEPT ME WARM IN THIS COLD PLACE.
WAKE UP, TOMMY.
DID SOMEONE MENTION MY NAME?
YOU HAVE A GUEST.
HA HA! DON'T GO. EVEN HELL ISN'T SO BAD WHEN YOU HAVE COMPANY.
YOU REALLY ARE JUST CRAP, AREN'T YOU?
BECAUSE I WANT VENGEANCE?
I'M THE WOUNDED PARTY, MISSY. WHAT HAD I EVER DONE TO YOU?
YOU KNOW WHAT YOU DID.
AS DO YOU, GIRL.
AS DO YOU.
HUH?

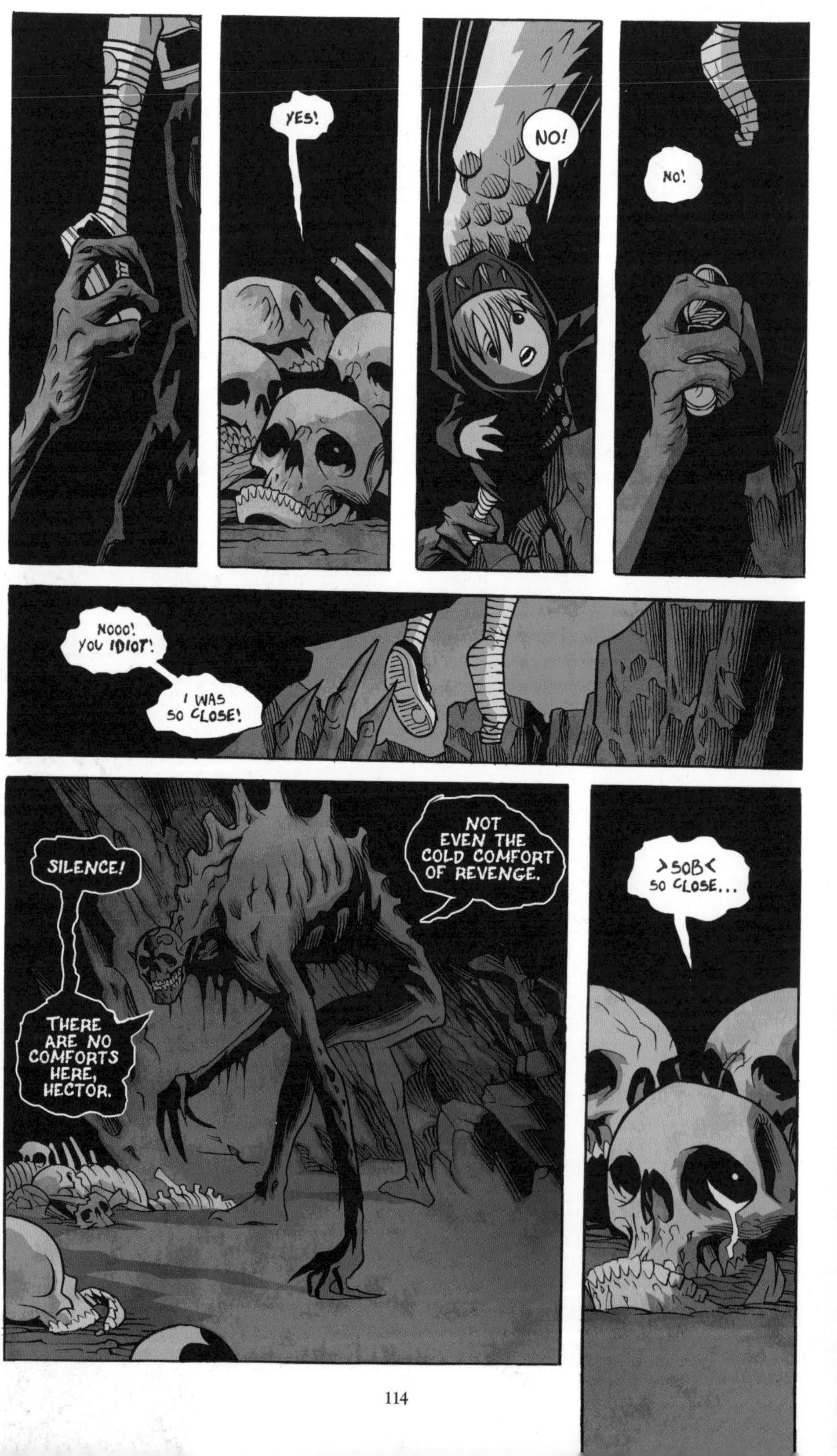
YES!
NO!
NO!
NOOO! YOU IDIOT!
I WAS SO CLOSE!
SILENCE!
THERE ARE NO COMFORTS HERE, HECTOR.
NOT EVEN THE COLD COMFORT OF REVENGE.
>SOB< SO CLOSE...

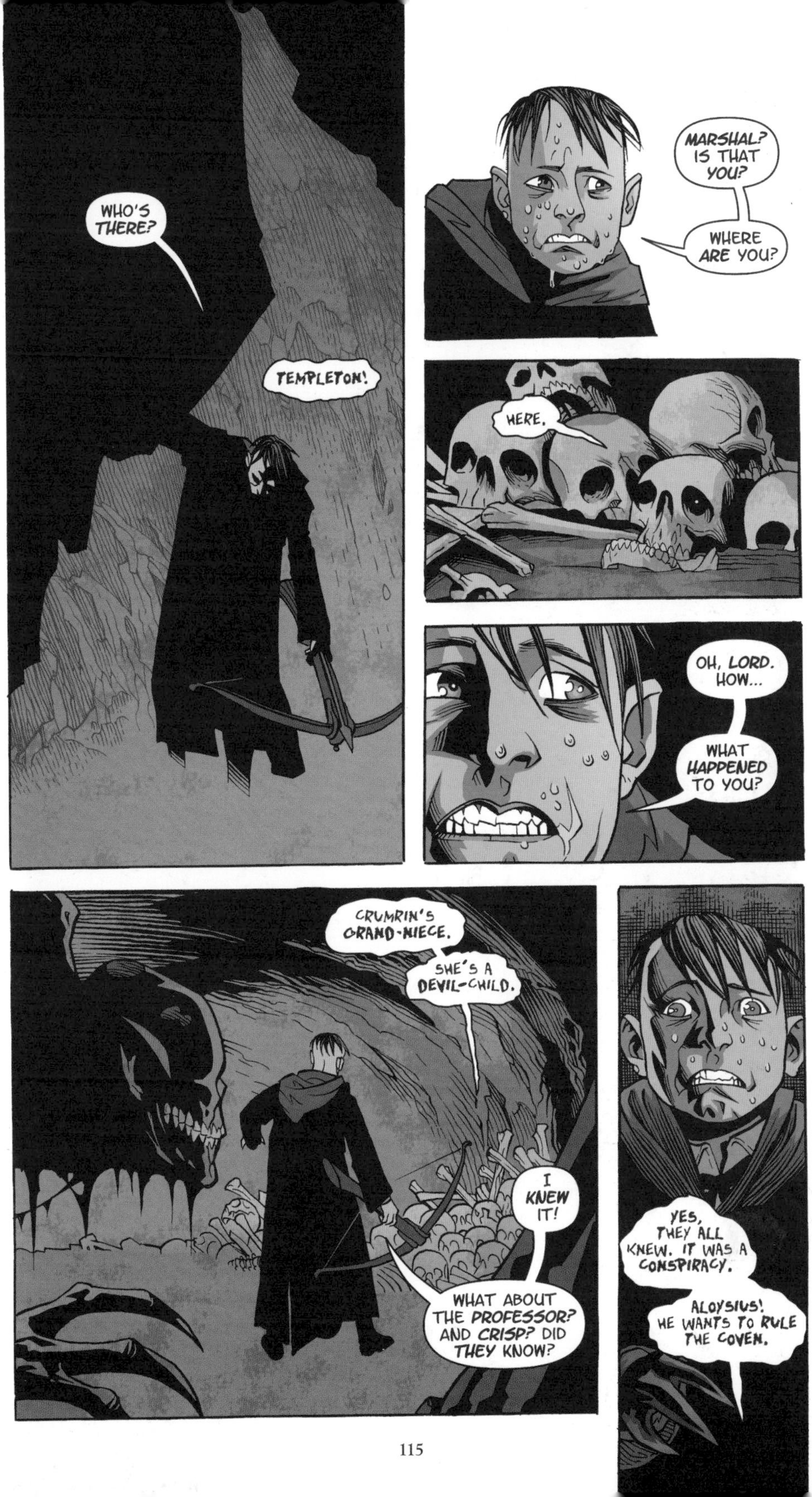
WHO'S THERE?
TEMPLETON!
MARSHAL? IS THAT YOU?
WHERE ARE YOU?
HERE.
OH, LORD. HOW...
WHAT HAPPENED TO YOU?
CRUMRIN'S GRAND-NIECE.
SHE'S A DEVIL-CHILD.
I KNEW IT!
WHAT ABOUT THE PROFESSOR? AND CRISP? DID THEY KNOW?
YES, THEY ALL KNEW. IT WAS A CONSPIRACY.
ALOYSIUS! HE WANTS TO RULE THE COVEN.

BE WARY OF THE WORDS OF THE DAMNED, MORTAL.

NO!

THEY'LL LEAD YOU TO NO GOOD END.

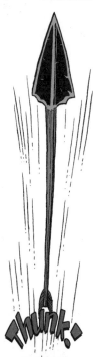

Thunk.

HHHHSSSSSSSSS

RUN, TEMPLETON. GET THEM!

GET THEM ALL!

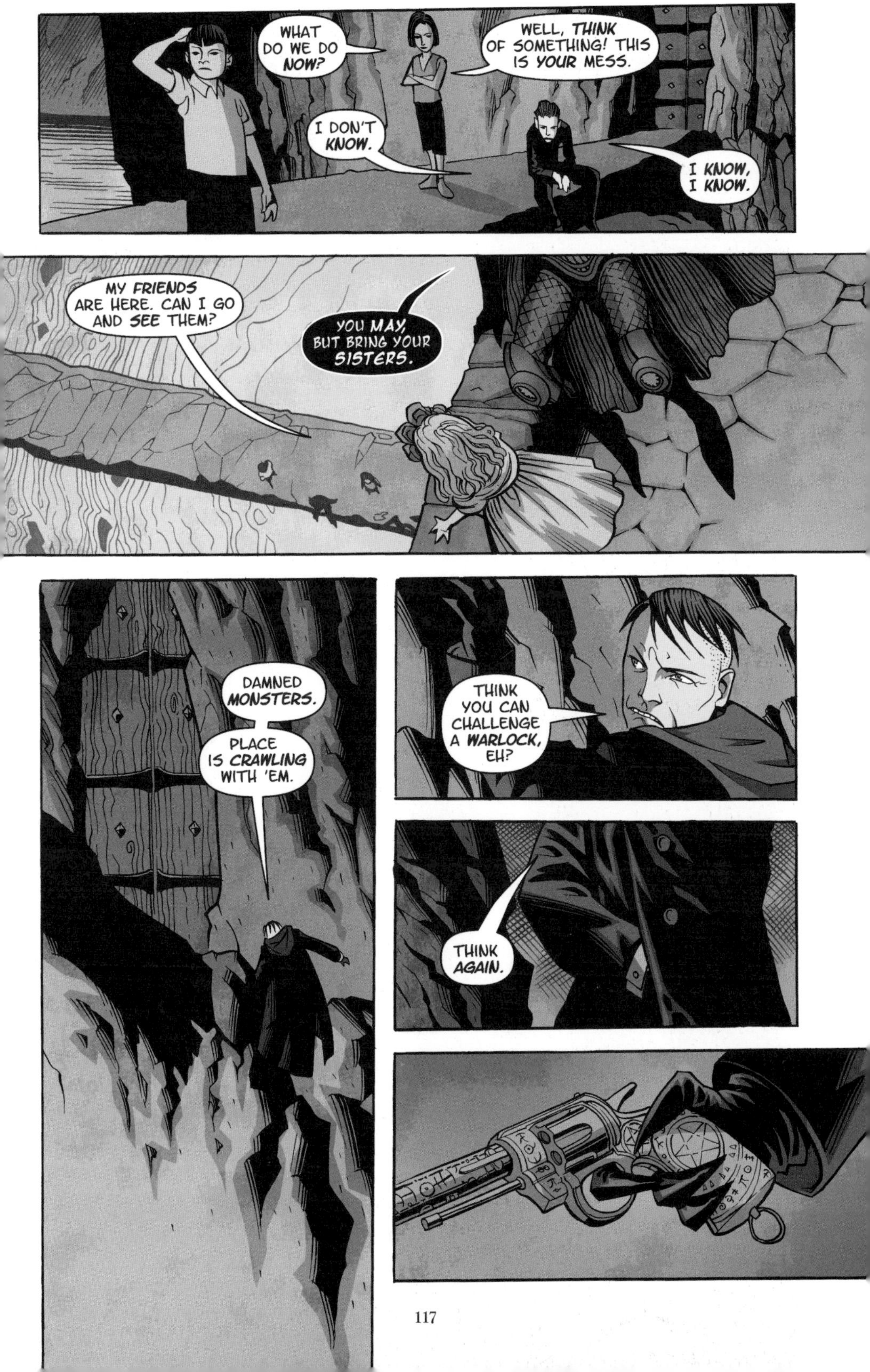
WHAT DO WE DO NOW?
WELL, THINK OF SOMETHING! THIS IS YOUR MESS.
I DON'T KNOW.
I KNOW, I KNOW.
MY FRIENDS ARE HERE. CAN I GO AND SEE THEM?
YOU MAY, BUT BRING YOUR SISTERS.
DAMNED MONSTERS.
PLACE IS CRAWLING WITH 'EM.
THINK YOU CAN CHALLENGE A WARLOCK, EH?
THINK AGAIN.

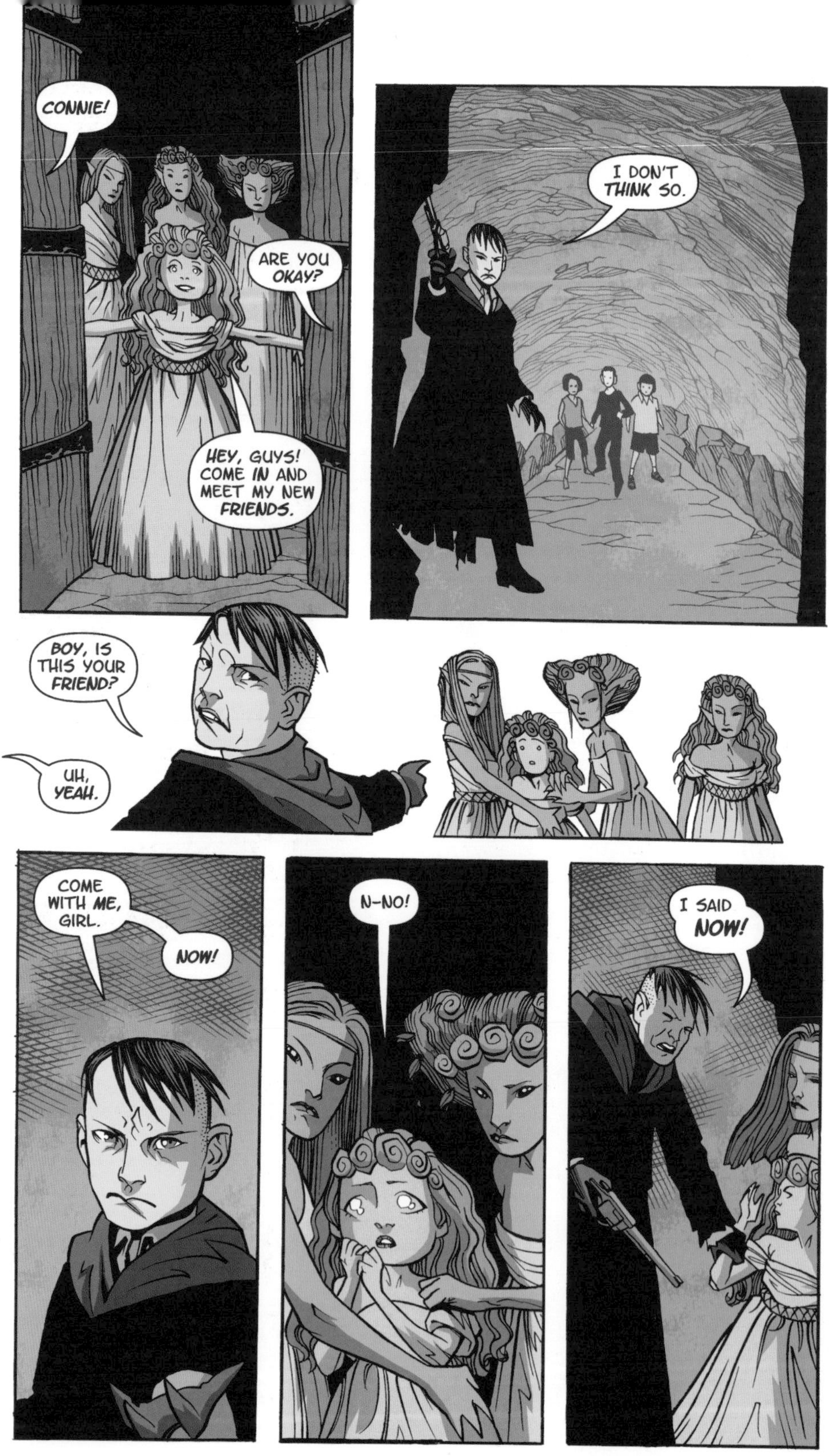
CONNIE!
ARE YOU OKAY?
HEY, GUYS! COME IN AND MEET MY NEW FRIENDS.
I DON'T THINK SO.
BOY, IS THIS YOUR FRIEND?
UH, YEAH.
COME WITH ME, GIRL.
NOW!
N-NO!
I SAID NOW!

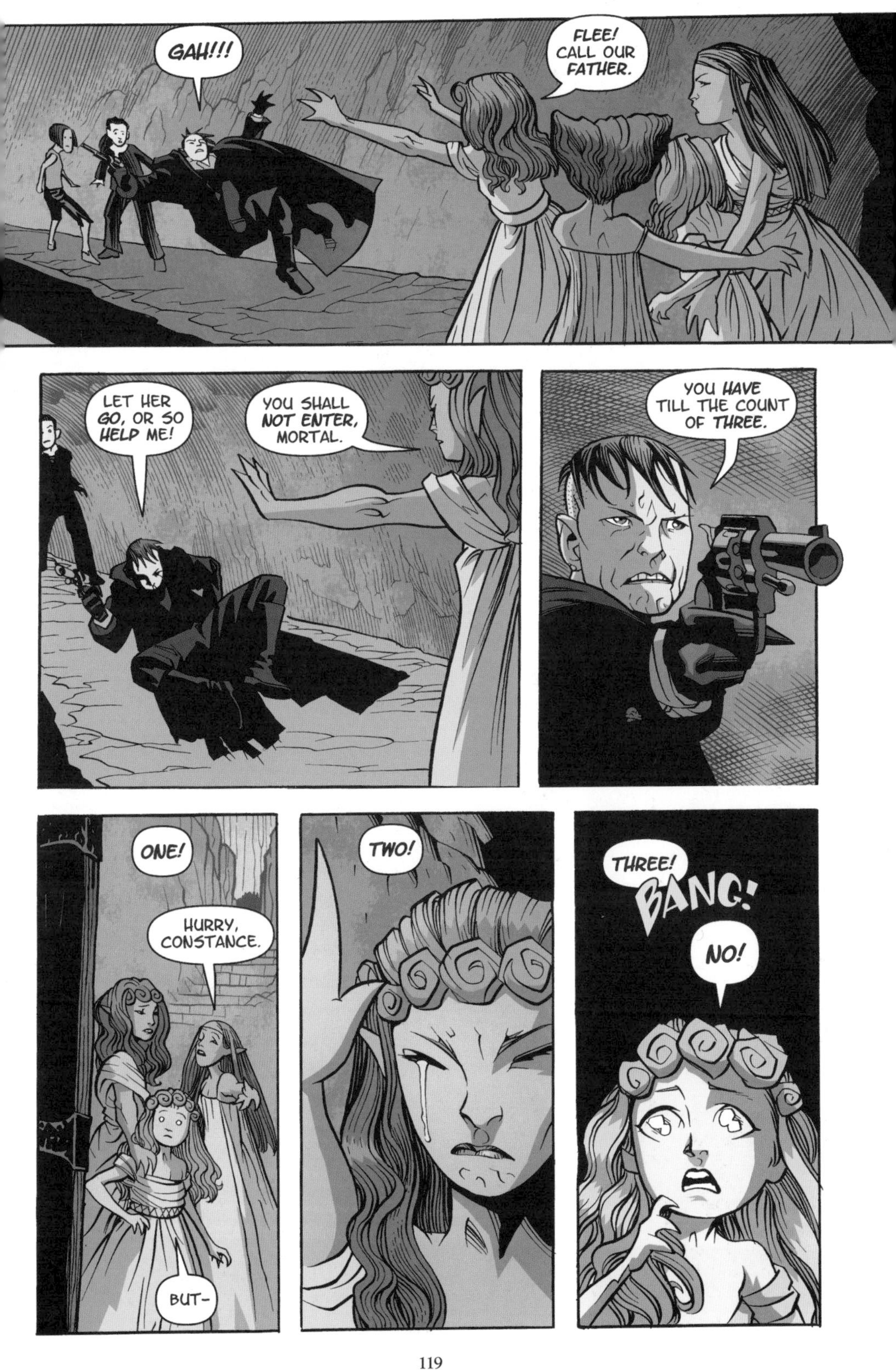
GAH!!!
FLEE! CALL OUR FATHER.
LET HER GO, OR SO HELP ME!
YOU SHALL NOT ENTER, MORTAL.
YOU HAVE TILL THE COUNT OF THREE.
ONE!
HURRY, CONSTANCE.
BUT-
TWO!
THREE!
BANG!
NO!

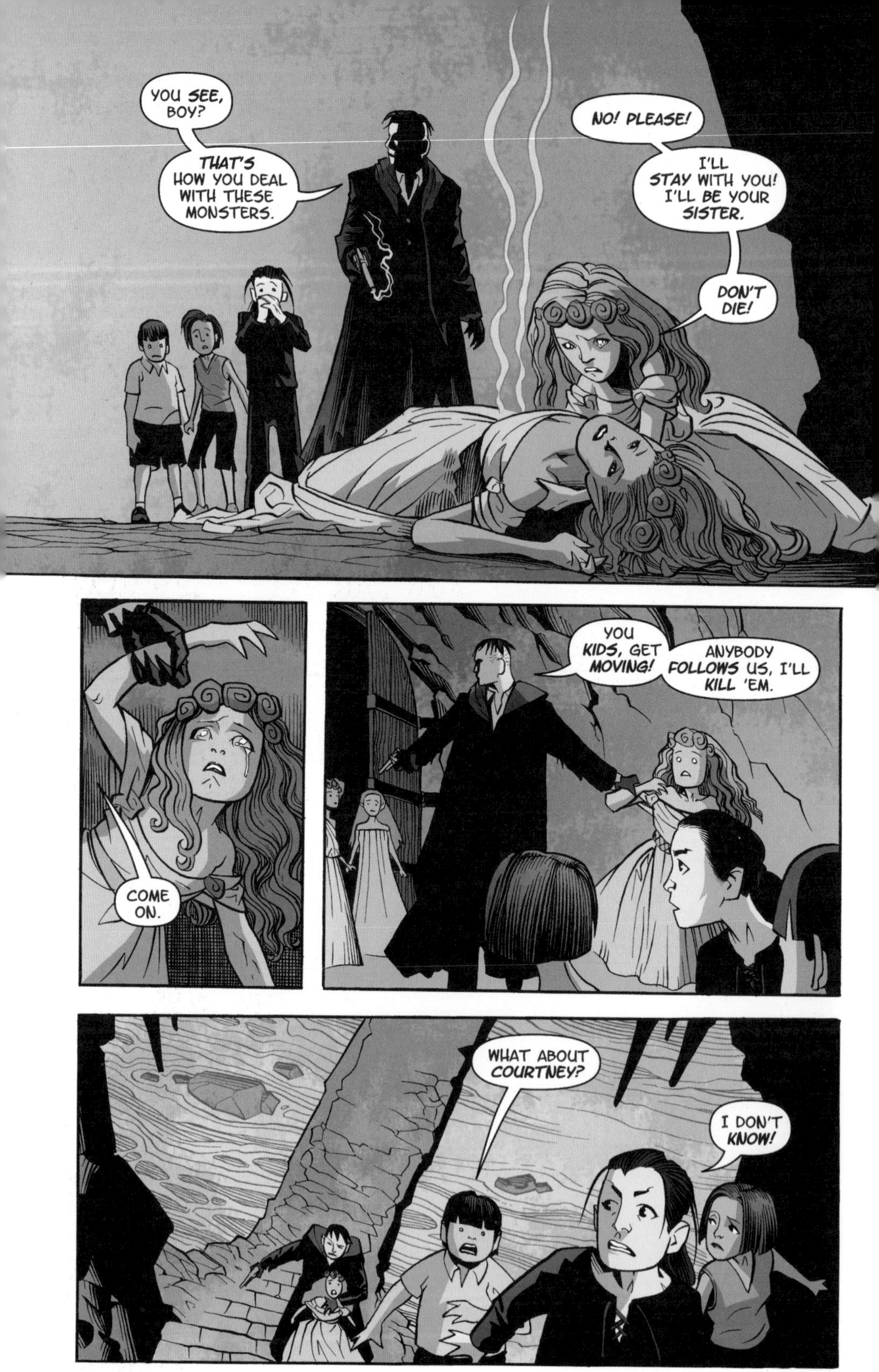
YOU SEE, BOY?
THAT'S HOW YOU DEAL WITH THESE MONSTERS.
NO! PLEASE!
I'LL STAY WITH YOU! I'LL BE YOUR SISTER.
DON'T DIE!
COME ON.
YOU KIDS, GET MOVING!
ANYBODY FOLLOWS US, I'LL KILL 'EM.
WHAT ABOUT COURTNEY?
I DON'T KNOW!

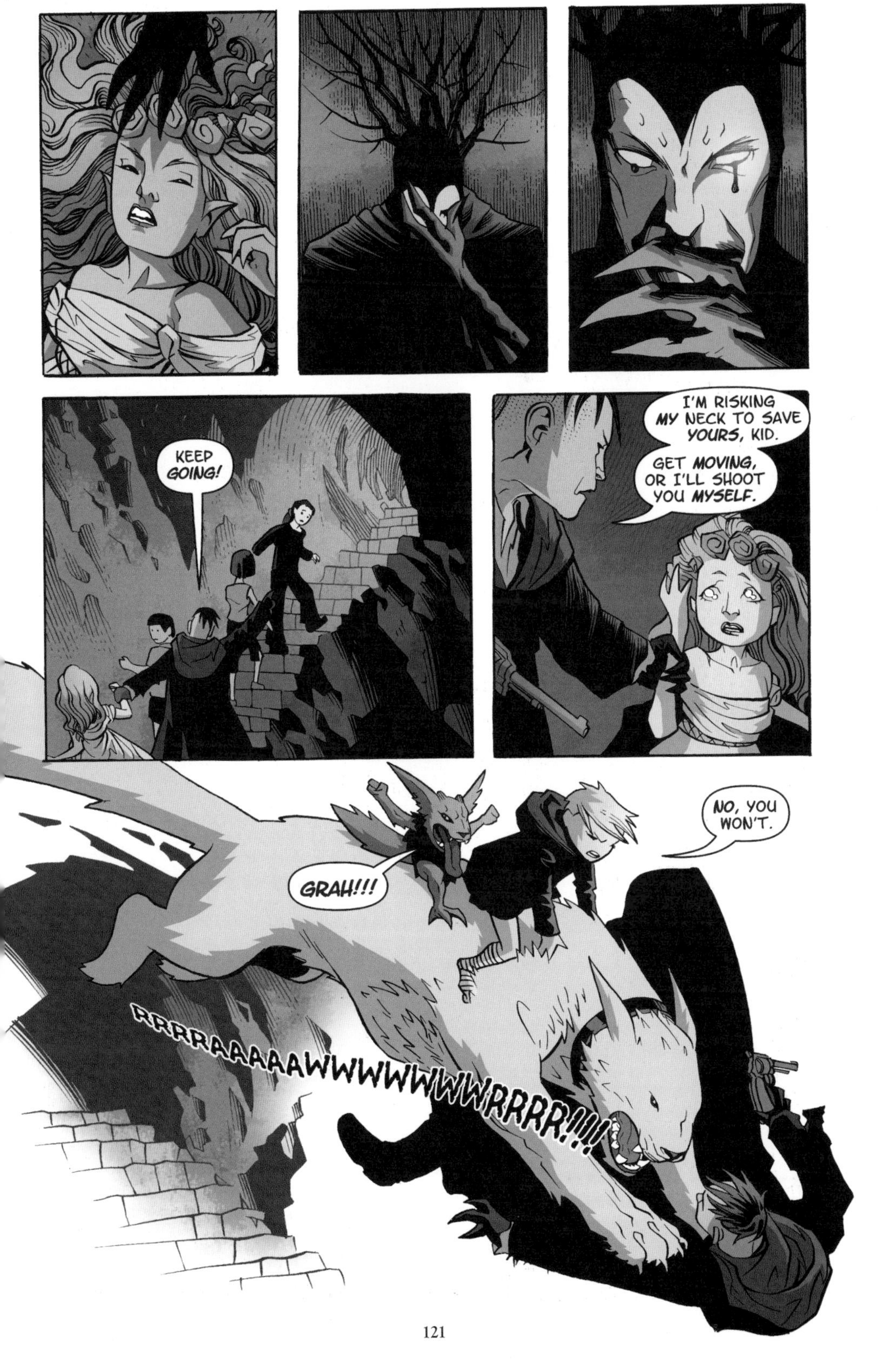
KEEP GOING!
I'M RISKING MY NECK TO SAVE YOURS, KID.
GET MOVING, OR I'LL SHOOT YOU MYSELF.
NO, YOU WON'T.
GRAH!!!
RRRRRAAAAAAWWWWWWWWWRRRRR!!!!

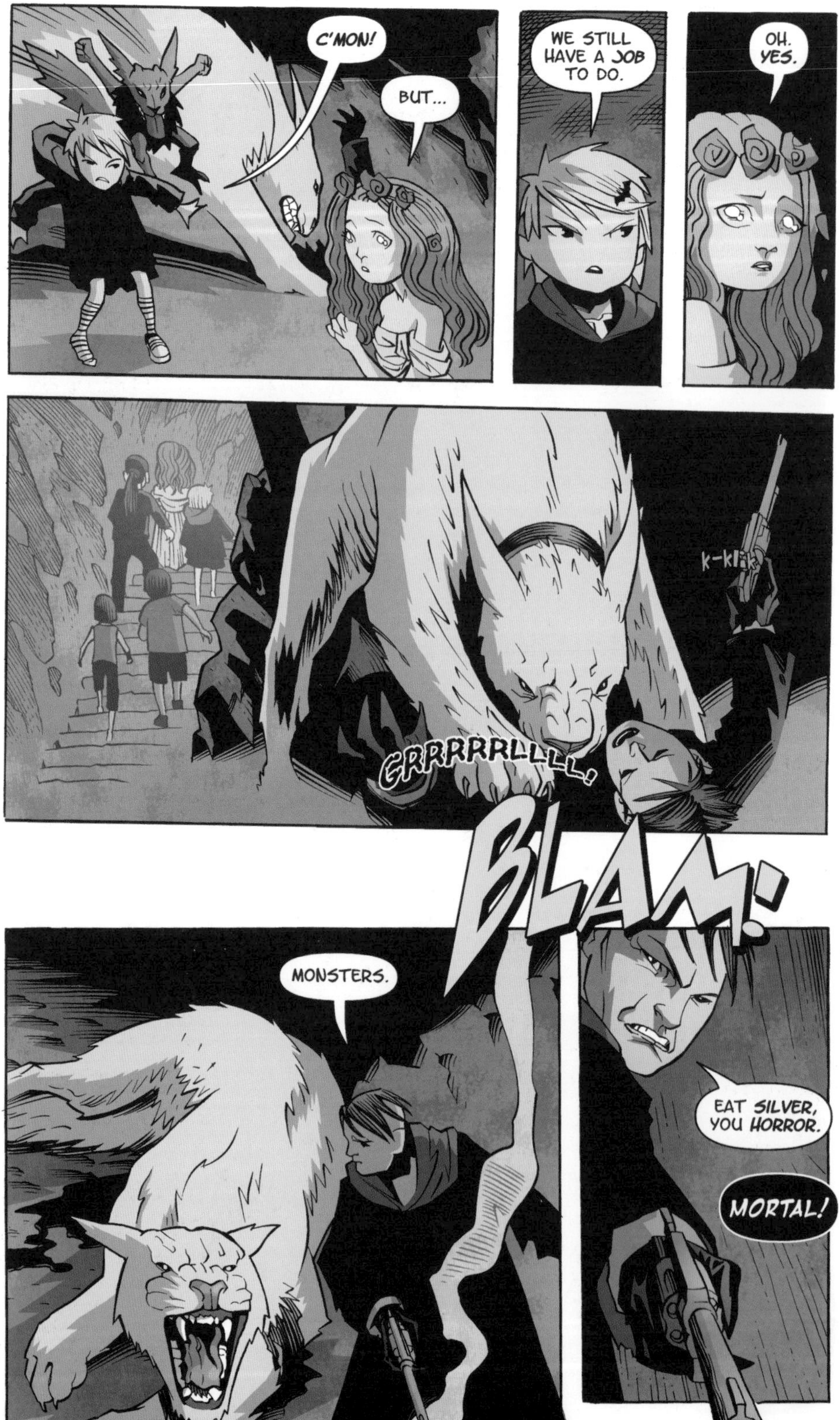
C'MON!
BUT...
WE STILL HAVE A JOB TO DO.
OH. YES.
k-klik
GRRRRRLLLL,
BLAM!
MONSTERS.
EAT SILVER, YOU HORROR.
MORTAL!

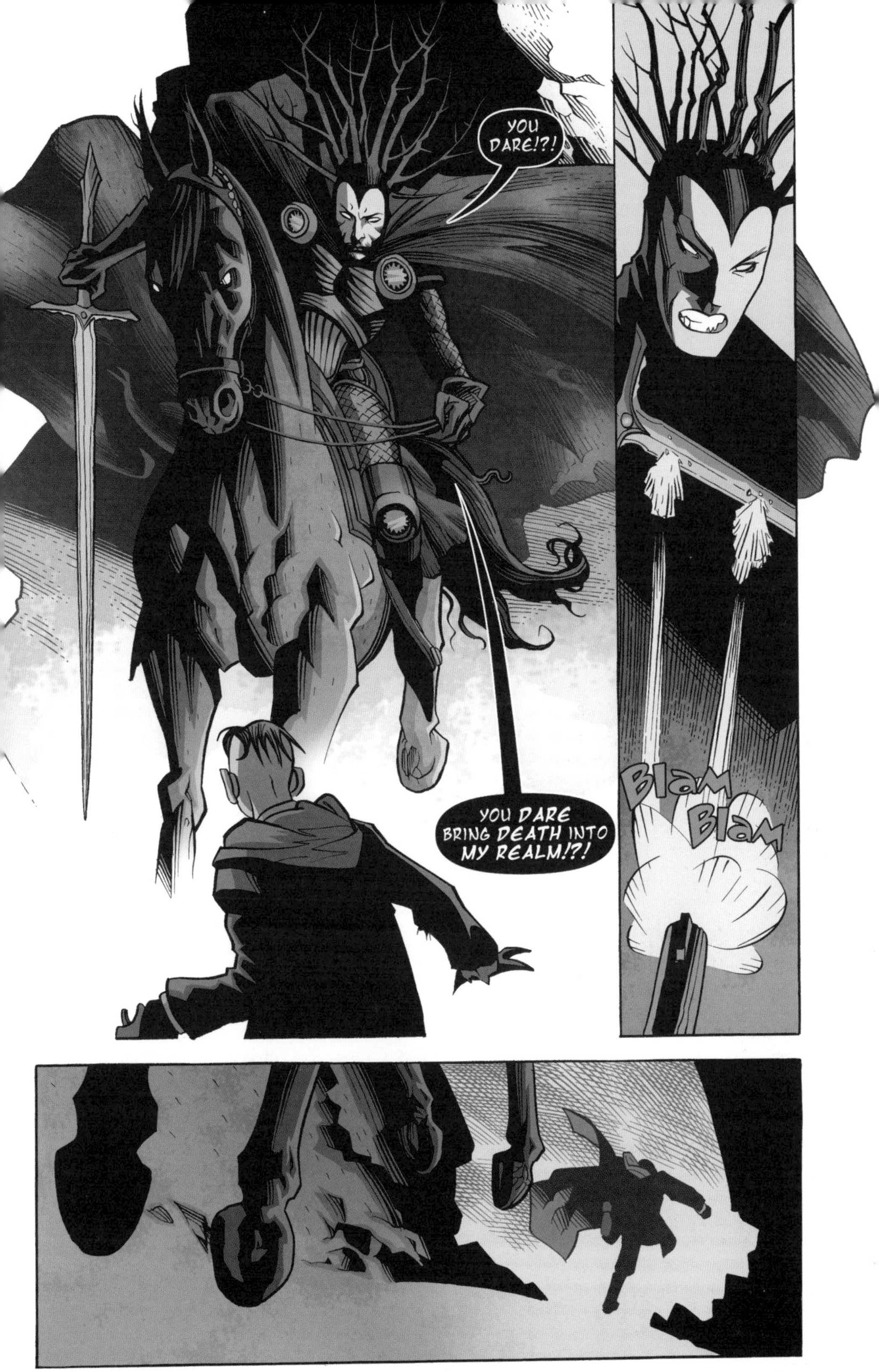
YOU DARE!?!
YOU DARE BRING DEATH INTO MY REALM!?!
BLAM BLAM

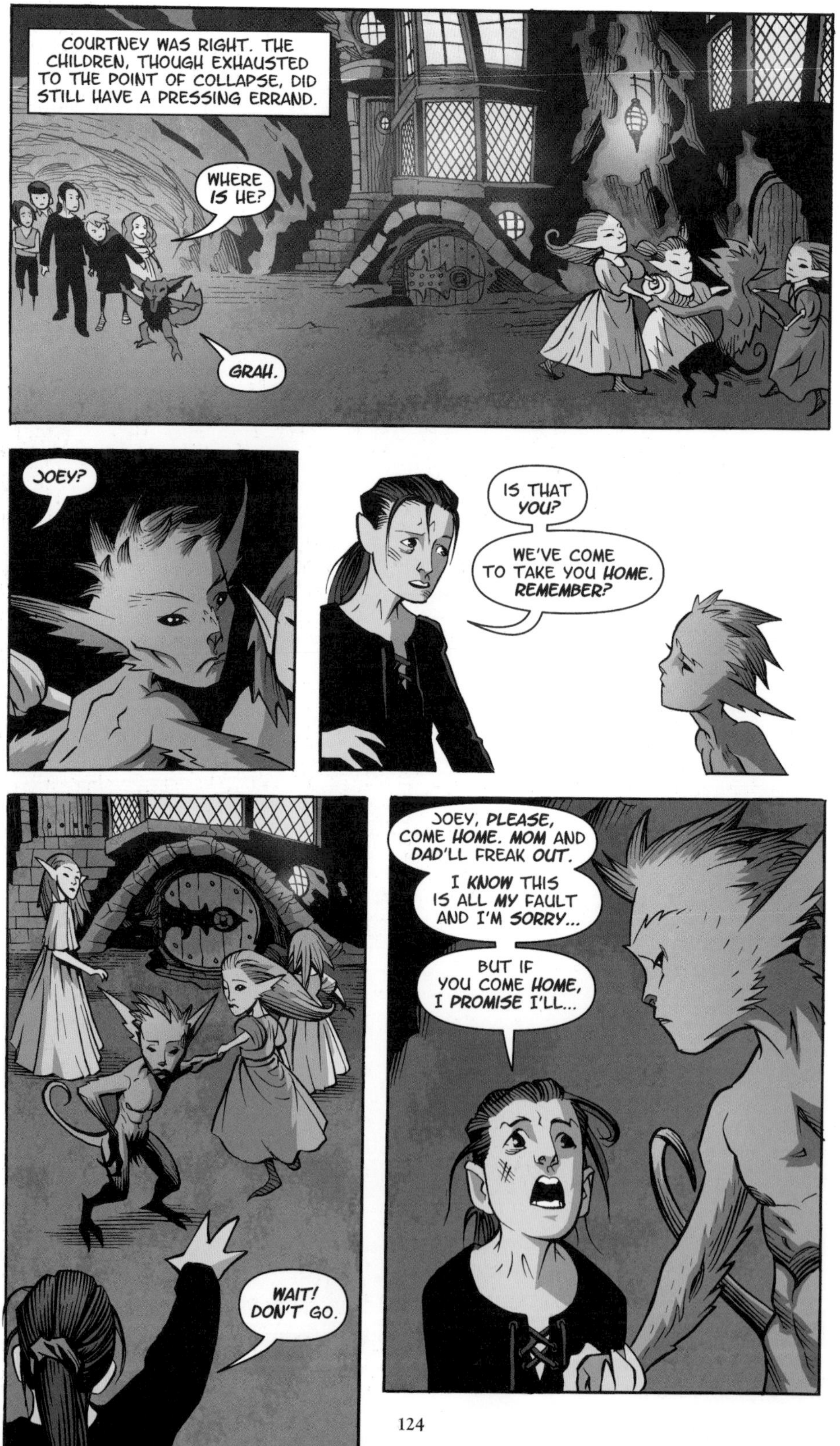
COURTNEY WAS RIGHT. THE CHILDREN, THOUGH EXHAUSTED TO THE POINT OF COLLAPSE, DID STILL HAVE A PRESSING ERRAND.
WHERE IS HE?
GRAH.
JOEY?
IS THAT YOU?
WE'VE COME TO TAKE YOU HOME. REMEMBER?
WAIT! DON'T GO.
JOEY, PLEASE, COME HOME. MOM AND DAD'LL FREAK OUT.
I KNOW THIS IS ALL MY FAULT AND I'M SORRY...
BUT IF YOU COME HOME, I PROMISE I'LL...

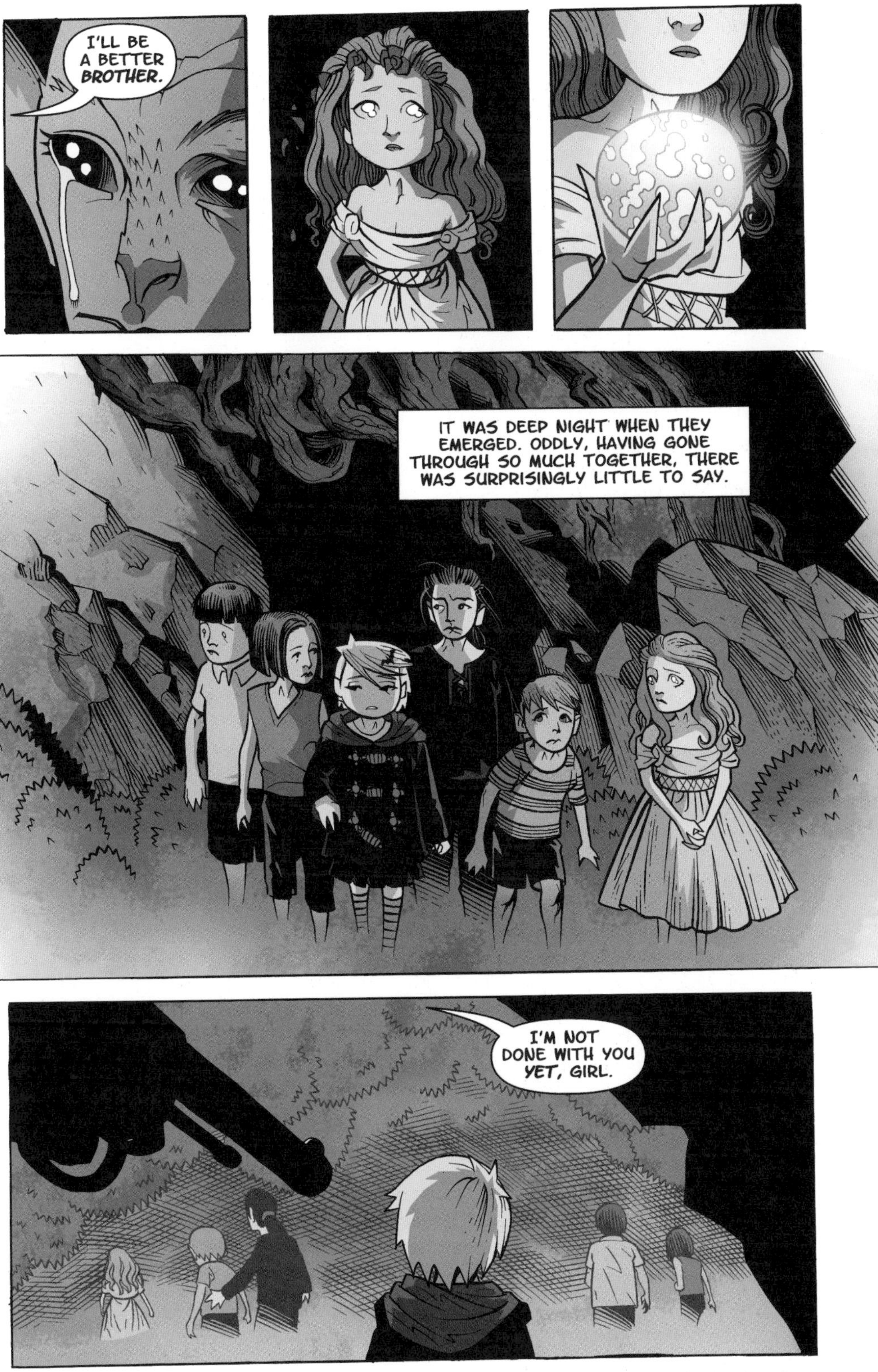
I'LL BE A BETTER BROTHER.
IT WAS DEEP NIGHT WHEN THEY EMERGED. ODDLY, HAVING GONE THROUGH SO MUCH TOGETHER, THERE WAS SURPRISINGLY LITTLE TO SAY.
I'M NOT DONE WITH YOU YET, GIRL.

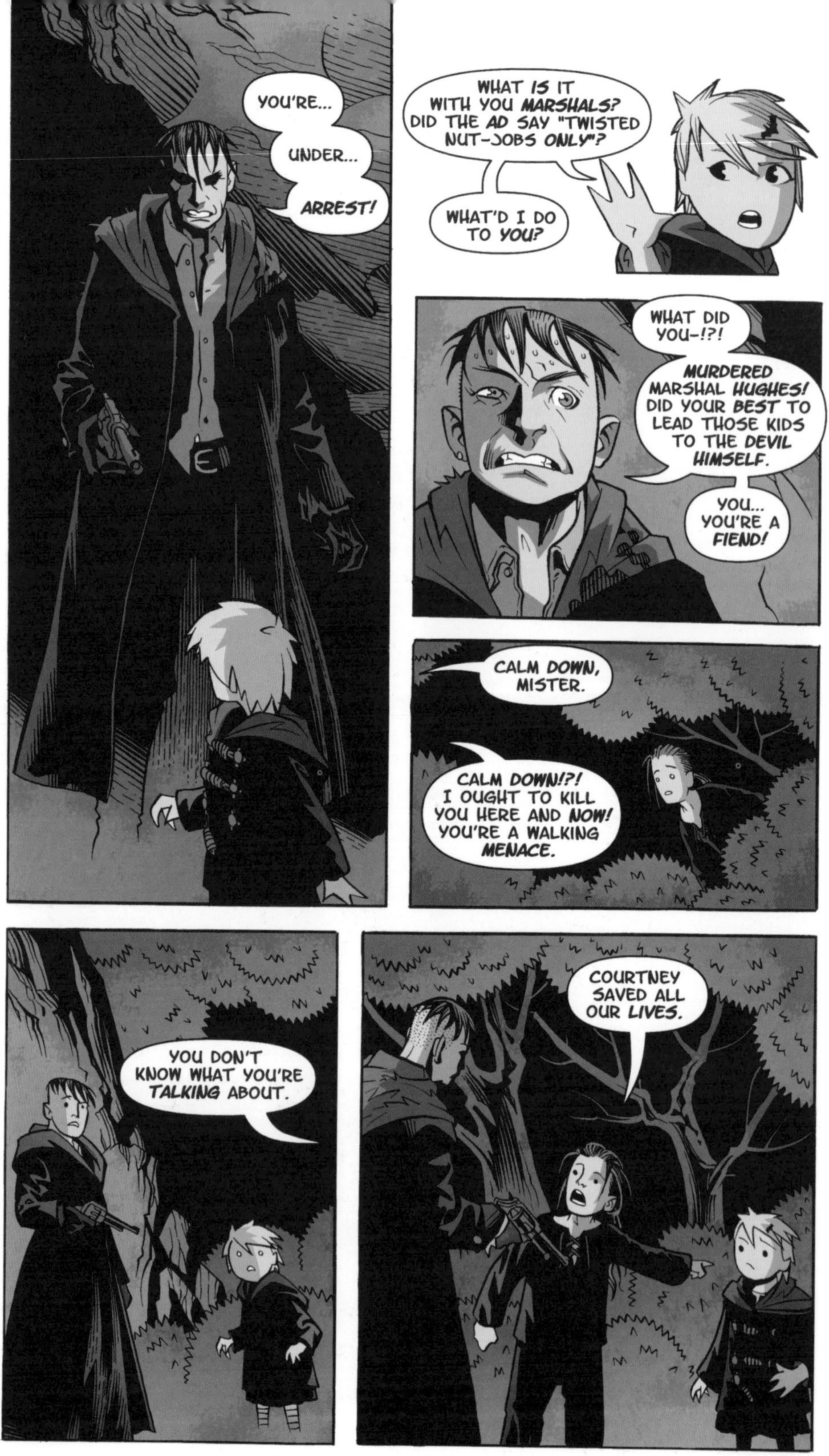
YOU'RE...
UNDER...
ARREST!
WHAT IS IT WITH YOU MARSHALS? DID THE AD SAY "TWISTED NUT-JOBS ONLY"?
WHAT'D I DO TO YOU?
WHAT DID YOU-!?!
MURDERED MARSHAL HUGHES! DID YOUR BEST TO LEAD THOSE KIDS TO THE DEVIL HIMSELF.
YOU... YOU'RE A FIEND!
CALM DOWN, MISTER.
CALM DOWN!?! I OUGHT TO KILL YOU HERE AND NOW! YOU'RE A WALKING MENACE.
YOU DON'T KNOW WHAT YOU'RE TALKING ABOUT.
COURTNEY SAVED ALL OUR LIVES.

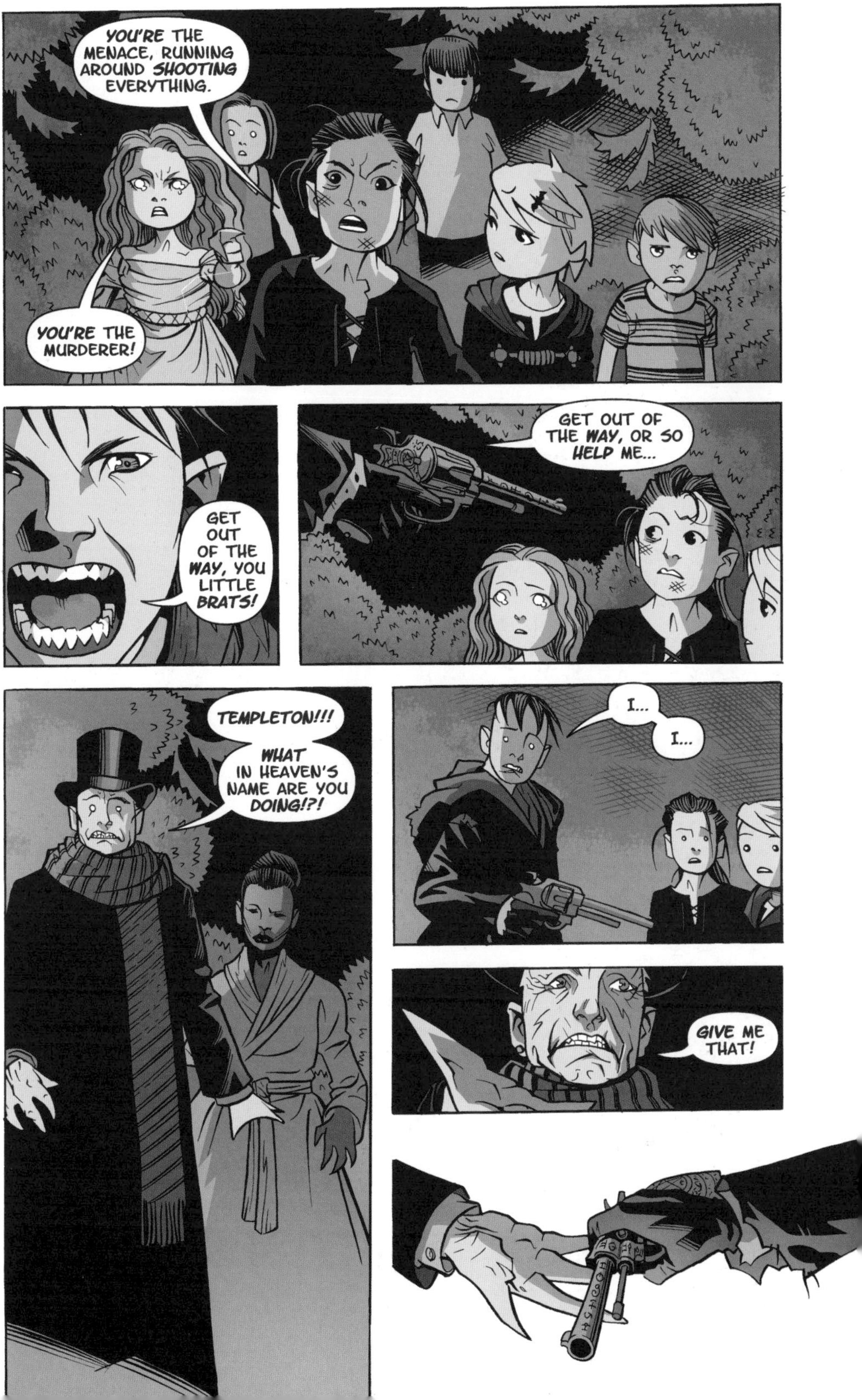
YOU'RE THE MENACE, RUNNING AROUND SHOOTING EVERYTHING.
YOU'RE THE MURDERER!
GET OUT OF THE WAY, YOU LITTLE BRATS!
GET OUT OF THE WAY, OR SO HELP ME...
TEMPLETON!!!
WHAT IN HEAVEN'S NAME ARE YOU DOING!?!
I...
I...
GIVE ME THAT!

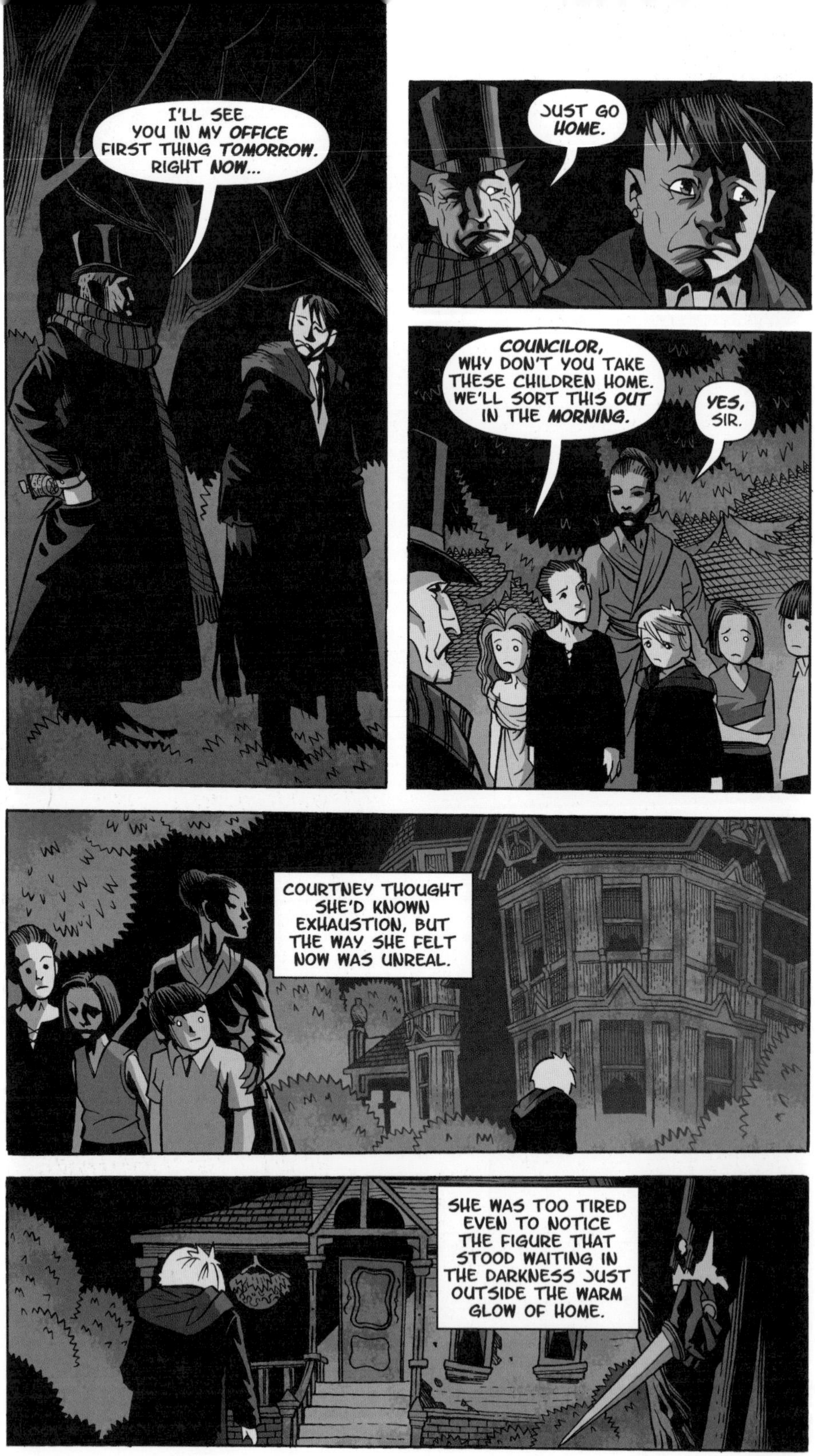
I'LL SEE YOU IN MY OFFICE FIRST THING TOMORROW. RIGHT NOW...
JUST GO HOME.
COUNCILOR, WHY DON'T YOU TAKE THESE CHILDREN HOME. WE'LL SORT THIS OUT IN THE MORNING.
YES, SIR.
COURTNEY THOUGHT SHE'D KNOWN EXHAUSTION, BUT THE WAY SHE FELT NOW WAS UNREAL.
SHE WAS TOO TIRED EVEN TO NOTICE THE FIGURE THAT STOOD WAITING IN THE DARKNESS JUST OUTSIDE THE WARM GLOW OF HOME.

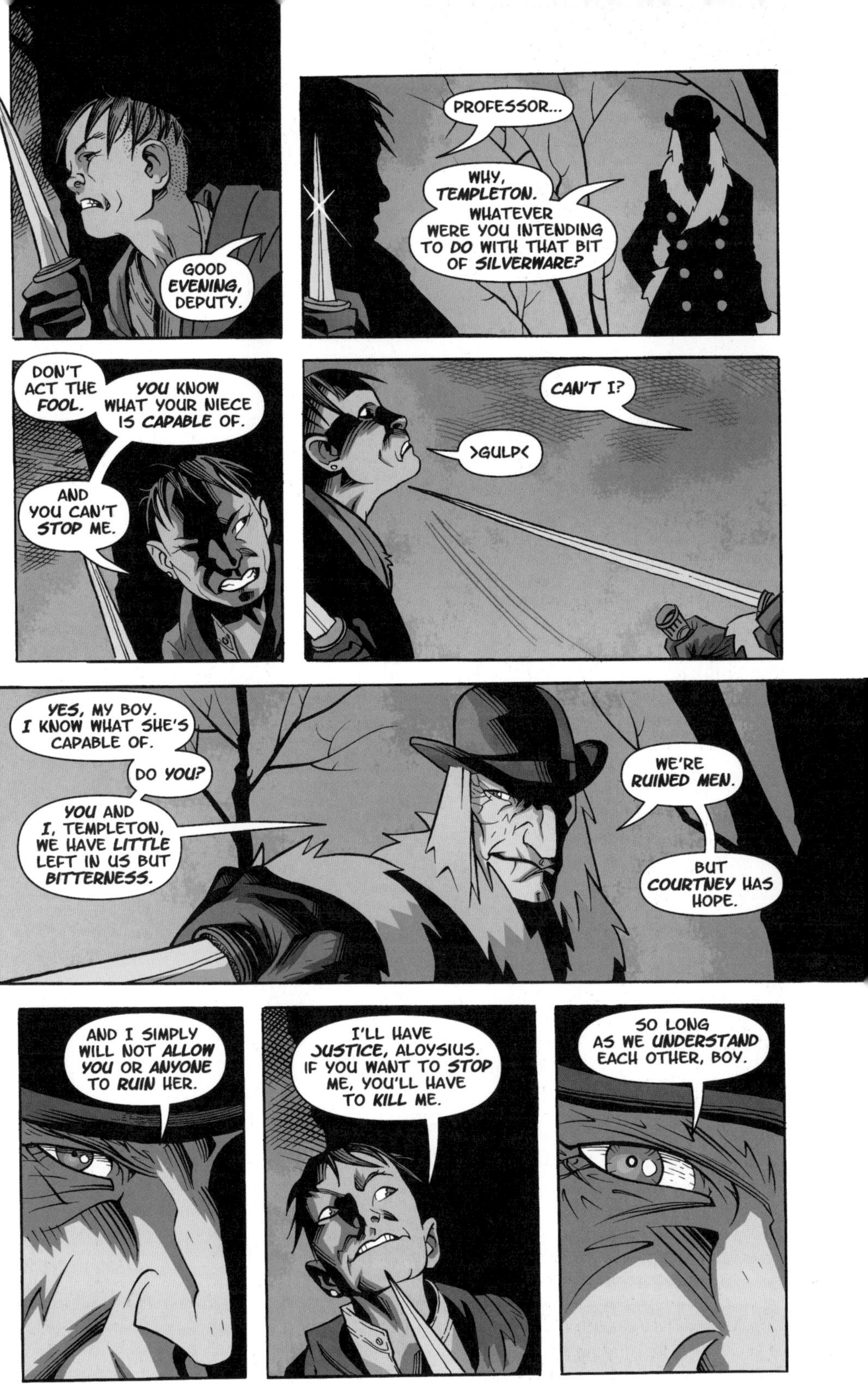
GOOD EVENING, DEPUTY.
PROFESSOR...
WHY, TEMPLETON. WHATEVER WERE YOU INTENDING TO DO WITH THAT BIT OF SILVERWARE?
DON'T ACT THE FOOL.
YOU KNOW WHAT YOUR NIECE IS CAPABLE OF.
AND YOU CAN'T STOP ME.
CAN'T I?
>GULP<
YES, MY BOY. I KNOW WHAT SHE'S CAPABLE OF.
DO YOU?
YOU AND I, TEMPLETON, WE HAVE LITTLE LEFT IN US BUT BITTERNESS.
WE'RE RUINED MEN.
BUT COURTNEY HAS HOPE.
AND I SIMPLY WILL NOT ALLOW YOU OR ANYONE TO RUIN HER.
I'LL HAVE JUSTICE, ALOYSIUS. IF YOU WANT TO STOP ME, YOU'LL HAVE TO KILL ME.
SO LONG AS WE UNDERSTAND EACH OTHER, BOY.

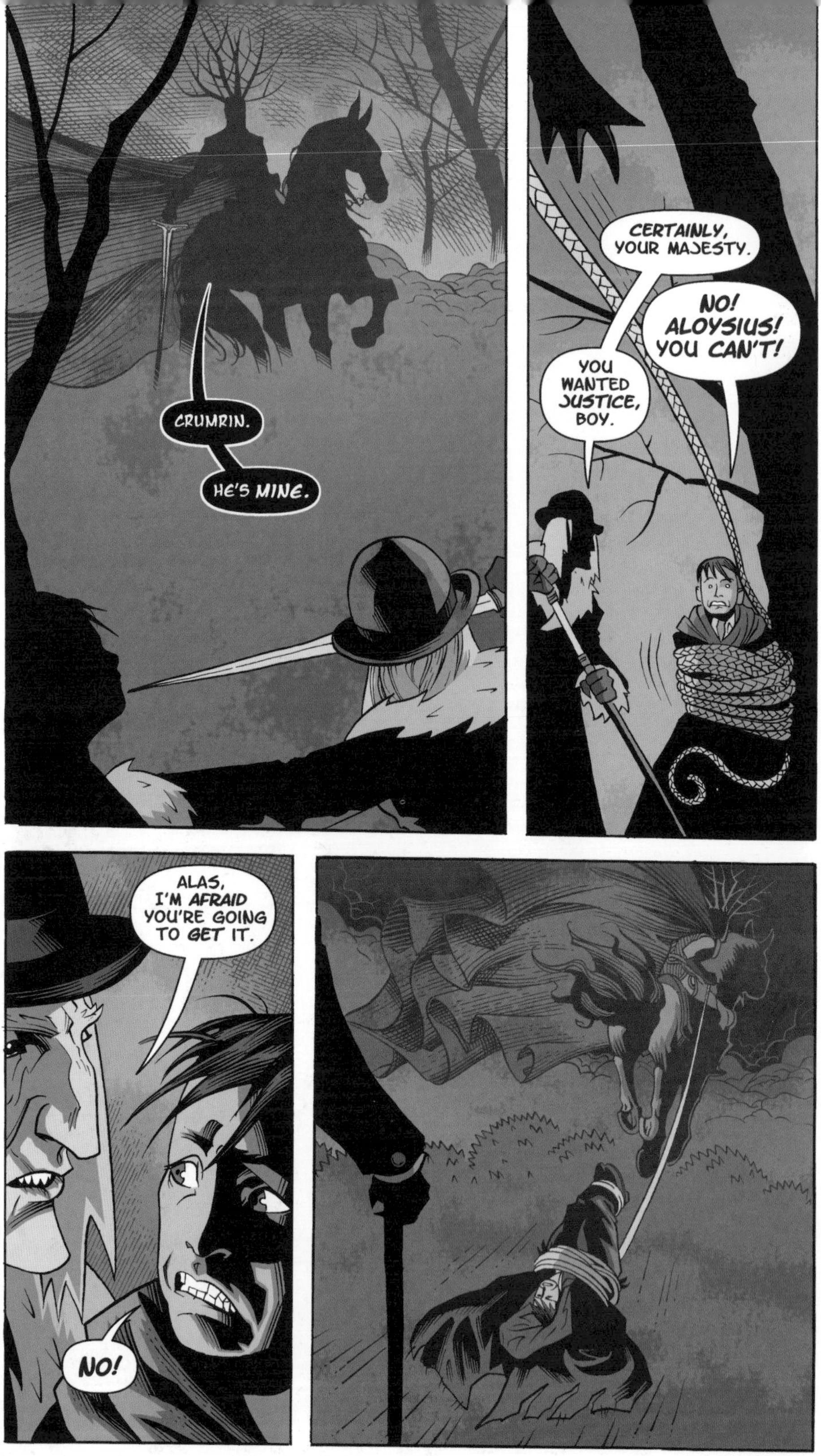

CRUMRIN.
HE'S MINE.
CERTAINLY, YOUR MAJESTY.
YOU WANTED JUSTICE, BOY.
NO! ALOYSIUS! YOU CAN'T!
ALAS, I'M AFRAID YOU'RE GOING TO GET IT.
NO!

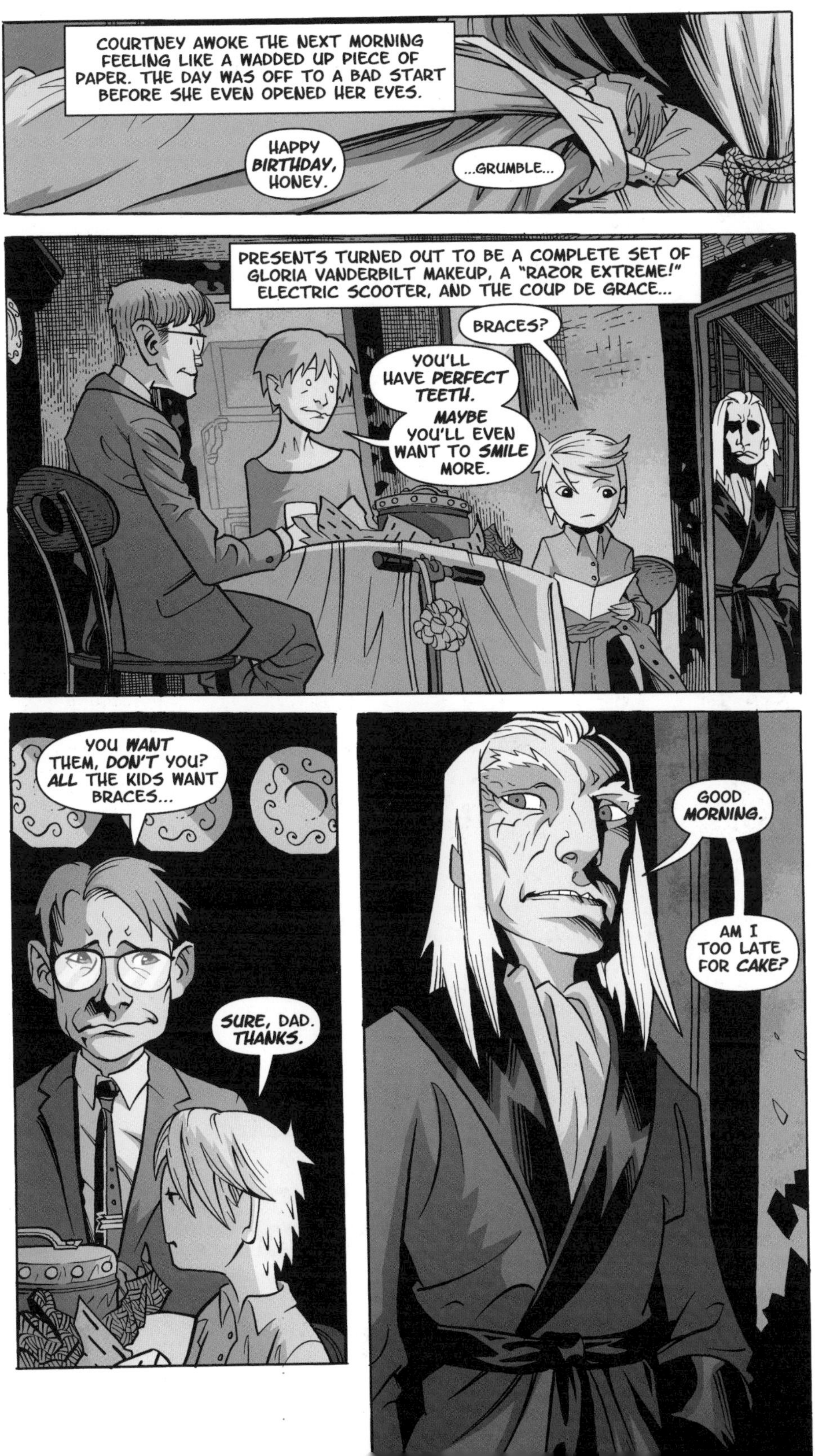
COURTNEY AWOKE THE NEXT MORNING FEELING LIKE A WADDED UP PIECE OF PAPER. THE DAY WAS OFF TO A BAD START BEFORE SHE EVEN OPENED HER EYES.
HAPPY BIRTHDAY, HONEY.
...GRUMBLE...
PRESENTS TURNED OUT TO BE A COMPLETE SET OF GLORIA VANDERBILT MAKEUP, A "RAZOR EXTREME!" ELECTRIC SCOOTER, AND THE COUP DE GRACE...
BRACES?
YOU'LL HAVE PERFECT TEETH. MAYBE YOU'LL EVEN WANT TO SMILE MORE.
YOU WANT THEM, DON'T YOU? ALL THE KIDS WANT BRACES...
SURE, DAD. THANKS.
GOOD MORNING.
AM I TOO LATE FOR CAKE?

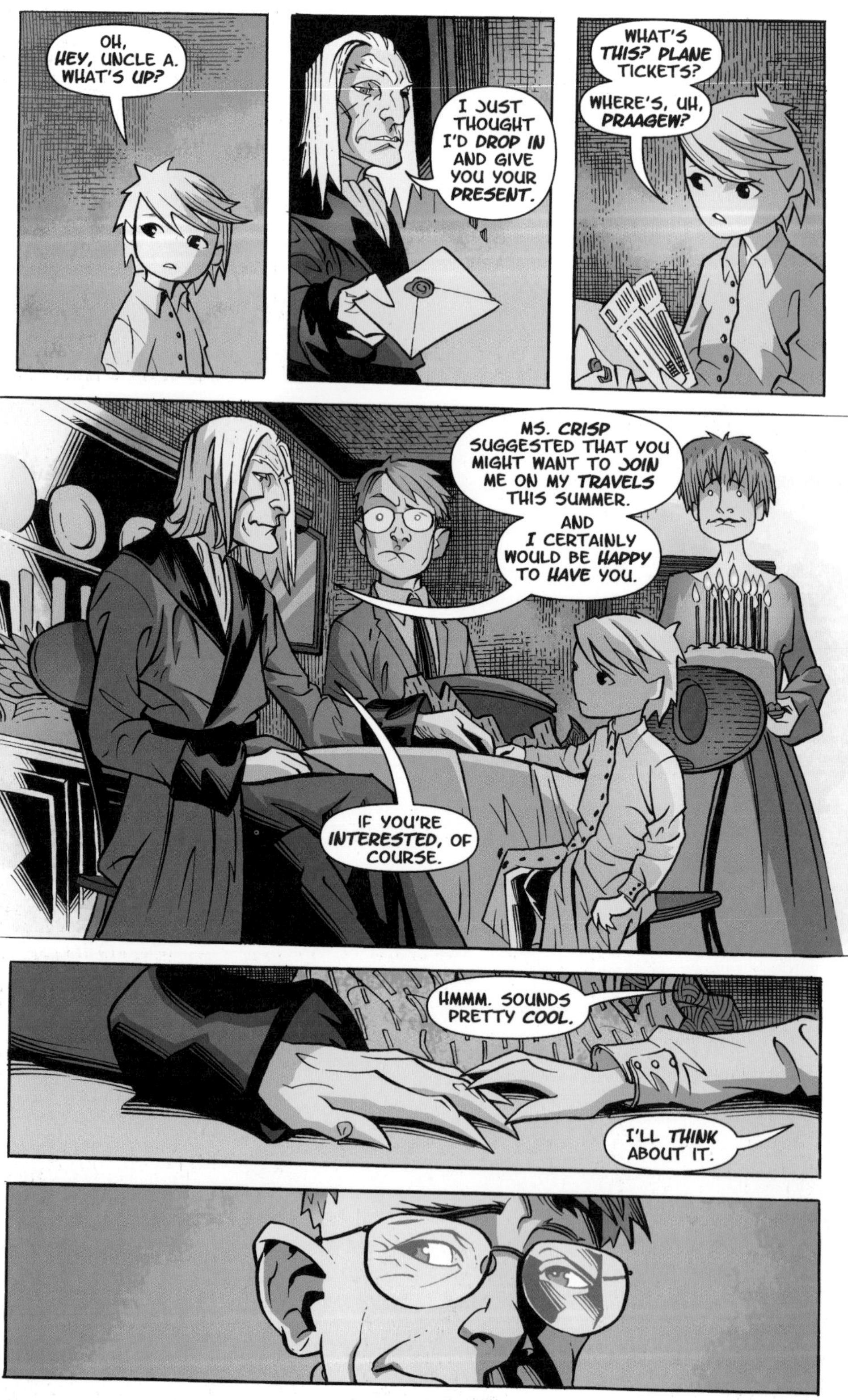
OH, HEY, UNCLE A. WHAT'S UP?
I JUST THOUGHT I'D DROP IN AND GIVE YOU YOUR PRESENT.
WHAT'S THIS? PLANE TICKETS?
WHERE'S, UH, PRAAGEW?
MS. CRISP SUGGESTED THAT YOU MIGHT WANT TO JOIN ME ON MY TRAVELS THIS SUMMER.
AND I CERTAINLY WOULD BE HAPPY TO HAVE YOU.
IF YOU'RE INTERESTED, OF COURSE.
HMMM. SOUNDS PRETTY COOL.
I'LL THINK ABOUT IT.

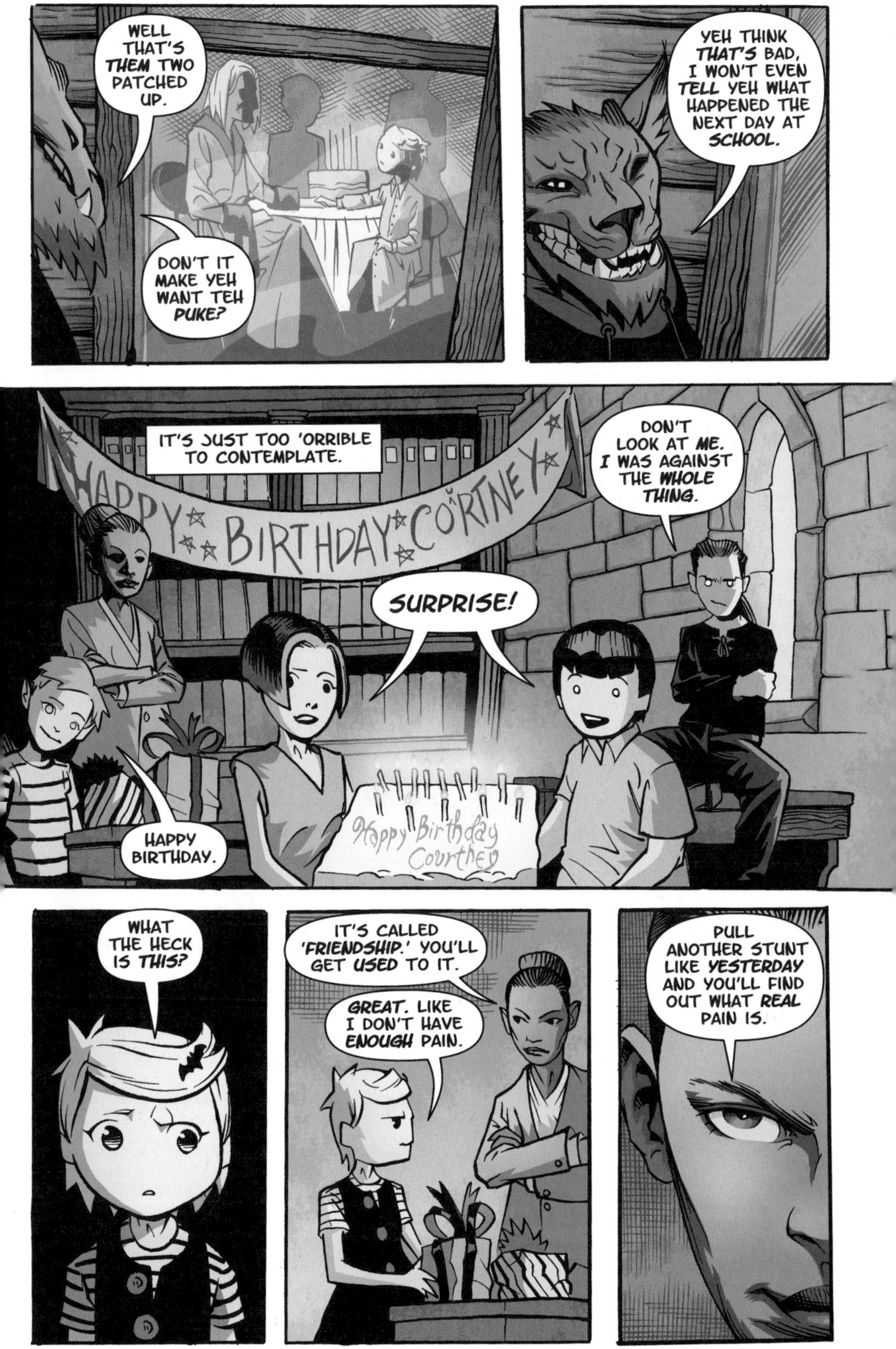

WELL THAT'S THEM TWO PATCHED UP.
DON'T IT MAKE YEH WANT TEH PUKE?
YEH THINK THAT'S BAD, I WON'T EVEN TELL YEH WHAT HAPPENED THE NEXT DAY AT SCHOOL.
IT'S JUST TOO 'ORRIBLE TO CONTEMPLATE.
HAPPY BIRTHDAY COURTNEY
DON'T LOOK AT ME. I WAS AGAINST THE WHOLE THING.
SURPRISE!
HAPPY BIRTHDAY.
Happy Birthday Courtney
WHAT THE HECK IS THIS?
IT'S CALLED 'FRIENDSHIP.' YOU'LL GET USED TO IT.
GREAT. LIKE I DON'T HAVE ENOUGH PAIN.
PULL ANOTHER STUNT LIKE YESTERDAY AND YOU'LL FIND OUT WHAT REAL PAIN IS.

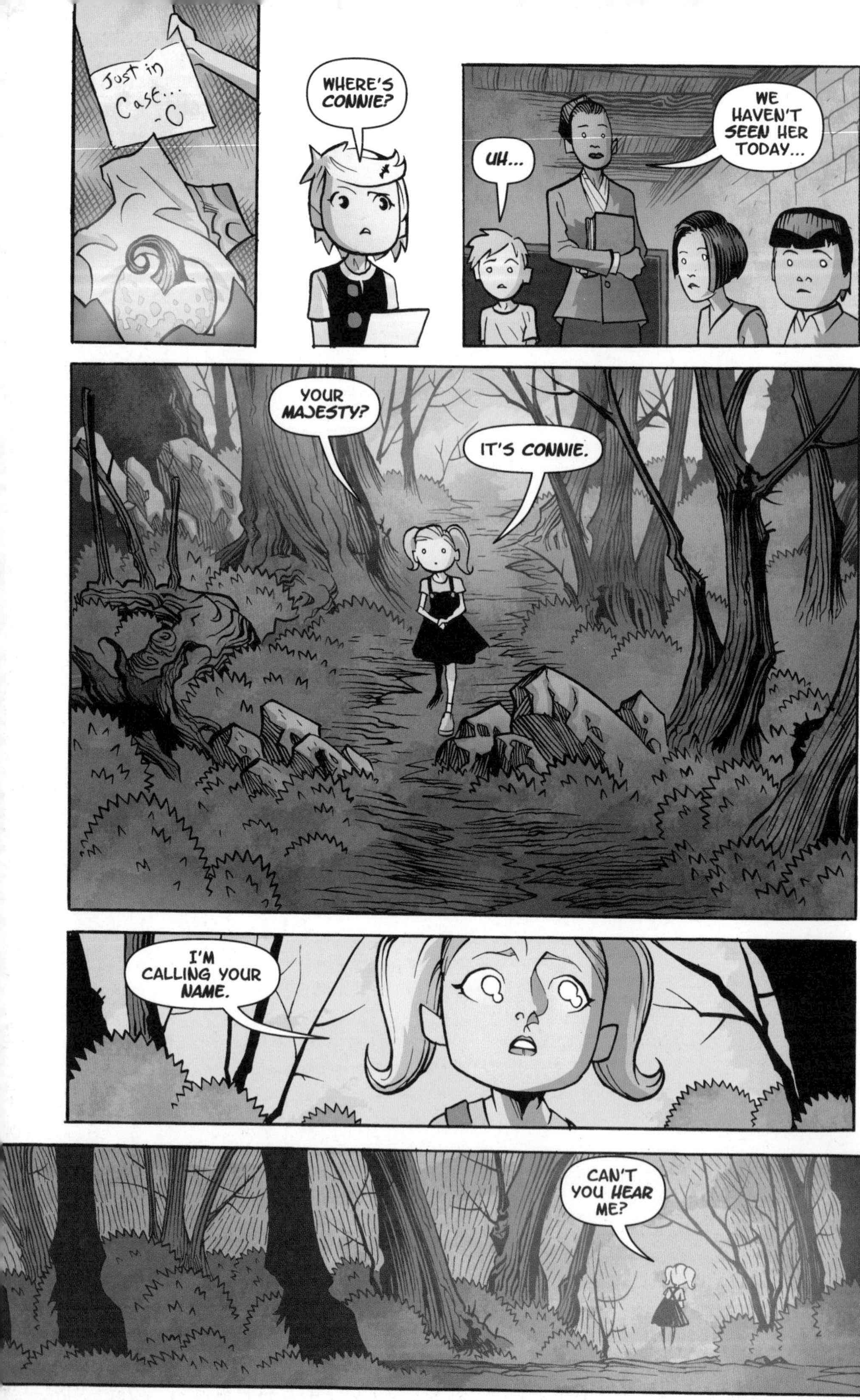
Just in Case... -C
WHERE'S CONNIE?
UH...
WE HAVEN'T SEEN HER TODAY...
YOUR MAJESTY?
IT'S CONNIE.
I'M CALLING YOUR NAME.
CAN'T YOU HEAR ME?

Courtney Crumrin

By Ted Naifeh

Crumrin

The Twilight Kingdom

Bonus Material & Cover Gallery

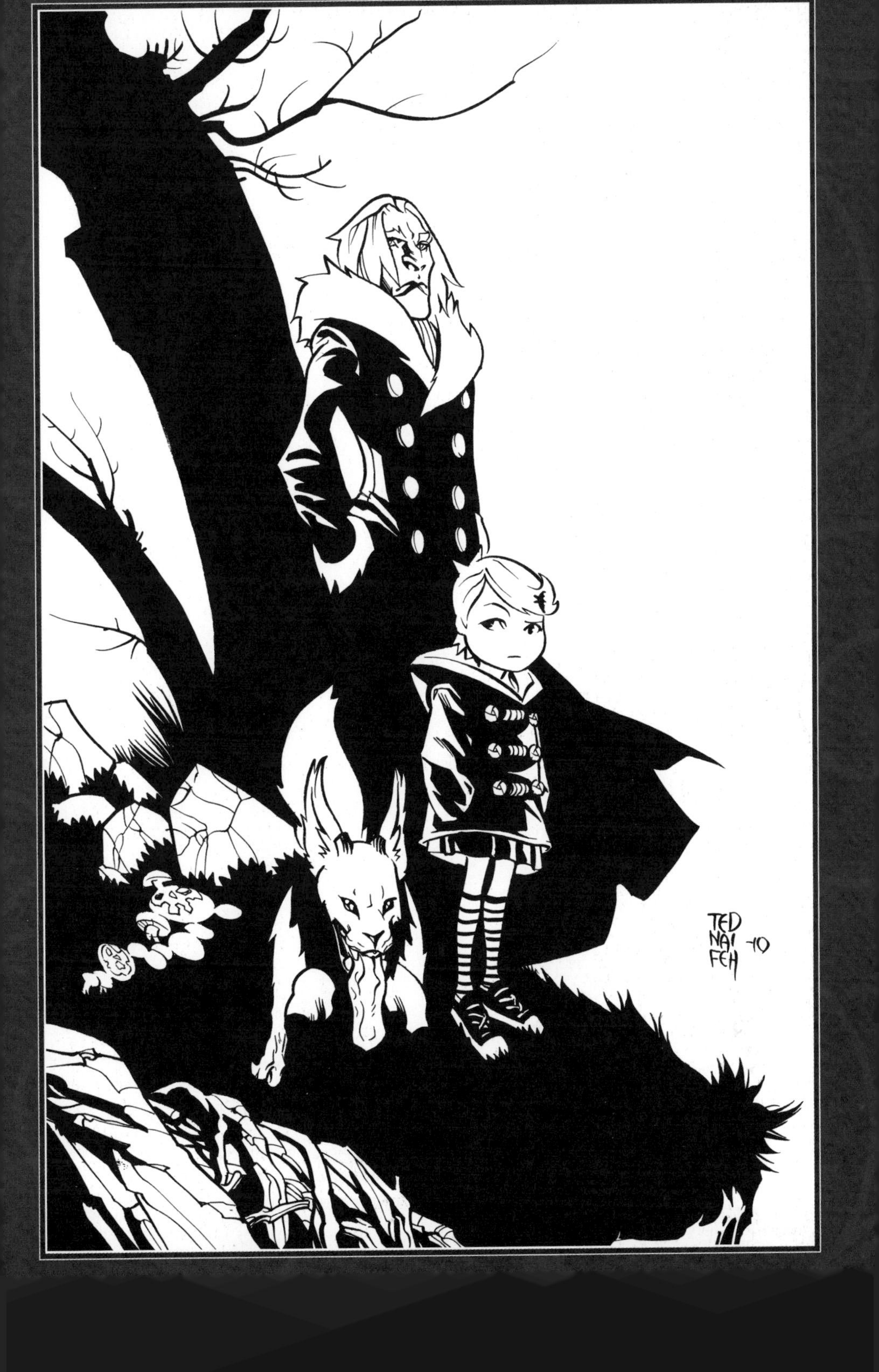
TED NAI FEH -10

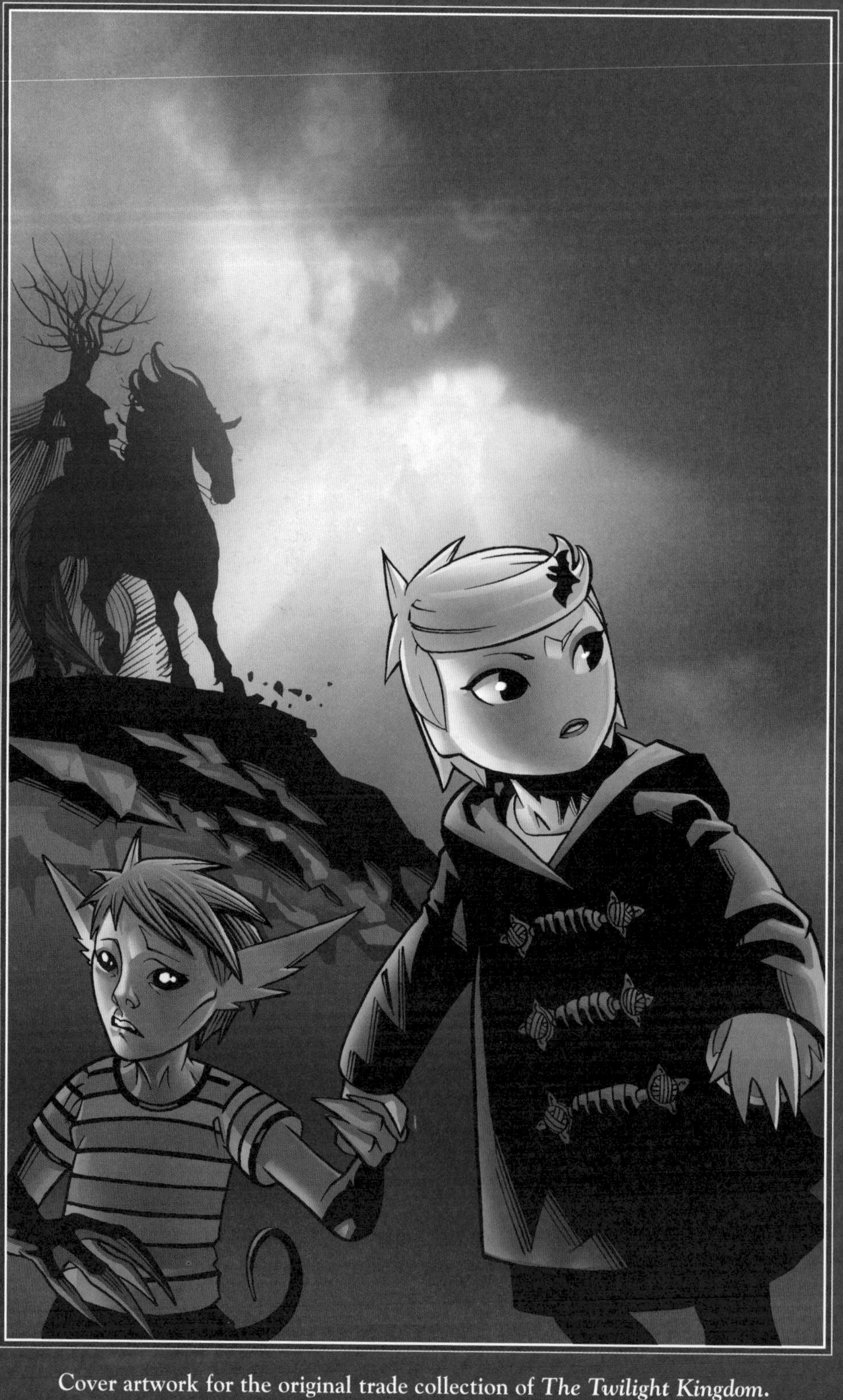

Cover artwork for the original trade collection of *The Twilight Kingdom*.

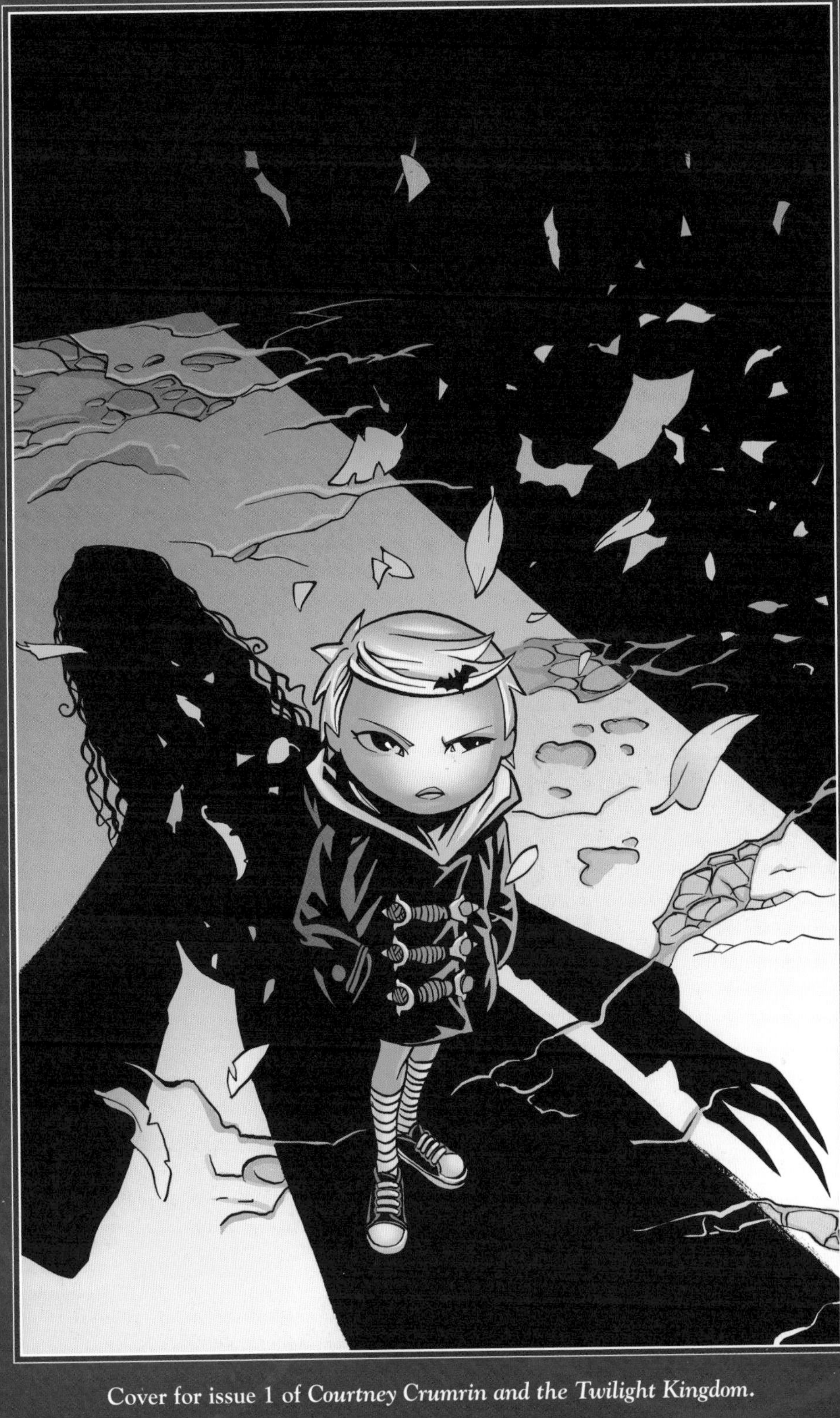

Cover for issue 1 of *Courtney Crumrin and the Twilight Kingdom.*

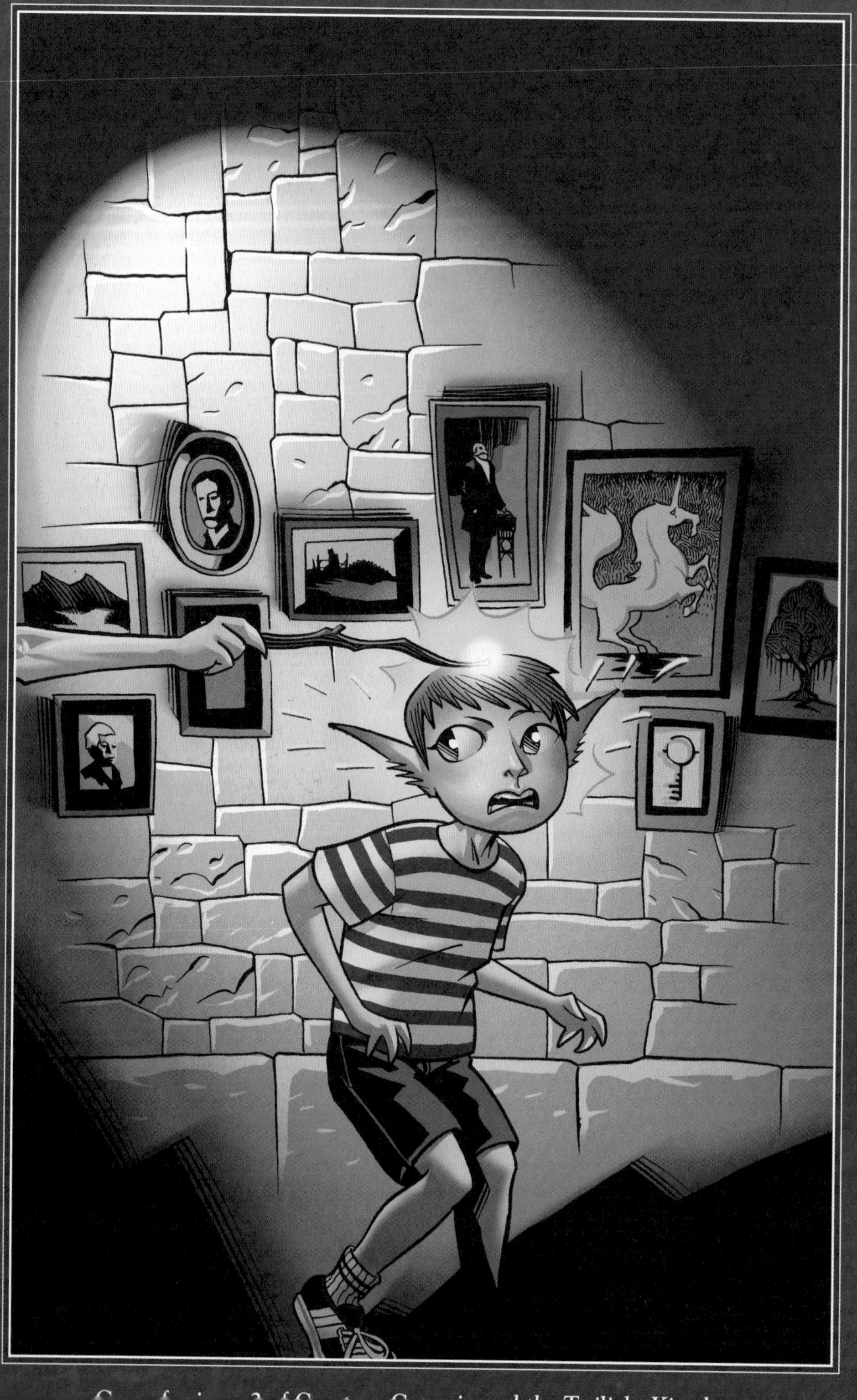

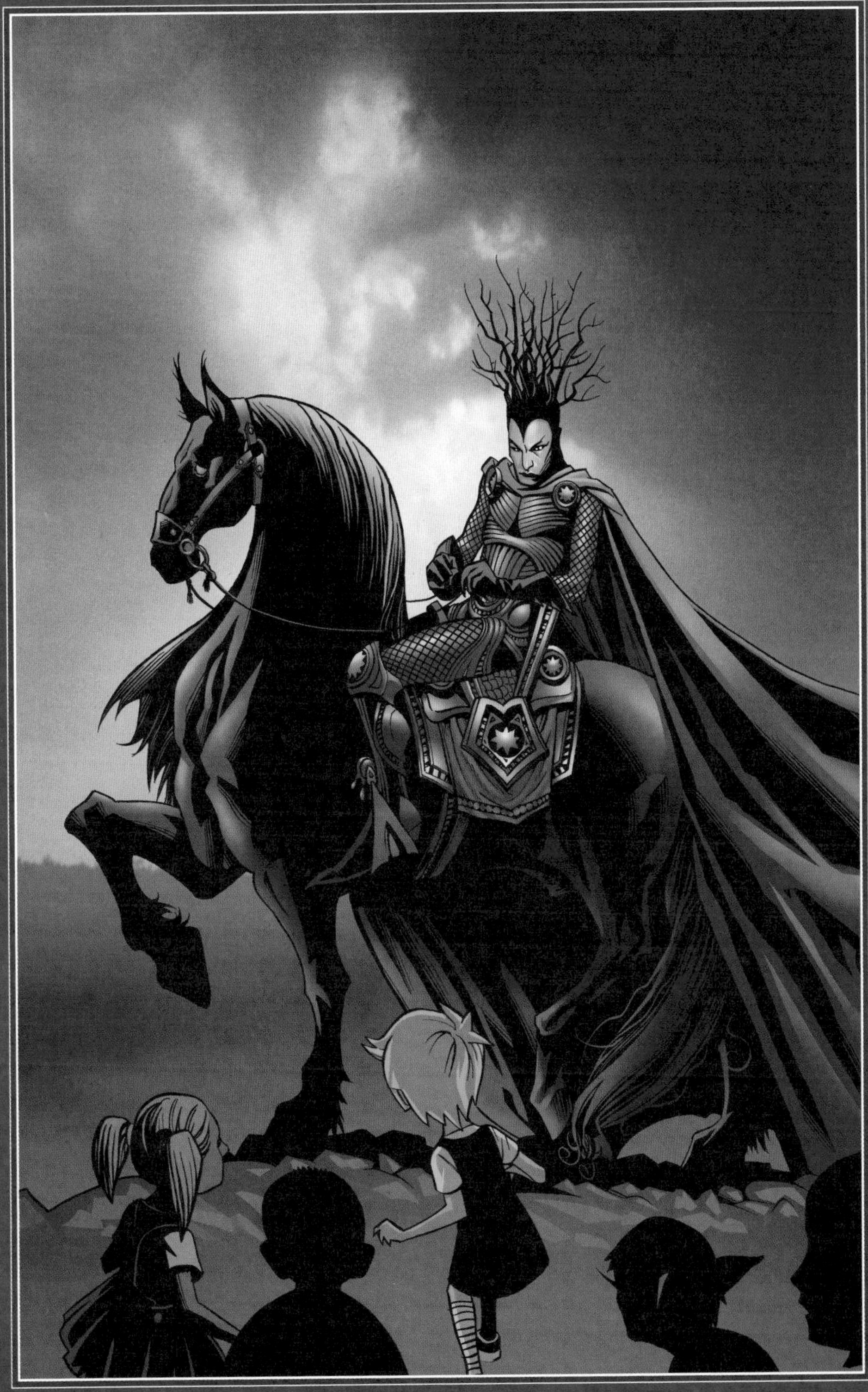

Cover for issue 3 of *Courtney Crumrin and the Twilight Kingdom.*

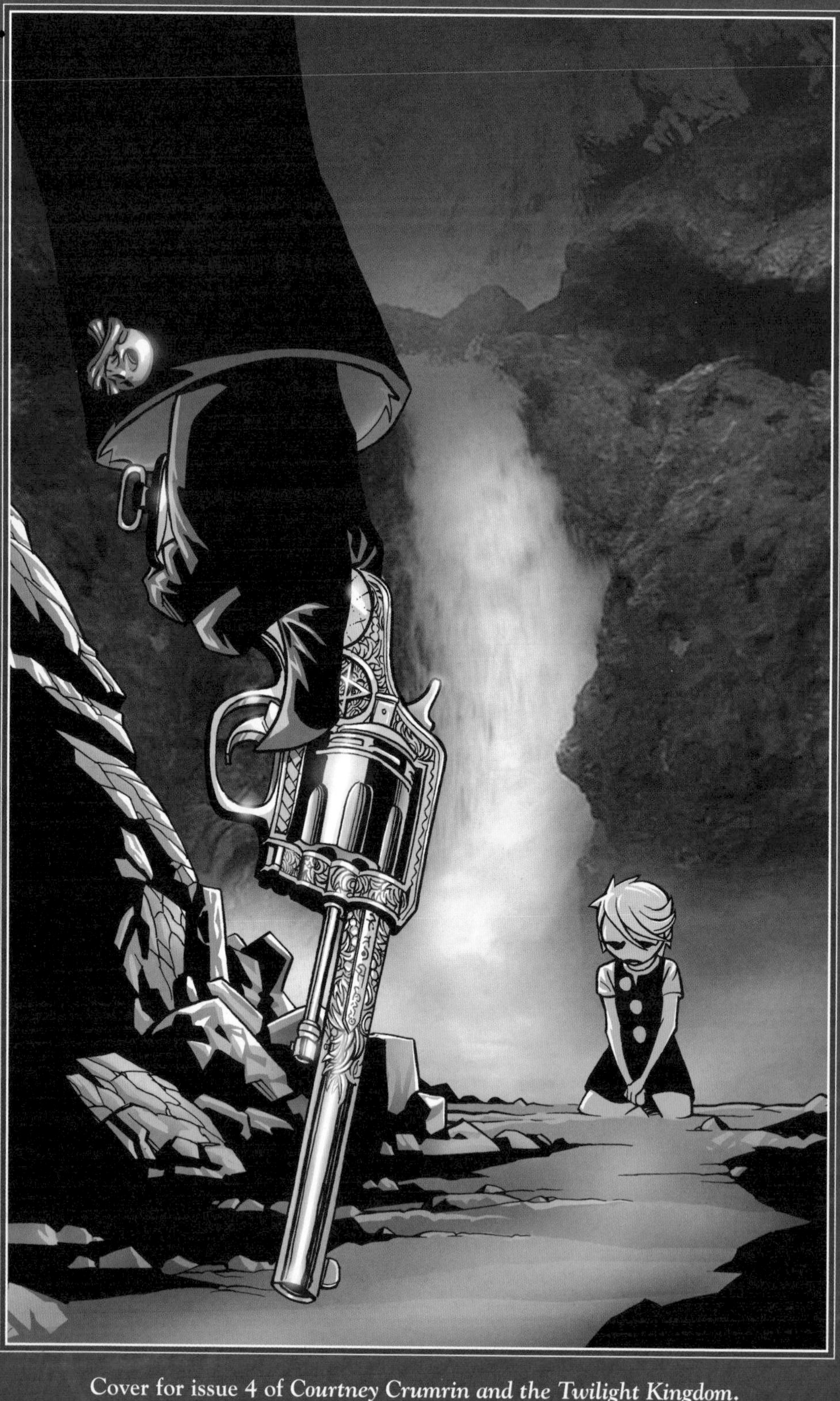

Cover for issue 4 of *Courtney Crumrin and the Twilight Kingdom.*

TED NAIFEH

Ted Naifeh first appeared in the independent comics scene in 1999 as the artist for *Gloomcookie*, the goth romance comic he co-created with Serena Valentino for SLG Publishing. After a successful run, Ted decided to strike out on his own, writing and drawing *Courtney Crumrin and the Night Things*, a spooky children's fantasy series about a grumpy little girl and her adventures with her Warlock uncle.

Nominated for an Eisner Award for best limited series, *Courtney Crumrin's* success paved the way for *Polly and the Pirates*, another children's book, this time about a prim and proper girl kidnapped by pirates convinced she was the daughter of their long-lost queen.

Over the next few years, Ted wrote four volumes of *Courtney Crumrin*, plus a spin-off book about her uncle. He also co-created *How Loathsome* with Tristan Crane, and illustrated two volumes of the videogame tie-in comic *Death Junior* with screenwriter Gary Whitta. More recently, he illustrated *The Good Neighbors*, a three volume graphic novel series written by *New York Times* bestselling author Holly Black, published by Scholastic.

In 2011, Ted wrote the sequel to *Polly and the Pirates*, and illustrated several *Batman* short stories for DC comics. In 2012, he wrapped up the *Courtney Crumrin* series in time for its tenth anniversary, and in 2014 he published two volumes of *Princess Ugg*. Currently, Ted is writing and illustrating two creator-owned series for older audiences: *Night's Dominion* and *Heroines*.

Ted lives in San Francisco, because he likes dreary weather.

Courtney Crumrin
Volume Two

Keep Reading Courtney Crumrin:

Courtney Crumrin, Volume 1:
The Night Things
By Ted Naifeh
136 pages • 6"x9" Softcover • Color
ISBN 978-1-62010-419-4

Courtney Crumrin, Volume 2:
The Coven of Mystics
By Ted Naifeh
144 pages • 6"x9" Softcover • Color
ISBN 978-1-62010-463-7

Courtney Crumrin, Volume 4:
Monstrous Holiday
By Ted Naifeh
136 pages • 6"x9" Hardcover • Color
ISBN 978-1-934964-92-7

Courtney Crumrin, Volume 5:
The Witch Next Door
by Ted Naifeh
144 pages • 6"x9" Hardcover • Color
ISBN: 978-1-934964-96-5

Courtney Crumrin, Volume 6:
The Final Spell
By Ted Naifeh
152 pages • 6"x9" Hardcover • Color
ISBN: 978-1-62010-018-9

Courtney Crumrin, Volume 7:
Tales of a Warlock
by Ted Naifeh
128 pages • 6"x9" Hardcover • Color
ISBN: 978-1-62010-019-6

More by Ted Naifeh

Polly And The Pirates
By Ted Naifeh
176 pages • Digest • Black & White
ISBN 978-1-932664-46-1

Princess Ugg, Volume 1
By Ted Naifeh
120 pages • Softcover • Color
ISBN 978-1-62010-178-0

Princess Ugg, Volume 2
By Ted Naifeh
120 pages • Softcover • Color
ISBN 978-1-62010-215-2

For more information on these and other fine Oni Press comic books and graphic novels, visit www.onipress.com. To find a comic specialty store in your area, call 1-888-COMICBOOK or visit, www.comicshops.us.